Carlos E. Rivera

Balckout: White Harbor

Book 2

SLASHIC HORROR
PRESS

Other titles by Carlos E. Rivera

Esperanza
I am the Door: A White Harbor Story
The Local Truth: White Harbor Book 1

Originally published in Australia by Slashic Horror Press in 2024.

SLASHIC HORROR
PRESS

ISBN-13: 978-0-6457638-9-8
Cover design by Greg Chapman
Interior design by David-Jack Fletcher
Edited by David-Jack Fletcher

Author's Note

One of the hardest things to do when you're a new author is actually finding someone who will believe in your story enough to spend their time and effort on actually publishing it.

Do you know what's even harder? Finding someone who will believe in a three-book story enough to spend their time and effort across said three books, while trusting that the nameless guy writing them knows where the hell he's going with it and isn't just winging it (I'm just about 30% winging it, I swear).

When David-Jack Fletcher and Leeroy Cross James said, "We'd like all three books," I was over the moon, but also terrified. It was like I had two imaginary RuPauls in my head going, "Don't fuck it up." I'm, of course, joking. They're super nice and never pressure me like that… I *do* like to picture them in fabulous wigs, though. The pressure mostly came from me. This intensified as I approached Book 2 of the trilogy (*Hello anxiety, my old friend*), because of the dreaded middle chapter syndrome. So, I focused on telling a story that advances the overall plot, sets up the stage for the big insane final book, but also contains a story in it that feels like an arc has closed by the end.

Did I accomplish that? Up to you, dear reader, but I can say I'm thrilled with how it turned out. I like Book 2 a lot more than I like Book 1, and I feel this is when my favorite characters and plots come into their own. This is when the real powers beneath White Harbor come to the forefront. This is when people really start dying. So, if that's my measure of success, I'd say I kicked ass.

I'm so thankful to everyone who's taken the time to read this. I hope you've found your visit to White Harbor rewarding, and as Book 3 looms on the horizon like a portent of doom, I hope you'll make that last visit to this seaside Oregon town. No guarantee you're coming out alive, though.

*This and the other two books in this
trilogy, are my love letter to those creators
who inspired me to write horror,
including but not limited to:
Stephen King, Guillermo del Toro,
Junji Ito, Neil Gaiman, Mike Flanagan,
Masahiro Ito, Edward Gorey,
and so many others.*

*You will probably never read a word of this, but
thank you.*

"'Something like a spot of leprosy has become
visible to me in the house.'
It is a malignant spot in the house; it is unclean.
The owner shall therefore tear down the house,
its stones, its timbers, and all the plaster of the house,
and he shall take them outside the city to an unclean place.
This is the law of leprosy."
– Excerpt. Leviticus 14:35-54

"Never be bullied into silence.
Never allow yourself to be made a victim.
Accept no one's definition of your life.
Define yourself."
– Harvey Fierstein

VANEK HOUSE (from the records of Callum Baker)

1-F

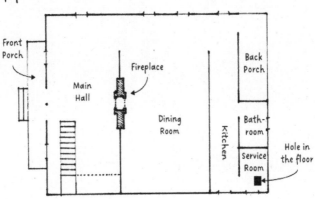

2-F

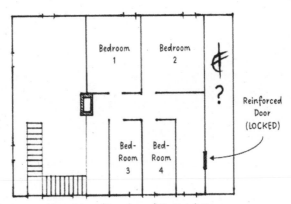

*Note: There are no blueprints or floor plans of the Vanek House, so I've drawn this on memory. Proportions may vary from the actual house. - C.B.

Prologue

In Water

1993

Days were never perfect when your entire family was cursed.

This day, however—to Freddie's utter shock—was perfect.

A bright sun glowed in a cloudless sky, such a joyful blue it could uplift the soul of any cynic. The singing of birds in the dense mass of trees and the crystal waters of the Pargin River added to the beautiful scenery. The waterfall—a short distance away—completed the awe-inspiring view, and fed the river, coming down from the mountain and traversing the town of White Harbor from its northeastern edge. The rumbling of the falling water reached them as only a pleasant relaxing murmur at the stony riverbank where they all sat.

Freddie's dad, Neal Parham, had been light on his drinking for about a week and was in a surprisingly good mood. Sure, he'd had a beer here and there, but the demon that kept whispering in his ear to have another and another and another—until he became the demon himself—must have been on vacation. He had a beer bottle in his hand right as he sat shirtless under a tree that cast a refreshing shadow on the stones and gravel. It was only the second beer he'd had all morning.

They had set up a picnic blanket at a spot where the river widened and the current slowed to an ebb, forming a big, roundish pool. They called this pool The Eye (Harborites had never been particularly creative with names) because there was a smaller pool made with rocks at the edge of the larger one, which made it look like a circle within a larger circle. This had always been a favorite picnic spot for people from town, but today was a workday; Freddie's dad had taken a day off, made some excuse or another for the kids to miss school, and they had the pool all to themselves. It was an annual Parham family tradition, but it had never been as wonderful, or as

(*Perfect!*)

joyful as it was this day.

Freddie's five-year-old sister, Laurie, was playing in the smaller, shallow pool with their mom, who was sitting in the water with her. The water rose only up to his mom's waist, and he could see the pale, freckled skin on her shoulders was already showing a bit of red from being under the sun. She splashed water on Laurie who laughed as if this was the apex of fun, and she slapped her tiny hands on the water, sending it flying everywhere and making their mom giggle.

The small pool had been delimited long ago by people who came here. Stone by stone, they'd made it so that small children, such as Freddie's cute baby sister, had a safe little circle where the current slowed down even further and they could play to their hearts' content.

Freddie, of course, didn't need the Pargin River kiddie pool. He was swimming and diving and floating along with the current in the deeper portion of The Eye, then standing and wading back upstream to let himself float back down. He was a talented swimmer and letting the water wash over him filled him with a combined sense of excitement and relaxation.

They hadn't had a *good* day in so long, and a *perfect* day was something unheard of for the Parhams. On any other day, his dad would be drunk, or his mom would be sad, or he would be grounded, or Laurie... No...Laurie was always perfect.

"Freddie?" Mikayla Parham called. "Freddie, honey?"

He didn't hear her at first, because he was busy doing a handstand, head underwater, legs kicking out over the surface, then flipping over. When he emerged with a splash, he heard her brisk voice trying to rise over the sound of the current. He shook his head, sending a thousand drops of water flying everywhere, catching the sunlight like tiny glass marbles. He blew his nose and looked at his mom, who was waving at him.

"Take care of Lolly for me for a second while I get the bug spray and put some more sunblock on me," she said. "I got half my body out of the water. I'm getting burned, and the bugs are eating me alive."

"Sure, mom." As he waded toward Lolly and his mom, the water covered less and less of his body, becoming shallower near the edge. He reached them and lowered himself into the kiddie pool, sitting next to Laurie. She greeted him with a grin. He grinned back and said, "You better not pee in the water."

The sound of Laurie's animated giggle was like music to his ears, and he couldn't help but smile.

His mom stood and walked away from the pool. She reached his dad, who was enjoying the shade with a pleasant, lazy smile on his face. She gave him a kiss and sat next to him. Was that a third beer? *Hmm, that was quick,* Freddie thought. Was the demon back? He watched his parents' lips move, but couldn't hear their conversation over the sound of the river. The exchange seemed pleasant and full of smiles. He watched as his dad set the beer aside as his mom handed him the sunblock, which he then applied on her skin. *Good,* he thought.

He turned to his sister. "So, what are you doing these

days, Lolly? Things okay at the office? Do you foresee a promotion in your near future?"

She looked at him, giggling. "I want you to be my water horsie."

"Hmm." He arched his eyebrows comically. "I was not expecting that."

"Like this." Laurie stood and started walking around the shallow pool, stomping her feet, causing the water to splish-splash with each stomp. Her laughter was so contagious it filled the air with pure joy. "Water horsie! Water horsie! Water horsie! Woo!"

Freddie couldn't help but laugh as she did this, shielding his face from the splashing water. "Fine! Fine! Fine! Water horsie it is!"

He went down on one knee, ready to lift her and sit her on his shoulders. "You may mount your noble steed, M'lady."

"Yaaaaaay!" she cried with delight, raising her arms. He picked her up, turned her in mid-air, and sat her on his shoulders.

Seconds later, Freddie was walking in circles around the tiny pool, splashing his bare feet into the water, shouting, "Water horsie! Water horsie! Water horsie! Woo!" as his dear Lolly chanted in unison with ecstatic laughter when the water splashed so high, the drops broke on her skin.

It was then Freddie had a brilliant idea.

"Hey, Lolly? Do you wanna play Water Horsie over there?" He signaled with his head toward the deeper pool where he was swimming before. The water in the deeper area reached his chest, and he knew the pool like the back of his hand. The only dangerous area was about three quarters of the way across, where four red flags lined a deep sinkhole at the edge of the pool; they had plenty of space to play in, without even coming close to that area, so Lolly was perfectly safe. "Lots more water for you to kick from up there!"

"Let's go!" she shrieked with unbridled joy.

Seconds later, Freddie was taking jumping strides and wading through the deeper area, with Laurie on his shoulders, kicking at the water and squealing with elation. He knew his little sister had always wanted to go where there was "bigger water", as she said every time they came, but the only one allowed to take her there had been their dad.

As he strode upstream, toward the upper end of the big, wide pool, he thought he heard something over the murmur and gurgle of the water, so he turned his head in the sound's direction. There was his mother, standing under the tree, shouting something at them. "...out of there! Freddie, get your sister out of there!"

"It's okay, Mom!" he shouted and motioned with his head toward Laurie, whose exhilarated giggles and cries were at their zenith. "I got her!"

"No! Bring her out here! You're not supposed to do

that. It's dangerous!"

He scrunched his face in displeasure. "No, Mom! C'mon! Look at her! She's having fun!"

His mom turned her red face toward his dad, who was still sitting in the shade without a care in the world. Based on his expressions and gestures, he was probably saying something along the lines of, "Don't worry. He's got her."

His mom turned back to glare, pointed a finger at him and said, "Frederick Parham, you listen to me right now, bring—"

Freddie tripped.

As he went down, he felt his foot slide off the stone he'd been standing on, loosened by his weight. His ankle rolled, his knee bent, his body toppled. His vision blurred with swirling water—bubbles drawing uneven curves as they rose toward the surface. Water rushed into his open mouth and his breath caught. Unable to find his footing, the current dragged him and rolled him, making him feel like a turtle on its back being spun by some cruel kid. And—

Lolly! Where's Lolly?

He couldn't feel her on his shoulders anymore.

Freddie scrambled under the water, trying to force his limbs to position his body in some semblance of upright. With a mighty heave, he propelled himself out of the water and took a deep breath. He wiped the water off his face, turned his head this way and that. Glimpsed a tiny hand emerging from the surface several feet away.

Too far! Too far!

"Lolly!"

As he swam with wide strokes toward Laurie, he caught sight of his mother running toward the water, then diving, then swimming. Freddie used his own strength and the push of the current to propel himself toward his sister, but his body felt shaky and cumbersome from terror.

His mom swam toward the spot where a small hand emerged from the water. She stood upright just for a second, then cried in pain. She had stepped on something. She got hurt somehow. He saw her lose balance and fall sideways. She splashed clumsily, but in seconds, she had picked herself back up and continued swimming.

Laurie appeared so far away, so out of reach, but in a last-ditch effort, he stretched out a hand and—

"Got her!" He felt his hand grip Laurie's wrist. He pulled. Got his arm around her. Pulled her out of the water. She coughed and let out a horrible wail of terror. Part of his mind was relieved he'd caught up to her, but another part fired out alarms the moment he saw two red flags a few feet upstream, near the area he'd swam past. He'd made the mistake of wandering into the off-limits portion of The Eye, where his feet soon wouldn't touch the ground, and the current pulled the hardest as it readied to fall a short but important four feet to the lower level downstream. If they fell through, rapid, rocky waters would carry them tumbling through a merciless stretch of river they'd have no chance of surviving.

The current kept pulling him, even if he tried his hardest to swim with one hand and kicking water to move toward the safety of the flags. His legs ached under the water, the cold water pressing in against him, and he felt it stealing his energy. Like a life force of its own, it hated him, it wanted him, wanted Lolly. He struggled to stay above the water, his mother's desperate voice distant and gurgled. He felt the last touch of rocks against his feet and knew it was too late.

The edge of the pool!

The fastest he could—with his sister still wailing in his ear—he turned right and gave four hard kicks, which moved him far enough away from the sinkhole, and allowed him to plant his feet. Swimming sideways, however, had let the current push him closer to the edge. His left foot slipped and, for a microsecond, touched nothing underneath. He scrambled to latch on to something, knowing the inevitable was coming. Knowing they were too close to the deadly fall, too weak to stop it. His lungs burned, his free arm reached and grabbed and flailed. Lolly was tight in his grip, still wailing, eyes wide in terror. Freddie tried to move his feet to walk away from the edge, but try as he might, he was hit by that terrible moment of realization.

They were going over.

Lolly, I'm so sorry.

Just as he prepared to tilt and fall, however, he felt a pair of arms going around his and Lolly's bodies.

"Mom!" he cried, the sudden relief mixing with the panic, resulting in a vulnerable, mewling cry.

With strength he didn't know his mom had, she got between them and the edge, lifted them, and threw them as hard as she could to get them away from The Eye's boundary. As he fell back toward the water, he saw his mom tilt backward and go over, arms spinning in the air. He thought it looked like one of those series, where the hero goes off the edge of the cliff before a "TO BE CONTINUED" screen appears, and you find out the week after, they'd managed to grab an outcropping rock and were still alive. But as he plunged back into the water, he heard an impossible sound, the most revolting sound he'd heard in his life: a blunt *thunk!* Which he assumed was his mother's head hitting a rock. It was impossible for him to have heard it from this distance, but he was sure he had.

Then, the unimaginable. The shock of that terrible sound made him loosen his grip on Laurie, not fully, but just enough. It was just for an instant, but the little girl squirmed and slipped off his grasp like a wet fish. "No, Laurie! No!" he screamed as he emerged from the water.

His dad's arms appeared out of nowhere.

Neal Parham's fingers wrapped around his daughter's arm, but just as the little girl had slipped from Freddie's grip, she slipped from his. She was pulled by the current beyond his grasp and went over the edge.

Now standing in frozen horror, Freddie could see his mom's unconscious body and Lolly's barely visible shape past the edge, being carried away by the current, as his dad screamed a guttural, primal scream.

Neal Parham climbed a rock at the edge, and hopped down onto a large stone below, then leaped to another with agility Freddie would've never imagined his alcoholic father to have. He jumped from one to the next, and for a ridiculous second, Freddie thought his dad would reach Laurie and pull her to safety, then skip from stone to stone until he reached his mom and rescued her, too. Thirty minutes later, however, Freddie was sitting at the bank of a smaller pool, further downstream, looking at the bodies of Lolly and his mother lying on the gravel, covered by blankets brought by first responders.

He couldn't let go of the mental image of a swollen bump in his mother's head, which had probably not been enough to kill her, but had knocked her unconscious, taking away any chance she might have had at fighting for her life. She'd drowned, sacrificed to the river, to The Eye.

Both of Lolly's arms had been broken as she'd banged against the rocks going down the river. He'd seen his dad in rabid madness trying to give her tiny body CPR. He'd seen water gurgle out of her mouth and nose, as if he had been squeezing an untied water balloon. She'd drowned, too.

Their bodies had gotten stuck in the rocks in the shallower part of the river, and they had been easy for his dad to pull out of the water.

His dad was talking to one of his colleagues, a policeman named Leo Fuentes, several feet away, and bystanders all around stared and commented about the tragedy that had unfolded. He'd heard the word "cursed" a few times, referring to the Curse of the Parhams; that not-so-much-a-legend that had plagued his family since the day Dorothy Parham hanged her teenage son for murdering the town's priest. That word didn't hurt so much, though. Every Parham since the late 1800s knew they were cursed, and it was something they didn't dispute. The proof was under those blankets on the riverbank. However, he'd also heard the word "drunk" a few more times; and that hurt because it was an incorrect assumption. Neal Parham was one of the most famous "barely functional" alcoholics in town, along with Yvette Giffen—Barry's mom—but that morning his dad had only had two beers and got started on the third. He wasn't drunk. Not that it mattered to all those people feeding Blight Harbor with their gossip and innuendo; but his dad hadn't been drunk when this tragedy had happened.

From a distance, Freddie glimpsed his dad pulling at his own hair, his face red with grief, eyes bulging, wide, confused, staring at nothing. Unlike his dad's more outward expression, there was a numbness in Freddie's skull. He couldn't even process what was happening. He couldn't cry. He couldn't speak.

He remembered giving Lolly a box of crayons and a drawing block a couple weeks earlier so she could go crazy drawing to her heart's content. He wanted to see if maybe there was another artist in the family besides himself. All she'd managed were weird, shapeless doodles and spirals and squiggly lines that made no sense. Regardless, he'd told her the drawings were very cute, and she'd celebrated as if that were the highest praise.

She was dead now.

No opportunity to see if her art would improve with time. Now all she would have created in this world would've been nonsensical lines and doodles.

Freddie was lost in his thoughts, so he didn't notice his dad marching in his direction. He looked up just in time to see his fist flying toward him. He punched him hard in the left temple. Freddie saw the world tilt sideways as he flew off the rock he'd been sitting on. He hit the ground and scraped the right side of his head on the gravel. As soon as he regained awareness of his surroundings, he turned his head to where he heard noise, and saw his dad being restrained by Leo Fuentes.

"You stupid fuck!" Neal Parham shouted. "Why did you take your sister to the deep part? You killed her! You killed your mom! Stupid fuck! You killed them! Damn you!"

The month that followed, Freddie hadn't gone to

school. He hadn't gone to The Pines with his friends, or to The Vigilantes' (the stupid name Peter Lange had picked) gatherings at the Vanek House, which had become their creepy club house. He didn't deserve an education. He didn't deserve friends. He had killed his mom. He had killed Lolly; robbed her of a chance to live past the tender age of five.

All he did all day was sit and draw his monsters, which had now taken on fresh new forms since the tragedy. When he ran out of paper, he started drawing on his bedroom walls.

His dad had taken a leave of absence from the police to dedicate himself to his true calling of getting stupid drunk 24/7. Not a day went by that his dad didn't remind him of what he'd done—as if there was a chance he'd ever forget. Freddie woke up each morning wondering if all he'd have to deal with that day were insults and blame, or if his dad would once again beat him until he got tired. His friends came to visit. He never opened the door. They called on the phone. He never answered. They slipped letters and messages through the mail slot. He never read them. Over time, with his dad's drunken threats, they'd stopped coming. This house had died with Lolly and his mom. It was his mausoleum, and he planned on staying there, decomposing.

That all stopped one morning, when the doorbell rang, and rang, and rang, and it wouldn't stop. Freddie looked outside to find Leo Fuentes, the policeman who had restrained his dad at the riverbank, with a woman he didn't know. By the time he opened the door, squinting against the harsh sunlight, and saw both their faces, he knew what had happened.

The previous night, his dad had gotten drunk—no surprise there—and he'd left Cunningham's on foot. He'd wandered toward Creed Road, and he'd walked along the side for a while in the darkness. A truck came through town at high speed, finding the road had no intersections and there were no other vehicles. His dad had shambled into the oncoming lane just at the exact wrong moment to meet the headlights of a truck. It hadn't been able to avoid him. He'd taken every single wheel on the driver's side, crushing him to death.

"He was killed instantly, son," Leo Fuentes said, but his tone, Freddie realized, actually meant: "He didn't die as horribly as he could have for the Curse of the Parhams' standards. Remember your grandma, who got eaten by coyotes?"

The woman, some social worker, or whatever, explained he'd go live with his uncle Bryce—who wasn't a Parham, as he was his uncle on his mother's side—for the moment. She'd asked him to pack up his bags.

His stay hadn't been long.

The second night at his uncle's, Freddie woke up to a man standing by his bed. Before he could recognize him, the man slipped a bag over his head and tightened it around his neck until he passed out.

When he woke up, he realized he was tied to a chair in a place he recognized. He was in one of the empty rooms inside the Vanek House, and standing in front of him was an elderly, tall, Black man. Old Man Curling.

"Hello, Freddie," Ben Curling said. "How would you like to put an end to your family's curse?"

Chapter One

Birth

2022

From inside the nursery, Freddie Parham watched in awe as the black cocoon containing Steve Felton shuddered. He was still reeling from the sight of the black tendrils that crept from the hallway wall, wrapping themselves around the helpless, terrified man—enveloping him, choking him, penetrating him, invading every interstice of his body, until all that was left was a cocoon stuck to the wall. Its surface was so black it was as if a void had formed and gained volume, creating an irregular, egg-like protuberance, a pregnant belly

17

ready to burst.

A bulge appeared on top of the cocoon, then receded. It reminded Freddie of his mother's stomach, back when his unborn baby sister kicked from within. Another bulge appeared near the bottom and vanished in an instant, followed by a larger bulge in the middle. Something wanted out, something wanted to be born. The first inhabitant of Blight Harbor—that "other place" where the darkest thoughts and fears of the townspeople became the building blocks of the world itself.

A small slit opened near the top of the cocoon, the skin sliding to the sides, wet and slimy, growing wider, until it was a gash dripping gangrenous blood. The surface receded, folded, wrinkled, and, little by little, gave out the contents of its dark womb.

What emerged first was a hunched back that was swollen like an enormous round belly. The outline of vertebrae was visible under the skin, running down the center. The skin was distended, covered in blackened veins and bruises, and had a yellowish hue, as if from jaundice. As the cocoon sloughed off, it left behind a translucent, viscous substance, like saliva, but thicker, hanging in drooping strands.

The next thing Freddie saw were the legs. It appeared, on first impression, like they were bent the wrong way. However, Freddie was reminded this creature of his creation walked backward, leading with its hunched back as if it were a drinker's protuberant beer gut. The legs looked human, but with varicose, greenish-black, sickly colored skin, from where the hunched back pushed the blood down, swelling its feet, giving them a gangrenous look.

It staggered out of the womb, the remains of which hung in black, limp, slimy tatters, revealing the creature's full form, and for a moment, it stood there, swaying, seeming confused about what to do after its unholy birth. All hair had dissolved, and all clothes had disappeared from Steve Felton's body. All that remained was his new form in all its naked, perverted nature.

Felton's body was bent over, rolled into itself to the point his head was fused into his abdomen. His arms had been bent backward and merged with the sides of his bulging back, holding it up as it walked. As a whole, Freddie thought it looked like a man carrying a huge, round sack on his back, whose weight made him hunch over.

He didn't understand why the Exiles—the source of the black tendrils that formed the cocoon and overtook Steve Felton's body—needed to transform the human body in such a dramatic way to exist in this world, but it wasn't his place to question the Lord's designs. All he knew was his job was to prepare the world for the coming of God, and these beings— His servants—could only exist in physical form by using a human host.

Watching his first creation stagger to life before his

eyes, Freddie pondered whether this was a chicken-and-egg situation. He wasn't sure if his drawings had shaped the Exile's physical manifestation, or if the Lord had transmitted to him the images of what the Exiles would look like once they were born.

He looked up as the wall texture of this incarnation of Blight Harbor spread from the hallway into the baby's nursery. The wallpaper wrinkled, tore apart, and became soaked with blood and other fluids, while organic tissue was revealed underneath, looking like pulsing flesh, skin, offal, parts that appeared to belong to a larger body he couldn't fathom the full shape of. Freddie had no notion of whether the body was the room, or the house, or the entire town, but he knew this was just one of infinite manifestations of Blight Harbor, which was both the body and the world of God, shaped by the minds of the townspeople.

The toys, the furniture, the baby clothes, the cabinet where the diapers were kept, all twisted and deformed until they turned into strange, wriggling organs that could have belonged only to a being not of this world. The curtains in the nursery now resembled long black hair stretching from the top of the window to the floor, and the window itself became a circular hole, like a tube made of flesh leading out of the house, into endless darkness.

The floor in the nursery looked almost the same as before, but as if it had been in a high-moisture environment for years. It cracked, molded, and became stained and deteriorated before his eyes.

The only thing that didn't change at all was the crib.

And the baby in it.

The crib's pastel colors, cleanliness, and delicate lines clashed with a world that was the complete opposite.

Freddie turned his gaze back toward the hallway. The creature that used to be Steve Felton was about to enter the room, holding its hunched back forward. Freddie stepped aside and stood in a corner near a strange, knitted web of gristle—what only a moment ago had been closet doors—letting the creature pass unimpeded.

It stopped next to the crib. It swayed, as if it had difficulty keeping itself upright. This made it look vulnerable in Freddie's eyes. *It's only a newborn*, he thought with pride.

From where he stood, he couldn't see the baby's face, only glimpses through the crib's bars. What he could hear, however, was calm from the infant, not a single cry of fear or any other sound but lazy, contented cooing. Freddie theorized the baby boy had no notion of what he was seeing; he didn't know it was a thing to fear. Or maybe there was a deeper reason for his behavior.

Does he still recognize his father?

The bulge of the creature's back jerked, an orgasmic shudder running through its entire body. The bumps that were its vertebrae separated, one left, one right, little by little, and an opening took shape in the center of its bulbous mass.

I want to see it, Freddie thought with excitement. *Oh, Lord, I want to see it!*

The monster's back opened like an enormous carnivorous plant readying to catch flies. A huge, slimy mouth, with a fleshy interior of exposed membrane and organs. The texture of the ribs was outlined underneath the flesh and ended in the vertebrae that stuck out, lining the edge of the maw, like teeth.

As the mouth opened, the arms, which were at the sides, were pushed through, leaving only wrinkled skin behind, like rolled sleeves, as the bloody, skinless hands now emerged through the insides of the mouth. The hands reached, the elbows bending at an unnatural angle, until bony fingers gripped the infant.

The creature picked up the baby. Freddie was fascinated by the tenderness in its touch. He was amazed the baby was still quiet. On instinct alone, a creature like this should've been perceived as predatory, an abomination, but the baby seemed to recognize his father in it. This touched Freddie's soul more than he could put into words. Tears welled up in his eyes. He brought his hands to his face, weeping with passion.

The creature pulled its arms back into its interior slowly, carrying the little one, bringing him into its great, waiting maw.

Despite that, the baby did not cry.

Abruptly, its jaws slammed shut like an iron maiden,

engulfing the baby whole.

Freddie's ears were filled with the grotesque sounds of flesh being mashed and bones being crushed within the creature. The wet, horrifying grinding of mastication was like music to his ears. He could no longer contain himself and fell to his knees so he could weep in adoration of his God for allowing him to take part and witness his glory. The first of the four sacrifices to take place that night—the Four Offerings—representing the cycle of life, growth, death, and rebirth.

The first was now complete. The Waxing Crescent. A child under four months, son of godless parents, taken from the cradle and delivered to the Lord.

The Full Moon was next. An adult man, son of faithful parents, chosen at random, delivered to the Lord under the blue moon.

Then would come the Waning Crescent. An elderly woman of The Faithful, willingly sacrificing to the Lord on her sleeping bed.

Finally, it would be the New Moon. A pregnant, godless adolescent, delivered to the Lord in her first trimester.

These would fulfill the First Night. The first of four nights, which would awaken God to remake the world.

Chapter Two

The Vigilantes

1992

Raymond Chang went into the crawlspace second to last, Barry Giffen standing lookout like a bouncer at those clubs they saw on TV. He went down on hands and knees and crawled under the old, wooden house. The smell underneath was musty and earthy, in stark contrast with the clean and Lysol-scented spaces of their homes and classrooms. After crawling two feet in, there was a ragged hole in the floorboards above his head, about three feet long, and two feet wide.

"Watch the broken floorboards," Callum Baker said, peering down into the hole through his big horn-rimmed glasses, as Ray put a hand up to climb inside. "We sanded off some of the more jagged ones, but you can still end up catching a splinter from time to time."

Ray's head came up through the hole in the floor, and the shorter teen took his hand and pulled him up, even if he didn't really need it. He was unimpressed at first; he was surrounded by old, wooden walls and an old, wooden ceiling, all quite plain. There was a small boarded-up window facing the direction he'd come from, but along with the entire wall on that side, it was covered in yellowed-out newspaper and magazine pages, crudely glued to the wall, most likely to block all view from the outside through any cracks or windows.

He was in a tiny room that would hardly fit a small bed and a minute desk. By today's standards, this was more of an empty storeroom than a bedroom, and there was an ancient closet with no doors against the longer wall.

There was a grunt from below and he turned as Barry emerged from the floor, his hands covered in dirt, like a zombie crawling out of the grave. Ray put out his own dirty hand to help him up, but the larger, bulkier teenager waved him off and climbed inside.

Once he stood, Barry brushed his hands together and twisted his lips. "Ugh, this is what I hate about this place."

Callum looked at Ray, since Barry already knew his way around. "C'mon. You can wash your hands right outside."

He led them out the door and into what should've been a kitchen. There was an old counter with shelves and a sink that looked to have been installed in modern times but was still quite old. There was a bar of soap next to it.

"The house still has running water. See that door over there?" Callum pointed at a small door in the wall furthest from them. "It has a working toilet, even a shower—cold water only, though—and you sometimes get some rust with the water, so I wouldn't recommend drinking it."

"You first." Ray looked at Barry and nodded toward the sink, knowing the big guy hated dirt. Answering with a smile, Barry walked past him to wash his hands. Ray surveyed their surroundings with curiosity. The kitchen counter was spotless.

"If you see anything that looks too clean," Callum said, noticing this, "that's your big buddy over there." He motioned toward Barry. "Second day we came here, he showed up with two brooms, a mop, and a gallon of disinfectant."

"Thank me when you don't get the bubonic plague," Barry said, without an ounce of facetiousness. "Don't give me the 'well, actually' scientific correction. You know I'm right."

Callum turned to Ray, pushed his glasses up with an index finger. "Well, actually... The big guy might be right. There haven't been people living in this house since 1968, so there are probably mice and rats which might have plague-carrying fleas, but the odds of us actually catching the plague are quite slim. We're more likely to catch hantavirus from rat droppings."

"That's comforting," Ray said. Once Barry moved aside, he washed his hands with more vigor than he'd intended.

They then followed Callum out of the kitchen and into a spacious area with a large stone fireplace at the further end, most likely a dining room.

Ray's jaw dropped.

There were comforters, beanbags, and cushions on the floor of varied colors and prints—indicating they'd most likely come from several of their homes—there was even an old fold-out picnic table with fold-out chairs—umbrella and all—at the center of the room. In one corner, there was a small TV with a Super Nintendo plugged in. Bobby Novak and Jess Cunningham were sitting in front of the TV playing some futuristic racing game. On a pile of cushions in a corner were Peter Lange and Nadine Schaefer, reading some books and eating chips out of a bag. The twins, Royce and Leroy Howe, sat at opposite ends of the picnic table, both with their headphones on, one reading a Superman comic, one reading a Batman comic; one with a can of Coke, one with a can of Pepsi—Ray couldn't tell which of the twins was which. Finally, there was Freddie Parham, drawing some kind of crazy mural full of strange creatures using chalk. The ones he was drawing now were two child-like monsters feeding on each other's arms.

"What the fuuuuu…" Ray mumbled as he took in the surroundings.

"How do you like it?" Barry asked, smiling at last, motioning toward the open space.

"It's…" Ray couldn't speak for a moment. "This is so cool. How did you guys get all this stuff in here?"

"Hole in the floor," Barry said matter-of-factly, earning a confused look from Ray.

"There's a picnic table, man." Ray motioned toward it with disbelief. "How in the world?"

"Oh, well, it's square, but it folds down the middle. Just barely fit."

Callum stepped in. "We brought in stuff from home that was in storage, or really old, so our parents wouldn't miss it."

"I'm looking at a Super NES." Ray pointed. "Pretty sure if my parents gave me a video game console, they'd notice the electronic thingy they paid for disappeared from the house."

"Oh, no, no," Callum said. "That's Bobby's. He tells his folks he's going to take it to a friend's house and always takes it back home with him. Before you ask, the TV is Jess's. It's a spare in case the one in the bar breaks down. And don't ask me why there's still running water and electricity; my best guess is Old Man Curling never turned it off after the Albrights died here in 1968 and keeps paying for both properties together. We've kind of been expecting him to get smart about it and realize his bill is coming in higher, but…I suppose he just doesn't."

"Hey, Ray!" Nadine Schaefer said, noticing the new arrival. "Welcome!"

Peter Lange waved at him from the cushion next to her, a book named *Legion* by William Peter Blatty in his hand.

Leroy—or maybe Royce—looked up from his Batman comic and turned toward them. "Oh, hey, check it out! It's Fred Flintstone and Barney Rubble!"

Royce—or maybe Leroy—looked up from his Superman comic and said, "Nah, that's Yogi and Boo-Boo, man." He shot a gaze at Barry, then Ray. "Just kidding, brother, welcome!"

Leroy or Royce—whoever the other brother was— pointed at a large cooler by the picnic table. "Grab a drink. Only soft drinks for now, though. One of these days, we're thinking of bringing beer, but we're still trying to convince Jess to grab it from her dad's bar."

Jess raised her middle finger without turning around. "Fuck off! I'm not making my dad lose his liquor license to get you to puke, Royce."

Okay, so that one's Royce, Ray thought, studying the minutiae of the boy's face.

"Welcome to the most stupidly named club in the world, Ray!" Jess said, still without turning around.

Bobby looked at him over his shoulder. Smiled. "Hi, Ray. I guess what Jess means is, 'welcome to The Vigilantes.'"

29

Ray gave him an ample grin, but then turned toward Callum and asked, "Why are we called The Vigilantes, though?"

Callum shook his head. "Lange came up with it. It's an unfortunate misnomer that sort of stuck. None of us really knew what 'vigilante' meant, but we always heard it related to superheroes. We thought it meant we were a superhero team. Not my most intellectual moment."

"Oh, okay." Ray nodded. "By the way, shouldn't we be, like, keeping the noise down? I mean…" Ray motioned in the general direction of Old Man Curling's house, where the windows were boarded up, and the outside-facing wall was covered in newspaper.

Freddie, who was the closest to where he stood, giggled with his bizarre hyena laugh. "You're not asking the right questions, Plus-One."

Plus-One? Ray shot a look at Barry, then turned his head toward Freddie—one of the monster children in his drawing had the other's entire arm in its distended, slobbering mouth. "What questions?"

With a smug grin, Freddie turned toward the outer wall and, at the top of his lungs, shouted, "Hey, Curling!"

Ray panicked, eyes darting around the room.

"Yes, you!" Freddie continued without a care. "You incontinent piece of shit! My dad says you fuck your dogs in the ass!"

Frantic, Ray waved his hands in front of him. "What are you doing?"

Freddie continued, undeterred. "My name's Freddie Parham! In case you want to have a word, you ancient pussy!"

Ray stared in abject horror, already picturing his first time at the Vanek House ending up with one of Curling's black Mastiffs chomping down on his throat. It was only then he noticed none of the other kids were acting the least bit alarmed by what Freddie had done. In fact, they appeared to find it hilarious. "I don't get it... What the fuck?"

"I see Brickhouse hasn't brought you up to speed." Freddie nodded toward Barry. "Figures. He's got the communication skills of a cinder block." He shot a crooked-toothed grin at the larger teen, who simply frowned and huffed. "Anyway, I know you were expecting a dark, scary, haunted house... Souls of the dead roaming the halls, dragging chains... Ectoplasm dripping down the walls like the house was cumming, but"—he raised his hands, swiveled his head around, guiding Ray's eyes to look at the surroundings—"it's only a dusty, old house."

"Oh." Ray was disappointed. He'd hoped for at least a few ghosts.

Freddie grinned. "Except..."

Ray's eyebrows arched.

"There are two unquestionably supernatural things about the house."

"Nothing is unquestionably supernatural," Callum interjected.

Freddie gave him an annoyed look. "Look, Droopy... Why don't you go be boring over there with the others, and I'll take it from here?"

Callum rolled his eyes and walked toward the cushions where Peter and Nadine sat.

"Two *unquestionably* supernatural things," Freddie repeated, holding up two fingers, this time exaggerating the word 'unquestionably'. "For some reason, noise doesn't leave the house. At all."

Barry gave a curt nod, confirming this. Ray turned an inquisitive gaze back toward Freddie. "Do you mean like it muffles sound?"

Freddie shook his head. "No. I mean I could bring Iron Maiden to play a concert in here and you wouldn't hear it outside."

"Bullshit."

"Hey, Bobster!" Freddie called.

"What?" Bobby looked back over his shoulder.

"Bring the boombox. We have a non-believer." Bobby paused his game and picked up a silver boombox off the floor, looking quite eager.

Ray followed him and Freddie, Barry close behind, back to the small room with the hole in the floor. Once there, Bobby set the boombox down.

"*You Could Be Mine*. Full blast, please," Freddie said.

"You got it!" Bobby grinned.

Seconds later, the room was filled with the sound of Slash's electric guitar and Axl Rose's yowling vocals. Ray stared at Bobby, who was banging his head as if this song was the epitome of rock excellence. It wasn't, as far as Ray was concerned. To him, this sounded more like the final death cries of the 80s hair-rock era. *Don't they have any Nirvana?* he thought. "Now, what?" he shouted, pushing his voice over the music.

"Whaddaya mean 'now what?'" Freddie shouted. "Down the hole, then go outside!"

"Are you kidding me right now?" He thought of his hands and knees getting dirty again down there. These people had thought of cushions and game consoles, but not of placing a tarp under the floor to make crawling less messy.

"Go!" Freddie said.

Ray did as he was told. Once he went down the hole and was on his hands and knees, he peered up at the other three. "I'm out of the house now!"

Freddie shook his head. "You need to move beyond the walls."

"Yeah, yeah." Ray shook his head. "'Run to the light, Carol Ann', and all that bogus shit." The music was still going on full blast above his head, and, as he started crawling outside, he wondered for a second what the hell it meant to be "bitch-slap rappin'" and having a "cocaine tongue", and how that related to *Terminator 2*—he knew the song was part of the movie's soundtrack. He stopped crawling when his head crossed the boundary of the Vanek House's wall and the sun shone in his face.

Birds chirping.

The wind blowing through the overgrown grass surrounding the house.

The Doppler sound of a car passing by.

No music.

This is impossible. Is Freddie pranking me? Did he drop the volume?

He crawled all the way out, turned around so he was facing the house, then poked his head into the crawlspace as quick as he could, certain this wouldn't give Freddie time to react and crank the volume up again. The second his head crossed the threshold, there it was again: Axl Rose telling someone to count their stars because he was home again. *What the hell?* He pulled his head out. Silence. He waited. Counted to seven. Poked his head back in. Axl Rose singing the end line of the chorus, the song's title leading into a guitar solo. He crawled back in and gawked at the others in astonishment.

The other three smiled down at him with "told ya" expressions on their faces.

He smiled at them, fascinated, then shouted, "What's the second unquestionably supernatural thing?" over the sound of the electric guitar.

Ray followed Freddie back through the kitchen and the dining room—where Bobby had gone back to play Nintendo with Jess—Barry, still playing silent bodyguard, followed close.

They walked into the main hall of the Vanek House, a wide-open space with a roof two tall stories up, which made its height feel daunting. The fireplace he saw in the dining room opened toward the main hall as well, and he figured, because of its size, if it were ever lit, it would warm both spaces quite well. It made no sense lighting it, though, since the smoke coming out of the chimney would be seen by everyone in the surrounding area—and at that point, no supernatural noise cancellation would prevent Ben Curling from coming over with his two huge Mastiffs. Ray also took in the large double doors across the hall, with two boarded-up windows on either side. In this space, newspaper was glued to every surrounding wall, making him feel like he was in some gigantic papier-mâché figure—a huge, creepy piñata.

He nodded toward the double doors. "Aren't you worried Curling's gonna come in through there one of these days to check on the house and find you all here?"

"First couple months we were," Freddie said. "Then we just kinda stopped worrying because he never comes. We're never in the main hall, so we'll hear him if he does come one day. Also, that lock and chain outside those doors? That's going to be freaking noisy when he tries to open it. We'll hear it. And even then"—he pointed at the fireplace—"the hole in the fireplace would let us see the moment the door opens, because the sun will shine through."

"You thought of everything, huh?"

Freddie shrugged. "It's more like we took some mild precautions, and if he catches us, then he catches us. What's he gonna do? Kill us?"

Ray stared at him.

"I'm joking. He can totally kill us." He followed this with his weird, high-pitched hyena laugh. "Emergency plan is we all run into the service room and lock the door and hope it gives us time to escape through the hole in the floor, or we chuck Brickhouse at him and hope he can tank him and knock him unconscious." He grinned at Barry. "I mean…if he's still up to it. Word is Brickhouse got all cushy after Norman tenderized him with a T-Square last year."

"Keep that shit up and find out," Barry said.

"Relax, dude. I'm just teasing. So uptight all the time!"

"Uh, Norman?" Ray asked.

"That's Peter Lange," Freddie said. "You know. *Norman? Psycho?*"—he moved his arm up and down in a stabbing motion—"Schwee! Schwee! Schwee! Yes, Mother. No, Mother. Oh, God, Mother! Blood! Blood!"

"Freddie, stop it," Barry said.

Freddie sighed. "Jeez. Why don't cha get that stick out of your ass, man? C'mon."

They followed Freddie up a set of stairs without a railing going up one flight, reached a landing, turned ninety degrees, then continued to the second floor. Once there, they followed the balustrade to the left—looking down at the main hall—then turned right at the corner into the next hallway, where there were two doors on either side; bedrooms, Ray supposed.

"Hey, Plus-One," Freddie said without turning around.

"My name's Ray, Freddie."

"Have you already heard about the Albrights?"

"Dad stabbed his whole family and ate them?"

"You got it!" Freddie raised his index finger, then pointed it at one of the closed doors to the right. "This is the room where he killed his little girl and his baby boy. You can still see where the blood was absorbed by the floorboards. Forty-four times, he stabbed each. They said the little baby looked like ground beef." He let out that weird laugh of his. "Guess that made it go down easier." He continued to giggle, then turned right at the next corner. "Almost there."

Ray shot an uncomfortable look at Barry, who responded with a shrug, and said, "The Hyena's not really a bad guy, he's just…creepy."

They followed Freddie around the corner.

37

There was a single door halfway down the hallway. It looked different from the others. "This is it." Freddie gestured toward the door with a flourish. "The second unquestionably supernatural thing in the Vanek House."

It was a wooden door, made from sturdier, thicker wood than the walls, reinforced with metal, which—though somewhat rusted—still looked tough. There was a metal plate by the handle with an old keyhole. It was ancient, like looking at a door in a dungeon of some kind, hiding treasure, but other than that, it was simply a door.

Ray shot a glance at Freddie. "Is the unquestionably supernatural thing *behind* this door?"

Freddie shook his head. "Open it."

Ray turned the knob, but it didn't open. "It's locked." He shrugged, indifferent to this. At the moment, he was more disturbed and fascinated by the room Freddie had pointed at a moment ago, thinking of going in there and seeing the bloodstains, morbid as that might be. A locked door wasn't enough to earn his attention. Had the corpses of the little girl and the baby been found behind this door? *Oh, no, that's right,* he remembered. *Their dad ate them.*

He turned his gaze to Barry, who already knew the story behind the door, kind of pleading for him to tell him what he was missing.

Barry rolled his eyes. "He wants you to point out you need a key, and then he'll tell you there's no key, and then you'll ask him what the deal with the door is, and then he'll get all spooky and tell you the door is haunted 'coz nothin' can open it, and you'll give him ideas to try to open it, and he'll say he's already tried them all, until you realize in a whole year we haven't been able to open the goddamn door."

"Well, thanks for ruining the fun, Brickhouse. Anyway, yeah, he's right. Door doesn't open, no matter what you do. We've tried to pick the lock, undo the hinges... We've tried hammers, drills, crowbars. Once, Jess brought this heavy ax she took from her dad's cellar. Bounced right off. Nothing works on the door."

Ray stared, unconvinced. "Have you tried—"

"Yes." They stared at each other for a second. "I mean it. We even had Brickhouse charge the door, putting his full weight behind it. Didn't even shake."

"Okay," Ray said. "How about the wall? The wood looks old, not very durable. No one outside will hear it if you use a sledgehammer or a saw to open a hole in the wall."

"Won't work." Barry shook his head, arms crossed over his chest.

"Whatever's protecting the door is also protecting the entire wall," Freddie said. "I took my dad's drill to the other walls in the house. This one is the only one we can't crack. Didn't even leave a dent. Now, here's the cool part. We prepared a demonstration for our newest member. If my beautiful assistant will please...assist?"

Barry rolled his eyes and approached a boarded-up window at the end of the hallway. Resting on the sill were a hammer and a few nails. Barry took them and stood in front of the wall to the left of the door. He shot a glance at Ray while holding the tip of one nail against the wall. "Um, better take a step back, just in case. See the tip?"

Ray nodded.

The big guy reared the hammer back and, with absolute precision, hit the nail square in the head. For a minute, Ray expected to see the flat head of the nail visible on the wooden wall, but it wasn't there. Barry took a step back, crouched, and picked up something off the floor; he held it up and showed him it was the nail. It was bent at a jagged angle. "Check the wall. Where the tip was."

Ray studied the surface, but where he should've seen at least a pockmark, there was only the untouched wooden wall. He saw the wooden texture, but no sign of the tip of the nail having pushed even slightly into it. "That's impossible."

"And that concludes our supernatural tour of the infamous Vanek House!" Freddie grinned proud of himself for some reason Ray couldn't figure. "If you'll accompany me back downstairs, we have snacks, beverages, and entertainment! No gift shop, though."

Other than Sylvia Nguyen demanding to join the group sometime in the fall—under threat of telling their parents where they spent their weekend afternoons and, sometimes, their after-school hours—1992 had been fairly uneventful for The Vigilantes, at least within the confines of the Vanek House. Through the ribbing, and the jokes, and the secrecy of it all, 1992 had taken what they had built and solidified it in ways none of them could have predicted. They had gone from a group of kids who had almost nothing in common to a veritable team whose differences helped them support each other where their strengths failed.

Despite having joined using coercion, Sylvia had integrated perfectly into their dynamic. At school, she had always lived in isolation, labeled the nerd, the teacher's pet, the snitch, only because she needed to live up to unfair standards set by her parents. As one of The Vigilantes, she'd become the "inside agent", using her status as the exemplary student to extract information on tests and other schoolwork—a practice Callum had some qualms with, but held his tongue about.

Whether at school, at The Pines, at the small arcade by Seaside Park, or matinees at the Harrell theater, the group had become inseparable, and as 1993 dawned on the horizon, the future within their little world looked bright.

Peter and Nadine had become an item, to their friends' utter surprise. They spent a lot of time together at school and could be seen handholding at lunch and at The Pines, and always sat together in their little spot on the cushions at Vigilante Headquarters. They had never made an official announcement or made a big deal of it; it was this small, pretty thing that had grown between them.

Bobby had brought in his old VCR, since his parents had bought a new one at home and shelved the other one in their garage. They'd watched *Batman Returns, Reservoir Dogs*—a bootleg recording, since the VHS version hadn't come out yet—*Alien 3, Candyman*, and, at the request of the Howe twins, *Encino Man*, a comedy about a caveman in modern times, starring some unknown actor named Brendan Fraser.

Freddie had completed his creepy little mural, and it had astonished them all how detailed it was for something drawn with cheap chalk purchased downtown at Greene's. It served as a reminder their HQ was still in the bowels of a house where dozens of people had died horrible deaths—it also returned a certain creepy vibe to the house their cheerful presence threatened to take away. He'd done an uncharacteristic memorial to Gerardo Valencia, the kid who had died in 1989 and who had been friends with both him and Jess. She, in particular, had been moved by the gesture. It was the only joyful, colorful part of the mural: a small yellow house with flowers on the front lawn.

Ray had started mowing lawns to make extra cash, even getting hired by Peter's mother, of all people, to mow hers. For the most part, she left him alone, but when interactions happened, he could count on a racist comment or two to issue from her mouth, which made Peter so embarrassed he wouldn't stop apologizing. She paid well, though. Ray's contribution to The Vigilantes consisted of bringing food and snacks from his parents' restaurant free of charge.

As for the others, Jess was always good for a large bottle of Coke or Sprite from the bar. The Howe twins, having the larger allowance, carried the bigger portion of snacks, drinks, and comic book expenses. Callum's under-the-table job at the shoe store meant he was next door to Becker's, so he was the one that did the shopping each Saturday before coming over to HQ, making a monthly stop at Merrill Yates's Pharmacy to stock up on comics and magazines—old Mr. Yates was always really cool and threw in an extra comic for every five he got. Nadine and Barry were the easiest deterrent from any bully who'd want to get cute and try to cause trouble for the little group of weirdos who gathered in the Vanek House—Nadine on account of her popularity and maturity, Barry based on his intimidating size and reputation.

Then, there was Peter, who brought nothing in particular to the group, but was considered the de facto founder, since his coming to The Pines over a year and a half earlier had been the catalyst for them coming together. He'd also been the one who gave them the way into the Vanek House. He'd even named the group, and it was a name most of them found ridiculous, but they'd given him the right to pick, so now they were stuck with it.

Perhaps their biggest reason to be optimistic had been that in all this time, they hadn't had a single encounter with Old Man Curling and his dogs, and he showed no signs of suspecting they were there. If he'd come during their absence, he would've no doubt noticed all their stuff, and would've discovered the hole in the floor. But this never happened.

And so, 1993 was looking bright for The Vigilantes.

However, as summer drew nearer, and the Parhams began planning their family picnic at the Pargin River, they would all learn life had a way of taking sharp turns into dark places.

Chapter Three

Remember?

2022

"How has Freddie been?" Royce asked, slapping Bobby on the shoulder.

Bobby, who sat to his right at the makeshift long table formed by combining three smaller ones, eyed his old friend with a mix of intrigue and surprise. He took a sip of beer and smiled at him. "We've been here for half an hour and you're already drunk?"

Royce chuckled. "I'm asking for real, Mr. Psychiatrist." His expression shifted from relaxed to serious. "I don't hold a grudge against Freddie, you know? After what happened to his family, I can't imagine what got scrambled in that head of his. Almost thirty years, he's still locked up. I don't think he was really aware what he was doing."

Bobby nodded. "I want to agree with you. I do. Sometimes, though, I'm not so sure." His face showed a slight hint of sadness and defeat. He ran a hand through his blond hair and let out a sigh. "In any case, you know I can't tell you anything I discuss with him. There is such a thing as doctor-patient confidentiality."

Royce let out a sarcastic snort. "True, technically, if you were actually his shrink, but from what I understand, his actual doctor is some other guy, and you're an assistant."

"Consultant."

"Same difference."

"I'm sorry, man. Even if, technically, I can talk about it, it just wouldn't feel right." Bobby caressed his mug of beer, which was almost empty—only a few strands of foam still clinging to the glass.

"How about an exception, just between us, friends?" Royce gave him a salesman's grin. "I can invite you and Angie to the next gig I play. Drinks on me."

Bobby chuckled. "Sure, because I look like the kind of guy who frequents rambunctious electronic dance parties, and getting drunk won't kill my sick girlfriend."

"C'mon, brother!"

Bobby gave Royce a slanted glance. Suspicion hung

from his eyelids. "Why so much interest?"

"Did you notice the thing with the birds earlier today?"

Bobby's eyes opened wide with surprise, lighting up his face. He'd thought the phenomenon had only happened in Lighthouse Rock, or that he'd been the only one who'd noticed it. In either case, this was not a topic he'd expected to come up that night.

His friend continued without waiting for a response. Bobby's facial expression was the only confirmation he needed. "Today I spent all afternoon trying to remember the last time that happened. I was sure it had happened at least once before. Let's be real. Normally, this wouldn't have even registered. Birds going quiet? Who even notices that?"

I did, Bobby thought.

"And then it hit me: it happened at two specific moments I'll never be able to forget. The first time was when the Vanek House burned down."

Bobby licked his lips. He replied with all the tact his profession afforded him. "You mean when Leroy passed away."

"Right," Royce said, the solemnity in his expression driving home the sheer weight of that event.

Bobby knew losing his twin brother had been the defining moment of Royce's life. He'd described it as waking up one morning and realizing half of your body was paralyzed. The Howe twins were your stereotypical twin pairing but augmented. Leroy and Royce. Left and Right. L and R. The Stereo Twins, suddenly in mono.

"There's no way I'd ever forget that day. I can still see it in my mind. All of us, standing in front of the Vanek House, flames coming out of every window and every crack… Leroy's corpse lying in front of me in the grass." Like in a trance, Royce motioned with his hand to the right. "Freddie lying there unconscious, after Barry punched his lights out."

He took a sip of beer. Swallowed.

"I was stunned. It was like I had tuned everything out. The roar of the fire, the police, the firemen, the noisy crowd. Barry cursing at Freddie. Jess crying on my shoulder. I knew all of those sounds were *there*, but I just couldn't really *hear* them. I was focused on the fact Ben Curling's house was surrounded by trees and shrubs, and there should've been birds calling out in alarm because of the fire, but there weren't any. All of these noises, but no birds."

"It's not uncommon," Bobby said, "for people in shocking, traumatic situations to focus on a single environmental factor: a flower that caught your eye, a strangely-shaped rock, or in your case, the lack of bird noises."

Royce responded with a grave nod. "That brings me to the second time I remember this happening. It was during Leroy's funeral. Weird, right? Why do I remember that specific fact about it?" He glanced at Bobby with a raised eyebrow in an inquisitive expression. "There were more important things that should've been stored in my mind. Not freakin' birds. Even if I noticed the birds both times, back then, why would I remember that today, thirty years later? Well, here's the thing: I remembered because today the birds went quiet at noon. Leroy was buried at noon."

Bobby canted his head to one side, thinking about this. "The Vanek House burned down at around four in the afternoon, though. I don't see the relation."

"Me either, but I want to test a theory tomorrow at noon. I was asking about Freddie, 'coz the first time I remember it happening was when he did what he did at the Vanek House. So, I had this stupid, shot-in-the-dark idea that maybe *he* knew something. You know how supernatural stuff was always his jam? Has he mentioned anything about it, like noticing that before?"

Bobby paused for a moment, putting his own theories together with what he was getting from Royce. "Not specifically about that. But every time I've seen him at noon, he's in these silent, solemn moods. They last, on average, fifteen minutes. Like he's praying in silence."

Royce shot a knowing glance at Bobby. "Do you think that's a coincidence? Not in this town."

Bobby considered his old friend, and, instead of answering the question, asked something back. "Have you seriously forgiven Freddie?"

Royce thought about it for a moment. He raised his

head toward the bar and signaled to Louis Foley. "Hey, Lou!" he said, and the rookie bartender looked back. Royce flashed two fingers. "Whiskey, gold label, neat, two glasses."

Louis nodded, but then shot an unwitting nervous glance toward his boss, Jess, who was sitting at a corner table having a fun chat with Bobby's girlfriend, Angie.

Royce reacted as if he'd made a social *faux-pas*, then shot a look toward Jess, making a face in her direction, asking for her permission to get a couple glasses of the mid-top-tier liquor. Jess looked straight into his eyes, smirked, then turned to Louis.

"Louis!" she said. "Bring them the bottle."

Royce gave Jess a thankful smile. "Thank you, baby."

"Don't mention it, Daddy," Jess replied in a playful, high-pitched, girly voice that always felt bizarre coming out of her. It was part of this strange, non-sexual, little S&M play she and Royce had, in which she acted all subservient, when in fact, she was always the one calling the shots.

Louis approached with a bottle of whiskey and two wide bottom glasses. Set them in front of Royce and Bobby, poured two fingers in each. Without hesitation, Royce downed his glass in a single shot and raised it toward Louis, motioning for him to pour another.

"First one's a palate cleanser," he said, grinning at Bobby. "It's the second one that really counts. Least that's how I do it."

Louis poured more whiskey into Royce's glass. This time Royce moved it in a gentle circle, making the golden liquid swirl. He brought it close to his nose and took a whiff of its smoky aroma. Took a single small sip. Smiled. "Thanks, Lou."

"You're welcome." Louis nodded with a smile, set the bottle on the table, and walked away.

Royce studied his glass, just a little emptier than Bobby's—as if it contained the answers to all of life's mysteries—then gazed into his expectant eyes. "I think I can never forgive Freddie completely. He killed my brother. Stole half of me. I'll never recover what he took. But I don't hate him, either. The person who did those things is not the Freddie we knew."

Bobby nodded, now taking his own glass between his fingers and raising it to his nose. "That seems just."

He took a sip, taking in about half of the whiskey.

"I don't want my daughter to know grudges," Royce added. "I especially don't want her learning them from me. I think I can teach her an important lesson: if her father can forgive her uncle's murderer, she can also have a kind and forgiving heart, but she should never *forget* who hurt her and always seek to understand why."

Bobby raised his glass toward him. "Here's to seeking to understand."

Royce smiled. They clinked their glasses together and drank until they were empty.

Callum peered over at Peter, who was sitting in the next chair over, his back to the wall, under a glowing Coors Light sign that made him wonder if those were a requirement at every town bar—could you *not* get a license to open a bar if you didn't put one of those up? The chair next to Peter was empty, since Barry had stood up and followed Raymond to the restroom. Callum had gotten the "shitty seat"; the one they'd set right at the corner because the three tables they'd put together could only fit eight chairs, but they needed nine. Raymond, the last to arrive, had asked him to switch places, and he'd smiled as he gave up the seat where the table corner poked under his sternum and one of the wooden legs was right between his thighs.

"Hey, Peter?" he said, moving to Barry's vacated chair and putting a hand on his shoulder. His friend turned his dark blue eyes towards him and smiled.

"Hey, Cal," he said. "Nadine was telling me earlier you're working on a book. We're going to have two published writers in the group. That's so cool! Nonfiction, I suppose?"

"Uh, yes, sort of." Callum cast an unwitting glance past Peter, toward Nadine.

"Oh, crap… I-I'm… I'm sorry," she said, stammering. "Was it a secret? Did I screw up?"

"That's okay," he said, and turned his attention back to Peter. "That's actually what I wanted to talk to you about. I... Well, Sylvia and I"—he glanced toward the end of the table to his right, where Sylvia was busy intimately acquainting herself with a glass of wine, just letting him do his thing—"we've been working on a book about the history of White Harbor. You know, all the weird events and stories? And, of course, it covers the origins of that weird religion you and your mother belong to—"

"My mother." Peter was quick to intervene, putting great emphasis behind his words. "Not me. I'm not part of that."

"No, wait, wait," Callum said, palms raised, realizing he'd touched a nerve. "Bear with me for a minute. I know you're not, but here's the thing. I'm very interested in the subject of the Vanek House, the history of the Parhams, and how it all relates to Blight Harbor, and it all seems to lead to that religion of hers."

Peter tried to get a question in, but Callum kept going, not giving him a chance to interject.

"Rationally," he said, "we think Blight Harbor is just superstition, right? But it's not. Not really. Blight Harbor is more than just this local folklore thing. It's not just this old wives' tale to scare children. For us"—he waved his hand around, gesturing toward everyone in their surroundings—"for all of us living here, and those of us who grew up here, it's almost objective reality."

He saw the confusion in Peter's eyes.

"Wait," Peter said with an intrigued, crooked smile. "You, Callum Baker, librarian, science and history buff, you are telling me you believe Blight Harbor exists?"

"Don't you?" he retorted.

"Uh…" Peter averted his gaze to one side, as if trying to come up with an answer that wouldn't make him sound crazy.

"Never mind," Callum said. "Let's say I do and *don't* believe in Blight Harbor. Let me explain from a psychological and philosophical standpoint. Let's not get into the supernatural…yet. Think of it as 'thought turned into action'"—he did air quotes—"and the action is what makes it real. For instance, you can *think* about eating a chicken sandwich; the elements to make a chicken sandwich exist in the universe, but it's not a reality until you actually *take* those elements, *make*, and *eat* a chicken sandwich. Thoughts. Action. Superstitions. Action. You know what I mean?"

He looked at Peter with an expectant expression.

"I get it," Peter said. "I don't mean to be dense, Cal, but I—"

"Okay, bad example." He continued. "In Japan, hospitals don't have a fourth floor; they go from the third to the fifth, because 'four' in Japanese—pronounced 'shi'—sounds like the word 'death'. This is also prevalent in many other Asian countries, where the number four *also* sounds like death. You can even jump from there to the Americas where there are buildings that don't have a thirteenth floor, or even go as far as building a thirteenth *mini-floor* to leave unused, like a buffer zone, all because the number thirteen is the number of Judas, the thirteenth apostle of Christ, and so, it's considered an unlucky number.

"It's like they took a superstition—which is something psychological, cultural, or spiritual—and turned that superstition into a building; into something physical, something solid. Something you can touch and inhabit. Actions. Do you understand now? Blight Harbor is like that. Here, people are afraid of Blight Harbor, as if it were an actual physical place that exists in all our houses. Like, regardless of where we are, it's in the next room over, listening to everything we're saying so, one day, when we open that room, all of those things we said will be there waiting for us. The moment we move dirt to build our homes, our streets, our buildings, we are setting our very foundations *in* Blight Harbor. It's fascinating!"

"Cal," Peter chimed in at last, "I can see this is very exciting for you, but I think you're losing me a bit. I get all of these concepts you're talking about, but I still don't understand what you're getting at. What's all of that got to do with me and my mother?"

"The story of Walter Parham," Callum said with an enthusiastic grin. "Do you remember telling us about that?"

Peter shot him a nostalgic smile. "Of course. It was the first time I spoke to all of you guys. Kinda hard to forget."

"I remember you said the place where Reverend Burgess raped Walter Parham—"

"Cal!" Peter looked around with visible discomfort, as if Callum had shouted the "r" word into a megaphone.

Callum coughed and lowered his voice. "Where Walter Parham was *hanged*. You said it was a place people called Blight Harbor. Remember?"

"Vaguely? I remember telling the story, but not the details. It *has* been a while."

Callum nodded. He loved his friends, but it could sometimes frustrate him they weren't as detail-obsessed as he. "John Ellis, the man who set up the 'kill spot' for Walter Parham and set up the rock where Burgess was going to...'r-word' him? The man who took him down from the tree where he was hanged and buried him in that same spot? Remember that part?" Peter looked lost. "Sorry, Cal. Just barely."

Callum narrowed his eyes, as if trying to determine if Peter was just being facetious. He saw no trace of humor in his expression. "Interesting. One would expect a horror writer to have an excellent memory for creepy stories and folklore."

Peter shook his head. "I wasn't a writer back then."

"Right," he said, his eyebrows furrowed in suspicion. "Anyway, I *do* remember. There's mention of Long-Lived John Ellis all over accounts of the town's origins and history. He was famous because he lived to be over a hundred—some say, even longer. He came with the people who colonized White Harbor. I found plenty of documents in which he's mentioned, and that's when I remembered your story. My point is, John Ellis called the spot where Walter Parham died 'Blight Harbor', meaning Blight Harbor was first a *physical* place, then it became this psychological concept in local folklore, and now, we're again turning it into a physical place we inhabit, and it's not just this hidden spot in the woods, it's the whole town. Don't you think that's fascinating?"

Peter nodded, with less enthusiasm than Cal had hoped.

"But, anyway, since you don't remember, maybe I'll ask you about something you probably *do*. Your mom was teaching you to read a book, a book with a leather cover. Something like the Bible of her religion. You remember that?"

Peter nodded. He shifted in his seat and avoided eye contact, showing discomfort. "Yes, she has it with her in the hospital. What's the question?"

"Really? She does? Great!" He looked at Peter with eyes so thrilled they almost glowed. "I wouldn't imagine your dear mother would be willing to lend it to you for a few days, would she?"

"Do you want to go ask her? I'll take you. If you touch that book, though, I can't guarantee you'll leave the room with your hands still attached."

Callum shook his head. He brought his hand up to his lips, taking a deep, discouraged breath. Pondering. "Oh!" he blurted. "Do you happen to have another copy of the book lying around? At your house, here in town? If your mom is part of this cult, I figure every member must have one. Maybe there's a copy somewhere with a dedication reading: 'To Peter. Love, Mother' or something like that?"

Peter pressed his lips together, not looking too happy with Callum's remark. He probably had to remind himself Callum hadn't meant it as a dig at his relationship with his mother. He shook his head. "I don't think so. Though there are some boxes in my attic with some stuff I took from the old house before renting it. Maybe there's something in there. Why the interest in the Uolminar? What does it have to do with fourth floors, and foundations, and hanged children? Damn, that question got dark."

"Uolminar? Fascinating! Well, in the historical documents I've found about the town, I have also found phrases and notes in which they mention the language of the cult."

"The Circle." Peter was quick to correct him.

"Yes, the Circle! Sylvia's the linguist, not me, so she's been developing a key to translate the language, based on those documents. The key is very empirical and rudimentary, but we've figured out certain things about it. For example, that the God of the Circle—or well, they call it God, not that there is such a thing—is called Uolmin. Which means, if the

Circle's Bible is called the Uolminar, that would mean—"

"It means the 'Word of God,'" Peter said. "Uolmin means God, but they use it as a proper noun."

"Like the Christians," Callum replied, intrigued.

"Something like that."

Callum leaned in closer, a smile tugging at the corners of his mouth. "How much do you know of that language?"

"Too little to be of any use, to be honest." Peter shrugged with a crooked lip. "I didn't learn enough before they took me from my mom's house." He squinted, as if a realization had popped into his head. "There *is* one phrase. It's repeated a lot in that book, and it's the first one they made me learn. I said it so many times, I have it memorized."

"Wait!" Callum hurried to take out a pen from his shirt pocket and reached for a napkin. "Write it down."

Peter eyed the pen with some trepidation. Unbeknown to Callum, the words Peter often heard from his mother were now running on a loop in his brain as he considered taking that pen.

"You won't be worthy of writing the Word of God until you are baptized at sixteen. You must never write it down, or the wrath of the Lord will be great."

When his friend took the pen from his fingers, Callum saw he was paler than usual. His face was paper-white, framed by black hair that only increased the contrast. His eyes, two blue dots under the shadow that fell over his brow. In a quick, decisive motion, he jotted something on the napkin and slid it back to Callum.

He read it with an intrigued expression on his face, trying his best to pronounce it. "*Tjenaf egoikaat gozun-Uolmin yggshe.*" He then read the translation. "God will feed." He turned to Peter, arching his eyebrows. "Ominous. Do you have any free time tomorrow to meet up? Just for a moment. I want to show you some things I have compiled, see if they jog your memory. It would really help me a lot."

"Sure." A hint of color returned to Peter's skin, and the darkness in his eyes dissipated. "I don't know how much I can help, though. By the time I left White Harbor, I knew very little about the Circle or its members. I never met any other than my mom. I wasn't supposed to know who they were until I was baptized at sixteen, and that never happened."

Callum flashed him a smug smile. "I know of two members."

Peter's eyes widened. "What?"

"One of them is dead, though. Barry's dad was a member of the Circle. The suicide letter he left had a pretty big hint, though he gave no details. I guess he didn't flat out say it because he didn't want to put Barry or his mom at risk, but I'm a hundred percent sure Barry's parents were in the Circle."

Peter cast a quick glance toward the bathroom, where Barry had stomped off just a couple of minutes earlier, chasing Ray. "Is Barry in the Circle?"

"No," Callum said. "If he is, he's doing one hell of a good job pretending, but his mom died of liver cancer before he was sixteen. It's likely he was never baptized, same as you."

"Who's the other one?"

"Hey Cal!" Royce said, interrupting. "Stop hogging Pete. Let him talk to us for a while. We want to catch up, too."

"Um…" Callum stammered a bit. "Yes, of course. How inconsiderate of me." He stood up, ready to return to his previous seat, but before walking away, turned to Peter. "Tomorrow?"

Peter nodded.

Chapter Four

Once in a Blue Moon

Sam Becker Jr. had just closed the supermarket, changed into his running clothes, and was now taking a relaxing night jog around town like he did five days a week. He found it both soothing for his mind and energizing for his body.

His parents had excused themselves a little earlier that afternoon and left him to take care of their last customers. By nine, Harbor Grocers was closed, and by nine-thirty, he'd put the cash in the safe and pulled down the shutters. It had been a slow afternoon and night. It usually took him longer to do the entire closing routine, but it had been pleasant and quick that night. Restocking the aisles and cleaning was something his mother liked to do early in the morning, since they lived next door to the supermarket. She planned on doing this until she died, but Sam had already decided to hire some extra hands. Not only were his parents getting a bit long in the tooth and slow, but no grocery store with plans for national expansion should close at nine, even in a small town like White Harbor.

He had a full five-year plan of where he wanted to take Harbor Grocers, and it would not stop at this little corner of the world—no way—he was going to take Harbor Grocers to the national level. Hell, who said he didn't have what it took to turn his little family business into the next Walmart, the next Amazon? The mom-and-pop store was a defunct concept and had been for a long time now. He was determined to modernize and grow what his parents had started decades ago.

Speaking of Mom and Pop, he thought, hearing the ringtone of his armband-strapped iPhone on his AirPods— he'd sold his Apple Watch recently, but he'd get the newest model soon. It was the ringtone he'd assigned to his dad's phone. He tapped twice on his left AirPod and heard the voice of his dad, who sounded a bit agitated.

"Junior!" his dad said the moment he heard the line open. "Are you home?"

"What was that?" Sam said, a bit confused by his tone. His dad knew he always went jogging after closing up the store, then headed back to his place.

"Are you home?" Sam Becker Sr. repeated.

Sam made a puzzled face as he turned a corner, his

Nike Air Zoom shoes bouncing up and down on the pavement, the breeze cooling his sweaty face, where a neon-lime Nike bandanna collected as much sweat as it could from his forehead, strands of blond, wet hair bobbing with the motion.

"What do you mean, 'Am I home'? You know I'm not, Dad. I'm out running. You and Mom should go out for walks, you know? It's good for your—"

"Go home! Now!"

Sam could hear the panic in his father's voice. He could also hear his mom in the background, rambling and whimpering. He stopped. Listened. He adjusted his armband, as if it had gotten tight all of a sudden.

"Whoa," he said. "What's gotten into you? Calm down. What the hell?"

"Samuel!" his mom cried from the background. "This is your mom!" She always announced herself as if he wouldn't recognize her voice. It annoyed him to no end, but right now it was sending a prickling sensation through the hairs on the back of his neck. "Please, honey, go to your house, or come to ours, whichever's closer! Stay in tonight! Please!"

Sam looked around, trying to see if there was anything strange going on. Just a normal night, like any other. "What's the matter with you two?"

"It's the First Night, Samuel!" his dad said, his panic laced with just enough parental condescension to sting. "How could you forget, son?"

"Oh, God, *please!*" his mom hollered in desperation. He could picture her clamoring toward the ceiling. "Please, not my baby!"

He realized he couldn't move. Memories of the stories his parents had instilled in him since birth resurfaced, followed by a deluge of bizarre images linked to his upbringing in their peculiar faith. That odd room they called the Sanctum. The prayers. The weird language. The creepy chanting. He'd never taken any of it seriously. Yes, he saw some bizarre things he couldn't explain during the Circle's gatherings, but wasn't that the whole dog-and-pony show every religion put on to keep people coming?

But the First Night, he thought. *Isn't that like the big one? The beginning of that ritual they kept waiting for. When that fanatical Lange woman spoke of the First Night, it chilled my blood. The Ritual of the Four Nights. Yeah, that's what it was called. And on the First Night—*

"Oh, shit," he said in a breathless voice.

—the Four Offerings.

"Run!" his father shouted into the phone. "Son, please, run!"

It took only two seconds of listening to his mother's wailing sobs in the background for him to conclude this was real. He spun on his expensive shoes, and the first thing that caught his eye was the blue moon, full, large, and menacing. A cold blue. A dead blue that made everything around him dark and otherworldly. The eye of a merciless god, peering down at a speck of dust that happened to draw breath. A speck of dust named Sam Becker…Junior.

An adult man, son of faithful parents, chosen at random, delivered to the Lord under the blue moon.

The world had changed. It had stopped making sense in a blink.

"Honey, please, run home!" his mother shouted, every word soaked with panic. "Honey, hurry! Get—"

Static.

Before Sam Becker's eyes, what used to be a town street had transformed into an abandoned, impoverished shantytown under the moonlight. Ancient buildings made of splintered wood, mud, and torn fabric stretched as far as the eye could see—which wasn't very far, considering the complete lack of streetlights or lamps from within the ruins.

There was no vegetation other than the remains of dead trees, gnarled and cadaverous, and everything was covered in mold and decay. The ground beneath his feet was no longer made of asphalt. It felt uneven, and—

Wet?

He realized now he was standing in about eight inches of foul-smelling water. A stench like sewage and decomposing fish violated his nostrils, making him gag.

If he hadn't been so aware and certain of every single thing he'd done in the day, leading him to this very street, he would've been sure this was a nightmare. He would've sworn he was lying in bed, sleeping, having a horrible dream. Instead, he was certain of the opposite. He'd changed inside the store and gone jogging. He'd never made it home. This was real.

Everything his parents had taught him. Every single insane rambling from Martha Lange had been true. *This*, he thought. *This is the First Night. This is Blight Harbor.*

Sam pulled his iPhone from his armband and stared at the screen. He was shocked to see it was still lit up, and the call was still connected. In a hurry, he took off his AirPods and pressed the device against his ear as if it would make him feel his parents' warmth against his skin. His entire body shook with terror.

"Dad?" he said, whimpering, almost in tears. "Mom?"

Static.

Then voices, deep in the static. Whispering. Whispering about *him*. It was hard to make out any actual phrases in the cacophony of whispers flooding his ear, but he could pick out individual words: Loser. Egotistic. Arrogant. Parasite. Then, from the chaos, the distinct recognition of his mother's voice saying, "*...lots of plans, but never accomplishes a thing.*" And his father's voice saying, "*...boy's half the man I hoped he'd grow into.*"

His breath caught in his throat.

"Dad?" His voice was a thin, mewling whine. "Mom?"

The answer was not something he could've expected.

There was the sound of uneven steps, splashing in the shallow water, coming from behind. Not two feet. Many.

When Sam spun around, only darkness greeted him. All he heard were the strange footsteps, fast approaching.

"Hello?" he said, but took a step back because his body knew, even before his brain reconciled with the idea, that whatever was walking in this horror of a world could not be another person.

Splash, splish-plosh, ploosh-splosh-splash.

SPLASH!

Closer now.

SPLASH-SPLOSH-PLASH! SPLASH! PLOOSH! SPLASH!

Closer. Closer. Closer.

His heart racing, without hesitation, he turned on the flashlight on his phone and raised it toward the sounds advancing with noticeable intent. He only glimpsed what looked like the deathly pale arm of a child—but moving as if it were crawling on all fours toward him—before he took off running in the opposite direction. He flew down the block and rounded the corner, his expensive running shoes soaked in water, mud, and filth.

Sam could now feel water falling on his face, which couldn't have come from his feet splashing in the swamp below. A violent downpour had begun out of nowhere. No gradual increase in the frequency of raindrops, just entire sheets of rainwater falling on him from the sky. The raindrops struck his face and his eyes, stealing his visibility as he ran. The cone of light from the phone's flashlight spun around with no aim, like a spotlight tumbling down a precipice. He was sure he'd lost the creature by now, but he kept on running.

Then the unthinkable. He brought his right foot down, and instead of hitting the ground, it passed straight through the water, followed by his entire body as he fell into a flooded hole. He plunged and sank into deep, filthy, dark water. No notion of where up or down were. He opened his eyes—his mind flooded with the infections that would by now be seeping into his eyeballs from the revolting pool. He caught sight of his phone floating above him; its flashlight still glowed despite the murky waters. Its waterproof case kept it afloat with two tiny air pockets on the sides.

He emerged and grabbed hold of the phone, shone it around. The driving rain didn't allow him to see far. And there was the blue moon, peeking through a black-clouded sky. He waved and slapped his free hand around, trying to find the edge of the sinkhole—invisible in the flooded street—but to no avail. As far as he knew, the sinkhole could stretch forever in every direction.

Little by little, through the droning sound of the rain, a chilling noise arose: *splash, splish-plosh, ploosh-splosh-splash, splish-plosh, ploosh, splash.*

He couldn't get out of the hole.

Ploosh-splosh-splash, splish-plosh.

"Help me!" he shouted, swallowing water and spitting it out in disgust, feeling his taste buds assaulted by a bitter, revolting taste, as if he'd bitten down on some rotten mollusk and let its juices run into his mouth.

Splish-plosh, PLOOSH!

"Somebody! Mom! Dad! Somebody help me!"

SPLASH-SPLOSH-PLASH! SPLASH!

The sound of the rain grew louder, and soon it was as if he could hear faint whispers mixed in with it, just like the ones he'd heard on the phone.

"*Parasite.*"

"*Loser.*"

"*Half the man I hoped.*"

SPLASH! PLOOSH! SPLASH!

"Please! Help me!" His voice was suffused with terror, his tears disappeared in the rain.

"*Arrogant.*"

"*Egotistic.*"

"*Never accomplishes a thing.*"

SPLOSH-PLASH! SPLASH!

PLOOSH!

It stopped.

Sam could feel the ripples in the water coming from the direction of the thing or things. Even in his panicked state, he could now determine where the edge of the sinkhole was. It was close. On his right. But he could not approach it anymore, because whatever was pursuing him was right there.

Reacting as fast as he could, Sam held the phone against his chest, trying to cover its light. Doing his best to stay afloat in the darkness, hoping to remain unseen and unheard. From his right came a low, guttural growl that sent shivers down his spine. It sounded like a snarling dog, but there was an unnerving human quality to it, like a child imitating a wild beast. Then there was another distinct growl, and another, each with different voices. Three individual creatures snarling in a human yet beastly tone.

Then, a sound like a woman choking.

Sam couldn't stop trembling. His breath was shallow, ragged. He wasn't sure of it, but he believed he had pissed himself. What he was hearing was illogical. He didn't know what was hunting him or why.

After seconds of nothing happening—still hearing the growls and the woman's choked gurgling—Sam went against every instinct in his mind. *Either I move and it gets me, or I don't move, and I drown.* He risked moving the phone from his chest until he could finally see the light reflecting off the oily, disgusting water he was floating in. His arm trembling, he turned the phone to the right, but before he could even shine the flashlight on the thing, or things, on that side, something attacked, fast as a striking snake, biting into his arm.

Sam screamed in searing pain, feeling a set of sharp teeth clamp down and pierce his skin. He pulled and shook his arm in a frantic struggle, letting out peals of terrified shrieking, but whatever had a hold of him wouldn't let go. The phone fell from his hand and began floating away. Despite the terror and pain, he caught it with his free arm just as the creature pulled him toward the edge with such force, he was certain it couldn't be a dog.

Crying in pain, struggling for his life, he was pulled to the edge in violent jerks. He felt his body hit a wall of earth and rocks under the water. The creature continued pulling. His elbow bent sideways and broke against the rocky edge. Before he could let himself believe the pain couldn't get any worse, Sam felt the teeth of another creature sink into the flesh of his left arm. He let out a shrill cry, but still kept his fingers closed tight around the phone. He was convinced if he lost the light, he was dead.

He was dragged out of the hole, filthy water flooding his shrieking mouth, and more than likely infecting the bite wounds the creatures had inflicted on him. As soon as he could gather enough strength to resist at least some of the pain, he raised his eyes and, in the shaking light of the flashlight, he saw an obscene image that made no sense in this or any world.

There were three creatures at ground level. Two, biting down on his forearms. Their heads resembled dog skulls, but covered in sickly, wrinkled, spotty human flesh, their eyes were empty sockets. Their bodies, however, were human, but their proportions were all wrong, and they were crawling on all fours. The creatures were naked and hairless, with no sign of reproductive organs. The two on either side were larger—one more than the other—to Sam, the size of their bodies registered as that of children, or teenagers. The one at the center had the body of a small child—three or four years old—but still covered in wrinkled skin, and with that unholy dog skull for a head. In a frenzy, the baby creature tried to crawl toward him but was held back by something Sam couldn't yet determine.

Speechless, stupefied, his pain numbed by shock, he was pulled closer to the creatures, and the flashlight revealed they were not individual monsters attacking as a pack, but part of a single entity. Appendages covered in veiny, wrinkled skin came out of their backs and bound them together to a core body.

In the shaky flashlight beam, he caught fleeting glimpses of the monster's body. It appeared to be an elderly woman, but twisted and malformed. A hint of wrinkled, sagging skin. A flash of a swollen, tumor-filled belly. Then, he saw the woman's face, eyeless, swollen, stretched into a skin-mask; a strange goiter had grown in its neck, so big it bulged out of her open mouth, fleshy, purple, covered in veins, like a tongue swollen to ridiculous proportions, choking her. The old woman's breasts sagged and stretched until they became the wrinkled-skin appendages attached to the dog-children on the left and right. The appendage fused to the small child's back grew out of the woman's vagina, as if she had given birth to it.

The dog skull on the right pulled on his broken arm, causing Sam to squeal in pain again. He saw the woman creature raise an arm, the only arm it had. It ended in a large, black, scythe-like claw. The other dog creature pulled on his left arm, digging its teeth deeper. His screams, he knew deep in his being, were getting lost in the wind. He had the full knowledge no help was coming. The black claw came down. His right arm was gone as if it had never existed, leaving only a ragged, bloodied stump. He could see the dog creature bite, and crush, and chew, and swallow what used to be a part of his body.

The other creature continued to pull on his left arm and shook its head with fury, trying to detach it, like a hungry dog struggling with a delicious piece of gristle that just wouldn't come off the bone. Down came the black claw again. He took in a breath for another mindless scream as he felt his left arm ripped away at the shoulder, but this new scream was interrupted by the small dog creature, which jumped and sunk its teeth into his throat, letting out copious amounts of blood.

He could almost feel himself emptying, as the blood flowed from the savage bite.

The phone had been released once his arm was severed and floated in the water—the flashlight shining upward, casting sinister shadows on the monster's full body.

As he felt himself dying, Sam saw four things:

First. The dog creature on the right had finished devouring his arm, bones and all, and now had its muzzle deep in his guts, chewing and feeding on his intestines. He could barely feel it now.

Second. The strange mass pushing out of the woman's mouth stretched out, swelling, growing, unfurling, moving down toward his face. It looked like a gigantic earthworm that ended in a revolting toothless mouth.

Third. The rain had stopped. The clouds had cleared, and the blue moon was watching him die.

Fourth. The woman's skin, though wrinkled, seemed to have a texture in places, something like a faded tattoo. It looked like a pink tracksuit.

Freddie Parham sat where the sidewalk would've been in the other town—the "normal" town. He couldn't feel the water he was sitting in; he was intangible if he so chose. His eyes turned up to gaze at the sky, and the rain stopped. He hadn't made it stop, of course; in His infinite grace, God had granted his request, just as He made it possible for him to be intangible. Freddie wanted to bear witness to everything, unobstructed. The clouds parted and he could finally see the blue moon.

Inside Steve Felton's home, he hadn't been able to see the moon since he'd been indoors.

Out here, however, it was an enthralling vision: God's eye upon the world.

He could bask in the beauty of God's work and the light of His moon, which now shone on the creature Freddie helped bring into the world. It fed on Sam Becker Jr.'s body. The tube appendage from its mouth swallowed him little by little from head to toe. He'd come up with this design while watching a documentary in which snakes fed on large prey, but felt a snake coming out of its mouth wasn't really his style. That worm-like tube looked so much better. It looked great on paper. It was breathtaking in reality. There would be nothing left of Sam Becker once it was all done.

Freddie had a smile on his face as he watched his baby feed. If anyone had seen this creature on his canvas, they would've found it silly, and with good reason: an old lady with dogs tethered to her breasts and vagina? But people were shallow. They didn't understand. The important thing wasn't what it looked like—it was what it stood for. This being was beautiful and tragic, like all his creations. Others wouldn't see what he saw: a mother who had lost her three children, now reunited with them as they grew from the most intimate parts of her body.

So beautiful, he thought, his eyes moist with tears. *My gift to you, Mrs. Knox.* He hoped this would set things right with Maria Knox after what he'd done to her children thirty years ago.

Once Maria Knox finished devouring Sam Becker Jr., he'd have to leave the Moonlit World. With the second sacrifice complete, the full blue moon should now be visible, not just here, but in the world the Harborites thought of as home. He had to prepare for what would happen next and hurry to his next destination.

The third sacrifice required a more involved, personalized approach.

Chapter Five

A Single, Tiny Frame

Callum returned to his previous seat. Peter watched him start chatting with Sylvia, most likely about what they had just discussed. He wondered how advisable it was to share details about the Circle with them. They planned on publishing them, after all.

All around, his friends held their own little conversations: Jess and Angie, at their separate corner table; Nadine—who had gone silent after the discussion about him moving back to White Harbor—was now chatting with Bobby; and here was Royce, sitting across the table from him, ready to be the next interviewer of his "comeback tour". It was a byproduct of seeing them only once a year. They always wanted to make sure they asked every question before he left. He hoped once he moved back, the number of questions would decrease, and his relationship with his oldest friends would stop feeling like speed-dating.

"Say, Pete," Royce said, as Peter was about to bring his mug of beer to his lips, stopping him halfway. Royce made a gesture of apology by waving his hands. "Oh, no, no, man, go ahead, have your drink. Sorry I interrupted!"

"Uh…" Peter looked awkward, the mug half an inch from his partially open mouth, not sure what to do.

"Drink, man!"

He put the mug to his lips, tilted it, and gulped a mouthful. He put the beer mug down and turned a considerable foam mustache toward Royce.

"You're literally the most awkward human in the world, aren't you?" Royce said, with a shake of his head, then pointed a finger at his mouth. "Foamstache."

Peter rolled his eyes and wiped his lips with the back of his hand. "How's that?"

His friend chuckled and shook his head. "So, Lillian wanted me to ask you something. I promise it's the only work-related thing I'm going to ask you about. After that, we can get drunk until we pass out or puke out our chicken wings—whichever comes first. Thing is, if I don't ask you, I won't be getting any lovin' at home for a month."

Peter let out a brisk, pleasant laugh. "You didn't need to do a whole preface, man. You can just ask."

"Lillian loves your books. She's read them like five times each."

Peter feigned a ponderous nod, with a grave look on his face. "So, what you're telling me is Lillian likes shitty literature?"

"Well, a little." He chuckled. "Not gonna lie. She really loves *Echoes in the Sanctuary.*"

"Then that confirms it. She likes shitty books. That's the worst I've written so far. Let me guess, she also loved *Twilight*, right? Does she like her vampires glittery?"

Royce nodded, laughing.

"Anyway, speak, my friend. What answers may this humble wordsmith provide for your beautiful wife, she of the lousy taste in literature?"

Royce tilted his head forward, making a suspenseful shadow fall over his face, raised an eyebrow, and stared into Peter's eyes, then uttered a single name. "Melinda?"

"Oh, shit…" Peter looked away and sighed.

"You told me to ask!"

Peter rubbed his eyeballs with his fingertips, looking like he was regretting entertaining this conversation. "Fine. Just so your wife doesn't leave you *without lovin'* for a month."

"Melinda is based on your mom, right?"

"That's your question?"

"No, man. Even Lillian, who isn't so familiar with your personal history, caught the parallels. Divorcee, religious fanatic, locks her daughter in a trunk with rats? My kitchen sink knows Melinda is your mom. Remember, you're a celebrity here, bro."

"Still not hearing a question."

"Alright. In the book, Melinda ultimately sacrifices herself to save her daughter's life. She admits she was wrong, tells her she's sorry she wasn't a good mother, and uses her sacrifice to close the portal to hell. And the last thing she hears from her daughter is, 'I forgive you, and I love you.'"

Peter nodded. "Yup. I know what happens. I wrote it."

"Stop being a dick, man." Royce gave him an annoyed stare. "My point is, Lillian *loved* that ending. She cried for like half an hour, hugging our baby girl, telling her she would give her life for her, and she would never hurt her. But, as I said, she doesn't know the background as intimately as I do." Royce's facial expression and his tone of voice got more serious. "I was there. I saw what your mom was like. That's why I was so surprised to see you redeem your mom in the book. Sorry about saying it like it is, but the shit she did to you? So, I've been wondering why? Why do that?"

"I thought the question was from Lillian."

Royce's eyes shifted left and right. "Uh...no, no, the question is mine. I just didn't know how to broach the subject, so...um...yeah."

Peter was in no mood to get into the subject of his mother, and his friends seemed intent on bringing up mother-adjacent topics. However, he couldn't escape the fact she was forever linked to who he was. He knew if he was going to base characters on people in his life, those who knew him best would ask about it. It was only natural.

Royce squinted. Peter could tell he'd noticed the question had made him uncomfortable.

"Look, brother, you don't have to answer if you—"

"Sometimes…" He started, then trailed off, choosing his words with purpose. "Sometimes, you write the people who hurt you most as relatable characters, and you allow them to find redemption, because the only way you'd ever see yourself forgiving them is in fiction."

His friend across the table regarded him for a moment, lowered his gaze, and nodded, grasping the full meaning behind those words.

Before either of them could say anything, they were startled by the sound of a voice.

"What the fuck? NO!"

Everyone turned their heads toward the voice. It was Jess, who stared in horror toward the bar area. All heads now turned in that direction to see something that made no sense.

A man who had been sitting at the bar had Raymond in his grip, arm locked around his neck. A gun pointed at his head.

"Maryann just doesn't want a big, bad homosexual coming into her house and being a negative influence on her children."

As Barry stood broken and alone in the men's room, gazing at his own face in the mirror, Ray's words bounced around his skull like a bullet fired into a bank vault.

"Issue is the big, bad homosexual already lives in her house."

His balled fists trembled with rage. Not at Ray, but at himself, at his weakness, at his cowardice.

"Don't fucking touch me."

Each word stung with vicious intent. Each a dagger to his heart, to his soul, to his very sense of worth; especially considering he deserved every single one.

"All I do is hurt people," he mumbled to himself, head down, voice tinged with defeat. He tried to steady his breathing, but his broad shoulders heaved with the effort of holding back his emotions, fighting back tears he refused to let the others see.

Then came a sound from outside. A sudden, shocked cry pierced the air. "What the fuck? NO!"

Jess?

Other voices joined in. Sounds of consternation and

panic. Barry turned in a hurry, pulled the bathroom door open, and stepped into a scene that was beyond incongruous.

When he followed Ray into the bathroom, he'd passed a customer sitting with his back toward the door. He'd noticed this person because there were still plenty of other seats available in the bar. Nobody ever sat by the restroom door unless there was no other place available. It was a man with a shaved head, Black, wearing a jacket over what looked like a security guard's uniform. If he was someone who had just come for a drink after work—as the uniform seemed to suggest—he was probably from town, but Barry was sure he'd never seen this man before. In either case, from town or not, the stranger had Ray in his grip and had the barrel of a gun pressed against his temple.

"Don't shoot!" The words came out of Barry on instinct, filled with confusion and panic. He stood just outside the bathroom door, large hands outstretched toward the stranger, trying to appease him. "Don't shoot! Please! Don't shoot him!"

The sight of a gun pointed at Ray's head paralyzed him in place. He couldn't risk startling the stranger. If the finger in that trigger moved just an inch, Barry's world would end. There was something beneath the panic and confusion, though. As he tried his best to process the situation, something awoke in him, something primal, whose only purpose was to protect his loved ones, the way he'd promised to do so many years ago. Barry wanted to charge forward and beat that man's face into the floorboards for daring to touch one of the people he loved—for daring to touch Ray—but he knew from experience, whenever he let himself fly off the handle, things never went well, so he did his best to keep control.

"Listen," he said to the security guard, taking slow, measured breaths. "I don't know what this is, but please, can you just point the gun away from him? I know you don't want to hurt anybody. Point it at me if you want."

The security guard cast an indifferent glance toward him. He didn't say a word at first. He appeared to be assessing all the people present.

Louis, Jess's server, was standing halfway from the bar with a tray and several broken bottles lying at his feet in a puddle of spilled alcohol, his arms raised. The other two regulars, sitting at the bar, were staring at the security guard, panicked looks on both their faces. Barry could hear murmurs and cries from his friends at the opposite end of the locale.

"Please," Barry repeated, forcing calmness into his voice. "Do. Not. Shoot."

"Quiet," the man ordered, paying no heed to him. "You two." He motioned toward the two customers at the bar—Riley Estrada and Mason Owen. "And you." He nodded toward Louis. "Into the bathroom."

The three men exchanged confused glances, but considering the gun in the man's hand, they were quick to comply.

"Giffen." The man turned to Barry, who reacted as if he'd been slapped by the sound of his name coming from this stranger's lips.

He knows my name.

Barry locked eyes with Ray, who—besides looking terrified—also seemed bemused by this.

"Take that mop," the guard said, nodding toward a mop and bucket in the corner. "Use it to bar the door."

"Okay." Barry nodded, taking nervous breaths. "Whatever you say. Just...don't hurt him."

"Stop blabbering. Do it quickly, if you don't want to see Chang's brain come out the opposite side of his head."

Barry and Ray exchanged another look. This guy knew both their names.

Following the man's instructions, Barry took the metal handle of the mop and put it diagonally through the door handle. "I did what you asked," he said. "Now, let him go."

The security guard responded with an amused snort. "You're in no position to negotiate, young man."

"Young man?" Barry was taken aback by this. The stranger looked over a decade younger than him.

The security guard motioned with his head toward the table, from which Barry's friends stared back in varying degrees of consternation. "Go over there with your friends, Giffen."

Barry struggled to keep a lid on his mounting anger.

"Let him go," he insisted through a clenched jaw. "You better not hurt him."

"Really?" the stranger said. "Why's that?" He applied pressure to the gun barrel against Ray's temple.

Ray let out a pained grunt, which got an immediate rise out of Barry. "Stop that, you son of a bitch, or I swear I'll rip your fucking head off!"

The young security guard let out a low chuckle upon hearing that. "*There's* the real you," he said. "Listen. I take no pleasure in doing this. The quicker we get through this nasty business, the better. I know you, Barry Giffen; don't let that temper get the better of you. This is a 48-caliber pistol. So, you're going to stop acting a fool and do what I tell you, or would you prefer to see what one of these bullets can do to Chang's pretty little head?"

The anger and indignation pulsed through Barry's head—as if his blood had expanded, thickened, and clogged his veins—but he applied what he'd applied so many times at home, with Maryann and her bitch of a mother. He forced the rage down. Pushed it deep. All the way to his feet. "No," he said at last, deflating, trying as hard as he could not to look at Ray's terrified eyes, because he wouldn't be capable of keeping his cool if he did. "I'll do whatever you want, just don't hurt him. I beg you, please, don't hurt him."

The security guard once again motioned with his head toward the table.

Barry nodded, lowered his head, and started walking. He knew Raymond was staring straight at him, but he didn't dare meet his gaze. Otherwise, he would do something beyond stupid. He shuffled beside them, one step at a time, his hands raised, arms forming ninety-degree angles.

Ray grunted from the pain of the gun pressed against his temple, the sound of his voice sending electric shocks through Barry's brain.

He turned his head toward him.

The moment he got a glimpse of the fear in his eyes, it was like his body took over for him. He had no say in the matter. Barry pivoted toward the security guard and, with one of his meaty hands, pushed the man's arm from below, so the gun pointed up. If this had been a movie, there would've been a dramatic blast, the bullet flying into the ceiling, plaster dust falling on their heads, but there was no shot. With his other hand, Barry pushed Ray out of the man's grip and out of the way. The bulk of his body crashed into the security guard, and soon they were both falling to the floor. He could hear the echoes of everyone around them screaming and shouting.

When they both hit the floor, Barry was ready. He went up on one knee, straddling the guard, and raised a solid, balled fist, ready to bring it down against the man's face. "How dare you touch him, you piece of—"

He froze, faced with the dark hole of the gun barrel pointed straight at his face.

"You just made this choice a lot easier," the man said. "Get off me. Stand up. Move over there so I can keep all of you in sight."

Barry did as he was told. Taking scared, shallow breaths, he stood up, hands raised, and took two steps back. His back was turned to the rest of his friends.

"That's far enough," the stranger said. The gun, its aim unflinching, pointed between Barry's eyes as he stood back up.

"No," Ray said, standing up a few steps away. "No, no, no. Stop!"

From the corner of his eye, Barry saw Nadine hurrying to Ray's side. She took him by the arm and pulled him to where the others were.

Jess held on to Angie's shoulder. It was an instinctive, protective reaction. If anything happened, or things got out of control, there was no question in her mind she would punch, kick, and claw the eyes out of anyone who'd dare threaten her life.

She felt Angie flinch at her grip and heard her draw a swift breath through her teeth.

Jess regarded her fingernails. They were short, but she was pressing them so hard into Angie's shoulder she was hurting her. Trying to keep her focus and control, she released her grip a little.

The security guard turned his expressionless eyes toward them and nodded in Angie's direction.

"The girl in the wheelchair stays in that corner," he said. "I don't need her. Cunningham, move to the table with your other friends. I need you all in the same place."

Jess obeyed and walked over to her friends. As she did, she made a mental note that the stranger knew Barry and Ray's name, and also seemed to know hers.

"Look, buddy." Jess remembered getting a furtive glimpse of a name sewn over the uniform's breast pocket under his jacket. John Hitch. "John, was it? John? Look. My idiot assistant, Louis, left the cash register open. You can take everything you want from there. Liquor, too. The place looks shitty, but there's some expensive booze there for the tourists. You can take whatever you want. Just don't hurt anyone and go away. Please."

The young security guard chuckled. His unblinking stare as he did this was enough to make her feel uncomfortable and on edge. Like he knew the first, second, and third things that were about to happen, and they were completely escaping her notice.

"This isn't a robbery," Hitch said. "As you can see, I have a job, thank you." He opened his jacket with one hand and canted his head toward his shirt pocket.

Jess saw Bobby's shocked reaction upon noticing the Lighthouse Rock security staff uniform.

"C'mon, hun," Jess said. "I'm just confused here. I don't know what's going on. Just trying to make sense of it."

She stood next to Royce, who, without delay, put an arm around her shoulder. "Stop talking," he said. "Stop calling attention to yourself."

John Hitch regarded the whole group.

Keeping the gun trained on Barry, he directed his attention toward Peter. "You should never have come back here, Lange. This wouldn't be necessary if you had just never come back." He motioned with the gun from Peter to Angie's table. "Move over there with the girl in the wheelchair."

Peter hesitated, but obeyed, not taking his confused eyes off his other friends as he made his way to Angela's side of the bar. Just like Jess had a moment earlier, he put a reassuring hand on her shoulder.

Jess couldn't hold her tongue anymore. "Why are you doing this? My friend over there's got cancer. You're terrifying her. What is this all about?"

"This isn't personal." Hitch trained his gun on Barry again. "I wouldn't be doing this if I had any other choice. It's important to me you understand this. This should've stopped thirty years ago, the day you burned my house."

Confused glances were exchanged all around. In Jess's baffled thoughts, the security guard might have said, "My name is Iñigo Montoya. You killed my father. Prepare to die," and it would've elicited the same reaction. His words made no sense.

"Still, the moment Lange was taken from his mother, it looked like it would stop." Hitch continued. "All he needed to do was not show his face in town during a very specific time window, but here he is—oblivious to just how badly he fucked up."

Peter's eyebrows furrowed as he shot a confused stare at the security guard. Just from looking at his face, Jess could tell he didn't know what he was going on about.

"She arranged for you to be here," Hitch said, then gave him a derisive grin. "Mother always gets what she wants, doesn't she?"

Peter's indignant reaction was immediate. "What the hell are you talking a—"

"No time to dwell on that," Hitch said. "You're here. It's done. Now things must happen. My point is, this could have been prevented. I tried to talk Freddie Parham out of leaving his room, but he wouldn't listen. Now he's out there."

"Wait!" Bobby interjected in alarm. "Freddie? What do you mean he's out of his room?"

The security guard tilted his head toward Peter while keeping his eyes on the group. "Your friend, there in the corner. His mother helped him escape the loony bin."

"You're insane!" Peter said, agitated, laughing in disbelief. "My mother's in the hospital. She can't get out of there, much less go to Lighthouse Rock to help Freddie escape. Also, why *would* she? None of this makes any sense!"

"And what's all this about us burning down your house?" Jess asked, pivoting away from Peter's mother—a subject that would lead nowhere constructive—and drawing attention to herself. That angry glint in Peter's eye worried her. She wanted the man's attention on her, not on any of her friends. If she could get him to point the gun away from Barry and toward her, it would be ideal.

"You're talking about the Vanek House?" Sylvia asked, looking as if the notion had clicked in her head, even though it was complete nonsense.

Sylvia, you stupid bitch, Jess thought. *I need his attention on me.*

Hitch nodded.

Jess took a step forward, trying to draw his attention back to her. "That was thirty years ago. You couldn't have even been alive."

"That house was in my family for nearly a century."

She could see he was serious, lucid, no sign of insanity or confusion. If John Hitch was insane, he was at least convinced he was telling the truth.

"It went from Amias Vanek to Long-Lived John Ellis, to Rickward Curling, to Jenelle Curling, to Osmin Curling, to Ben Curling. If you hadn't burned the house down—and

Curling with it—it would be mine."

"You're a descendant of the Curlings?" Sylvia asked, nudging Callum with her elbow.

The man grinned. "You could say that. It's not about the house, though." He once more turned his attention to the gun he still held pointed toward Barry. "Explanation over."

Barry flinched, hands raised.

Everyone reacted and cried, "No!"

Ray shouted, "Don't!"

"John!" Jess said, desperate. "John! Here! Look at me! Point your gun here! Not at him! Point it at me!"

Hitch ignored her. His gaze bore into Barry's as he spoke, his words meant for everyone. "I hate doing this. I just wanted you to understand I did everything in my power not to get to this point. Because now, the only way to stop Martha Lange and save White Harbor is for four of you to die right here and now. Starting with Mr. Giffen."

She saw the terror in Barry's light blue eyes. Despite his size, he looked like a scared little kid.

Hitch stared at Barry with intent; finger on the trigger, barrel trained unwavering on a point between his eyes.

Everyone shouted at once.

Barry's thoughts—as he prepared for the oncoming nothing-ness—were of his children, Daniel and Gabe. He had made so many mistakes in his life, wasted so much time; he had ignored so much of himself, but his boys were the two things he was proud of, those two perfect little kids. They would carry on after the bullet erased all consciousness from his mind, and the world would simply move on without him in it.

His beautiful kids were the only bright spot in an otherwise regret-filled life.

The only thing I haven't fucked up so far.

He pictured an endless landfill where every single action he regretted had piled up and been festering for years. It stretched forever until it disappeared into a thick, stagnant mist that made the air near-unbreathable. His light blue eyes swiveled toward Ray, who was now shouting in desperation at the gunman while Nadine and Bobby held him back.

Don't let him go. Keep him there. Keep him safe.

So much wasted time.

For a moment, Ray's beautiful brown eyes met his. He hated the despair he was seeing there and hated that he was the cause of it. Again. Other than desperation, there was a mixture of a thousand other emotions in his face, all of which added up to one thing: futility.

It's better this way, Barry thought.

Ray swung an arm and broke away from Nadine and Bobby's grip.

NO!

He charged toward Hitch.

Barry's breath caught in his throat as he saw the gun now swiveling toward Ray. He came to a sudden stop, just a few feet from Hitch.

"Ray!" Barry said. They were back at square one. All for nothing. He was going to have to witness the one person in the world who mattered most to him, besides his children, be shot to death. *Why couldn't you just let me die, you stubborn asshole? Why couldn't you just let me take the damn bullet for you and move on?*

"You two can't seem to decide who wants to go first, can you?" Hitch said. For all his claims that he wasn't enjoying doing this, there was an undercurrent of delight underlying each word. "Love turns people stupid, at least in my experience."

Barry flinched. *Did he just say… How does he…*

Hitch looked at one, then the other. "Now that I think about it, if I have my facts straight, Giffen would've killed Freddie Parham the day of the fire. He would've put an end to this little problem, except *you*"—he nodded toward Ray—"stopped him. Didn't you, Chang?"

How could this man know what happened that day? Barry wondered. Even if he knew about the Vanek House burning and what Freddie Parham did, how could he know these details?

"Maybe I'm just rationalizing things to justify doing something as messed up as this," Hitch said, gun trained on Ray, "but this wouldn't be happening if you hadn't stopped him from killing Freddie. So, maybe, you *do* deserve to die more than him."

"You're crazy," Ray said, doing his best to sound brave, despite looking paralyzed with fear. It made Barry's insides twist with anger.

Hitch shrugged. "Well. It's as good or bad a justification as any." He straightened his gun arm, ready to fire.

The mental image of what would happen the moment that gun went off flashed in Barry's mind like fast-forwarding through a movie, but somehow being aware of every single frame in acute detail. If Barry died, his family would move on, his children would move on, Ray would move on. He could see their entire lives in that movie reel, and grieving for him would be just a single, tiny frame in an otherwise long and happy story. If Ray died, however, all that would be left for Barry's existence would be this burned-out hole in every frame of the film; a hole in the world he'd always be able to see, from any location, from any distance, whether awake or asleep.

Ray needed to exist in the world, Barry decided. *He* didn't.

He rushed forward, letting out the loudest roar he could, trying to draw Hitch's attention. Like before, the gun swiveled in his direction in what felt like a fraction of a second. He dropped to the floor and went into a slide—his body remembering when he used to do this as a teenager, playing soccer—sure, this wasn't as soft as grass or AstroTurf, and he wasn't twelve anymore, but Jess kept the linoleum floor slick enough to go the distance, allowing him to kick Hitch's feet from under him.

The grooved heel from one of his Timberlands struck Hitch's shin. For a second of sudden panic, he saw the gun barrel line up perfectly with his face. He saw the finger on the trigger, ready to fire. Then, the security guard lost balance and tumbled to the floor. Before the man could get his bearings, Barry flipped onto his stomach, went up on one knee, and leaped toward him, grabbing his arms.

He noticed Ray hurrying toward them.

"Stop!" His voice was an angry growl. "Go back with the others. I got him!"

Ray hesitated.

"Go! Now, dammit!" he shouted. Ray took only a couple of steps back. *Not far enough*, Barry thought. *Not nearly enough*. He had a tight hold on Hitch's arms, but the man still had an iron grip on the gun.

"C'mon!" Peter shouted at the others, taking a step forward. "What are you waiting for? We gotta help him!"

"No!" he said. "Stay back!"

The gun was still at play. He was being reckless, but he didn't matter.

I'm a single, tiny frame, that's all I am.

His friends mattered. If any of them got shot for trying to help him, he would never forgive himself.

Putting his muscles behind it, he tried to twist Hitch's arm to get him to drop the gun, but the young security guard was wiry and strong. He didn't find him as easy to subdue as he had expected.

Hitch bared his teeth at him, grunting as he tried to free himself, a blank shark's look in his eyes that terrified him. He let go of one of Hitch's arms and punched him once, twice. The man looked dazed. Barry's fingers strained against the unyielding grip he had on the gun, trying to wrestle it away with no success. Hitch retaliated with a punch to the face, followed by another, stunning him, but he still held on tight.

If I let it go, I'm dead. My friends too. They matter. I don't. I'm nothing.

Out of options, he head-butted the security guard and, as if by miracle, he let go of the gun. However, the moment Barry reached for it, he left himself open, and the younger, more agile man buried his knee in his crotch with devastating force. Barry let out a pained groan and curled up in a ball.

Hitch scrambled toward his gun.

Everyone around cried in alarm.

Pushing through the pain, Barry threw a hand out and got hold of the man's leg.

Hitch's hand was a mere inch from the gun. He started kicking Barry's hand, using his free foot.

He was about to lose his grip when—

"Stop right there! You crazy piece of shit!"

Barry heard a familiar clicking sound and peered up.

Standing over a bewildered Hitch was Jess, pointing her shotgun—which she had named Peggy—at him.

The security guard, looking thwarted, gave her a withering glare over his shoulder. He lay down on his stomach and put his hands up.

Jess stepped around the man, keeping a safe distance, approaching the gun on the floor. She kicked it away toward Angie's wheelchair.

"Angie, sweetie," she said. "Are you strong enough to pick that off the floor and hold it for me? If not, Peter, you do it."

"I can do it," Angie said, bending down and reaching for the gun.

"Just be careful and point that away from everyone, alright?"

"Does it have like a safety button or something?" Angie asked.

"No," Jess said with a calm voice, her shotgun still trained on Hitch, "that's TV and movies for ya. The Glock 48 doesn't have a safety. It won't fire on its own, but he had it ready to fire, so let's just avoid any accidents and set it on the table, pointing at the wall." She shot a severe glance at

Peter. "Peter, I know you're like the guest of honor and stuff, but would you mind going to the bathroom and opening the door? Louis and the others might be feeling antsy from all the shouting and commotion."

"Sure, Jess," he said. He shot a glance toward Barry as he passed. "Are you okay?"

The only answer Barry could manage was a silent nod, followed by an aching grunt that contradicted the nod itself.

Peter offered him a hand.

Barry took it and stood up with difficulty, teeth clenched. He figured his balls were still orbiting somewhere in the vicinity of his lungs—or they felt like they were—and his hand was scraped and bruised from when Hitch had kicked him.

Peter gave him a reassuring squeeze on the shoulder and continued on his way to free the men in the restroom.

"Barr," Jess said, not taking Peggy off Hitch. "That was an astonishingly stupid thing you did, but thank you for do-ing it."

"Don't mention it." An aching grunt escaped him as he rubbed his hand. He approached Ray, who looked tense and confused. "Are you okay?" he asked in a diminished, awk-ward voice.

"Mm-hmm." Ray nodded, looking down at the floor, then gave him a dubious glance. "You?"

"Uh...yeah."

"Okay." Ray tightened his lips in acknowledgment, gave a single nod, and walked toward Callum and Sylvia; as far from him as he could.

Barry felt deflated. Heartache spread through his chest like acid, eating away at his insides, but he understood Ray's reaction wasn't any less than he deserved.

"Barr."

He turned.

Jess was looking in his direction, a kind look of concern in her eyes—the security guard wasn't trying to stand, fight back, or regain the advantage, faced with Peggy's barrel. "I'm glad you're okay." Jess smiled at him. "Don't listen to that voice in there." She tapped her temple twice.

He managed to give her a weak smile, but his eyes were filled with sorrow. A wordless understanding passed between them—she wasn't referring only to this night.

"We're *all* glad you're okay," she said, and cast a furtive glance toward Ray.

Chapter Six

Torch Song Trilogy – Part 1: "Shining Light"

1990

"**I** know you're going through something," Barry's dad said.

That night, they were sitting on the couch in the living room; on the TV there was some game show he would later have a hard time recalling when thinking of this moment.

"Unfortunately, son, I can't let this go just like that. This matters. Please, tell me you understand."

Barry nodded.

Logan Giffen got close to his son's face and flicked his thigh with the back of his index finger, which prompted him to meet his gaze. Barry knew his dad wasn't angry. He was smiling, in fact. That loving, understanding smile which only made him feel like he'd failed the best dad in the world. "Buddy? I'm gonna need you to say you understand."

"I understand," he answered under his breath.

"Now, help *me* understand," his dad continued. "You have good grades. You're one of the best players in the school's soccer team. You have everything you need here at home. So, why go around beating up other kids?"

Barry slid away from his dad and slouched, looking away. He returned a shrug.

"It might shock you, buddy, but I was your age, too. If there's one thing I know is, if I'm hearing of this once, it might be a single event. But if I'm hearing of it twice, it's probably been going on a lot more."

Barry sank deeper into the couch.

"What's going on?"

"I dunno," Barry said, in that pretend-unaffected mumble preteens master as if it were its own form of communication. "They just annoy me sometimes."

"Hmm."

He hated it when his dad made that sound. It meant he knew there was more to it. His dad looked back toward the bedroom, where his mom slept off yet another hangover. His dad sighed, nodded, then gave him *that* look. The look that let him know he was loved, even if he'd messed up. "Your mom promised she'll go to AA next week."

"She's gone three times already. She always drops it after a couple weeks."

"She's trying, buddy." He put a hand on his shoulder, prompting him to meet his gaze. "Sometimes, all you can do is try to be better."

Barry's eyes drifted downward, as he sensed the comment was directed at him and not just referencing his mother.

"I can't just let this go. You know that, right? You beat up a kid real bad and almost got kicked off the soccer team."

Barry's eyes widened, and he let out an audible gasp. His gaze dropped again, only more embarrassed now.

"Yup. Didn't know that part, huh?" His dad still sounded calm, loving. "Had to call in a lot of favors and make a lot of promises to keep you on the team."

"I'm sorry."

"I know you are. Now, please, look at me, son."

Barry obeyed, though he felt too embarrassed to look at his dad.

"Either you stop beating up other kids, or *I* will personally pull you from the team."

"No!" Barry blurted. "No, Dad, please!"

"Not just that. You can forget about the World Cup in '94. You do this again, and we're not going."

"No! I've been saving money! I've been keeping my grades up!"

"I know." His dad smiled. "And that's commend-able, son, but this other thing—beating up other kids—that trumps everything else. So, this is your one warning." His dad stood up from the couch, then took a step in the bedroom's direction, where his mom slept. He turned to look at him and gave him *that* look. "Try to be better, son."

Barry had promised and, from that day, made an hon-est effort not to disappoint his dad. For weeks he was a model student, and maintained a low profile at school, avoiding con-frontation and keeping out of trouble.

It all went to hell a month later.

One night, while his mom was out drinking, he walked into his parents' bedroom to tell his dad their pizza had ar-rived. He found his dad hanging from a beam near the closet, a belt around his neck and a revolting, inhuman, puffed-up expression on his face. His dad's skin had gone blue, and his eyeballs were bulging and red; all capillaries in them burst.

Barry didn't scream. All that left his mouth was a gasp, after which he ambled in a hypnotic dream toward the living room, holding his breath in. He stood in front of the living room phone and called 911, and letting out the air from his lungs said, "1011 East Hill Drive. My dad hanged himself," and put the phone down. After the call, he sat on his couch waiting for the ambulance to arrive, while his dad hung from the belt, his dribbling tongue sticking out of his mouth.

The ambulance arrived, the police arrived, his mother arrived. Whatever happened between them coming in and taking his dad away, he couldn't remember. It was all a sped-up blur in his head, lit by the flicker of the TV screen, which played yet another game show he couldn't remember anymore.

He was finally blasted out of his trance by his mother's hand, slapping him out of his stupor. She screamed, "How could you let him do this? How *didn't* you notice your dad had done this? Were you just looking at the TV like a fucking retard the whole time?"

The first sensory recollection he had at that point was the smell of alcohol on her breath as she shouted and slapped him again. He wouldn't recall the pain of each slap. Just the smell. Just her deranged, red face. Just a string of insults, ending in: "THIS IS YOUR FAULT!"

1992

When he opened his eyes, Barry's field of vision was filled with fuzzy figures, moving, floating, and blending together. The world around him was spinning, and he struggled to focus his eyes on the fleeting figures passing by. Different colors, twisting, doubling, tripling. The world just wouldn't stand still. The images and sounds were disorienting, seeming to come from different directions at once.

The moment his hand touched his temple, he felt the familiar pain and remembered everything that had occurred.

The soccer ball, he thought. *I'm gonna break both legs of the fucker who kicked that ball.*

"Yo, big guy!" a voice called out as a formless, amoeboid figure approached. "Sorry about the ball, but you were all distracted, and I thought you were going to get out of the way or, you know, *not* stop it with the side of your head."

This was the asshole who had knocked his lights off with a soccer ball.

"Soon as I get up, I'm gonna... Whoa..." As he sat up on the grass, a sudden wave of dizziness washed over him. "Ugh... I swear I'm gonna rearrange your ribs with my foot..."

"Okay," the amoeba said, which had begun taking the form of a person. The first thing in the general area of the face that looked human was a big, wide smile. "Would it be alright if, before you kick my sternum into my spine, I help you up?"

Barry saw a hand extended toward him and finally got a full view of the face of another teenager smiling at him with the most nauseatingly perfect teeth he'd ever seen in his life. It reminded him of his own crooked canine, and he closed his mouth in a stern and unfriendly line, slapped the hand away, and forced himself to stand up, even as the world still wobbled around him.

Seconds later, as Barry slapped the dirt off his shorts,

he was surprised to see the kid's hand stretched out toward him again. He gave the other kid an annoyed look. "You fuckin' blind? I'm already standing."

Amoeba Boy turned out to be a shorter Asian teenager with an athletic build, long black hair and the stupidest, brightest smile he'd ever seen. With his hand still forward, waiting to be shaken, he said, "I'm Raymond Chang. You're Barry Giffen, right? You're the guy who had his ass handed to him by some skinny kid with a T-Square last year. I can see that nasty scar on the side of your neck. Damn! He got you good, huh?"

"You're asking me to kill you, right?" Barry said. "Is that what this is? Suicide by Giffen?"

An image flashed through his mind of his dad hanging, the belt tight around his—

Laughter exploded out of Raymond Chang, so loud it startled him.

"What are you laughin' at, you little fuck?"

"'Suicide by Giffen?'" He doubled over with laughter again. It made him hate the kid with a passion. "Wow, man, you've got quite the high opinion of yourself."

Barry, already determined the boy was scheduled for a horrendous death, and knowing he had a reputation to maintain, took a step toward him. The afternoon sun behind him cast his shadow over the shorter boy. He flexed his arms a little, glanced at one of his biceps, then the other, bringing

Chang's attention toward them. "One of my arms is thicker than either of those skinny little legs."

The kid kept grinning, shooting a condescending glance at both of Barry's arms. "Look, big guy, I don't know if it's the concussion messing with your memory, but one of *these* skinny legs kicked the ball that knocked you out a moment ago." Once more, he stretched his open palm between the two, insisting on shaking his hand. "So, whaddaya say? Are we cool?"

Barry's face flushed red with anger, and it looked as if steam was going to shoot from his ears and nostrils. He got in close to the shorter kid's face. In a low growl, he said, "You're dead, stick figure."

"Hey, Giffen!" their coach's voice came from a few yards away. "If you're okay to go on, let's keep going. If not, hit the showers and go to the school nurse, stat!"

He curled his lip at the puny little kid. "You got lucky, bitch," he said, then turned and walked away. "I'm okay, coach. Let's go!"

The following days, Barry had to put up with Raymond Chang approaching him at random times of the day, trying to chat. Avoiding him had become a chore. He was like that annoying mosquito that waits until you're just about to fall asleep to begin whining around your ear, and you just can't kill it. He was in most of the same classes as Barry. He came to talk to him at lunch, in the locker room, in the hallways. Ignoring or threatening him didn't seem to do the trick.

Four days after the soccer ball incident, as he made his way to his next period through the noisy school hallway, a voice rose above the crowd, causing his neck to stiffen and an exasperated sigh to leave his chest.

"Hey, big guy!"

Fuck, Barry thought. "Go away."

"Wait, wait," the kid insisted. "Hold up!"

"You didn't hear me, did you? I said, go away."

He felt a hand hold on to his left shoulder. He turned his head, and there was Raymond Chang's big stupid smile, flashing straight at him.

"I wanted to ask you something," he said, keeping pace. "You're with that group that meets at that haunted house in town, right? The Vanek House?"

Barry stopped cold. He turned his angry face toward him. "You need to shut up now!"

Raymond grinned at him, visibly not threatened. "Or, what? You're going to pull out my lungs and feed them to me? Some other silly threat like that?"

"Keep grinning at me like that and find out."

"Look, big guy. I know you have a reputation and all,

but I've been asking around. You *used* to be the huge, scary cave troll at this school for a while, but it's been like a year since you've actually bullied or beaten anyone."

"The fuck?"

"Ever since you became friends with those other kids, you've been nothing but a big, gentle bear. What was that Disney bear called? From the Jungle Book? The TalesSpin guy? Baloo?" He looked at him with that aggravating grin. "I think a red pilot cap would look great on you."

"You're so dead."

"Give it up, Baloo. If I know you're harmless, being the new guy, I'm sure the other kids know, too. Embrace your newfound fluffiness!"

He stared in bafflement at the puny little insect with his irritating, absurd grin. "What are you, some kind of psycho?"

"Well…" The kid considered for a moment. "Maybe? But that Peter Lange guy is also supposed to be kinda crazy, and you're *his* friend, aren't you?"

"You don't talk about Peter." Barry squinted at him. He wasn't sure what the deal was with this guy. He only knew he didn't like him.

"Oh. I'm sorry. Is he, like, your boyfriend or something?"

"Shut up!" Barry's chest heaved with genuine anger. "I'm no fag. If you ever say anything like that again, I'll show you just how harmless I am."

The grin disappeared from Raymond's face. "I'm sorry."

"Go! Away!" Barry growled, turned around and walked away as fast as he could.

The locker room after soccer practice always felt crowded to Barry. He should've been more than used to it by now, but it was always one of the most uncomfortable moments of his day. Despite being larger and more muscular than most of the other kids, he'd always felt physically unwieldy and fat compared to them. Of course, none of them would dare say that to his face.

The locker room also brought with it the constant fear of spontaneous boners, which had become a concern since little over a year earlier. There had been incidents. Not four months prior, he'd been getting dressed, and he'd looked down to find his wiener standing up at attention, just as several of his teammates strolled out of the showers. In a panic, he'd scrambled to throw his towel back on and sit as fast as he could, barely avoiding their eyes. Since that day, he'd made sure to always put his underwear and pants on while still wearing his towel.

The day after the hallway encounter, Barry was in the process of pulling up his briefs under his towel when he sensed someone sit down next to him on the bench.

"Hey, man," he heard the person say. It was that voice again, grating on his nerves.

"I *know* you can't possibly be sittin' next to me while I'm getting dressed." He pulled his briefs up to his waist, despite how uncomfortable it was to do this sitting down.

"Look, I just wanted to say I'm sorry."

Barry turned to find Chang sitting there, already fully dressed after practice, in a blue T-shirt and yellow shorts, his gym bag resting on his thighs.

"I didn't mean to offend you with my comment about Peter Lange."

"Fine," Barry said. "You can go away now." He diverted his attention from him and hurried to pull up his pants under the towel.

"Can I, like, buy you a Coke and a burger on the way home?"

Barry gave him a weirded-out look, stopping halfway from unwrapping the towel from his waist.

Raymond Chang held his gym bag tighter against him, looking nervous. "To apologize for hitting you with the ball, and the thing I said about your friend."

Barry considered this instead of just flat out refusing but shook his head. "No, thanks." He threw on a T-shirt in a hurry, shoved his dirty clothes in his bag, and left the annoying kid behind.

His momma got violent again that afternoon. She came home drunk—the norm since his dad died, more than it had ever been. When this happened, he tried his best to stay out of her way, letting her take it out on the glassware, the walls, and the furniture.

He'd been sitting on his bed when he heard her outside struggling with her keys and the door. His eyes wandered toward his bedside table, toward the 1990 Italy World Cup alarm clock his dad had gotten him. The edge of the table and the position of the clock formed an angle that was driving him insane. He put out his forefinger toward one of its edges and pushed on it until the angle was gone and they were both aligned. Parallel. Perfect.

Footsteps marched straight toward his room.

His door flew open, startling him, even if he knew she was coming. She'd scared him so much he raised his feet off the floor and scurried backward onto the bed until his back hit the headboard. In his confused state, she looked to him like some horror movie beast crashing through a door, looming tall and terrifying, frothing at the mouth, waving a knife in the air. What she had been waving, though—he saw when he finally got a good look at her—had been a green notebook he'd never seen before.

"What is this?" she said, and threw the notebook at him, hitting him with the spine right in his face. It hadn't hurt much, but if throwing things was how she had started, this was only going to get worse. "WHAT THE FUCK IS THIS?"

Frantic, he grabbed the notebook and stared at it. The very first page read: "Diary of Hank Marsh". The moment he read the name Hank Marsh, his breath caught in his throat. He looked up at her. Swallowed hard. "I don't understand, momma!"

"Don't lie to me, you fucking FAGGOT!" she shouted, now holding up his paperweight, a heavy one shaped like a soccer ball.

"Momma!"

She hurled the paperweight at him, and he raised his arm to cover his face. It hit him on the side of the elbow, and pain sang up and down his arm like the vibration of bells hit by a hammer. Barry screamed and rolled in his bed, holding his elbow, and suddenly she was on him, rabid and out of control; the stink of booze wafting out through her bared teeth.

"I got that from Skylar Marsh!" She pulled him toward her by his ear, which reddened and throbbed with pain. She was so much smaller than him, and yet, the terror she filled him with made him feel so insignificant it would always make him freeze, like a mouse realizing it's been sighted by a cat. She wrested the diary from his hands with one hand, placed it on the bed, and hurried through the pages until she reached one near the middle. "Read that!" she commanded. "READ, YOU FUCK!"

The words on that page dragged a sharp icy claw down his back: "Today I kissed Barry Giffen in the locker room. His lips tasted sweet, like root beer. I hope next time we're not interrupted."

"It's not true!" he said in less than a second, terror flaring up in his eyes. "Momma! It's not t—"

She swung the closed diary at his face, striking him across the cheek. Upon impact, she lost her grip on his ear, and her fingernails left two red lines on his outer ear. He lost his balance and rolled off the bed, falling on the other side.

"It's not true! He's lying!"

He wasn't. It had been Barry's first kiss.

Little less than a year earlier, he and Hank Marsh had caught each other's awkward gazes throughout P.E. class. Barry hadn't been able to understand why, but he'd felt a warm sensation in his chest, climbing up his neck, toward his cheeks, and no matter how many times he'd tried to look away, his eyes had found Hank looking back, every time.

In the locker room, he'd made sure not to shower at the same time as Hank, because it would've been difficult for him to hide the fact he'd been hard just from the thought of it. He'd waited, folding, unfolding, and re-folding his clothes, until Hank stepped out through a cloud of steam. Only then had Barry gone into the showers.

He'd emerged, water dripping from his hair, expecting to find Hank already gone, along with most of his classmates, but he'd been sitting in the locker room—folding, unfolding, re-folding. Barry had gotten dressed as fast as he could, his back turned toward Hank, concealing the unwitting, but rather unmissable reaction brought upon by the whole situation. This had never happened to him before. Not the boner part—that had been happening every few hours since he was ten—but such a spontaneous, immediate reaction when looking at another boy.

There had been moments before that, in which he'd looked at another boy and thought, *He's so pretty*, but he'd only ever considered it a visual qualification, nothing sexual about it—he'd only begun to grasp the concept of sex a few months earlier and still wondered why people would even do that. It sounded gross. In his mind, these other boys were just "pretty". However, what was happening—what Hank Marsh was *making* happen; first, with a few exchanged looks, and now, by staying in the same room as him—was terrifying.

Why couldn't he just finish putting on his shirt, pack his things, and go home?

Why was he stalling, waiting for everyone but Hank to leave?

118

The answer came the moment the last of his classmates walk out, and he turned around. Hank was now standing two feet in front of him, gazing at him, his green eyes looking into the light blue of his, an extra bit of red in his cheeks.

The image of the shorter, curly-haired kid became etched in his memory: Hank had been wearing a red shirt three sizes too big with some abstract image printed on the chest, and a pair of olive-colored cargo pants. One of Hank's white-and-red sneakers moved as he took a step toward Barry, bringing them face-to-face.

Barry licked his own trembling lips, then tried to speak. "I—"

Hank did a hesitating twitch, then rose on the tips of his toes and pushed his face against Barry's. It was an awkward, graceless motion that shocked him, but the moment he felt Hank's lips on his, he didn't pull back. Every voice in his head was screaming to push the scrawny kid off, threaten to punch him into a coma if he told anyone, and run away. Instead, Barry pushed his lips against his.

Neither of them seemed to know what they were doing at first. It felt like just smooshing their lips together for no apparent reason, but then it was like their minds took over. Their lips parted, and their tongues touched—an irrational act of teenage discovery. It was clumsy and wet and imperfect, not like the movies—particularly since, in movies, it was always a man and a woman—but from that point on, it all clicked in his head. He grabbed Hank's face and held it as he continued to kiss him. He felt Hank's hands grab on to his hips and pull him against his body. He realized with trepidation he was blushing, but he was enjoying the heat of the embrace and he didn't want to let go.

Questions filled his head: *What now? What's next? How does this work?*

Then, the world came crashing down.

"Oh my god, I'm s-sorry!"

They both turned to see Peter Lange standing at the locker room entrance, staring agape at both of them. Barry recalled in a second: Peter always showered last, so no one would see him, but he *also* came in to change first, before everyone else from his period arrived.

After a few bumbling explanations, Hank excused himself and left, swearing on his mother's life not to say anything.

Barry had only recently become friends with Peter, but despite that friendship, after all the hell he'd put him through, there was no one in the world more deserving to ruin his life. However, Peter had promised he'd never tell, and had kept that promise. The loyalty and support he'd shown him had become the driving force behind Barry's own loyalty toward him. He'd became one of Peter's closest friends and his staunchest protector. No one would dare mess with him as long as Barry was around.

Hank had approached Barry several times since then, but he'd been too afraid to get caught—this time by someone not as loyal as Peter—so that one kiss had been the first and last. After months of rejection, Hank had given up and never spoken to him again, except to assure him he'd tell no one. He'd held true to his word until this diary entry—dated a little less than a year earlier—had come out of nowhere to ruin everything.

A kick in his thigh brought him back from the memory as his momma continued to yell. "Do you want to embarrass me more than you already have?" She kicked him again as he lay on the floor. "Well, do you?"

"No, momma! It's not true! I swear it's not true!"

"LIAR!"

She kicked him again, then turned around and stomped out of the room. Instead of being relieved the attack was over, Barry knew what her walking out meant. His eyes darted around the room, searching for an escape like a trapped animal. He could hear his momma moving things around in her closet. He knew what she was getting. He looked at the window, his only escape from the room, but he knew he wouldn't have enough time to get out, and she'd be waiting for him when he came back.

"You will tell me the truth!" she said, striding through the door, and his entire soul sank to his feet as he saw her wielding exactly what he'd expected. In her right hand, wrapped in a single loop, was his dad's belt—the same one he'd used to hang himself.

"No, momma!" he pleaded as tears spilled from his eyes. "No, momma! Don't! It's not true!"

Before the phrase was done, she was standing over him, and she belted him once, pulling a pained cry from him. She belted him again and again. Each strike punctuating each word as she said, "You. Will. Tell. Me. The. Truth!"

"It's not true, Momma!" He held his arms up toward her, a pathetic, futile attempt to protect himself.

"Liar! You lying faggot! You AIDS-ridden faggot! You lying shit! LIAR!" She continued to strike him with the belt, over and over, and in his mind was the bright image of his father hanging from a beam from that same belt. Had she even cleaned it after? Or was that part of the punishment? Those tiny skin particles from his dad's neck coming in contact with his own skin as it bruised and ruptured, becoming a permanent part of him, as if his dad's death wasn't already a permanent part of his being.

"Tell me the truth!"

"Okay!" he shouted, now blubbering, trembling, his arm covered in red welts, stretched out toward her. "I did it, momma. I did it. It was only once. It was only once. I swear on dad's life. I swear. Please don't hit me anymore!" His last word stretched into a low, keening, quavering sob. He could feel the burn of one strike that had gotten past his arm and had whipped him right in the jaw and cheek.

In terror, he looked up, and what he saw in her eyes went beyond simple anger. Something had broken inside her at that moment. She made a growling sound at him, then turned around. Before his horrified eyes, his momma started ripping his soccer posters off the wall.

"No! Momma! Dad gave me those!"

She turned a crazed glower toward him that stunned him into terrified silence. She resumed tearing off the posters, then went after his player statuettes, his World Cup scale model. To the floor they went, then under the heel of her shoe, breaking. Then she went for his trading cards, which she removed from their cases and ripped in half. Everything she found, she tossed, ripped, trampled, and broke. He watched as the room he'd arranged and tidied with such love and care turned into a disaster zone.

She pointed a forefinger at him, the belt still in her hand; the finger moved this way and that in a drunken sway. "Be thankful I told Skylar Marsh if she or that queer of hers even *breathe* a word of this, I'll make sure Martha Lange knows the things she said about her in the PTA meeting. And you... Don't think I don't know you've been hanging around her son."

Barry stared at her in terror, rubbing the burning welts in his arms.

"Are you fucking Peter Lange, you faggot?" she said,

not understanding Barry only had a preteen's superficial understanding of what the concept entailed.

"No, momma." He panicked again. He could see it in her face. She didn't believe him at all. *Think of something. Think of something.* "You told me not to bother Peter Lange again, 'coz you didn't want his mother to hurt you like she hurt dad." This one had gotten through. He saw it in her face. He had to keep going. "I became his friend. He's my friend. Just that!"

She studied his face.

"Yes, I kissed Hank Marsh. Well, he…uh…he kissed *me*… Took me by surprise. I was confused. Not anymore. I'm"—he swallowed hard—"not a fag. I swear."

She watched him for a while, then, still pointing an unsteady forefinger at him, said, "You get *one* pass. I will not have you shame your dad's name, or mine. Don't let me *ever* find out you've gone queer. I won't hesitate to drag you by your balls to Martha Lange and tell her you fucked her son. Then I'll just watch as I let *her* take care of it. Would take one hell of a fucking burden off my shoulders." She looked around the room. "My head hurts. Clean up this mess. Don't want to see any more fucking pictures of men hanging on your walls."

After she left, seeing his room in shambles, his body aching, Barry wanted to curl into a ball and sob, but he was terrified she would see his tears as another reason to question his manhood, so he wiped his face dry and held it in.

It was almost six. He figured there were still a few people inside the school building up the slope, mostly staff, but adults never came to The Pines, and students came here straight after class. They were never here this late.

Barry was all alone.

It had become his own little spot in town. This small clearing in the woods made him feel protected, away from all danger. The one place where he could let himself be vulnerable and really cry. He sat at the foot of his usual pine tree, a small stone held in his hands. It was oval shaped, porous, with a crack running down the middle. He'd found it in the same pile as the one in his bedroom—and thank god, his momma hadn't thrown that one at him—but this one wasn't fully cracked open. He couldn't see inside, like with the other one. That one was unique.

In a burst of rage, he roared as he hurled the rock toward the pile at the edge of the clearing, where he'd found it. It bounced off with a loud *CLACK!* but it didn't break, simply rolling on the grass before coming to a stop. He let his head fall and tucked it between his knees, then let out noisy, painful sobs and sniffles. He used his forearm to wipe the snot off his nose, and he felt the red belt marks on his skin burn upon contact.

"Hey, big guy."

Barry heard the voice and closed his eyes, his jaw clenched. *Goddamn it, not now!*

"I'm sorry," that annoying Chang kid said.

Barry saw with aggravation he was now lowering himself to the ground to sit beside him.

"I was riding my bike near here, and I saw you go through the fence. You looked a bit…shitty… I got worried."

"You don't need to worry about me. You don't know me."

Chang stared at him. "Dude, your eyes are red, your face is covered in tears and snot, and your arms and face are covered in belt marks." Ray reached into the pocket of his cargo pants and brought out a handkerchief, raised it to his face.

"Who the fuck has a handkerchief now?" Barry said, turning his bloodshot eyes toward him. "Are you someone's grandpa or somethin'?" He took the handkerchief anyway and wiped his face. "You're weird, Chang."

"Call me Ray."

Barry nodded but said nothing.

"Look," Ray said. "I know my family just moved here a couple months back. I don't have many friends. I've been talking to some people, but none of them like soccer like I do, and they're all very standoffish about talking to someone from out of town."

"How's that my problem?" Barry said, but his words

lacked aggression. They were a pathetic attempt at distancing himself.

"I heard about you from some other guys on the soccer team. I meant it as a compliment when I said people used to be scared of you, but not anymore. Dude, you actually have a cool group of friends. So, I thought, 'hey, that's the kind of guy I'd like to be friends with—someone who isn't afraid of trying to be better.'"

(*Try to be better, son*)

Barry stared at him, slack-jawed. Had the Chang kid really said that?

"I know we got off on the wrong foot," Ray said. "I know you already have friends, and you've made it clear you don't need me as one." He looked around at the empty clearing of The Pines. "But I'm guessing, since they're not here, you don't show them this part of your life. They don't usually see you this way." Barry shot him a painful glance. "I just kinda stumbled upon you having a moment. So, maybe, I could be your friend during these moments. If you don't want me to meet your other friends, that's cool. I can be here for you for the times you don't want them to see. Least you know we have soccer in common. We can talk about that if you don't want to talk about what happened to you. You can cry, and I can sit next to you, and when you're done crying, we can talk about, like, who's the best soccer player of all time, or which team should've won which World Cup… Stuff like that."

Suspicious, Barry looked at him, but then softened and gave him the beginnings of a smile. "Sure," he said with reluctance, but flashed a full smile. "I still think you're kind of a psycho, though."

Ray smiled at him and placed his hand on his. Barry didn't move it for two seconds, but then pulled it away.

"I'm sorry," Ray said.

"That's okay," Barry answered. "It's not you."

The shorter kid nodded, and they sat in silence for a while.

"So," Ray said. "I get the whole legend of The Pines, and—"

"Not a legend."

Ray regarded him with just a hint of disbelief. "Uh, sure. I mean, the whole deal of how no one can hurt anyone here because they will be cursed and all that, but why come here alone?"

Barry gazed around, wistful. "I don't feel scared here. It's kind of like my safe place."

"I get it. Nice and quiet. Smells of pines and earth."

Barry nodded. "Yeah, I like that about this place."

"I think you should have more than one safe place, though," Ray said, and before he could ask what he meant by that, he added: "I have a great idea. Come to my house for dinner tonight."

"What? No! That's crazy. No."

"My mom's making dinner. She's one hell of a cook—my dad, too. You know King's?"

Barry was confused at first, then returned a look of recognition. "Wait. Your family took over the Chinese place downtown?"

"Korean," the shorter kid said. "Used to be Chinese. We bought it from the previous owners. We kept the name, changed the menu. My mom and dad, they take turns in the kitchen; they're incredible cooks. Once you try their fried chicken in *yangnyeom* sauce, you'll get addicted."

"Well, I don't know what '*yum-yum*' sauce is. Love fried chicken, though." He gave him a pleasant smile, but then it faded, as if he was remembering something. He looked down at the red marks on his arms. "I, uh… I don't want them to see me like this."

"Oh." Ray looked like he was thinking of a solution. He looked down at himself and unzipped his light blue hoodie, which looked several sizes too big. "This is my older brother's hoodie. He left it when he went to college. It's huge on me, so it might fit you, even if it's gonna be a bit tight around the shoulders." He shuffled out of the hoodie and held it up for him, indicating to put his arm through the sleeve. "Try it." Barry hesitated at first, but then he put his right arm through the sleeve. Ray threw the other one over his shoulder, and Barry grabbed it and put his left arm in. He looked at Ray with a nervous stare. "Well? How do I look?"

Ray gave him that stupid, wide smile of his and said, "You look ready for *yangnyeom* chicken."

Looking at the shorter kid's smile, Barry reconsidered his previous assessment. He thought it looked quite pleasant.

Two days later, Barry would introduce Ray to The Vigilantes.

Chapter Seven

Xavier

2022

"And we're back, believers and skeptics!" Xavier spoke into his mic with a joyous grin. "In case you're just joining us, welcome to Paranoid-Normal, the show where we know we're being watched, but we're watching *them* right back! You know me, I'm your paranormal curator, Xavier PK, and we're about to kick off the second half of Telltale Thursday!"

There was an expectation that came with being known as the town weirdo in a town like White Harbor. Xavier Poe Kane, however, reveled in being the owner of the title, several years running. It wasn't enough he lived in an isolated little cabin in the western end of the Crescent Mountains and almost never showed his face in town. He made it a point to exaggerate what other people perceived as strange about him. Every social encounter with Xavier was sure to end up with him blurting out theories about aliens, ghosts, and conspiracies with gleeful abandon. He rejoiced when people avoided eye contact—lest the "mountain crazy" engage them in conversation.

He once told a very uncomfortable Faith Harvey—a supremely religious and nosey seventy-year-old—while in line at the Harbor Grocers cashier, he was proud of being a card-carrying resident of Blight Harbor, and he planned to remain King Oddball until old Ben Curling came back from the grave and dragged him off his throne. Mrs. Harvey reacted as if Xavier had spoken about the Devil himself.

He was an eloquent, witty, and well-read man, but part of his mystique was maintaining an eccentric persona.

Locked in a soundproof, windowless room in his home, the real Xavier Poe Kane came out. To every watcher and listener tuning in to his live stream and chiming in on his group chat, Xavier was a voice of reason, an impartial judge of truth and lies, an asker and answerer of questions. This was where Xavier had found his niche: he was earnest and unapologetic about wanting to believe in paranormal phenomena, but he refused to take the easy road to Believertown. Where other voices on the subject saw a close-up of a dust particle on a video recording and started going nuts about "orbs" and "spiritual manifestations", Xavier didn't hesitate to ask: "How do you know it's not just a fucking speck of dust floating too close to the lens?"

His listeners respected his way of challenging them, combined with his enthusiasm for the subject matter, and the no-bullshit way he spoke to them. And so, despite being just some guy from a nowhere town who lived in the mountains, Xavier was making a killing on the different live streaming and podcasting apps, making a comfy six-figure income from home, while people like old Faith Harvey believed he spent his time locked in a cabin making pickled squirrel preserves and talking to the buried bodies under his floorboards.

Before going on a quick sponsor break, Xavier had been talking to his latest caller for his Telltale Thursday livestream; a college student from Notre Dame, Indiana, who hadn't sounded like the sharpest tool in the shed, abused the word "bruh", and had identified himself as simply Cris, without an "h".

Cris without an "h" had gone on for quite a bit regarding the story of a glowing orb of light traversing the hallways at a building on campus. The story had been the usual haunted building fare Xavier had heard a thousand times before, and Cris hadn't struck him as the most trustworthy—or not-high-at-the-time-of-events—source, and Xavier had been ready to bring down his Bullshit Hammer on it, until the very last moment, when someone on his live chat with the login Liv2008, had pointed out a strange inconsistency in the story.

Xavier, however, had a fairness rule: he'd give every person a platform and allow them to tell their story, unless its stupidity was so abject it didn't deserve the airtime, like that guy from Atlanta who said he bought one of those talking Japanese toilets that kept giving him a doomsday prophecy in the most offensive mockery of a Japanese accent he'd ever heard. With Cris, he was glad he'd listened to the full story before dismissing it.

Near the end of Cris's otherwise convoluted, clichéd tale, the five terrified—and, "like, totally not high"—college students who'd Scooby-Doo'ed their way into the haunted building had run out, chased out of the building by the ghostly orb of light they'd been trying to record with their phone cameras. This—Xavier had believed—had been the focus of the story.

That was when Liv2008's message had popped up on the chat window.

Liv2008: What do you mean 'the five of us ran out of the building'? You said SIX of you went into the building. [poo emoji]

Xavier had stared at the message for just two seconds, but it had felt like an eternity. He felt embarrassed he'd missed this key piece of information in the story. Cris *had* mentioned six people had gone into the school building. Five had run out. Had Cris made a mistake? Was the inconsistency proof of it being a bullshit story? Or was it something else?

Xavier adjusted his glasses, ran a hand over his long, brown beard, and confronted his caller. "Thank you so much for that interesting and creepy story, Cris without an 'h' but an esteemed member of my audience, Liv2008, has a very interesting question. You mentioned six of you had gone into the building, but only five of you came out."

"YES!" the caller said, triumphant, not even waiting for Xavier to ask his question, which confused the crap out of him. "Someone caught it!"

"Huh?" Xavier eyed the call on his screen, puzzled.

"I owe my girl Lindsay ten bucks. She said someone in your show would catch it."

"So, you had a plot hole on purpose?"

"No, man. No plot hole. Guess what happened?"

Xavier pondered on this for a moment. "Uh, I guess, you mentioned you paid the security guard to let you in the building at night, so maybe the guard followed you in, but stayed inside after you ran out?"

"Nice guess, X, that's why you're the best, man."

"Thanks, Cris without an 'h'," he replied, losing his patience a little.

"You're wrong, though, bruh."

Something in the caller's conceited tone made Xavier want to throttle the guy, because he was stealing his spotlight, but he could tell there was no malice behind it. "Okay? Care to elaborate?"

"The guard was sneaking a smoke outside and was startled when we burst screaming through the front door. He wasn't expecting us out until much, much later, so we gave him a big scare."

"And you're sure he didn't follow you in?"

"No, bruh. I mean, yes, I'm sure. He was almost done with his cigarette when we came out. We would've smelled him if he'd been smoking inside."

"Also, it would've triggered the smoke alarm, I guess?"

"Exactly! See, the thing is, we all remember six people going in, but only five of us came out."

"So, someone was what? Lost? Abducted? Is this where you pull some alien abduction out of your hat?"

The caller's voice took on a confused tone. "I ain't wearing a hat, X."

Xavier ran a hand over his face in frustration.

"It was a figure of... ugh... How are you in college, seriously, man?"

"What?"

"Nothing. Get to the point."

"We all remember it wrong, X." The caller's voice sounded now assured, convincing. "That's the creepy thing about what happened, bruh! We all remember going into the building with DeShaun's brother, Matt. No, let me correct that. We all remembered six of us had gone in, right? But my friend Priya was Matt's girlfriend. As far as she knew, Matt was with us, but when we came out of the building, he wasn't there! She thought he was walking right behind her, but he wasn't there, bruh! They had hugged, and talked, and even made out, and he wasn't there! Gone! Just *pfft!* and only *she* remembered him specifically. The rest of us remembered six of us, but we didn't know who the sixth was."

"And what happened to Matt? Is he okay? How do you know he didn't just stay inside to mess with your heads?"

"My girl Lindsay called him. Now, listen to this. He was staying at his mom's, which is on the other side of town. Lindsay was sure he was pranking us, so she FaceTimed him, and he really was at his mom's! Here we had Priya having a full breakdown because she'd spent the last couple hours with him, and he was all the way across town! Priya was so creeped out she broke up with Matt, because she was too scared of him, even though he didn't even know what happened."

And just like that, what had started out as a spectacularly boring ghost story had evolved into a full discussion on perception, mind-manipulation, and even interdimensional travel. *You never know how these stories will end,* Xavier thought.

He glanced at the calls waiting and allowed himself a satisfied grin. It delighted him that so many people shared in that ethereal world few people let themselves wander into.

He took a sip of his Black Butte XXX (just because he lived in the mountains, it didn't mean he had to settle for trashy beer like Keystone), let it slide down his gullet, and tapped on his desk twice, ready to continue.

"Alright! I see five, six, whoa! Nine calls waiting! Wow, those anal probers in the sky are working overtime, it seems!"

He read a message on the chat.

DungeonPig69: It's not work if you enjoy it! [eggplant emoji] [peach emoji]

Xavier let out a loud cackle. "Ha! Well, congratulations, DungeonPig69, wasn't talking about you, but sounds like you have a more interesting sex life than I'll ever have. Good for you!"

He clicked on a button on his screen and a remixed version of the opening theme for the TV show *Fringe* played for a few seconds, followed by the loud, booming noise you often hear in suspenseful movie trailers—Xavier always insisted *Fringe* was superior to *The X-Files* in almost every way, and he'd fight anyone on that topic, gun duels being an acceptable option.

"Enough chitchat! Our last story will be hard to top, but let's move on to our next caller." He drank from his beer bottle until it was completely empty. "He's from right here, my hometown, White Harbor!" He stopped. Noticed a message on the live chat. "Hold on, we have a question on the chat."

Masahiro99: Should I visit White Harbor? Looking for a spooky vacation place.

"No! No, dude, do yourself a favor and don't come here. It's a boring Podunk town in the middle of nowhere. Sure, some nice scenery, a tiny amusement park, plenty of creepy history, but nothing to write home about. If the Vanek House was still around? Maaaaaybe? Other than that, you'll be bored to tears. Anyway, let's talk to my buddy on the line. I'd say he's my neighbor because everyone in White Harbor lives close to each other. Welcome to Paranoid-Normal, Dominic Willis! How's it hanging, Dom?"

"Hey, Xavier," Dom said, with a voice that sounded like he wasn't the brightest bulb in the Christmas tree. "I always listen to your show here at the gas station. Big fan."

"Well, of course you're my fan! I'm awesome!"

"One sec... uh... What was that?" There was the sound of another person's voice in the call's background. "Oh, okay, I'll... I'll tell him... Okay... um... Xavier, this is not what I called about, so this is not coming from me. It's Gunnar, being a jerk." He hesitated. "Gunnar said to tell you to get an actual job and stop chasing after little green men."

"Well, thank you, Gunnar!" Xavier said, without missing a beat. This hadn't been the first time Gunnar Bilson tried to make fun of him while broadcasting. Xavier took in a deep breath. "You mean an actual job like yours? What does a gas jockey do nowadays, exactly? Help Mrs. Riley when

139

she's sliding her credit card upside down in the pump, because credit cards didn't exist when she learned to drive? Also, the men I chase are not green, they're gray, unlike the men *you* chase, who aren't green, they're white trash. And no, my dear listeners, this is not a homophobic rant. This is an intervention for my friend Gunnar's horrible taste in men, who may or may not be his cousins. This is 2022 America, not *Game of Thrones*. You *can* find plenty of sex partners you're not related to, Gunnar. I say this because I care."

"Uh…" Dom sounded uncomfortable, listening to his coworker, then came back to the phone. "Gunnar says he don't fuck men, and they're not his cousins."

"Alright." Xavier put on a joyful grin. "Alright, dear listeners, for time's sake, I won't dissect Gunnar's sentence. I'll just let syntax be syntax. Now, Dom. You had something for me tonight on this Telltale Thursday, before getting so rudely interrupted by your buddy. Spit it out, my friend—which, coincidentally, is something Gunnar never does."

He could hear Gunnar Bilson cursing at him in the background.

"Well," Dominic said, bashful. "I know in your recording room you ain't got no windows, but, uh… Have you seen the moon?"

"Have I seen the moon?" Xavier enunciated each word slowly. "Dom, buddy, have you been drinking on the job? I mean, anyone would drink at a gas station in this boring town with no better company than Gunnar, but—"

"No, Xavier, I'm serious!"

Xavier was taken aback by the sudden assertiveness in Dom's voice.

Dom, a soft-spoken, affable individual, never raised his voice. "The moon is blue," Dom said. "It's a full moon, and it's blue."

"Uh… Okay?" He sounded puzzled. "The moon is blue." Xavier considered how to answer his friend, since it was obvious he was talking nonsense. "Alright, Dom, I'm going to bring the Bullshit Hammer down on this one right now, save time, and spare you the embarrassment. I get it, you think this is clever because 'once in a blue moon' refers to something weird that rarely happens, but let's stick to the facts here, my friend, there's no such thing as a blue moon—it's just a saying, not an actual thing. A blue moon is the third full moon of a season that has four, and blah, blah, blah, blah. It. Is. Not. Blue."

"You should probably go outside and check it out, Xavier," Dom said. "Like…it's blue, man. Dark blue."

"Dom, I can't actually step out of the room right now since we're in the middle of recording, but I'll ask my listeners on the chat. In the counties around White Harbor, what does the moon look like to you right now? Is it blue? Let's see…" He surveyed the answers on the chatroom. "White. White. White. Silver. White. White. Silver. White. White"—he noticed something—"oh… OH…"

His eyes widened as he read the interesting message.

"My dear believers and skeptics, we have someone who didn't just answer the question, but added the answer to the question I forgot to ask. Our buddy, AntAfterlife, located merely ten miles from White Harbor, just threw down the Bullshit Hammer—no, the Bullshit Anvil—on this one."

He clicked on a sound effect and a drum roll played, followed by a cymbal crash.

"There isn't a full moon outside at all!" he said, triumphant. "What are you doing to me, Dom? We have a waning gibbous right now, and there are zero, hear that: *zero*, people saying the moon is blue. What do you have to say for yourself, Dom? I expected better from you, buddy. Gunnar, he's the spawn of Satan, but you? What's your excuse?"

"Please, Xavier," Dom implored. "Please, take a moment and go to your window. I'd send you a picture, but then you'll say I put like a filter on it, or something."

Xavier considered for a moment. "Alright, alright. Let's do this. I'll step out of the recording room for a minute, if you, my dear believers and skeptics, will pardon the interruption. But, Dom, I'm warning you. If this isn't worth my time—and I'm guessing it isn't—you're giving me a full tank of gas on *your* dime next time I go to the gas station."

"Fine," Dom said. "Just, please, go. People need to know this is happening."

Xavier removed his headphones and rolled his chair back. He scratched the top of his head with a tired expression and scoffed at the very notion that what Dom was claiming could be true. It couldn't be. And yet, if he was so convinced, what was this strange void in his stomach? Why were his fingers tingling? Anticipation? *Ridiculous!* he thought. *Anticipation for what? Sore disappointment?* He wished, all of a sudden, he hadn't finished his beer so quickly.

He stepped out of the recording room and strode next door to his bedroom, where large windows, covered with wood-textured horizontal blinds, looked out toward the east. He pulled on the collar of his jacket as he felt a cold breeze come in, which made the blinds sway, making cracking noises against the wall.

It's summer. Why is it so cold?

Xavier approached the windows and reached for the hanging stick that opened the blinds and turned it. The horizontal blinds swiveled, revealing the outside.

He looked out toward the mountain; the slope falling toward the ocean. The town lights to the left, and the dark waters of the bay at night, reflecting the moonlight.

He peered up at the sky.

Minutes later, Xavier reentered the recording room and closed the door behind him. He couldn't lift his gaze. He kept looking down at the floor, and thoughts swirled around in his mind, but they didn't feel like his thoughts. They felt more like overhearing a scientist in a separate room, speaking out loud while measuring, weighing, reading, and comparing—coming up with theories, explanations, and hypotheses that led to no logical conclusions.

He sat and rolled his chair up to his desk, put on his headphones, licked his lips, and leaned in toward the microphone. He inhaled to speak, but let the air out without a word, staring toward an empty portion of wall to his left, as if reconsidering his words, while the scientist in the next room continued to pore over numbers, and calculations, and definitions, and coming up with nothing.

Anything? one part of his mind asked.

No, the other one answered.

He inhaled again.

"I… uh… My dear believers and skeptics, I… I owe my buddy, Dom, an apology." He paused. Looked at the chat feed. No one typing. Expectation. "I… I don't know how to explain it, but I looked out the window, and…there's a full moon over White Harbor, and…it's blue. Like a dark silver blue I've never seen in my life." He once again stopped and pondered on what to say next. "I've talked about ghosts, and UFOs, and unknowable creatures in this podcast, but this, uh... This left me stumped... No, no, I see a bunch of you guys already typing 'Bullshit'. I get it, but you know me. Xavier Poe Kane would rather be proved wrong than to lie to you guys. I have no explanation. The phases of the moon can't change. They completely depend on the position of the moon relative to the Earth. They can't... They can't just be changed. I have nothing. Dom, I'm so sorry, man."

There was no answer.

"Dom? You still there?"

"I think he hung up and my call came through," an unfamiliar voice said. "But I was calling about the moon, too, Xavier. I think I might have something to add."

"Uh, sure!" Xavier answered, his voice absent, but eager, glad to know he wasn't the only one who had lost his mind. "Sure, man. I'm sorry, I'm a bit shook, so I'm not super talkative right now, but go ahead. You're from White Harbor, I suppose? Since you're seeing the blue moon, too? Who am I talking to?"

"I'd prefer not to say my name. I don't want my neighbors thinking I'm crazy because of what I'm going to tell you."

"Why would they think you're crazy?"

"Dude, are you for real?" the caller said. "Xavier. To half the people in town, you're crazy and should be locked up in Lighthouse Rock, and to the other half, you're a potential serial killer. My sister switches sidewalks when she sees you coming. The old people don't like you because you keep digging up old secrets and refuse to leave Blight Harbor well alone."

"Fair enough... I'm flattered. What do you got for me?"

"I've been listening to you for five years, and I can't believe, in all this time, you haven't covered the UFO crash that happened in White Harbor three hundred years ago."

The face Xavier made was comical. He looked perplexed, as if the person on the other end of the line had suddenly belted out an impromptu opera performance. "Say what?"

"You know all the creepy, crazy shit that keeps happening in town? People dying too young, going crazy, deaths and murders, all the stories about ghosts and disappearances?"

"Yeah?"

"It's all related to that. I have it on good authority there are coinciding tales by Native American tribes in the area, of a colossal explosion, as if from a UFO crash, or a meteorite, or *something*, releasing a huge burst of blue light somewhere in the Crescent Mountains long before this town was founded. There might be a thing from space or from another dimension buried somewhere in town, emitting radiation and mind-waves that influence us and cause all the weirdness in town. It covers the entire town like an area-of-influence bubble. That's why we're seeing a full, blue moon, while everyone else sees a waning gibbous, because we're *inside* the bubble."

Xavier heard himself let out an odd snort that surprised even himself. What this person was talking about ticked all the boxes of a made-up story. Using very general terms like "UFO crash", "a thing from space", "another dimension", "mind-waves", providing vague sources, and having it happen so long ago, it was impossible to corroborate the information. It certainly was within the type of stories one could expect in his show, but it felt so ridiculous, he could've started laughing right then and there. However, if it was that implausible, why wasn't he dismissing it already? What made this story more ridiculous than the glowing orb at the university building, or five people thinking they were six?

After all, the moon was blue. He'd seen it with his own eyes.

"Alright." He composed himself and put the blue moon aside in a separate compartment of his mind. "I can subscribe to that idea, as much as any theory presented here, but I'm assuming you don't have any actual evidence for this event that happened three hundred years ago? You know, seems kind of convenient all corroborating sources are dead."

"C'mon, man, I'm not gonna do your job for you. Talk to Callum Baker, the librarian at Anne Summers. He can tell you about it. It was in a book he had among some papers on his desk once, while he was helping my daughter find this novel for class. I found it very interesting, but I don't remember the actual name."

"So, I'm supposed to go sleuthing in a library for a hypothetical book you don't remember the name of, only because you said, 'aliens crashed in town three centuries ago?'"

"I never said aliens. Look, I'm not trolling you. I'm your fan, alright? I actually want you to find something cool for your show. The reason I think you're going to do it is, if it turns out to be true—even if it's not an actual spaceship, even if it's like just a meteor, or the freakin' second coming of Christ, falling from the sky in a weather balloon—you know it will be big for your channel. Also"—the caller's voice made it sound like a challenge—"because the goddamn moon is full and blue, Xavier. Don't you want to be the one to find out why?"

Xavier looked down at a small notepad on his desk. He grabbed a pen and jotted on it: *Callum Baker. Library. Anne Summers High.*

Chapter Eight

Lights Out

The town air was thick with the smell of humanity, lingering traces of the day, still clinging to the wind. It put Freddie in a wistful mood as he ambled through the empty streets, peering in on the lazy lives in the surrounding homes as they unfurled. It was a subtle, dignified kind of existence that continued on after the sun had abandoned this side of the world. The sound of people, of civilization, retreated but didn't disappear altogether. It overwhelmed him, even now, in the quiet hours of the night. He heard someone playing a piano. He didn't recognize the tune, but it sounded mournful, lonely, gliding into his ears from somewhere distant.

Freddie could see light from lamps and TVs in the surrounding houses, diffused in the fabric of closed curtains, the streetlights casting their warm glow on the sidewalks, the headlights of an old passing car. He realized he'd forgotten the smell of engine exhaust from spending so long on an island; he could almost feel it cling to the yellow pajamas and robe he had to wear at Lighthouse Rock and crawl up his body and into his nose, yet even that seemed pleasant, because of how long it had been since he'd last felt this.

The moment he crossed over from the Moon-lit World—Blight Harbor as the townspeople, and even he sometimes called it—Freddie was met with the sight of Maria Knox, lying unconscious in the middle of the street in her pink tracksuit, her little Pomeranian—Dottie III—licking her face and yapping with worry. She was alive, but her mind was elsewhere. He hoped a car wouldn't run her over, but he doubted it; nighttime in a small town like this often meant the streets would be empty.

The next thing he'd noticed was the blue moon, which, for the first time in well over a century, glowed not only over Blight Harbor, but on this side as well, watching over the town itself. For the first time since Walter Parham surrendered his body to the Exiles and killed his rapist, there was a blue moon shining over White Harbor.

Freddie now stood in front of his next stop. A two-story home, on the northern side of town, whose key features were its large windows on both floors, looking out toward the beach. In front of the house was a car. He knew little about car models, given his almost thirty-year stay at Lighthouse Rock, but he could see it was a red Dodge SUV.

The lights in the house were on, and there was the shape of a woman sitting at a window on the first floor, looking out. She couldn't see him right now. She would soon. Freddie would be surprised if she wasn't already expecting him.

Before walking up the front steps, Freddie glanced around once more at the lights that had so fascinated him. Not the pale, impersonal lights of his prison in Lighthouse Rock, but the lights of a living, thriving town. Human lights. Living lights. Soon to be extinguished.

As if in response to his thoughts, every single light around him went out. Every house was flooded with darkness, every streetlight devoid of its glow—even a parked idling car about five houses away had its headlights blinded.

The sound of people murmuring and exclaiming in their homes filled the air, mingling with the gentle sound of the waves on the beach. He heard agitated and confused voices, people searching for flashlights and cell phones. Freddie knew, however, none but the most rudimentary sources of light would work tonight. The thought came to him, then: wasn't that chatter and excitement—awakened in darkness— considered life as well? Life wasn't exclusive to the light, after all. In the dark, there was a peculiar sort of life; a subtle, dignified kind of existence, as he'd been musing just minutes earlier. He thought it was ironic the darkness often illuminated the things people kept hidden from others.

The blackout had begun.

John Hitch sat on the floor, his back against the wall, knees bent, arms resting on them. His face had little to no expression. He looked thwarted, but there was a cornered-animal quality to it; a snake waiting for the right moment to strike.

In front of him, a few feet away, Jess sat on a chair; legs spread, body leaning forward—Peggy pointed at him to ensure a swift, direct shot, should the snake attempt its strike—her friends were around her, some standing, some sitting, observing the interaction with mounting curiosity.

"Alright, asshole," she said. "It took some convincing, but Louis and my two forcibly sober customers agreed to go home. They will give the police their statements tomorrow at the station if they're needed, and that's what I'll tell the cops when I call them. Before I do that, though. Let's have a quick chat. It's just us now, the people who"—she did air quotes—"burned your house."

"Um." Angie raised her hand.

Without looking in her direction, Jess sighed in annoyance. "Yes, Angie. We know you weren't there."

"Sorry. Objections are kind of force of habit."

"Fine," Jess said. "Sustained." She once again spoke to Hitch. "We were all there, except for my friend Angie, who—now that I think about it—is the only one you spoke to whom you didn't call by name. I don't think you know it."

Hitch gave her a sideways glance but didn't speak.

"But you *do* know all of us, don't you?"

No answer.

"And not just passingly." Jess stared at the man's face, studying his every expression, every twitch, every blink. She thought the years of observing people here at the bar had given her at least some insight into their many tells: This one had a bad day at work. This one is cheating on his wife. This one's getting laid tonight. This one had a fight with her husband. It was all in the face and the body language. Sometimes words weren't necessary. She would, of course, love a few words about the insanity this man had just put them through. There was only so much she could infer with twitches and snorts. "You kept Angie on the corner table, made me move with the rest of the group. You only separated Peter because your beef is with that crazy sack of badgers he calls a mother."

The security guard turned his bald head toward her, stared at her with piercing, knowing eyes, and looked away again.

She was on the right track.

"I see. So, Peter's off limits, *and* you knew Angie wasn't part of the core group. You also knew Barry almost killed Freddie the day of the fire. You knew Ray stopped him. Who the *fuck* are you?"

She could hear Hitch's angry breathing, but his head remained turned away. His lips didn't move. Not a word of acknowledgment, but she could see the wheels turning in his head. He was debating something with himself.

"Shouldn't we, like, restrain him, or something?" Royce said. "Citizen's arrest? Like that thing crazy white people do when they see a Black person parked on their street, minding their business?"

Jess gave him an annoyed look. "Be my guest," she said, tilting her head toward the man on the floor. "He nearly kicked Barry the Brickhouse's ass, and here you are, all pudgy and soft. Wanna try it?"

He considered for less than two seconds before answering, "Rather not."

"He didn't kick my ass," Barry added in a dejected tone. "Just my hand a bit. Doesn't hurt anymore."

Jess sighed at the unnecessary macho posturing. "Tell me, Barr, have your balls already dropped back down, or are they still tangled in your ribs?"

Barry rolled his eyes.

She turned back to the young security guard and

forced a big grin. "Sorry about the interruptions, hun. My friends and I do this thing, in which we try to get funny when we're nervous and insecure. It's a completely unhealthy coping mechanism and I love it. Now, I really want to know. What's your deal?"

Hitch's head cocked left, then right, releasing two audible cracks. He sighed. "You wouldn't believe me," he grumbled, avoiding eye contact.

"Look, hun. Even if you don't live in White Harbor, you said your family passed the Vanek House on for almost a hundred years. You know what living in this town is like, just as much as we do. You know about the town's colorful history, most of which is painted in shades of red. So, try us." She pointed at Callum and Sylvia. "See those two people over there? The tall lady with the perky boobs, and the short gentleman with the perky butt?"

Callum huffed, looking self-conscious.

Sylvia only smiled.

"They're two of the smartest people I know. They might find a solution that doesn't involve you killing a bunch of us like a psychopath. So, is there a reason you're doing this? Or are you just another nut who listens to Xavier's podcast way too much and reads online rumors about this town being paranormal Mecca?"

Hitch scoffed, rolled his eyes. She saw he hadn't fully closed down. The fact he'd reacted meant he was listening.

"I'll tell you something about me, then. All day, I've had this feeling, like something's been building up, you know? When I say 'Blight Harbor', you know what I'm talking about, right?" She regarded him, paying close attention to his every expression.

He returned a single nod.

"Well, John, if my customers and the gossip on the vine are any sign, Blight Harbor has felt sort of *awake* today. Am I wrong about that?"

The security guard held quiet for a moment. He raised his face, those big eyes of his surveyed the faces around. Stopped on Peter. Tilted his chin toward him. "His mother. She's going to kill a lot of people."

"What?" said Peter. "No, wait a minute—"

"Peter," Jess said, raising a palm toward him. "Let him talk."

"You all know who Martha Lange is." Hitch scanned the reactions of the group. "What she can do."

Awkward glances were exchanged all around. Most eyes avoided lingering on Peter too long.

"Not just that, you've heard rumors about her."

Jess held quiet. She'd gotten him talking. She had to let him get it all out. There was something so old in the young man's voice. A tired tone she'd only heard on unhappy, elderly people.

"You've wondered if there's any truth to them. Well,

there is. Everything you've heard about Martha Lange is true. And now, she's going to kill thousands of people, and she's using Freddie Parham to do it."

"That's impossible," Bobby said. "Freddie is locked in a room in—"

"Lighthouse Rock?" Hitch said. He reached into his shirt pocket—causing Jess's grip on Peggy to tighten and her trigger finger to be back at the ready. He pulled out his access badge, with "Lighthouse Rock Mental Health Facility" under his name and picture, and tossed it on the floor in front of Bobby. "Well, I got news for you, Doctor Novak. Freddie Parham is free now." He tilted his chin toward Peter again. "His mother let him out."

Peter opened his mouth to retort, but Hitch cut in before he could.

"You know she can do it, Lange. Don't even act like you don't."

Peter tightened his lips, giving the man a contemptuous look.

The young security guard swiveled his head toward Bobby again. "Freddie has killed two people tonight already."

"No! You're lying!" Bobby said. "That's not—"

"I needed to kill four of you before he killed the second one."

Horrified faces all around.

Jess was appalled at the casual way this man could say

something like that without even flinching.

Hitch swiveled his eyes toward Ray, who was standing at the opposite end of the group as Barry. He flashed a wicked grin at him. "Those deaths are on you, by the way, Chang. If you hadn't stopped *that one*, thirty years ago"—he motioned toward Barry—"those two people might still be alive."

"Fuck you!" Ray's eyes were full of rage as the words exploded out of him. "No way that's my fault. Fuck you!"

Hitch held his grin. "There's good news, though. There are rules to this. I didn't make those rules. But if I was going to kill four of you, it needed to be before the blue moon rose."

"There you go with the crazy shit again," Jess blurted, sounding tired of the whole supernatural mumbo-jumbo.

"What I'm saying is I failed. I needed to kill four of you before Freddie killed two. It's too late now. I have no reason to kill you anymore. You're safe from me."

Jess let out a loud, sarcastic cackle. "Oh my god, hear that, you guys? We're totally cool now! Our buddy, John, here doesn't need to kill us anymore. We don't need to call the police or anything! We can just let him go! We're safe!" She turned back to Hitch. "Sorry, hun, not getting many supporters here. It's the police and a cell for you tonight and the foreseeable future."

Hitch smiled. There was hostility, as well as amusement, in that smile. "You're talking like they'll come," he said. His tone gave Jess the chills. "The blue moon is out, which means, anytime now—"

Darkness.

Every lamp, every neon and LED sign on the walls, the red exit signs, even the tacky Christmas lights that surrounded the mirror behind the bottle shelves. Everything went out at the same time.

"What the fuck?" Jess shouted.

All around Peter, there were shouts, alarmed calls, shuffling footsteps, confusion. He couldn't see anything, only dense, complete darkness.

"Hitch! Where did Hitch go?" he shouted.

"Angie!" Nadine's voice, from his left.

"I'm here!" Angie responded, further on that side.

Footsteps. Shuffling noises. Chairs being dragged on linoleum.

"Someone grab him!" Barry shouted. Far left, moving toward the front. "Don't let him get away!"

"Who brushed against me?" Callum said from the near right. "Was that him?"

"The gun!" Sylvia said, close to Callum's voice. "The guard's gun! Who has it?"

"I have it!" Royce said from the front. He'd been close

to Jess. "Where's the guy?"

Shuffling. Grunts.

"I think I got him!" Barry said. "Here! Here!"

"Barry, that's me!" Royce said.

"Fuck!" Barry said.

Footsteps. Shuffling. Deep breathing.

"Phones aren't working!" Ray said from the far right. "No flashlight!"

A whisper in Peter's ear.

"Mother?" Peter said in shock.

"What?" Bobby said, nearby.

"Oh god!" Peter said, panic at once seizing his mind, a chill running up his back as sudden terror gripped him. "Mother? Is that you?"

"Peter, what the hell are you talking about?" Nadine said. Her words sounded distant.

But he'd heard Mother. He'd heard her. Peter heard Mother whisper in his ear. He hadn't been able to make out her words, but she'd been there. He could've sworn he'd even felt her breath in his ear. He would recognize that voice anywhere, that resentment, that disapproval... That love.

"I got you, you son of a bitch!" Jess's voice, stealing back his attention. She sounded far from the others, like she'd made a beeline for the door, even in the darkness. Jess grunted. There was a sound like someone crashing against the bar.

"Jess!" Angie shouted.

He heard glass breaking on the floor. A second later, there was the sound of the front door opening and slamming shut. A brief glimpse of blueish light; there, then gone.

"Fuck!" Jess shouted, then the sound of her stomping footsteps.

A vertical rectangle of dim, blueish light appeared in the darkness as Jess opened the door and her silhouette passed through it as she stepped outside.

"Fuck!" she repeated, raging from the sidewalk.

Mother wasn't there, Peter assured himself, even in all of this confusion. He had imagined it. The light from the door was dim, but he could recognize the contours and forms of the surrounding people. He'd imagined her. Mother wasn't there.

"Peter?" Nadine shook his shoulder, giving him a start.

"Nothing," he said, in a hurry. "It was nothing. Just got scared, and my imagination ran away with me. You know I'm still scared of dark places."

"Don't worry," she said in a soothing voice. "We're all here."

Peter saw Jess's silhouette drawn against the blue rectangle of light, then the silhouette disappeared into the darkness as she walked toward the bar, leaving the door open. He heard her angry footsteps walk deeper into the darkened space.

In the dim blue light that only just allowed any visibility, Peter saw something move in front of him. Like small tendrils taking shape out of the darkness itself. Knitting into each other with purpose, roiling like solid smoke. A form appeared before his eyes, against the dim blue background.

He gasped.

Mother!

She was standing mere inches from him, the hint of a disappointed look on her face, disapproval visible even in this, the most minimal of illumination. Her face wriggled and shifted, as if thousands of worms crawled under her skin. Or was it the worms themselves that gave shape to her face?

"Peter?" Nadine shook his shoulder again.

He didn't respond. He was petrified.

"Peter!"

There was the sound of Jess throwing things around, over by the bar.

He could only let out a shaky breath in response. In the darkness, he'd heard Mother whispering in his ear, and now here she was, in the flesh, standing in front of him. He realized Nadine couldn't see her, even if she was right there. He even thought he saw a hint of Nadine's arm passing through Mother's body, as if moving through nothing but a shadow.

"You will come back to me," Mother whispered. "God has promised."

Suddenly, a spark. A flame. Small but blinding in this darkness.

"Here we go!" Jess said, holding a long-neck lighter right in front of him and Nadine.

Mother disappeared, as if the light itself had blown her image away.

"Bought these a while back in case someone ordered their drinks flaming," Jess said, forcing some humor into her voice, though deep down she sounded pissed off she'd let the security guard escape. "Guess what? In this little nowhere town, people only drink beer and cheap rum, nothing fancy, like flaming cocktails. Ever. These seem pretty useful right now, though. Fucker escaped. Nothing to do about that. I guess."

"Peter, are you okay?" Nadine asked, ignoring Jess, a look of worry on her face. "You're sweating."

"I'm okay." His tone was ill, deathly. "Just thought I saw something."

"Did I hear you right, Petey-boy?" Jess said, the light from the tiny flame casting shadows on her face. "Did you say, 'Mother?'"

Before he could answer, Sylvia held the black screen of her phone up, which reflected the small flame. "Am I the only one concerned the electricity went out, even on our cell phones, which makes no sense at all?"

"This isn't a normal blackout," Ray said, tapping his thumb on his own phone to no avail. "This is going to sound ridiculous, but maybe an EMP?"

"Ray," Royce said. "Does it look like we live in a town in which people would know what an EMP is, let alone be in the vicinity of *anything* that could produce one?"

"Maybe it's the blue moon," Callum said, with a hint of insinuation. The entire group went quiet and turned to look at him. "Do you all remember Peter's story about Walter Parham? At the Pines?"

"The blue moon," Barry said. "Now that Hitch mentioned it, I remembered I'd heard of that too. Don't remember where, though."

"Your dad, maybe?" Callum said in a surreptitious tone.

"My dad? What's that supposed to mean?"

"Forget it." Callum shook his head. "Peter? Any details about that come to mind? The blue moon? Walter Parham's story?"

All heads now turned toward Peter. He was still agitated. Still reeling from seeing his mother standing in front of him in the dark. He didn't know what to respond.

There was a blue moon when Jenny died. It wasn't in White Harbor, but I saw it. While the blue moon was out, there was no one else around. The firetrucks and the neighbors didn't arrive until after the moon turned back to normal.

"I don't know," Peter said. "Right now, I don't know."

"Let's pause there for a minute," Jess said.

Peter could see, by the tiny lighter flame, her keen bartender instincts told her he wasn't in any condition to answer questions.

164

"I have some Coleman lanterns in the cellar. I'll get them. Then, we can talk." She handed Nadine a second lighter. "Here, Nadine. Take this for now. I'll be right back. Royce?" She motioned with her head. "Help me?"

"Sure thing," he said.

She cast a concerned look toward Peter, then turned around and left for the deeper areas of the bar, followed by Royce.

Nadine turned on the lighter, just as the light from Jess's faded into the gloomy space.

Nobody spoke a word for a long while.

Chapter Nine

Tali

"Alberto!" said the voice on the other end of the phone. Carlos Alberto Ruiz, whom those close to him called "Tali"—pronounced "Tallie"—could have written an entire thesis on his mother's present mental and emotional state, just from the tone in which she'd said his name. His nickname came from a cute mispronunciation by his Nicaraguan grandmother, who wanted to call him "Charlie", but not knowing how to pronounce English well, called him "Chali" (Challie), which later evolved into "Tali".

"*Mami*," he said, his tone serious and somber, his voice deep and formal, even though he was speaking to his beloved mother. "What happened? Are you okay?"

"No, Alberto," said his mother's old, troubled voice. "It's the First Night. The blue moon came out. White Harbor is in the dark. You have to come! I can't do this alone!"

Tali sighed, frustration creeping up on him. In just a few short sentences, his mother had crammed so many ridiculous beliefs, superstitions, and legends that it was hard for him not to ignore her and change the topic right away.

The only reason he'd joined the Order of the Rising Sun—his mother's offbeat religion—was that it had been passed down by his parents. He'd never had a choice as a child, and then, for most of his existence, it was the only truth he knew. He had been born in Burley, Idaho, the son of immigrant parents, and if he was being honest, the fact his mom and dad had abandoned the staunch Catholicism they'd learned from *their* Nicaraguan parents meant they had in fact seen something valuable in that small local religion, which they had embraced with open arms. He thought it benign, at least.

Tali learned the texts, the prayers, the protection charms and, during his high school and college years, he'd let himself be carried away by the lure of magic—although it wasn't really magic, it was using drawn sigils to harness what was already there in nature. He liked the concept, though. It had become an obsessive hobby of his until one day he concluded none of it worked. Any perception of success in casting a charm or spell could be dismissed as seeing what he wanted to see. He'd become disillusioned, decided it was all a bunch of gobbledygook, and renounced his parents' religion. His books now collected dust in an enormous bookcase in his apartment's storage room.

Now, here was his mother, speaking of one more thing he thought he'd left behind: that silly rivalry between her Order and the Circle—that doomsday sect in White Harbor that, like the Order, showed nothing concrete to support their beliefs. At least, he always took solace in the fact the Order was peaceful in its methods—their motto, almost copied from the Hippocratic oath, was: "We shall never harm". He could respect that at least, even if he no longer shared their beliefs.

"*Mami*," he said, "it's just a regular blackout. White Harbor is on the coast; it's not uncommon for the grid to get damaged sometimes."

"It's not that, Alberto. Even the phones are down!"

Tali was silent for a moment, confused. Did his old mother realize what she had just said? "*Mami*. You're calling me from your smartphone."

"It works for me," she said in a stubborn tone, sounding almost offended. "I drew a protection charm on it, so it works for me."

Tali's eyes drew a full arc, rolling from left to right.

"Wait a minute, I'll show you," she said.

In his apartment's living room, sitting on his couch,

some contrived Netflix cooking competition paused on his TV screen, Tali waited. He respected his mother's beliefs, but at times, she could be as stubborn as a stone wall about them. His eyes wandered toward the door to his left, the door to the storage room, where so many books on sigils and glyphs and spells longed for the touch of curious fingers.

A notification appeared at the top of his phone. When he opened his messaging app, he saw his mom had sent him a video recording. *I have to give her credit*, he thought. *With how long it took me to teach her how to use a smartphone, sending a video so quickly means she* really *wants to show me this.*

The video thumbnail was a blurry view of White Harbor from the mountains, where his mother was right now, in the house of that writer she worked for. The town below looked almost like a black hole, but he guessed, when playing the video, he might see cars moving with their headlights on and other light sources in the distance.

Tali tapped the "Play" icon.

As much as he tried to focus on parts of the image, there were no headlights, no sections of town with electricity, nor lights from the usual places that would have emergency generators in most towns—not even the hospital, which he found bizarre. Except for the occasional dim, flickering light of a candle or lamp indoors, darkness enveloped the town of White Harbor.

Then the camera angled up, and he heard his mom

say, "See it? The moon?"

The full moon was dark blue with silvery highlights, which disconcerted him for a second, until a notion, a hysterical idea, touched the back of his mind like a ghostly lace curtain sliding down the nape of his neck.

Tali turned his gaze toward the window to the right of the couch. He could see the moon from where he sat. Even if he attributed the coloration of the moon to an effect of the recording or the lens of his mother's phone, the moon in White Harbor was full, the moon in Burley was a waning gibbous. That was impossible.

"You have to come, *m'hijo!*" his mom insisted. "But don't come tonight. If you cross the Crescent Mountains, your car will stop working. Only four die tonight, but we can't know what that deranged woman can do to make sure she gets what she wants. Come tomorrow. I don't want anything bad to happen to you."

"*Mami,*" he said, still looking at the waning silver moon, stupefied. "What do you mean, only four die tonight?"

"I told you, it's the First Night," she said, as if, just like that, it should be a recognizable concept for her son. "The Four Offerings. If Martha Lange does the ritual as written, only four will die tonight. But the one who's helping her is that crazy Parham man. The Cursed Man. They're both unpredictable. We don't know what they'll feel like doing between sacrifices or after. Then there's Curling…"

"Curling?" The name sounded familiar. "Who is—"

"The man from the Vanek House. He's still here. According to him, he's doing the Order's work, but like Martha Lange, we don't know what methods he's using. I don't trust him not to do harm."

Alberto took one last look at the moon outside his window and looked down at the blue moon in the paused video.

"I'll be there tomorrow, *Mami*. What should I bring with me?"

Chapter Ten

Coral

Maddie Cunningham's life hadn't yet been enveloped by darkness in its entirety. Legally blind didn't mean the same as completely blind—not yet, anyway. If anything, her weak bones were more of a hindrance than her blurry eyes. Whenever she thought of her bones, what came to mind were those dried pieces of white coral you sometimes found on beaches: bleached white, filled with millions of tiny holes, and oh so brittle.

She remembered when she was a little girl, before it was illegal to take coral off the beach. Maddie would often come across these tiny gems and would bring them home to create a beautiful display in her fish tank next to her bed. She loved arranging them to form different abstract shapes. She recalled their sensation in her fingers, both rough and smooth at the same time. One thing she'd noticed, however, had been that her fish kept dying, and she couldn't figure out why. She made regular water changes, fed her fish well, and always made sure there was a proper source of oxygen in her tank; even if back in the day, the devices available for this were rudimentary, they worked if used as instructed.

Maddie couldn't shake the feeling she was doing something wrong, but never related her fish dying to the presence of the coral. After all, they were just these pretty white pieces of soft rock. That was until one day her biology teacher talked about the importance of coral in the ecosystem. She realized then she wasn't keeping coral in her fish tank—not exactly—it was *dead* coral, and dead coral had the property of changing water chemistry.

At the end of class, Maddie approached her teacher and expressed her concern about her freshwater fish dying every other day. Her teacher smiled in a commiserating way and explained she'd put bleached coral from the beach in a freshwater tank, and it had released calcium and bicarbonate into the water. This changed the hardness and pH of the water, turning it into an environment her fish could not survive in.

It was a terrible realization for Maddie. She'd felt stupid in not knowing the coral did not belong in a freshwater tank, and even stupider to realize she'd thought there was still life in that coral. It was dead, however. Dead and decomposed. Devoid of color and function. Remains of what used to be a living colony of animals. Even worse, her dead coral had killed her fish. *She* had killed her fish. The idea of something she'd found so beautiful was now tarnished by the thought of it being dead and causing death. The thought of her sleeping next to a bunch of dead bones disturbed her to no end. She'd taken all the bleached coral, put it in a bag, and next time her family went to the beach, she tossed it on the wet sand. The pieces broke against each other as they fell with muted, raspy clacking sounds.

Her bones, she thought, were like dead coral.

The Circle was also dead coral.

The Circle had seemed so beautiful, so beneficial. She had felt proud of being invited in by her husband. Now, thanks to the Circle, her son was years in the grave, and what remained of her family—her husband, Chuck, and their daughter Jess—was in deadly peril.

She sat on her favorite high-back chair by the window, looking out as far as her poor eyesight allowed. Maddie spent most of her afternoons listening to audiobooks, contemplating her life and the future, and she found the future was shrinking every day, much quicker than she'd ever considered.

Her husband tended to her every whim, always watchful of whether she was comfortable enough, if she wanted a cup of coffee, if she was hungry, if she needed him to adjust her lumbar pillow or hand her that wooden cane she kept nearby and help her stand. He took her on short walks along the beach—firm muscles helped compensate for weak bones, after all. Until recently, she struggled to walk for about eighty percent of the time, but those limited walks, leaning on her husband, increased her endurance. She could stroll short distances now, as long as she had her cane.

God bless his soul, Chuck was a good man. He'd never been the same since Jonah was taken from them. Neither of them had been, but Chuck had taken it harder. He blamed himself for it.

Maddie knew who was to blame, however, and it wasn't Chuck.

She peered out her window and, though the edges of her vision were blurred, the sight before her was undeniable. The blue moon cast its eerie glow over the unsuspecting town.

Oh yes, Maddie knew who was to blame for their Jonah's death.

Soon the entire town would go dark. It had already started, and it wouldn't stop.

She felt her husband's hand on her shoulder. She interlaced gentle fingers with his. She felt his warmth as he stood beside her, though he was to the left of her, where she couldn't see him as anything but a smudge.

"Now that I actually see it," he said in a breathless voice filled with dread, "it doesn't look divine at all. It looks hideous."

"It is," Maddie said, giving his hand a squeeze.

There was a brief silence between them, that strange telepathy that exists between couples who've been together for a very long time.

Chuck sighed, squeezing her hand back. "Please don't ask me to leave."

"I don't want you to be here when he comes." Her tone of voice conveyed they'd had this conversation several times already.

"He might not actually come." The slight tremble in his voice revealed he didn't truly believe that.

"You know it's going to be me." An ironic smile tugged at the corners of her lips. "That woman—"

"You don't *know* that, Maddie!" He sounded like a child throwing a tantrum about his homework. It made her love him even more. After a moment of silence, he spoke again, his voice resigned, but angry. "This is all my fault."

"Chuck," she said, with a gentle, reassuring tone. "I wanted it, too. You spoke for both of us."

"Yeah, hun, but I had been part of this thing longer than you."

She could hear tears building in his eyes as he spoke.

"I should've known the Mo—"

"Don't call her that," she snapped. There was no wavering in her conviction about this. "She's no such thing. She's not a mother. Not even to her own son."

"Right. But I should've known that woman wouldn't take kindly to us wanting out. I should've just kept quiet, stuck to the program. It's my fault she took our Jonah from us, and now—"

"Charles Gareth Cunningham." She turned her head toward him to get at least a blurry look at her husband's sorrowful face. "Stop."

He nodded. His eyes spoke volumes about the grief that ate at his soul.

"I want you to go be with our girl," Maddie said. "Our Jess can't know this is happening."

"No!" His tears spilled over and ran, leaving fat streaks down his cheeks. He brought a hand up to his mouth and shook his head. He sputtered, face crunched up and red. "I can't leave you alone! I can't!"

She turned on her chair, eased off the hand he'd placed on her shoulder, held it between both her hands, and kissed it. "I don't want you to be here when it happens."

"Maddie, you don't know if—"

"Yes, I do. You know that Lange woman is nothing if not spiteful. 'An elderly woman of The Faithful, willingly sacrificing to the Lord on her sleeping bed.' Who else do you think it's going to be?"

"There are others!" He raised his voice. His despair spilling over the brim with every word.

"No, there aren't," she said, with a kind smile, and caressing her husband's rough, wrinkled hand. "Not to Martha Lange. She is *nothing* if not spiteful. Remember what happened to the Rockwells? An entire family wiped out. When we tried to leave, we wronged her. We spurned the 'gift' of that thing she calls 'God', and by extension, we rejected her. She took our son. Now, she's sending that Parham boy for me. I don't want you to be here when he comes. What if she told him to take you as well, not as a sacrifice, but to punish us? Who will protect our Jess?"

Chuck reacted to this, his instincts spiking. He took a deep breath and held it.

"That's right." Maddie nodded. "You know what's going to happen to her if one of us isn't there. You know that horrible woman selected Jess, too. She will sacrifice our baby girl."

"I won't let her," Chuck growled. "I'll kill her if she touches our girl."

"That's right." Maddie nodded.

With difficulty, Chuck went down on his knees and rested his head on his wife's lap, weeping in soft, quiet jerks as Maggie caressed what little hair remained in that head of his.

She turned her gaze to the window, toward that blurry blue eye in the sky. That evil thing staring at her now with vicious hunger. Even if her sight was hazy and weak, she stared back fiercely. *You're going to lose,* she thought at it. *My girl will kick your ass. You're going to lose, you motherfucker!*

She looked down at her weeping husband. "Go now, while there's still light and you can use the car."

"What should I tell her?" His voice shook. He used the collar of his shirt to wipe his face.

"You can't tell her about this. She can't know what's happening to me, or she'll come here. Just stay by her side while the ritual passes. Protect her. Don't tell her anything that might cause her to look for me, or Martha Lange, or Freddie Parham. She needs to see the end of this alive, so the less she knows, the better. Tell her you took me to her aunt's in Bay City for the weekend and you just got back. I haven't gone to visit in a while, so she won't suspect. Ask to stay with her for the weekend, or to let you work the bar."

"Work the bar?" He gave her a bewildered look. "There might not even be a functioning bar to open by tomorrow night."

"She doesn't know that."

"She'll see right through me, Mads!" He gestured with his hands toward his grief-stricken face. "I mean, look at me! I'm a fuckin' mess!"

She placed her hands on his cheeks. She could see him clearly now that she held his face this close. "Do it for our girl. Do it for me."

179

He hesitated, gave a curt nod, his conviction still wavering.

"C'mon, old man, kiss me now," she said, moving her face down toward his.

Chuck wiped the tears off his face, grunted as he stretched his body toward his wife, and kissed her on the lips, placing his arms around her. He kissed her as if they were a newly married couple. He'd always kissed her like this, though. His love for her hadn't declined one iota in all their years together. The only difference in this kiss was the desperation and the grief that came with it—the knowledge that it was the last one.

They remained like that, forehead to forehead, both with tears in their eyes.

"You've been a good husband, Chuck," she said. "Never forget that."

He took her hand in his. As was their custom, he laced his fingers with hers and squeezed, softly, with care for her frail bones—that telepathic "I love you" passing between them as she squeezed back.

Chuck stood before her, his eyes fixed on her face as if he were committing every line to memory.

As if he needs any help remembering me, Maddie thought. She did the same.

With great effort, Chuck turned and left. She heard his steps recede as his image blurred in front of her eyes. There was the sound of his coat's fabric rustling as it was picked off the rack. The sound of keys jingling, and the door opening and closing signaled his departure from the house. A minute later, she heard the Dodge's engine turning over and the crunching of rubber on asphalt as it rolled up the street, past her window.

Her husband was gone.

Maddie sat there, waiting in the crushing silence of her empty house.

The only noise inside the house was the low hum of the fridge starting its cooling cycle. Not even creaking boards adjusting to the temperature shift of the night. She became acutely aware of the sound of her own breathing. The air leaving her nostrils came out as an extended huffing that almost synchronized with the effervescent hissing of the waves from the beach outside.

She could see the outline of the waves, a shape made of reflected blue moonlight turned liquid. The blue moon stared at her—her one spectator as she waited for the inevitable. She saw, to the southeast, the lights from the houses, and she felt the slow, increasing rhythm of her breathing as she waited for what she knew would happen soon.

The minutes passed.

One...

Two...

Three...

Four…

Darkness swallowed White Harbor.

Every light vanished, save for that dreadful moon and its dark glow.

The hum of the fridge came to a halt.

Maddie's next breath came out with a raspy sound to it, like her body wanted to hang on to every bit of air in her lungs.

She heard a board creak behind her. There had only been that one single creak, as if the foot that made it had materialized on the spot as its owner stopped walking.

"Hello Maddie," a blithe voice behind her said.

"That's Mrs. Cunningham to you, Freddie."

She heard him chuckle.

"Are you ready?" he asked.

She reached to the right of her chair. Her fingers touched the handle of her cane. With determination, Maddie placed it in front of her and pushed herself up, supporting her weight, one hand on the cane and one hand on the armrest. She turned a withering look toward her unwelcome guest.

"That's quite a superior glare for a bartender's wife," Freddie said with a deriding smile.

Maddie strolled toward him, taking short steps, supporting herself on her cane, but holding her head up as high as she could. As she passed beside him, she said, "Son, this bartender's wife can pour an Old Fashioned that has more dignity to it than you'll ever know in this life or the next." She turned left toward the stairs. "Bedroom's this way."

The bedroom was her final destination, the place where her life would be forfeit to a deity she no longer believed in. There was one opportunity, though, if she played her cards right.

One slim chance of survival.

Chapter Eleven

The Cellar

Jess descended the creaking stairs toward the bar cellar, the tiny flame of the long-neck lighter held in front of her, Royce following close behind. "Watch your step," she said.

The cellar was old, far older than the bar up top. It had a red-brick vaulted ceiling and brick walls. Wine racks stood against the deep wall ahead, only half-occupied by dusty bottles that reflected a tiny spot of light from the lighter that moved along with them. Beer kegs on shelves to the right. Sacks of flour, cans, jars, and other food, also on the right-side shelves.

Some walls were reinforced with concrete pillars,

which were newer than the cellar itself, and cracks on the walls were filled in with cement. Despite that, the space looked sturdy.

"Damn, Jess!" Royce said, casting a surprised glance at his surroundings. "This place is ancient."

"My great-grandpa chose this spot to build the bar *because* of the cellar," she said. She reached the bottom of the stairs, turned around one-eighty, and walked toward the back end of the cellar. "He was kind of paranoid the government was gonna come for him. He used this place during Prohibition. So, he figured if police raided the place, he could hole up in here for a 'final stand' of sorts." She looked at Royce and rolled her eyes. "No one said I come from a line of geniuses."

Royce followed her until he could see a wall with shelves loaded with supplies. In the dim light of the flame, he could see containers with clothes, toolboxes, huge water bottles, a couple of car batteries, first aid supplies, walkie-talkies, books on assorted topics, and many other items—too varied to commit to mental notes.

"Um," Royce started, stopping to look around, standing in front of a tall, metal cabinet, with a combination lock, "was this your great-grandpa's, too?"

"No." Jess grabbed a box and started loading some Coleman lanterns into it. "My dad's."

"Any reason you keep this with a lock if only you and your dad come down here?" Royce held the combination lock in his hand, turning the little numerical discs randomly in his fingers.

"Uh…" She stared at the lock. "It's just security. Stop doing that."

"Is Chuck secretly a survivalist or something?"

"Nope," Jess said, then pointed at a lower shelf to the right. "Pick up that car battery charger, will you? Uh…the… black, yellow, and red box thingy with the cables."

"I know what a car battery charger looks like, you dick." He bent down to pull out the somewhat heavy box. "What's the plan with this? Everything with a battery died."

"See the crank?" She pointed to a handle protruding from the battery. "You're gonna take that upstairs and use that hand of yours to crank more than your cock for a change."

"Oh, ha ha," he answered humorlessly.

"You do that for a while, and soon the battery has enough charge to at least jump start one car. I have a theory about how this might work."

"This what? The battery?"

"The blackout." Jess drove a piercing gaze into his eyes. "That security guard said there are rules. I'm pretty sure the cars won't start now, but it doesn't mean their batteries can't be charged. Worth a try."

"Absolutely," Royce said. A white light illuminated the entire space, coming from Jess's direction. "I'll take this upstairs and…start cranking."

"No, wait." Jess looked at him, her face shrouded in shadow from the lit lantern in her hand. "I asked you to come down with me for another reason. Look...I don't know how to say this, but..." She paused, trying to choose her words with care. "I don't think the crazy guard was actually that crazy."

Royce responded by squinting at her. The lower position of the gas lantern casting upward shadows from the lines of his face.

"This isn't a normal blackout. We all know it."

He nodded in agreement. "Phones and batteries don't just go dead like that."

"It's more than that, Royce." Jess ran her hand down her face while she gathered the courage to say something she wasn't even done processing herself. "I saw her. Peter's mother. I saw her when he went all crazy saying, 'Mother', just a moment ago." Royce looked at her as if she were demented. He swatted a hand at the air in front of him. "Get outta here! You didn't. That's impossible."

"You're saying that to me," she said, fixing both her eyes on him, as if daring him to keep dismissing her words. "You. After everything we went through in the Vanek House."

"That's different, Jess." A slight but visible shiver shook his shoulders. His eyes flitted left and right. "The Vanek House was haunted. This—"

"This whole town is haunted, man!"

187

His lips tightened as he gave a nod.

"She was there. Nadine, Bobby, and Angie didn't see her, but *I* did. I had the moonlight from the front door behind my back. I could see her. She was there. Even if the light was dim, I know what I saw. Peter's face was"—she considered—"his face was twisted in terror, and she was standing in front of him. Even from what little I could see of her face from the angle I was, I can tell you, it was her. Then, soon as I turned on the lighter, she vanished, in mid-fucking-air."

"Why didn't you say anything?"

"That's what we need to talk about."

"So, not about the creepy witch apparition, but about why you didn't point out the creepy witch apparition?"

"Shut up. We have to go back soon. We have to talk about Peter. That face of terror I was telling you he had? The moment the light came on, he forced himself to put it away, like that"—she snapped her fingers—"sure, he looked agitated, but I could see the way he pushed down the terror, like it was a practiced impulse or something. I saw him do that, and I acted as if nothing was going on. I poked at him once to see if there was a reaction, and that's when Sylvia cut in talking about the phones, but I saw his face. The reaction was there, and, Royce, he was really pushing it down, like really hard."

Royce squinted again. "Okay, so he didn't start screaming 'Mother!' at the top of his lungs. Maybe he was just confused and didn't want to make a scene."

Jess chewed on her lip, her uncertainty showing on her face.

"There's a thing I haven't told anyone." With a cautious expression on her face, she leaned in closer. "You know how I found Peter in that crawlspace under his house?"

"Mm-hmm." Royce nodded.

"There was a weird thing that happened while he was down there…then later, at the hospital."

1993

The wind whipped through Jess's hair as she pedaled across town, her mind filled with anger toward her friends and their families. It had been two weeks since the fire at the Vanek House.

Fuckin' cowards! she thought.

Leroy was now buried at Clive Memorial. So were Elijah Knox and his three children. Ben Curling was also dead, and Freddie had been taken into custody.

How? How is that asshole even alive?

Since that day, it seemed some unspoken agreement had happened among every parent in White Harbor—they had imposed a strict curfew.

Their time at The Pines was limited to lunch breaks, and a few stolen minutes after class before heading home. Their parents had gotten clingy, paranoid. Despite being adults who'd grown in the shadow of Blight Harbor, the events at the Vanek House had shaken the populace to the core. Six children, dead. Elijah Knox, dead along with his three children. Ben Curling, dead.

She gulped. Shook her head.

Even her parents, who were usually quite relaxed about most events in town, had felt it—what transpired at the Vanek House was different, worse than other events, even worse than Gerardo Valencia's death, which remained unexplained to that date.

Her eyes flickered to Gerardo's house as she passed it. It was now abandoned, a hopeless FOR SALE sign on the front lawn, which used to be so pretty and adorned with flowers. Now, it was unkempt, the flowers dead, the cute yellow of the house faded, the paint peeling and molding. She couldn't help but notice the vines and crawling plants already claiming it as their own.

Besides the curfew, the adults didn't want them anywhere near where the Vanek House used to stand. They didn't want them anywhere near the Lange house, either. Even Bobby, who lived a couple of houses up from Peter, wasn't allowed to walk near it. His parents, instead, made him take a small path that went all the way around, cutting through the foot of the hill when he went to school every day.

The few times they'd been able to speak at The Pines, no one had any news about Peter. Bobby said, when he looked out the window, he sometimes saw that bitch Martha Lange come out of the house to do her food deliveries, but not Peter. Never Peter. Two weeks, and he hadn't been at school.

Two fucking weeks!

Jess had tried her best to convince the others—Royce being the only exception, for obvious reasons, as he was still reeling from his twin brother's death—to just show up at Peter's house and demand to see him, but the proposal had been shut down by the rest of The Vigilantes—she even reminded them they wouldn't even *be* The Vigilantes without Peter naming them so.

Even Barry, who liked to pretend he wasn't afraid of anything, simply stood there, leaning back against his usual pine tree, knuckles still covered in scabs and bruises from smashing Freddie's face over and over, and newer bruises from sources he refused to discuss, but which they all knew he brought from home. He'd simply grunted and said, "We have to give it time. That bitch is crazy. If we just show up like that, she might pull a knife on us. Wouldn't put it past her."

"My mom said that woman showed up at the school to withdraw Peter from all his classes," Nadine said, grieved and agitated, shifting her pleading eyes over each of her friends. "She unenrolled him from all classes over a week ago. We haven't seen him in two weeks! What if she—"

"He's not dead," Bobby said in a matter-of-fact tone. "Her whole mess is that she's overprotective of him, that she"—he did air quotes—"*loves* him…in her own screwed up way. She wouldn't kill him."

"Easy way to know," Jess said, losing her patience with all of them. "Let's all fucking go there together!"

At this, everyone had exchanged uncomfortable glances in deep silence. It was obvious the events of the Vanek House hadn't just impacted the adults. She could see the fear and trauma on all their faces, the memories of everything they'd seen in there. The mental image of Leroy's lifeless body flattening the knee-high grass, covered in blood.

"Fuckin' cowards!" she said, this time through clenched teeth, as she pedaled up the gradual slope of Hill Road. Before, she would've seen the Vanek House from this distance, looming over the town, but now there was only empty space, and further up, the trees that surrounded what used to be Ben Curling's home. A strap from her rucksack slipped a few inches off her shoulder, but she shrugged it back into place.

Minutes later, she was passing by the burned remains of the Vanek House. The land was surrounded by a fence, like the ones they put around construction sites, an excessive number of KEEP OUT signs all over the fence. She saw some of the house's remains on the other side, blackened and splintered, sticking out like skeletal fingers creeping out of a grave.

From that corner, Hill Road became steeper, and she stood on her pedals to climb the short distance from there to Peter's house.

She dismounted and stood in front of the house, staring at the black, white, and gray residence with dread. The quiet outside was eerie. There was no one in sight. It was almost like the neighborhood knew she was about to do something monumentally stupid, and they wanted no part of it.

The sharp, straight lines of the one-story Craftsman appeared to warn her off—nothing *that* straight with perfect angles existed in nature, so whatever was kept inside the house could not be natural. She knew this was ridiculous. There were many houses in White Harbor that looked just like that one, but t*his* house was different, she assured herself. That woman lived in there. No place that contained her could be a good place.

Feeling her courage waver, Jess decided it was now or never. She slid her rucksack off her shoulders and pulled out her father's stun gun. If Chuck Cunningham knew his daughter was walking around with that, he'd first sigh—admitting to himself he should've expected her to take it and go pick a fight where she shouldn't—and then he'd be furious at her. It was his fault for keeping that in his nightstand drawer. What was she supposed to do? *Not* go rummaging through his drawers? That was bullshit; he'd taught her to handle more dangerous weapons—"Under supervision!" he'd say, chiding her.

She pictured that madwoman coming at her with scissors like she'd done with Nadine a couple of months earlier, and her sticking the head of the stun gun right under her jaw and watching the bitch dance, then collapse to the floor. She snorted with satisfaction at the mental image, but her smile disappeared as she walked up the two porch steps and reached the front door.

She glanced at the doorbell, as if it was this big, glossy, round, white blister in the back of a disgusting, naked man, which would burst the moment she put her finger to it, covering it with pus and infecting her with some kind of lethal virus. After coming this far, she couldn't turn into a pussy like the rest of her friends. She took a deep breath and pushed the button once with her finger.

Ding-dong!

(*Get away from my home! Get away from my son! You bitch! You whore! I'll kill you! I'll kill you!*)

Nothing.

She rang the bell again.

Ding-dong!

(*You want to take my boy! You whore! Whore! He's mine! Mine to love! Mine to torture! Mine to fuck!*)

She stood there, facing the inexpressive door, feeling thwarted. She was expecting Martha Lange to come out in full insanity mode, eyes blazing with rage, frothing at the mouth, ready to kill her for daring to ring her doorbell.

Her thumb twitched from the tension and the stun gun startled her with a loud *tak-tak-tak-tak* noise.

She raised her finger to ring the doorbell one more time.

There was a sound coming from inside the house. A voice. A familiar voice. Distant and weak.

It's not coming from inside the house. She wasn't sure exactly from where, though. "Hello?" she said. *Was that Peter?*

There was the sound again. Definitely a voice, she was certain now.

"Peter?" She walked to the left of the porch. The sound seemed to come from that side. "Peter? Is that you?"

"Motherrr," the voice said. It was coming from the deeper side of the property.

As Jess leaped off the porch, she could feel the incline of the slope beneath her feet, causing her to land with a jolt. She stopped herself with her palms on the fence that separated this property from the one down the slope, leaving a setback of about six feet between the fence and the house.

"Motherrrrrrrr," the voice said, sounding weak, slurring the word, as if drunk, or half-asleep.

"Peter?" It was him. "I'm coming!" It alarmed her that, even though she was standing a full five feet lower than the house's floor, on account of the slope, Peter's voice didn't seem to come from higher up. It wasn't coming from inside the house. It was almost as if it were coming from *beneath* it.

"Mooothhherrrrrrr…"

"Jesus fucking Christ, no way!" It *was* coming from beneath the house.

She ran, following the wall toward the back of the house, and stopped just a few feet from the closed gate that would lead to the backyard. The voice had come from this exact spot. She was sure.

"Peter?" She slapped the house's wall in front of her. She saw one support pile to the left and one to the right, both solid concrete, and while many houses left the space between these open, the Lange house had thick wooden boards between the piles, sealing the crawlspace. She opened her backpack and brought out a small flashlight she'd also borrowed from her dad, and she crouched in front of a half-and-inch space between two boards. She shone the light in and, before she could call Peter's name again, even before she could see him, she smelled him.

The smell of sweat and shit and piss hit her nose and made her gag, her eyes watering. She spat on the floor and covered her nose, breathed through her mouth, and even then, she could smell him.

"Moootheeerrrrrrrrr…"

She adjusted her light, following the voice, and there he was. Unrecognizable, but definitely him, despite her mind's protests that it couldn't be. Peter was in his underwear; a bag of bones and skin, paler than normal, covered in dirt and filth, scratches and blood all over.

"Peter, oh my god! Can you hear me? It's me, Jess!" She gave a few quick slaps to the wall to call his attention.

"Motherrrr, I'm sorrrry," the zombie under the house slurred in response. "I'm sorry I wassss bad... I'm sssorry I offffended God... I won't do... won't do it again."

"No, Pete, it's me. It's Jess!" In anger, in desperation, she kicked the wooden boards, roaring in anger with each kick. The boards wouldn't break or come off. She stopped. She could still hear Peter mumbling.

"Whateverrr y'want, Motheerrr... You tell me whut t'do. I'll do it. Want 'em gone? I'll make'em gone. All of 'em. Gone. Dead. I swearr... God dosssn't want'em. God dosssn't love'em, Mothherr... I get it noowww..."

Jess felt the blood freeze in her veins.

"Pete, you're scaring me. Talk to me. Please!"

"You love me, Mothhherr. God lovessss me...lovesssss me... Kill me, Motherr... Y'want me to kill me, Mother? I will kill me... I promissse... Will kill myssssself for you, Motherrr. For God, Mothherr, for God, for Mother... Kill myselffff... Annything y'want..."

The flashlight caught Peter's eye. His unnerving, sunken eye, which snapped shut as he raised his arms in front of his face, and started screaming with a raspy, worn-out voice—its sound dry and corpse-like.

"I'll get help!" Jess said, already feeling the onset of

tears. "I'll come back. I promise. I won't leave you there! I won't! I'll be right back!"

Jess ran out toward the sidewalk and ran uphill as fast as she could—her feet propelling her up the incline faster than her bike would—until she reached Bobby's house. She ran up his porch steps, then started slapping and banging on the door. "Bobby!" she shouted. "Bobby, open up! Open up! Open up, Bobby! Open up!"

The door swung open, and she didn't even acknowledge Bobby's face. As if sucked into the house by the gust of wind made by the door opening, she ran past him. She thought she heard him say, "Jess, what the hell?" but she didn't pay any mind to him.

She flew into his living room and picked up the phone. She looked at the handset, as if it were some ancient riddle and the numbers had turned into hieroglyphics, but after two attempts, she dialed 911. She started shouting at the operator about the horror she'd discovered. Bobby stood in front of her, looking more appalled by the second, as the details started painting a grim picture.

What felt like an eternity later, all of their friends— and all of White Harbor, it seemed—had learned of Peter's fate. Blight Harbor was eating. Blight Harbor was sending out tendrils, cables, vines, interconnecting everyone in town. Blight Harbor was feasting on her friend's misery, on the abuse he'd suffered, and the gossip coming off it.

A crowd had gathered around the Lange Home the way they had gathered around the burning Vanek House just two weeks earlier—her friends and their families included. Everyone who was available had turned up to see the show.

Jess pictured Blight Harbor as an enormous, sentient sewage treatment plant, and every word, every comment, every piece of gossip she heard passing through the crowd made it fuller and fuller with shit. She pictured it spilling over when a policeman emerged from the front door, a delirious Peter in his arms, wrapped in a blanket. Martha Lange—who had arrived almost at the same time as the police—spat and shouted all kinds of curses at them for taking her son. Jess pictured gallons and gallons of shit spilling over the rim of Blight Harbor, and filling out an even bigger treatment pool, and another, and another...

The Vigilantes stared in abject horror. What that policeman was now easing onto a stretcher was not sweet, kind Peter. It was a skinny, pale creature, starved and dehydrated, rambling incoherent words to God and Mother, pleading for their forgiveness, until the moment the ambulance doors closed. He'd become so inarticulate, she was sure her friends hadn't picked up anything quite as disturbing as what she'd heard him mumble in the crawlspace. She imagined him continuing his ramblings during the entire drive to Clarendon Hospital.

They all stood there, speechless, until the police took

Martha Lange away, and their respective parents forced each of them to go home.

During Peter's brief hospital stay, his aunt Constance from Oakland was wonderful and accommodating to all his friends. The woman and her sister couldn't be more different from each other. She welcomed their visits, hoping it would help him feel better soon. The Vigilantes knew there was another reason for this, however.

Jess had heard whispers that Peter's aunt planned to take him away to live with her and her husband in California. Jess's dad said it would be temporary at first, but that his aunt was sure to get full custody, since she was his only other known relative—Peter's dad having left years ago and being nowhere to be found. What Martha Lange had done to the boy had ensured she would not even get supervised visits. Once Peter came out of the hospital, it would be the last time he'd be in White Harbor for a very long time, if ever.

Jess's dad had then added a phrase she hadn't really understood. Chuck had lowered his gaze, shaken his head, and said, "Then, God help us all."

Jess visited Peter on the third day of his hospital stay and had found he already looked far better than she could've imagined after the horror show of the other day. His aunt had left them alone and said she'd go get them some snacks from one of the vending machines outside.

"You look so much better," Jess said. "Pete, you scared

the hell out of me."

He gave her a bashful smile and said, "Thank you. For saving me."

"What was I supposed to do? Leave you down there until you grew roots and ended up looking like a really ugly potato?"

"Potatoes *are* roots," Peter said.

She gave him a soft jab on the shoulder. "Stop trying to be smart. You'll start sounding like Droopy Baker if you keep that up. Also, potatoes are stems."

"How do you know that?"

"Droopy told me."

Peter chuckled, but his smile faded, and an awkward silence grew between them. It was the opening she needed.

"Look, Petey-boy. Do you...um...remember all the stuff you were saying while you were trapped down there?"

"What do you mean?" His expression conveyed genuine confusion. "What...stuff?"

Jess studied his face, looking for any signs of pretense. Saw none.

"Pete, you said some truly messed up stuff while you were there. I know you were starved and dehydrated, so probably up in your head you weren't doing all that great, but are you sure you don't remember anything?"

Peter blinked twice in quick succession. This was news to him, it seemed. "I don't remember even seeing you," he said, his face turning haunted. "All I remember was the darkness, the bugs…and the rats." His eyes stared past her, looking lost for a few seconds. "She—my mom—she only dropped a small bag with water after a few days…but that was all. I…" He stopped. Looked like the wheels were spinning in his head, like he was reconsidering words that had been about to come out of his lips, but pivoted and went in a different direction. "I know she was only doing what she thought best, even if it was wrong. She wouldn't have let me starve to death."

Jess squinted. Her jaw hung open in disbelief. Was he really trying to justify what that woman had done?

He looked at her, his eyes begging her to understand. "I get it, you know? In a twisted way, I get it. I disobeyed. She was punishing me. She went too far, but she didn't *really* mean to hurt me. It was just like being grounded. That's all, right? I mean, she's my mother, she loves me. She wouldn't have left me there to die…"

Jess sat by the bed, looking into Peter's dark blue eyes and she saw desperation, the *need* for it to not be as bad as it had been. He didn't want to believe his mother could do something that neglectful.

"Right?" he added.

Under normal circumstances, Jess would've told him everything she was thinking. She would run her mouth and let him know what a monstrous piece of shit Martha Lange was. How what she had done was unforgivable. How, if she could, she would kick the woman's face until she no longer had a face. She would've told Peter that, before being taken out of that crawlspace under his house, he had been rambling about forsaking all his friends, about killing himself for God, killing himself for "Mother". But then, that phrase her dad always said to her came floating out of the angry haze in her mind: *"Connecting your tongue to your brain is like pulling down your pants before you take a shit."*

In one of those rare instances in which she controlled her impulses, Jess said, "Right, Pete. She just got carried away."

2022

After Jess finished her story, Royce's brow furrowed in contemplation. For a moment, she was certain he would just dismiss it as what it sounded like—the raving words of a kid suffering through a physically and psychologically traumatizing situation—and not what she was worried it truly was.

Instead, Royce turned to her and said, "So, we're talking about Gollum-Peter, then?"

Jess was taken aback by this. "What?"

"Gollum-Peter. That's what Bobby calls what you just described."

"I'm gonna need you to explain that."

"Well, a long while back, Bobby and I had been talking about why Peter keeps coming here. What I'm saying is, yes, he comes to see us, but c'mon, people rarely stay in touch with friends they met in the sixth grade, you know what I mean? Not when they live in different cities, and not when their friends live in nowhere little towns like this one—*definitely* not when you're a famous writer with two movies and a miniseries based on your books. Let's be honest. Pete doesn't need us."

"Uh huh, uh huh," Jess said, her face lighting up. She shot a glance toward the stairs, realizing the rest of their group was waiting. "Go on."

"Don't get me wrong, I love Peter. We all do. I'm sure he loves us as well. But we ain't the reason he keeps coming back to White Harbor, and you can bet your ass we ain't the reason he's made this ridiculous decision to move back. The real reason's locked up in Clarendon, making Ray question his decision to become a nurse."

"Mother."

"Bingo," Royce said, pointing a finger at her. "That's where Gollum-Peter comes in. You know how Bobby and Angie are huge *Lord of the Rings* nerds? Well, he came up with the theory. And I quote, 'Peter both hates and loves Mother. He's addicted to her. He can't accept the fact she's dying when they have all of this unresolved bullshit. He can't forgive her for what she did to him, but he can't bring himself to just let her go. He wants Mother to love him. She can abuse him and treat him like shit all she wants, and he'll hate her every second, but the moment she calls, he goes—'"

"Yes, Precious," Jess said.

"Gollum-Peter," Royce said with a nod.

"So, you and Bobby already know he's not...okay?"

"I think we all know, on some level, he's not the most stable guy, but that's how he's always been. What can we do about that?"

Jess thought of the right word to use for just a second, then said, "Anchor him."

"Like tie him to an anchor and toss him in the ocean? Seems drastic."

She punched him in the shoulder.

"Ow... Okay, I deserve that. So, anchor him... Go on."

"Jenny was his anchor. She kept him with his feet on the ground. She made him feel valued, and loved, and important, but mainly, she kept that crazy bitch out of his head. Now, Jenny's gone. It's only been a month. No way he's okay, and here he comes visiting that fucking ghoul and talking about moving back to White Harbor. Then, all of this weird shit starts happening: the power goes out, a man tries to kill us, the goddamn moon is blue, for God's sake! Last thing I see is Peter crying 'Mother!' at supernatural apparitions." She stared into

Royce's eyes, a look of desperate concern plastered on her face. "I'm scared, Royce! I'm fucking browning my jeans, here!"

"Summing up, you're worried he's gonna snap and hurt himself?"

"Not just himself." She stared deep into Royce's eyes, trying to see if he'd been paying attention when she mentioned the part about Peter rambling about getting rid of *them* while he'd been in the crawlspace.

Royce shook his head. "Whoa, whoa, let me stop you right there! Peter would never hurt us, even at his craziest. Never!"

"Why don't you go have a closer look at Barry's neck? The T-Square incident would've landed an adult man in jail. Peter's lucky he was just a kid."

"That's different. Back then, Barry was a piece of shit, and he made it his mission to make Peter's life impossible. Jess"—he paused, and got close to her face to make sure she met his gaze as he spoke—"Peter would *never* hurt us."

"I know. I know!" Jess placed both hands on her hips, thinking. Then she brought a hand up to her mouth and nibbled on her thumb's cuticle. "I know," she repeated, sighing. "My mind's just a fucking mess. I just think he shouldn't be alone these days. *This*"—she waved a hand at the surrounding space, referring to the whole situation—"this isn't normal, and I'm worried it's gonna drive him over the edge." Her eyes were open wide, showing her fear and uncertainty. She stared at him. "I saw her, Royce." She said in a whiny whisper. "Martha Lange. Standing there, like I can see you now. I saw her!"

Royce nodded, a supportive expression on his face.

"Am I crazy?" she asked.

"No. If you say you saw her, she was there. I know what I saw in the Vanek House made no sense, but I saw it."

The image appeared—clear and undeniable—in Jess's mind. That room on the second floor of the house. The room that *changed*, the room that led somewhere else.

"So, bottom line is, you believe Hitch. You believe Martha Lange is going to use some magical, supernatural whatever to kill a bunch of people in town for that weird religion of hers."

Jess nodded fast. "And I think Peter is the key for her to do that. *And* I think whatever this is going to do to him is going to drive him crazy. Do I think he'd ever hurt us? No. But going by that weird nickname Bobby made up, do I have to remind you Gollum betrayed the hobbits because of how addicted to the ring he was?"

He stared at her for a moment. "You're such a nerd."

She punched him in the shoulder again, harder.

"Ow, fuck!" he said, rubbing his aching shoulder. "Don't get mad! So what, then? Do we tell the others about the crawlspace thing?"

"No! I don't want everyone to panic just because of a hunch I have. Let's play it by ear for now. I'll tell Nadine to be with Peter as much as she can manage. Him not hurting himself is the more immediate concern. We'll think of something else if we notice any more weirdness. Might be a good idea to find an excuse to check on Peter tomorrow." She cast a glance around. "That is, if it's not the end of the world, and electricity comes back, and this doesn't turn into a whole zombie apocalypse situation."

Royce nodded again, letting out a mirthless chuckle.

"Let's go," she said.

Royce picked up the battery charger, Jess handed him the gas lantern and picked up the box of lanterns with both hands. On their way to the stairs, Royce stopped, as if something had just popped into his mind. "Hey..." He looked at her over his shoulder. "So, that whole thing with Barry and Ray a moment ago... Did I interpret it right?"

"What? That they were probably fucking, and it ended badly?" Jess asked, looking annoyed.

"Did *you* know?" He raised a suspicious eyebrow at her.

"No! Why? So, there's a supernatural blackout, and your biggest concern is whether your two friends are banging each other?"

"Well, no...and yeah... It's just...the mental image, man. You know, in *The Wizard of Oz*, the house that crushed the Wicked Witch of the East? I picture it's like that, but the house is mounting the witch..."

"You're a fucking idiot," Jess said, doing her darnedest to contain her laughter. "I'm telling Ray you called him the Wicked Witch of the East."

"Do you think Ray wears striped socks while they do it?"

Despite all the disturbing events of the evening, she started laughing. They climbed up the stairs, the sound of her laughter echoing through the cellar. However, as they went up, she saw, through the space between two stairs, the lantern's light reflecting off the padlock on the locker, and she felt her humor grow sour.

2020

Jess closed the bar early that night. She was feeling under the weather. The holidays were coming up and White Harbor was seeing a constant flow of passing tourists, driving toward their holiday destinations, a lot of whom stopped at the bar. The weather in town had been a special kind of schizophrenic these past few weeks, too, which hadn't been kind to her health.

The regulars had stopped by—as regulars did—and she would always prioritize the locals: Mason Owen, Riley Estrada, who were there every day. Dominic Willis, who worked the night shift at the gas station, and his buddy, that unpleasant shit, Gunnar Bilson, had stopped by for a couple cold ones before work. Royce and Lillian stopped for a quick drink and got some wings to go. Nadine and a few teachers and staff from the school came for Happy Hour. Barry had stopped by in the later hours and had a couple beers before going home—he'd been more glum than usual and hadn't said goodbye. She felt tired down to her bones and just wanted to get home, wrap herself in her covers and sleep for the next twenty-four hours at least. She'd have Louis or her dad cover for her the next day.

The bar was now quiet, most of the lights were off, and she walked down the cellar stairs, carrying a crate holding large, half-empty jars containing assorted condiments, pickled foodstuffs, breading mix, and other items she'd brought with her from the kitchen. Each of the steps creaked as she set her foot down.

One of these days, I'm gonna build a damn dumbwaiter. My knees are going to kick my ass someday from going up and down these stairs.

The cellar light was on. She didn't remember leaving it on, but she'd come down here several times throughout the day, and it had been busy, so she convinced herself she'd just forgotten. She reached the bottom, turned around, and halted. The sole of her shoe squeaked as she came to a stop. A loud gasp escaped her chest, followed by the sound of the plastic crate hitting the floor at her feet. Three jars broke on impact and their contents spilled on the floor.

At the deeper end of the cellar, where she kept batteries and other supplies, she saw Barry. He was sitting on a foldout chair and had one of her dad's rifles in his mouth.

In a fraction of a second, she saw the open gun locker, saw his closed eyes, saw the tears streaming from them, glistening under the light of a bulb above his head, saw his thumb curled over the trigger, his hand trembling. She almost screamed "STOP!" but—also in a fraction a second—she saw in her mind her old friend getting startled and pulling the trigger, blowing off the top of his head, his eyes rolling up into his skull, never to see again. He hadn't reacted to the crate falling, though, which meant his attention was solely on what he was about to do, or he was so determined he'd willed himself to ignore her.

She had to be careful with how she would get his attention. She brought her emotions under control and said, in a soft voice, "Barr, it's me."

His eyes opened, light blue, bloodshot, wet. They swiveled in her direction. The anguish and despair she saw in them demolished her heart.

"Don't," she said, walking toward him. With each step, she felt the squish of pickles and preserves under her shoes and smelled their pungent vinegar aroma. "Please, Barr. Get your thumb off the trigger. Don't do this. Please, hun."

The big guy didn't move. He didn't disengage the trigger.

Jess took small, hesitant steps toward him, her heart pounding. Her eyes remained glued to his as she approached him, even though the look of hopelessness on his face felt like a knife in her heart. She could see his tense arm trembling.

She went down on one knee and slowly stretched a hand toward the trigger, placing it over Barry's. With a gentle touch, she wrapped her fingers around his and pried his thumb away from the trigger. He let her. She curled the fingers of her other hand around the gun barrel and, with slow, steady conviction, pulled on it. Barry's arms relaxed, and she saw the tip of the barrel slide out of his mouth, strands of saliva still clinging to it, to his beard, and his trembling lips. Once he let go of the gun, she put it aside, away from his reach.

Jess looked up at him, at his inflamed eyes and his heaving chest, which moved as if there was a void so great within it, he was struggling to breathe.

"Barr…"

"I'm sorry." His voice was a childish whimper. "I just… I'm…"

"Why? What's going on?"

Barry's lips trembled. He bared his teeth in a pained grimace. Tears and snot slid down his face, and before she could say a word, he let himself fall off the chair, to his knees, and buried his face in her lap. What followed were soul-rending wails of anguish, as Barry sobbed loudly, his large hands gripping her arms so hard she would have bruises on them the next day, and yet, she endured it.

Jess caressed his thick hair with her fingers, and she couldn't help but tear up.

"I'm sorry," he said again, his voice muffled against her thighs. "I'm sorry. I just can't. I can't. I just want it to end. I can't do this. It's a prison. I'm in prison. I have no escape. Pleeeease!"

"Oh, sweet baby." She wiped a tear away with the sleeve of her jacket. "I don't understand. Why?"

She knew why, she realized. *That woman and her mother. They're killing him. I never knew it had become this critical.* Her eyes glimpsed the gun cabinet, its door standing ajar, and she thought of how many times she'd asked Barry to please carry some heavy stuff down here, and she pictured the moment he might have noticed the unlocked cabinet, gotten curious, seen the guns inside, and seen the final "solution" to all his marital problems. How desperate did he have to be? How hopeless? To have even considered doing this and doing it here.

"Barry. Honey. Think of your son, and the little one on the way."

She felt his grip tighten on her arms.

"They're better off without me," he said, slurring between sobs. "I'm a coward. I'm a bad father. They're better off.

213

All I do is hurt people."

Jess weighed her next words. She thought she had the right thing to say, but it could also be the worst thing. She had to say something, though.

Barry's huge back convulsed with sobs.

"Were you better off"—she swallowed hard, hesitating—"after your dad took his own life?"

Barry looked up at her, the pure blue of those eyes in sharp contrast with the underlying, irritated red around them. He looked appalled, yet there was a glimmer of understanding in those eyes. Realization, perhaps a memory. His mouth worked. He tried to form a word, and Jess hoped with all her heart the next word out of it wouldn't be "Yes."

"No," he said in a soft breath. He shook his head once, a slow movement almost imperceptible. "No." He once more laid his head on her lap, now resting it on its side. "No."

She felt his hands slide off her arms until they were now on the cold concrete floor.

"No."

Chapter Twelve

Bones

2022

The blue moonlight filtered through the large windows, illuminating the bed in front of Maddie Cunningham. The bed reminded her of an open coffin.

An elderly woman of The Faithful, willingly sacrificing to the Lord on her sleeping bed.

She would die there.

No. There's still one chance. I can stop him, or at least delay him, and give Jess a chance.

"There's no rush," that mindless puppet, Freddie Parham, said. There was a calm joy in his voice that made her stomach turn. "Thank you for doing this for us. Those of us left will remember you fondly... Maddie." He said her name in a prideful, mocking tone to highlight the fact he wasn't planning to comply with her request to be called Mrs. Cunningham.

Slow and cautious, she turned and sat on the edge of the bed. She smoothed her sleeping gown, then turned a scowl toward Freddie, so disdainful it could've wilted flowers, turned wine to vinegar, and dried rivers, killing the entire ecosystem around them. He looked blurry in the dark, but what little she could see of him, she hated. She hated him with a passion. He represented everything she and her husband had tried and failed to escape from. She pushed past her disgust to stay on track toward her objective. She had to, if she was going to have any chance to change the course of events. Pulling in a deep breath, she exhaled and embraced her inner calm.

"I was close with your mom, Freddie," she said.

He snorted and smirked, as if spotting an obvious attempt to appeal to his conscience.

"She was a good woman. With your dad's drinking, and doing most of that drinking at my family's bar, we became close, she and I. We spoke often."

"Is that right?"

"It's only natural." She thought she was forcing regret into her voice, but she found, when it came to Mikayla Parham, she didn't have to force it. "My husband was poisoning hers. Not that we saw it that way at the time. It was more like, 'Here's your unconscious husband,' while she apologized for him making a scene." She looked down at the floor. "She apologized a lot, your mother, for things that were not her fault."

There was a twitch in Freddie's face. She might be almost blind, but she noticed it. It was his heart wringing in his chest, causing a chain reaction that climbed toward his face, making his eye give a single twitch of grief.

"Your mother fell in love with a man the whole town said was cursed, only to find out he was *not only* cursed, but an alcoholic, and not just an alcoholic, but a violent one that constantly humiliated her in public. And yet, *she* was the one who apologized constantly."

"What's this?" he said, that smug grin on his face. "Is this your way of making me change my mind? Too late for that, I'm afraid, Maddie."

She stared straight at him. Her eyes full of sympathy, not hate. "There was one thing she never apologized for. That was you. Your little sister, of course, but you were here longer. Many people wrote you off as another cursed Parham. They saw you as a screwup, even from an early age. A troublemaker. A weirdo. But Mikayla loved you for your weirdness."

"There's nothing you can tell me about my mom I don't already know."

"She was saving money to help you with the startup of your publishing brand."

217

His breath caught in his throat.

"Hyena Publishing?" she added, twisting the knife.

His face became stony. A mask.

"She always knew you didn't want to go to college. She knew you wanted to start your brand as early as possible. She was proud of your art, of your creations. She showed me. You were so good. Twisted, yes, but fantastic. So talented. In the end, all that money she saved went to your legal defense after you killed those kids. Even after death, all Mikayla Parham did was take care of her son."

He lowered his gaze for half a second. Mentioning his mother's name along with that story had stung, she could see. He opened his mouth to speak. "I—"

BANG!

The shot echoed through the room and lingered in the air.

Freddie screamed and went to the floor, holding his thigh.

Maddie stood up from the bed, supporting herself on her cane, and walked toward him, holding the handgun she'd pulled from the holster Chuck had installed on the inner side of her nightstand.

"Fuck!" Freddie shouted. "You goddamn, crazy b—"

She shot him again, this time hitting his forearm.

He bellowed.

"I gave my Chuck so much grief because I didn't want

this thing next to our bed," she said, barrel trained on him.
Freddie looked like a smudge in the dark, but all she had to
do was point the gun toward that smudge and put as many
bullets in it as she could. "I figured I'd never need it. I never
even loaded it, but I knew if there would ever be a chance to
use it, it would be tonight."

Freddie grunted. Doing his best to cover both wounds
and shield the vital parts of his body. He was afraid. She could
barely see it. He was a forty-something old man, but the stare
he gave her was that of an immature, scared child who had
never been exposed to the world. Despite everything he'd
done and planned on doing, Freddie Parham was just a scared
little kid. And she had to kill him to put a stop to this insanity.

"This was the only time this could happen, right?" she
asked, moving closer, not taking the gun off him. She had limited bullets, and she would get a better shot the closer she was.
"This was the one you had to take part in. No hiding in the
shadows like a voyeuristic fucking coward. No intangibility. I
was just hoping—hoping—that it would start counting from
the moment you walked into the room. And you can't kill me
either, is that right? This old bitch is supposed to 'willingly
sacrifice herself to the Lord', right? These ritualistic rules are
just a pain in the ass, huh?"

He gave her a scowl that almost matched the one she'd
given him just minutes earlier. She could see it clearly, standing just steps away from him, careful not to get close enough

to let him sweep her off her feet and steal her advantage.

"Stop talking," he said through clenched teeth. "If you're gonna shoot me, just shoot me."

"Gladly," she said, and aimed for his head.

"I just hope you're ready to be responsible for your husband and daughter's deaths," he blurted. It gave her pause. "Wasn't it enough that you and that husband of yours got your son killed for wanting to leave the Circle?"

"That's not—"

"Want a preview?" he said, his voice a vile hiss. He touched the floor, and the room changed in a matter of a second.

The smell of alcohol invaded her nostrils. She was in the bar's cellar, a gas lantern on a chair at the center of the room. The cellar looked ancient and dilapidated, flooded in about five inches of disgusting water. Some walls had caved in, earth had poured in through the holes, making piles of earth and bricks. She saw bones and body parts sticking out of the piles, as if they'd been buried under the bar for decades. Corpses hung from the ceiling and the walls, all in varying degrees of decomposition. Some were nothing but bones, skin, and ragged clothes. At the center of it all, though, was the worst thing she'd ever seen, and she saw it with full clarity, as if she'd recovered her 20/20 vision, or the images themselves were being broadcast directly into her brain.

She screamed in despair.

On the floor was her daughter, Jessica, naked, tied with ropes. She was covered in cuts and blood. She was missing an eye, a foot, and all the fingers on one hand. Jess cried for help, but her screams only echoed, bouncing off the bricks in the cellar's walls.

Out of the darkness appeared her husband, but she didn't recognize the man in those eyes—it was his face and his body, but the identity wasn't there. The eyes were empty and black, like dark caverns, and black veins formed webs all over his skin. His clothes were ragged and covered in blood. He carried a meat cleaver in his hand. Without hesitation, he dropped to his knees next to Jess, who now squealed in terror, calling for help, the panic in her eyes showing she didn't recognize this man as her father.

Jess screamed and pleaded for what felt like hours before being silenced by her own father bringing down the cleaver once, twice, right into her neck, then a final time that severed her head—the muted sound of the blade hitting the concrete floor through the few inches of water, was the most sickening sound she'd ever heard in her life.

The thing posing as her husband then raised the cleaver to his own neck, and just as the blade cut a deep line into it and blood sprayed, she saw her husband's eyes clear out and the shock set in as he realized he was bleeding to death, then the unadulterated solid horror as he noticed his decapitated daughter before him.

"NOOOOO!" Maddie shouted in a shrill, devastating pitch, as the surroundings disappeared and she found herself back in her bedroom, tears rolling down her eyes, and a stream of saliva running down the corner of her mouth. "No!"

She still had the gun pointed at Freddie, but as her sight blurred again, he stood up, aching and with difficulty from the wound in his thigh, but no longer scared.

"There are rules, Maddie," he said, that odious smirk drawn on his lips again. "You do the thing you're supposed to do; something good happens. You don't do the thing you're supposed to do; something like what you saw happens."

"You're lying," she said, under her breath. "You're manipulating me. That wasn't true."

"It *is* true. It's one of the many ways Jess and Chuck could die—and they *will* die—in Blight Harbor if you don't fulfill your duty. If you do your part, they will most likely survive. If you don't, they will die with one-hundred percent certainty, and trust me, this one isn't the most horrible way it can happen."

Her hand trembled.

"So, what will it be…Mrs. Cunningham?"

Maddie let the gun fall. It fell heavily, with a blunt thud and only the slightest clatter as it settled on the floor. Her arm hung limp at her side for a moment, then she raised her hand and wiped away the tears and drool from her face. Without answering Freddie's question, she turned, and, supporting herself on her cane, walked back to her bed and slid onto it, lying down on the side she'd always slept in. She took slow, measured breaths, staring at the ceiling, holding back new tears. She wouldn't cry. She was doing this for her family.

"I'm ready," she said.

She had failed.

Freddie opened a drawer from a nearby dresser and pulled out the first shirt his hand could grab. He wrapped it around his leg and tied it into a tourniquet. He'd only need it for a second, Maddie knew, while he was in this house. Once he became intangible again, the bullet wounds would disappear as if they'd never existed.

She had failed.

He grunted as he pulled the shirt tourniquet tight around his thigh. He then limped toward a chair by a desk near the window and pulled it closer to the bed. Sat next to Maddie.

"Thank you for doing this, Mrs. Cunningham," Freddie said, his voice now humble and respectful.

She turned her head toward him. His demeanor and expression had changed. There was now kindness in his eyes. Like her accepting her fate made him see her under a whole new light. She turned away. She didn't want to see him as a human being on account of this monstrous thing he was doing.

He placed a gentle hand on her arm, and she contained herself from pulling it away in disgust. "I know this is hard," he said, his voice warm and compassionate.

She breathed raspy breaths, holding back her tears.

"I meant it when I said if you did this, your family would most likely survive. It wasn't just to stop you from shooting. I know 'most likely' doesn't seem like much, but they'll have a chance. You're *giving* them that chance. You have my word I'll do everything in my power to ensure they see the other end of this alive."

Maddie didn't answer.

"Mrs. Cunningham, look at me."

She turned her eyes, filled with dread and resignation, toward him.

He pressed softly on her arm. "I mean it."

She nodded, ragged breaths coming from her chest.

"Tell me. Do you consent to be the Third Offering of the First Night? Do you willingly offer yourself to our Lord, so He may remake this world in his image at the end of these four nights?"

The tears flowed from her eyes now, unrestrained. In her heart she felt nothing but hatred for this man—for this misguided boy—but she put the image of her husband, her daughter, and her long-lost son in her mind. "Yes," she whimpered.

"Let's begin, then."

The wall above her head made a sudden cracking noise,

making her jump. Her vision—blurry at first, but clearing fast, like in that nightmare cellar—caught two small cracks opening in the wall. Tiny chunks of plaster and paint broke off to the left and right of the headboard until there were two holes. Another cracking noise startled her, this time at the foot of the bed—the sound of floorboards breaking, splintering.

"Be still, Mrs. Cunningham. It'll be alright."

Thin, black tendrils emerged from the cracks in the walls. They were like solid shadows that absorbed light. They crept down the wall and onto the headboard. Approaching her with purpose, and as they reached the mattress, they became liquid, pooling close to her left and right shoulders. Similar tendrils crawled up the foot of the bed and pooled by her feet.

"Give me your hand, please," Freddie said, his voice now different from the arrogant monster that had first walked into her home.

She moved her trembling right hand toward him.

"Palm up, please."

She turned her hand. Freddie leaned into her and reached toward the small black puddle on that side. Pinching a bit of the black liquid between his fingers, it formed a thread that he stretched before settling into a small pool in her palm.

"Thank you. The other hand, please?"

Maddie complied. Freddie leaned over her body to take another pinch off the black puddle on that side and put it in her left palm.

Limping toward the foot of the bed, Freddie repeated the process, plucking a thread from the right puddle and wrapping it around her ankle before doing the same with a thread from the left puddle.

He returned to her midsection and looked up. Another small crack opened in the ceiling and soon there was a black tendril hanging from it, low enough for Freddie to reach. He took it between his fingers and pulled it down, touching it to her abdomen, where it formed one last tiny pool.

"Everything's set."

Maddie continued to weep in silence. The fear was so powerful she couldn't speak. The thought of the coming pain overwhelmed her.

"The first sacrifice is about the pain of life cut short," Freddie said. "The second sacrifice is about the pain and struggle of adulthood. This one is about the pain of losing our eldest and wisest. The fourth and final one is about the pain of rebirth."

"I know all this," Maddie said, between sniffles. "I don't need you to—"

"Wait," he said, again placing his hand on her arm. "I know you're afraid of the pain you are about to experience, and I won't lie—I owe you the truth—it will be intense."

Maddie whimpered again. She took in air then blew it out of her mouth, as if readying to give birth.

"This pain feeds the Lord. This pain strengthens the

Lord. It's through suffering that we accomplish great things. Your faith can make this pain bearable."

"I don't believe any of that bullshit anymore." She found a voice where she thought she had nothing more to say. "Any god that feeds on pain and suffering is no god. It's just a fucking killer whale, playing sadistically with a seal before tearing it to pieces."

Freddie gave her a condescending smile. "In that case, if you're not doing it for faith, do it for your family. Keep them in your mind and know you're doing this for them."

She tightened her jaw, ready for what she knew was coming. She let out a confused, startled exclamation when the tiny pool in her left hand abruptly stretched into a long tendril that crawled up her arm like a centipede, wrapping itself around it all the way to her armpit. The thin thread swelled into a black tentacle as thick as a thumb. It grew, hardened like a snake's muscular body. Then there was a sudden blast of pain. Her arm lay broken in at least four places. She stared at the splintered end of a bone sticking out of a bleeding wound, as agonizing screams issued from her mouth.

Before her brain adjusted, she felt it now happen in her right hand. Stretching. Crawling. Wrapping. Swelling. Hardening.

NO, PLEASE!!!

Breaking.

Peals of screams, painful convulsions, rolled-up eyes,

saliva running down a raging, screaming mouth.

She felt the movement on her left leg. Stretching. Crawling. Wrapping. Swelling. Hardening. Her entire leg was broken in a crooked zigzag shape that resembled nothing human; followed by the tentacle on her right leg. Stretching. Crawling. Wrapping. Swelling. Hardening. Breaking.

By this point, Maddie's screams could not be heard. Just air leaving her lungs, where vocal cords failed to convey the pain overload of her every nerve. Soon her bed was wet as she pissed herself amid the feverish shakes of her body being pushed to the limits of human endurance.

There was another jolt of pain as the tentacles pulled and stretched her broken limbs taut. She felt a grating sensation on the inside of her limbs as the ends of splintered bones scraped against each other, like touching the tips of two electrical wires, sparking shocks that coursed through her body.

The black tendril on her belly pierced through the fabric of her robe, then pierced through her belly button, worming its way into her, sending out other branching tendrils she could feel crawling under her skin. It felt as if the black threads were anchoring themselves to her tissue, her muscles, and her bones, whatever they could cling to inside her body.

She was lifted by her abdomen. She could feel hundreds of minuscule hooks pulling inside her body as she now hung above the bed. Her body was in a tense position with the tentacles pulling from high in the wall, the others pulling from down on the floor, and the one pulling from the ceiling.

With the savage way her limbs were being pulled, the notion of how this was going to end formed in her mind. She would be stretched like on a rack at the Spanish Inquisition, and her limbs would come off their sockets in a disgusting spectacle of blood. Her penance for having rejected the Circle and Martha Lange. It was the only logical end to this horror.

What she didn't notice as she hung in the air was that from the holes in the wall and floor, more and more of the shadowy threads kept pouring out, pooling, more and more, on the bed, until it was covered in a rubbery, reflectionless shade of black. There were wet, slurping, disgusting sounds. Unfathomable noises came from below, when all that should've been down there was a mattress.

Then another sound rose above it. A strange, excited, weeping giggle from her right, and despite the unsurmountable pain, she turned her head to see Freddie Parham, hands over his mouth, tears of devotion running down his face, a smile stretching beyond his cupped hands. Whatever he was seeing, whatever the bed had transformed into, had driven him into a fanatical bout of tears. The surrounding room was no longer her bedroom, she realized. It was a broken and ancient ruin of what used to be her room, covered in desiccated vines, cobwebs, and dust. The windows were broken, and outside, a desolate, flooded landscape, from above which the moon—that horrid moon—witnessed her end. She realized

229

she was on that other side. She was in Blight Harbor. Her screams had not been heard by her neighbors. She would die, and no one would even know what had happened to her. Only that fucking moon.

She turned her bloodshot eyes toward Freddie. "I don't want to see," she whimpered, pleading. "Please, make me not see."

Freddie's expression was that of overwhelming emotion. He was moved by this request. He nodded, and her vision blurred, darkened, then was gone.

She filled her mind's eye—now her only sight—with the image of her family. Their last dinner together, all four of them. Chuck's birthday. Smiles all around. Laughter. The cake. Chuck failing to blow out the candles in a single try. Hugs. Kisses. Her beautiful son, still alive, and going to college soon. Her daughter, a woman she admired, working hard to take over the bar one day. Her family. Her everything.

There was another unbearable blast of pain as she felt the tentacles that bound her loosen their grip.

Gravity.

Falling.

There was a sensation like being enveloped by a warm, wet maw closing around her. A second of trepidation.

My family. My everything. My—

Sharp teeth driving into every inch of her body.

Then nothingness.

Chapter Thirteen

Cursed

1993

With his arms wrapped around his knees and his head tucked in between, Freddie sat in a corner of the square wooden room on the second floor of the Vanek House. He'd known it was that exact room when he'd noticed the door with the metal reinforcements. He had only seen the other side of that door during the two years he'd been coming here with his friends.

"They're not my friends," he reminded himself in a bitter, muttering voice.

There was the clatter of the bucket hitting the floorboards in the opposite corner from where he sat, like it had done every day for a month.

"What did you say?" the old man asked. The light from his flashlight swayed around as Curling turned to look at him.

"Nothing, old man, fuck off." Freddie's voice sounded weak.

"Talk to me like that again, and I'll leave your bucket here. See how you like to be locked with your shit and piss in the dark for an entire week." He turned toward the door and opened it.

So easy, Freddie thought. *Two years, we couldn't open the fucking thing and this asshole opens it like it's nothing.*

"We'll see if tomorrow you're ready to have a chat." Old Man Curling looked at him with disgust. Freddie spotted his two dogs standing outside the threshold. They never crossed to this side. If he were to make a guess, he'd say the dogs feared entering the room.

He caught a furtive glimpse of Curling's hand reaching for the door handle, prepared to close it again and leave him in darkness, and during the fraction of a second it took him to raise his head, there was a sudden rush of thoughts in his mind.

The ragged, swollen lump on his mother's head. The way her skin had become three shades whiter, with an underlying blue hue; veins like dark vines and scrapes all over, which no longer bled. There had been a large red ant crawling over her lower lip.

Lolly's broken arms. Her face with an expression he'd never seen it make: frozen halfway through a surprised gawk—one eye open, the other half-closed, like one of those plastic dolls with closing eyes when one of the lids gets stuck. One side of her face was covered in tiny pebbles stuck to her skin with moisture.

Purple teeth marks around Lolly's mouth. Neal Parham had become a desperate, panicking animal trying to save his little girl—he'd scrambled to find enough humanity and control to give his baby daughter mouth-to-mouth resuscitation, but in his desperation, he'd bitten down as he pushed air into her lungs.

His dad's closed casket. The lack of tears from the people at the funeral. His family's tragedy hadn't been surprising at all. Just the next bunch of Parhams who'd succumbed to their family curse. He'd peered inside the casket at the funeral home before it was sealed. His dad's head had been crushed like a melon.

He remembered the voices of his supposed friends downstairs. They couldn't hear him in this room, as he screamed and cried for help, but he could hear them. He could hear what those two-faced assholes had been saying about him now that he hadn't been there a whole month.

"What a shocker," he'd heard Royce say. Others had

a hard time telling the twins apart, but he knew Royce was the most soft-spoken of the two, but he'd still managed to make the remark hurt. "A cursed family died because they were cursed?"

"What were y'all expecting them to do, win the lottery?" Leroy, as per usual, completed his brother's remark.

"If you ask me," Jess said, and he could hear the gossiping tone in her voice, "Neal Parham was stinking drunk and drowned his family. All he did was talk shit about them at my dad's bar. He saw an opportunity, and he took it. Freddie got lucky the police got there before he could drown him."

"Too bad the truck got him before he could give it another try." That was Barry's voice, that old tone from back when he used to dunk his head in the toilet, had returned in full force.

"Um, actually..." That could only be Droopy Baker's mandatory annoying interjection. "According to witness reports, it was Freddie who drowned his mom and his sister, not Neal Parham. People on the bridge over the Pargin River saw him take his sister to the deep part of The Eye, and he dropped her, then when his mom came over to save her, he pushed her off the edge into the rocks."

Shut up, Freddie thought in a flash. Still watching Curling close the door in slow motion. *Stop saying that!*

"Well, I told you all how his dad used to beat the shit out of him every chance he got." Bobby. His best friend. How could he? "How else does someone get fucked up in the head enough to drown his little sister and his mom?"

Fuck you, Bobby! Freddie continued to think *at* them, trying to silence voices that weren't there anymore. *Fuck you! I loved you like a brother! You—*

"He used to say I was like a brother to him." Bobby scoffed. "Can you imagine? Being brother to a Parham? I don't want to have my head squashed by a refrigerated truck!"

Stop laughing!

He heard them all laugh and cackle and giggle, making little of his pain.

"When I heard the news, I was like 'Laurie who? Mikayla what?'" Nadine's voice, venom dripping from it. "It was only when they said Parham that my mind went, 'Parham. Dead. Well, sure, why so surprised?'"

"That's just what happened to me!" That bitch, Sylvia Nguyen, said. "I was like, 'Whatever, tell me when someone important dies.'"

Bitch! I should've never let you join! You poisonous bitch!

"I didn't know him enough to care, if I'm honest," Raymond said.

Fuck you! You'll know me one day, you asshole! I'll show you who I am!

"Well, look at it this way," Peter Lange said. He was the shiest, most reserved member of the group, so Freddie would never have expected the meanness in his voice as he completed his remark. "The one who got lucky there was the little girl. Think about it. She only had to put up with five years of being a Parham. She was probably glad someone put her out of her misery."

I'll kill you, Lange! I'll fuckin' kill you, you piece of shit!

He could hear them in his head, laughing in delight as they got everything off their chests. What they really thought, who they really were. Liars. Fake friends. Every time he heard these conversations, he screamed at the top of his lungs, first shouting for help, then cursing his fake friends for the way they mocked his loss. As the month passed, he thought he could see them, stepping out of the shadows of his small room, giving him leering glances, laughing, or saying something demeaning. He grew to hate them all during his time in this dark, smelly cell.

He looked at Curling—only a line of light two inches wide now—as he closed the door.

"Wait!" Freddie cried in desperation. "Don't leave me here! No! Don't leave me here! Please!"

Curling turned around.

"I'm ready to talk now. I'm ready to talk."

Curling watched him in silence for a moment, his hand still not leaving the doorknob. "Do you even know what I want to talk to you about?"

"You said you knew how to end the curse. I didn't believe you. I thought you were a goddamn nut, and you were going to kill me like you did all those people who came in the house."

Curling squinted. "I never killed no one."

"Oh, c'mon, old man!" Freddie's face filled with anger. "I'm not fucking stupid! How long has this house been here? Like a hundred years? Been in the Curling family for what, ninety? According to Droopy Baker, about ninety people have died or disappeared in this house. One person a year, sometimes several at once. You're *feeding* the house."

Curling scowled, but there was intrigue in those eyes. Freddie knew he was on to something.

"Or feeding whatever makes it tick." Freddie shot him a savage stare. "My head's full of scary stories. It's the only thing that makes sense to me. The Albrights? Four years' worth of house-chow in one go. No more deaths the four years after, I'm guessing."

A shadow of a smile passed over Curling's face. "Makes sense. Let me show you how much sense this makes. Then, we'll talk."

Curling strolled into the room, hand searching in his pocket, until he pulled out something similar to an intensely red piece of chalk or crayon—it wasn't dull enough to be the former, nor glossy enough to be the latter. He crouched in front of Freddie, who weighed his chances if he lunged at the old man, but then he remembered the dogs out there. If he touched the old man, those two animals would tear him apart.

237

Curling drew a strange symbol on the floor; something like the letter H, but with squiggly doodles crossing the vertical lines to form something like a sigil.

As Freddie stared in confusion, Curling's callused hand reached out and grabbed his, pulled it toward him, and slammed it flat on top of the symbol.

A flash of dizziness made Freddie close his eyes. When he opened them, he was sitting at the bottom of what felt like stairs. The wind howled outside, and a chill crawled up his bones, stiffening his muscles. Around him, utter darkness. He moved his fingers until they touched something made of fabric. It was a lump, a bag or sack of some kind. He touched a zipper—*A backpack,* he thought—and, as if he knew his way around this specific backpack, he unzipped it and reached inside, confidently feeling around for *something.*

Freddie became aware he wasn't himself. He wasn't in control of this body. He inhabited this person's body, their ears, nose, skin, and eyes—even if they couldn't see much in this darkness. The person's fingers grasped something slick, cylindrical, metallic. Their thumb clicked on a button, and there was sudden light emerging from inside the backpack, which blinded him for a moment. A penlight, he saw, which the person shone around, and now Freddie knew they were in the main hall of the Vanek House, sitting on the bottom step of the stairs. They shone the penlight toward the second floor, where shadows shifted with the moving light.

What the hell is this? Freddie thought.

"Hello?" he heard the person say and realized it was a boy, maybe his age, based on the squeaky voice, he surmised.

A noise responded from the second floor, faint but there. It sounded like shuffling, or some mass settling on creaking boards.

For a few minutes, he sat there, pointing the penlight at the second-floor landing and the shadowy hallway beyond. There was silence for a while, save for the wind crying out like the souls in hell. He hugged his body; he was shaking; his breath came out in a cloud. It was so damned cold. His eyelids felt heavy—so sleepy, so tired. Freddie could feel the boy's eyes close and his head nod, despite the fear. He'd been sleeping before he arrived in this body, had been woken up by the sounds upstairs. Now, in the unnerving quiet, he felt sleepy again.

Who is this? Who am I?

Minutes passed and he could feel the boy fighting to stay awake. The noises upstairs stopping didn't mean danger had passed. He blinked. Blinked. Nodded. Nodded.

He fell asleep.

Freddie was now at a barbecue in a huge backyard, so

expansive it got lost in the horizon on either side. *He's dreaming.* A large family gathered together around a grill. Sometimes, people changed places, or the boy shifted to a different spot in the backyard. Sometimes there'd be the wall of a house—*A yellow house*—sometimes he'd be at school. Sometimes he'd be eating, sometimes drinking, sometimes he'd be in the middle of conversations he didn't remember starting. Conversations in Spanish.

Wait. Blizzard. Yellow house. Spanish. This is—

"Gerardo!" A voice coming from somewhere in the endless backyard, a woman's voice. Freddie thought he was walking toward it, but in reality, he had blinked himself into a new location, and now he was standing in front of Roberta Valencia, the kindergarten teacher. "Gerardo," she said. "*Sírvete carne, m'hijo, hay bastante.*"

Inside his mind, Freddie understood what she said, even though he didn't speak Spanish. She said, "Have some meat, son, there's plenty." He gasped, and the thought hit him like a kick to the head. *I'm—*

THUMP!

His eyes flew open, startled. The dream faded. Darkness. Cold.

—*Gerardo Valencia!* He thought, Gerardo's heart beating quickly in his chest. *I'm Gerardo Valencia. This is the Vanek House. So...*

THUMP!

Gerardo's head spun toward the top of the stairs. The sound had come from the second-floor landing. It was—

THUMP!

—descending. Steps. Steps coming down. He could feel a presence in the darkness, but he couldn't see it.

Turn on the light! Turn on the light, you stupid moron! Freddie thought, as if he could change what he knew was about to happen, even if no one had been there to witness it.

THUMP!

Freddie could feel Gerardo's trembling hand reach into his pocket, bring out the penlight and click it on with a shaking thumb. He could feel his fear, his desperation. Then the boy shone the light upstairs, and two legs—a man's naked legs—appeared, partially covered in a strange black goo; like tar, but it didn't reflect the light, and it wriggled.

THUMP!

Move! Move! Move! Freddie thought at the hapless kid who was inevitably about to die, and it was then the thought hit Freddie: he was about to experience Gerardo Valencia's death firsthand.

THUMP!

He could now see the creature's body—under some strenuous description—was male, but it didn't appear human. Its appearance was that of a skin suit in the shape of a man, body hair and all, which had been filled with the black, moving substance, distending, and swelling its shape, until the black stuff had poured out of its mouth, nose, ears, and every other orifice. The living substance had coated most of its legs, arms, groin, and abdomen—making it look like a fat man who had been attacked with black paint balloons—and had formed smaller black tentacles coming out of holes throughout its body.

THUMP!

The boy was frozen. He was a statue watching this abomination lurch down the stairs toward him. Freddie could now see texture in the few exposed areas of skin on the creature's body, and on its chest, on the left side, there was something which made even less sense than everything in this picture. It looked like there was an old, blurry, faded tattoo of a police badge on the creature's chest. It was then Gerardo's eyes moved toward where a person's head would've been, and though it resembled a stretched latex mask with black caves for eyes and had a disgusting black tentacle coming out of its mouth, Freddie recognized his dad's face.

THUMP!

No! This isn't true!

The black tentacle monster wearing his dad's skin was now a few steps up from Gerardo's location, and at last, the boy reacted. Staggering in panic, he turned and ran for the front door. Through his screams, Freddie could still hear the thumping of the creature's feet on each step as it descended. Gerardo tried to turn the knob and pull the door open, but no matter how hard he tried, all that came from it was the clatter of the wood, and the chains on the other side, which hadn't been there when he'd come in. He pulled with all his strength, but they did not give way.

"Help!" Gerardo screamed. "Help! Someone!"

Thump! Thump! THUMP!

The vibration on the floorboards made his skin tremble as the creature reached the first floor. He sensed Gerardo getting frantic, banging and clawing at the door.

"HELP ME! PLEASE HELP ME! HELP MEEEE!"

Gerardo turned around and the trembling light of the penlight in his hand shone on the creature, which stood at the foot of the stairs, swaying back and forth, those horrid black tentacles moving every which way, as if searching. Then it turned its head in his direction. The boy raved with fear. He turned back toward the door, banging and clawing, banging and clawing, and screaming throughout. Even in the desperate motion of the penlight, he could see the marks the boy's fingernails were leaving on the door.

THUMP! THUMP! THUMP! THUMP! THUMP!

"HEEELP! MOOOM! DAAAD! MOOOMIEEEE!"

A slurping sound. Something wrapped around Gerardo's ankle. It gave a hard pull.

Freddie watched the door shoot upward in front of his eyes as Gerardo fell.

Gerardo's jaw—Freddie's jaw—hit the floorboards.

The dizziness hit him as the impact rattled his brain. There was light in front of him. The penlight on the floor pointed right into his eyes as he was pulled backward, dazzling him. Gerardo let out peals of desperate animalistic shrieks as his fingernails dug into the wooden floor. Pain burned in Freddie's hand as one of his fingernails got stuck in the floor and was savagely ripped out, but the boy continued to claw at the wood, as if there was truly something he could do to fight the force pulling him toward certain death. Another fingernail came off, then another.

"MOMMY! MOMMIEEEE!"

Gerardo's body was lifted, flipped, then slammed onto his back. Freddie was now staring into the stretched skin-mask resembling his dad's face, the creature's body weight holding Gerardo down, as the tentacle from its mouth swayed this way and that like a salted slug.

"MOMMY! MOMMY! MO—ulghff!"

The black tentacle went into Gerardo's mouth and Freddie felt himself choking as it crept down his larynx. It soon divided, sending tendrils crawling through his body. Freddie's mind roared with the raw, freezing, earthquaking fear that shook every inch of Gerardo's body. Even if he was choking, he wasn't suffocating. The tendrils filled his lungs; he could still breathe, but the way a person being waterboarded can feel themselves drowning, even if they're not. Rivulets of tears left his eyes as the tendrils continued to spread into his bronchi, into his stomach, creeping into muscles and organs, and Gerardo kept trying to push out futile screams against the abomination slowly killing him.

As he strained to let out a soundless scream through a stuffed mouth, the larger portion of the black tentacle jerked, and Gerardo's jaw dislocated. Every iota of intense pain made it from Gerardo's nerves to Freddie's. Through it all, he saw the indifferent stare of the black eye sockets on his dad's face. The smaller tentacles coming from his nose and ears merged into the main tentacle from his mouth and continued flowing into Gerardo's mouth.

Then the creature stopped. It looked puzzled. Freddie realized why.

Gerardo's heart had stopped. The creature knew it. It wasn't expecting it. It had probably wanted to tear the boy apart from the inside, but the boy's heart had simply stopped from the sheer terror before it could.

The boy was dying, which meant Freddie was dying. His vision blurred. The world faded away. There was no more pain, as he was overtaken by real darkness, and Freddie knew something then he'd never forget: after the heart stopped beating, after the lungs stopped breathing, after the body could no longer move, and the eyes could no longer see, you could still feel the fear and the terror; heightened by the lack of all other sensations, if it was the last thing on your mind as you departed, you left the world in the purest of horrors.

As soon as his hand came off the sigil on the floor, Freddie was back in his own body. The images were gone, but the fear was still sending cold spikes through his heart. His cheeks were wet and his breathing was deep and agitated. He fell backward, taking a deep breath, and scuttled away from the sigil until his back hit the wall, screaming as he did this.

"My dad." His voice slurred and distorted, as if waking from a fever dream. "My dad, why was... My dad... Why was..."

"He was drunk that afternoon," Old Man Curling said. "I left the door open to let that boy walk inside, let the house do what it does."

Still feeling Gerardo's fear buzzing in his mind, he gave Curling a revolted expression.

"Far as I know, your dad wandered in before the boy, made his way to the second floor, and passed out. The house just...did what it does."

Freddie thought of the events that followed. His dad coming to the Vanek House a couple days later; him taking the polaroid of the corpse; him showing it around to other people, being drunker than usual. His nightmares, his rants about kids dying, him becoming more violent afterwards, everything now made sense.

As if knowing what he was thinking, Curling said, "That damn picture." Curling ran his hand over his mouth. "I think there was a part of your father that remembered what happened, even if the house made sure he didn't."

"Dad felt guilty. He might have been showing the picture around, maybe to have someone tell him he wasn't guilty of something he didn't know he'd done."

Curling gave him another intrigued look.

"What's this got to do with my family curse?"

"Do you still want to talk after what you saw?"

"I lost everything, old man. I don't care what I have to do to get rid of the curse."

Curling nodded. "If your dad hadn't been a Parham, the house would've killed him. Instead, it used him to kill the boy." He let Freddie absorb this information. "This house is a gateway. I've spent a long time keeping it closed. Whatever you think is still spilling out into the town, it's nothing compared to what this house is keeping in."

Freddie raised his sleepless gaze toward him. The teenager in him was terrified of the notion of what Curling was describing. The horror freak in him was fascinated.

"There are two sides, two halves, to the power in this town." His usual grumble and short sentences had been pushed aside for now. "Always there, always present. Your ancestor, Dorothy Parham, served one half of that power. That's why the house used your father. You Parhams are servants.

You're slaves. One half of that power wants you all dead for what Dorothy Parham did to her son. The other half wants to use you. Fortunately for you, it can only do it in this house."

"You're talking about Blight Harbor, or the thing that created Blight Harbor. Which of the halves is that?"

"Both." Curling's face was expressionless.

Freddie raised an eyebrow, confused.

"You can never appease the half of this power that wants your family dead."

"But, I thought you said—"

"You can never appease that half. It will always want to kill you. But the other half, the one most people know of White Harbor, is more powerful. It has fed more. Serve it, and it will protect you."

"Is that everything?" Peter asked, standing next to a medium-sized box full of books. There were bags with cushions nearby. The picnic table had been folded, its umbrella closed. They had emptied the ice water from the cooler, and it was sitting in the corner with the rest of their stuff. The TV and the boombox were sitting on the lid, along with a backpack with Bobby's VCR inside.

"I think so," Bobby said. "We should start carrying

everything outta here."

"On it." Barry bent down to pick up the cooler and the items on it. He stood there, holding them in front of him. "Do you really think people will come here?"

Nadine nodded. The look of concern on her face was enough for the point to get across. An entire month had passed since Freddie disappeared, followed by two additional weeks in which two children had disappeared: Kayleigh Grant and Wilfrid Ingram, both of whom they knew from school or from The Pines.

Jess turned to Barry, a bag of cushions tossed over her shoulder. "After what happened to Gerardo? I'm shocked this wasn't the first place the police checked."

"They can't find all this stuff here," Nadine said. "It can all be traced to our families. That'd be a shit storm."

"Let's go, then," Barry said.

"Guys, wait." Bobby looked forlorn as he examined the wall where traces of Freddie's mural could still be made out. They hadn't been able to fully erase it. "Look...I know in this town, if someone goes missing, it's not a matter of whether they'll turn up, but whether a body will turn up. But"—he gulped, an aggrieved look in his eyes—"they might still find Freddie alive, right? He might not be dead." He cast a glance around, pleading with his eyes, trying not to cry. "Right?"

An uncomfortable look passed between all present. It lasted a little too long to be of comfort.

Peter realized no one else was going to answer with a lie, so he did the best he could. "We all hope he's okay."

"Um, actually…"

The sound of all eyes shifting simultaneously toward Callum was an almost audible *click*.

Cal, don't, Peter thought.

Callum, however, continued, almost incapable of reading the room. "The first seventy-two hours after a person disappears are critical. After that, it's an unspoken truth the police assume they're looking for a corpse." He stopped. Caught their glances at last. "But uh… Steven Stayner!"

Everyone stared.

Jess squinted. "Did you just pop an aneurysm, Droopy?"

"Steven Stayner was a kid from California that went missing in 1972." Callum looked at them, oblivious of why they were confused. "He was held captive by his kidnapper for eight years. The police thought he was dead. Then, he and another kid escaped alive, and they sent the kidnapper to jail."

"Oh…" Jess nodded with relief.

"Thanks, Cal." Bobby gave him an earnest smile.

"You're welcome. Though…uh…Steven Stayner died in '89 in a motorcycle accident."

Horrified stares all around.

"But he survived the kidnapping!"

Barry pushed past him with the cooler. "Let's go."

Jess approached Bobby and put a hand on his shoulder. "He's not dead until we know he's dead. For now, he's like that cat in the box, you know the one? Let's keep hoping he's alive when we open the box."

Bobby nodded, a weak smile on his lips.

Little by little, passing things to each other through the hole in the floor, they brought everything out of the house. Every single item that made Vigilante Headquarters their special place was now piled up in neat bundles in the overgrown grass of the Vanek House.

Nadine was standing lookout outside, while the others did a last sweep of the house. Her head swiveled on her neck from one side to the other, dreading someone might show up out of nowhere and see what they were doing. "C'mon, c'mon, c'mon, hurry."

The first to emerge from the crawlspace was Leroy, crawling with one hand, holding a comic against his chest. He stood up and wiped the dirt off his knees. He smiled and held the comic up. "Left a Batman comic on the toilet. Would've been kind of a fuck-up to leave it there!"

He was soon followed by Royce. Then out came Jess, Callum, Sylvia, Ray, and Barry.

She surveyed the group, then asked, "Where's Peter?"

"He remembered there were two bags of chips in one of the kitchen cabinets," Barry said. "He'll be right out."

"Can we pick all of this shit up?" Nadine was beginning to panic. "Please, we need to get it out of here, fast!"

The rest of the team scrambled to take some of the stuff off the grass when Peter crawled out from under the house, holding two bags of chips in one hand.

"Oh, thank god!"

He stood up and gave her a dorky smile. "Ready."

As Nadine was about to smile back with relief, a figure came around from behind the house. The shock made it appear as if a shadow on the wall had extended a claw toward Peter and pulled him toward it. The cracking sound of a slap startled her—had *she* been slapped? No—Martha Lange was holding Peter steadfast with one hand. She slapped him again.

"Holy shit!" Leroy was the first of the others to notice.

"Stop!" Nadine shouted.

"Shut up!" the woman said, pointing a finger at her.

Peter stared at his mother, paralyzed with terror. Martha returned her gaze to Peter, eyes boiling with rage. "How could you? How many times have I told you never to go into that house? You will atone before God! You disobedient, rebellious son! Do you know what you've done?"

She slapped him again.

"Stop that!" Barry stepped forward, fists clenched.

The woman turned a rabid stare at him, and he froze in place. They all did.

When you were a child, no matter how much disregard you felt about adults in general, there was always this barrier when it came to your friends' parents. Regardless of how horrible, they were owed at least some level of reverence. You didn't confront your friends' parents. That was, unless your name was Jessica Georgina Cunningham.

"Let him go, you old dried-up cunt!" She scowled. "I'll be fucked if I let you slap my friend in front of me!"

"How dare you?" Martha Lange hissed.

"Easy. I'm not scared of you."

The Lange woman, still clutching Peter by his shirt, glared at her, but then gave her a wicked smirk. "I don't need you to fear me. Chuck and Madelyn Cunningham already fear me enough, and you'll one day learn to fear me, Jessica Cunningham, because God is on my side."

A shocked expression took over Jess's face. Her eyes opened wide, her mouth gasped, and choking noises issued from her throat as her hands flew up to her neck, as if she had a lump of food stuck in her gullet.

"No!" Nadine shouted. "What are you doing?"

"What the fuck?" Royce shouted, running to Jess's side, clumsily trying to find some way to help her. "What the fuck? What the fuck?"

"Mother, stop!" Peter shouted. "Don't do this!"

"They have to learn. They have to learn to fear God."

"Stop, Mrs. Lange!" Nadine pleaded as Jess's face turned red. "You're killing her!"

"Mother, I'll go with you! I'll do anything you want. I'll take my punishment. Just please don't hurt my friends!"

Martha turned a snarling upper lip toward Peter.

"Anything you want, Mother!"

She responded with a huff.

Jess gasped and fell to her knees. Her friends formed a protective circle around her.

The terrifying woman turned her scowl now to the entire group and pointed a finger at them. "I curse you all." Her voice, a vicious sissle, snakelike and poisonous. "You have corrupted my son with the filth of the world. You have made him wish for a life he cannot have. You have pulled this irresponsible, weak boy away from the Lord's plan. You will all experience loss at the hands of the Lord. One day, I will come for you, and you'll feel my revenge. That is my curse on you."

She turned her gaze to her son, and, as if to spite them, slapped him again, and left, pulling Peter along with her, leaving them all standing there in fear.

Chapter Fourteen

Rules

2022

It hadn't been a long distance from Cunningham's to Callum Baker's house, and with the confusion caused by the blackout, no one in the neighborhood had noticed John Hitch picking the lock and letting himself in. People in small towns with low crime rates didn't often have complex locks on their front doors, so it wasn't shocking that Baker's door had been so easy to open. Baker's modest one-story home wasn't the type of place thieves would want to break into, anyway.

His office was a small, somewhat cramped square of

a room at the back of the house, with a single window looking out toward the Pargin River, just beyond the backyard. Though it was a stifling space containing nothing but a desk, a closet, and wall-to-wall bookcases, the view of the river, and the sound of running water, must make this quite a pleasant room to work, John thought.

This night, however, there was a sinister blue moon peering down through the window. Before inserting himself into the Lighthouse Rock security staff, John Hitch had worked for a stint as a TV technician; he mused if, while calibrating the picture settings on a screen, you were to bring the brightness and contrast to zero, and increased the blue balance to the highest setting, it would be exactly what it looked like outside: a completely dark world, with only the slightest blue hues in place of highlights. A mockery of light that made things darker instead.

He stood in front of Baker's desk, browsing through his perfectly organized files and the books on the desk under the light of a gas lantern he'd set on the varnished wood surface. He had to hand it to the young librarian—young being a relative term, in this case—he *had* compiled insane amounts of information about White Harbor, its origins, and the basic logic behind what the locals called Blight Harbor.

Baker knew a lot, but John knew more. John knew *what* the power beneath the town really was. While Callum Baker would pore over the piles of documents on his desk, hoping to uncover a *rational* explanation, the entity beneath the town was not something rational. Little by little, however, John realized the librarian was not as scientific as he'd assumed. Some of his hypotheses showed he was open to non-scientific explanations, even if he tried to filter them through the lens of science. Though Baker's accuracy wasn't spot on, he might have accidentally uncovered something useful about the rules of the First Night; something John might have missed.

As he sifted through the documents, one soon caught his eye. He paused. Re-read the title. The reason it caught his attention was not that it contained new information, but because it was a copy of a document he hadn't seen in years. The document was so rare it surprised him to find it in the cramped office of a nobody librarian from a small town.

"Zephaniah Emmit's letter," he mumbled, his eyebrows arching up in surprise. "Well, I'll be damned."

John had read this letter so many times before, he could almost recite it by heart, but he couldn't waste time on old memories. He did, however, feel a chill climb up his back. This, he thought, was how it had all started. The first party of settlers coming to what would become White Harbor, trapped in a cave, where 109 would starve or freeze, victims of a cruel blizzard. Five more would disappear in the depths of the cave.

He was mentioned in that letter, John thought, back when his name wasn't John Hitch, but John Ellis. Long-Lived John Ellis. How prophetic that moniker had turned out to be.

Callum Baker had even added a note about him in his notebook.

"By the time the storm subsided," the note read, "only thirty-two settlers remained, weak, scared, and nearly witless with grief and loss. No child was left alive and, of the elderly who came with the party—either by the stubbornness of their families or their own—only one remained. A man named John Ellis—who was mentioned in Emmit's letter. One account described Ellis as 'an old, husky pig rancher, with callused hands, a muscled body wrapped in a thick layer of fat, and skin that looked like old tree bark; a man likely to outlive them all and give God a run for his money.'"

John had to chuckle at that. He felt flattered by the description of the man he once was. Long-Lived John. Back when the nickname had been simply ironic, not a curse he had to endure. It made him sound almost mythical. The way things were looking, he *might* just give God a run for his money, indeed.

The notes appeared to be unfinished. There was a hasty scribble on a post-it note—a reminder, not as descriptive as the rest: "Long-Lived John Ellis. Important player in later events. Compile notes on Ellis in one place."

Interesting, Mr. Baker, John thought. *I wish I had more time to read through those notes, but there are more pressing matters right now.*

He spared one final thought, though, to the memory

of the cave. Of the stones piled up as a cairn in the woods over the mass grave where those 104 were buried. Stones *he* himself had helped set. Stones which would be surrounded by those horrid death-flowers that reflected the moonlight. The blue moonbuds.

As people are wont to do, the memories of the deaths in the cave quickly faded. The tragic tale of the Cave of the Dead was later reborn as a dark legend to scare children and adults alike, speaking of an evil that lived in the land. People in the late 1800s spoke of ghosts, spirits, and wights wandering the woods; the souls of those that had been buried too late to be allowed into Heaven and had remained earthbound, never to know rest. It was because of these tales that some had taken to calling that dark place in the woods "Blight Harbor", an area not to be visited, as it would curse those who dared venture into it.

It was because people never visited that spot that John Ellis—blackmailed by Reverend Douglas Burgess—had chosen it for the priest to rape and murder Walter Parham. What neither of them had expected was that the forces that lived in Blight Harbor would take over the boy and help him kill the evil priest. This, instead of aiding him, however, had gotten the boy hanged, and the Parham family cursed. John had been cursed as well that day. He had pleaded for God to let him die for what he'd done, and yet, he was still here.

John Ellis, Rickward Curling, Jenelle Curling, Osmin

Curling, Ben Curling, John Hitch.

Different body, same punishment.

I'm getting sidetracked, he thought, shaking off the memories, and shuffled around papers and notes, looking for something of use. *C'mon, Baker, don't let me down. I know you must have something here.*

He picked up another notebook and browsed through it. On one page, there was a pink post-it note, almost a throwaway scribble, that didn't fit the topic of the previous pages:

No reports of weird events in Lumenwood.
The Pines nearby. Might mean something?
Worth a look?

Lumenwood. The trailer park, he thought. *The only record I found of a teenage pregnancy in town at this time is in Lumenwood. The Pines are nearby. Yes, Baker. Definitely worth a look.*

He continued browsing through the notebook until he saw a handwritten note with a yellow post-it glued to it:

Is Jess part of the cult?

John removed the post-it and read what was on that page. According to Baker's musings, there were some vague hints that pointed at Chuck and Maddie Cunningham being in the Circle. John knew for sure they were. However, another post-it at the bottom of the page shone light into something he hadn't considered:

> *Jonah Cunningham. Dead.*
> *Gossip: Argument w/Martha Lange. Wanted out.*
> *Beef between Mother and the Cunninghams (????)*

Martha Lange was one of the most spiteful people John had ever known, back in his time as Ben Curling. There were other options for the third sacrifice from within the Circle, but this was his safest bet. Parham needed to assist the victim in performing the sacrifice. He needed to become tangible in order to do this.

Maybe, he thought. *Maybe.*

As fast as he could, John rearranged the papers, trying to leave them as he had found them. He stood up and pushed the chair in, placing it in the same position it had been in before.

Just as he was about to leave, he regarded the small closet built into one of the walls; the two doors were the only place in the room not covered in bookcases. He had an idea. He opened the doors and shone his lantern inside. He found shirts and jackets hanging, shoes at the bottom. Based on a thin layer of dust on everything in the closet, he could tell these weren't clothes Baker wore often—otherwise, they would've been in his bedroom—so it was unlikely he opened this closet very often. He pushed the hanging clothes, half to the left, half to the right, same with the shoes. He pulled a stick of red chalk from his pocket and drew a figure on the wall, something that looked like a combination of Celtic runes and strange glyphs. Once done, he left the clothes parted, closed the doors, and turned to leave.

He had to go to Chuck and Maddie Cunningham's house before it was too late.

He would arrive at their home mere minutes after it was.

The group gathered around the bar, now illuminated by soft, warm light from the gas lanterns Jess had brought from the cellar. Royce and Barry were the only ones not present; they had gone outside to try to recharge the car batteries using the crank-operated charger.

Peter sat with Sylvia and Callum. He fidgeted with his hands under the table, questioning his sanity; the thought of his mother appearing in the darkness with those empty eye sockets still lingering in his mind. There was no way in the world that could've been real.

"Do you think it will work?" he asked, nodding toward the door, attempting to break the silence and stop himself from thinking about the apparition. "Seems like a big assumption to—"

"It'll work," Callum said, sounding more secure than anyone had any right to be in these circumstances. "I think Jess has the right idea."

"I don't know. Seems like a stretch."

"Think of what Hitch said," Callum said, turning to him with a smile. "'There are rules to this', but he also said he didn't make up those rules. Then who made them up? How do people know the rules? Did your mom teach you any of those rules?"

Peter looked up toward the ceiling, where the lantern made the shadows of their heads stretch and split into lighter versions of themselves. "There were the rituals, which I never got to learn, but I remember they were very, 'if you do this, then this will happen, but if you don't do this, then this other thing will happen.' It was vague, but oddly specific at the same time." He turned his head to Callum, a confused grimace on his face. "I'm talking nonsense, aren't I?"

"You actually aren't," Sylvia said, sounding calmer than anyone had any right to be in these circumstances. She had been drinking wine, non-stop, and other than a hint of redness in her cheeks, she seemed almost completely unaffected by the alcohol. She waved a glass of wine in the air as she spoke, the red liquid balancing and shifting from one side to the other. "Think of it this way: in some places, the superstition is you have to toss salt over your shoulder to ward off evil, right? Well, there are other versions of the superstition that *specify* it has to be over the left shoulder, because that's the shoulder the Devil stands on to give you bad advice." She put on this spooky but silly expression as she said this, and moved her fingers, creating a shadow spider on the wall.

Perhaps, Peter thought, *she actually* was *drunk*.

"Now, for the romans, the very act of spilling salt was unthinkable, terrible fortune because of how expensive salt was. So, you tell me, which rules are right?"

Peter gave her an amused side eye as she swigged a drink of wine. "I think I get it," he said. "So, assuming we're saying for a fact what's happening tonight is one of those things we"—he did air quotes—"'leave in Blight Harbor', and assuming this means Blight Harbor is real—which I don't think I'm mentally prepared to do just yet. You guys are saying there are rules to how Blight Harbor works, but those rules were made up by people, then passed down to other people, who added stuff to them, and that creates loopholes someone can exploit."

Sylvia turned to Callum. "See?" she said with a smile. "I told you he wasn't dumb, despite the dumb books he writes."

Peter stared at her, taken aback.

Callum cleared his throat. "Um… Syl?"

"Oh, I'm sorry," she said. She put a hand on his arm,

trying her best to appear supportive, but coming off as conde-scending. "They're not dumb. They're fun. They're the super-hero movies of horror books."

"Thank you," Peter said in a flat voice.

"You're welcome!" She gave him her sincerest smile, raising her glass toward him, brought it to her lips and had a sip. She swallowed with a gulp.

"Back on topic," Peter said. "Doesn't that mean, then, that we can just make up our own rules about how this works and do whatever the hell we want, and nothing matters?"

"Not really," Callum said. "There would be constants that can't be changed—those are the consistent things in all versions of the rules."

"You have to use salt, not paprika," Sylvia added.

"Exactly, but there are the things that aren't covered. Whatever ritual John Hitch believed he was following, or try-ing to avert, was predictable enough for him to know he'd failed by not killing us before the blue moon came out, and that a blackout would happen soon after. Which"—he mo-tioned toward the dark surroundings—"it did. That's the in-variable part of it. Maybe whoever made up the idea of a full blackout in White Harbor didn't know one day there would be hand-cranked car battery chargers. At least, that's what Jess is betting on. All we know is something weird is happening in a town where weird things happen a lot, so we should be open-minded enough to make guesses on what this whole thing is, how it works…and how to subvert it in case it continues."

"If John Hitch is doing that," Sylvia said. "Who the hell says we can't do the same?"

"The difference is we don't know any of the rules," Peter said. "Hitch does."

Callum's face lit up with a big smile. "Maybe we do. That's why it would be good for you to come over to my place tomorrow."

"We really are having a conversation this casually after someone just tried to kill us, huh?" Peter said, giving a disbelieving chuckle.

"Welcome to White Harbor," Sylvia said with a shrug, pouring more wine into her cup. The bottle emptied. She shook it to get the last drops out of it.

An awkward silence followed.

"You guys don't really believe any of that, do you?" Peter finally said, turning to one, then the other. His expression begging for a return to logic and reality. "I mean…you don't really believe there's a god in White Harbor or some supernatural blackout going on." He noticed a knowing glance being exchanged between his two friends. "I know it's weird, and that moon is a bizarre natural phenomenon, but I think the key word here is 'natural'… Right?"

His friends shared another complicit glance.

"Peter," Sylvia said.

He knew Sylvia had a unique talent to be dismissive and nonchalant about pretty much any topic, like she was above it all, so it unnerved him whenever her expression and tone became serious and assertive.

"You *do* remember what happened inside the Vanek House, right? What we all saw?"

Peter opened his mouth to speak, then bit his lip and shook his head. "I don't know what I saw. I was too scared, and things were too confusing. Then the whole thing with me spending two weeks in my house's crawlspace happened, and it all became a jumble."

Sylvia raised an eyebrow. "Hmm."

"Peter?" Callum said. "I will give a disclaimer here. I don't believe any of the things we consider supernatural about the town are *really* supernatural. I just consider them unexplained. Science—and of course, *I*—might one day have an explanation for them. Let's forget for a minute what happened at the Vanek House. Let's say what happened there was isolated to that one location, like that house was some interdimensional anomaly or something. Let's look somewhere else, shall we? I suppose you know about the Rockwells?"

Peter turned his head toward him so fast it almost came off his neck.

"You have, I see. You have every right to think this is a coincidence, but Pam Rockwell, something like a year ago, went to visit a friend in Clarendon, and well... Disclaimer:

Ray decided not to tell you this, because he didn't want to worry you, but your dear mom wandered out of her room, and Pam—"

"No, no, no, no," Peter said, waving a hand to silence him. "You're not doing this."

"Peter," Sylvia said. Serious. Assertive. Unnerving. "Listen."

"According to Ray, Pam crashed into her by accident, hard enough to knock your mom to the floor, which, as you might guess, didn't go down well with her."

"Wait." Peter had an immediate, strong reaction. "My mother was injured last year, and Ray didn't tell me?"

Callum exchanged a quick glance with Sylvia, then eyed Peter with confusion. "Not the takeaway I meant for you to have at this point," he said in an appeasing tone, "but no, your mother wasn't injured. Ray would've definitely told you if she had. Your mom was fine."

Peter, seeing the expression on both his friends, realized he might have overreacted. "I'm sorry. Go on."

"Long story short, Pam helped Ray bring her back up to her feet and tried to apologize. Your mother wasn't having it. She mistook Pam for Stacy Rockwell, her mom, and there seemed to be some bad blood between them. She started shouting at her, blurting out all sorts of curses."

"Oh, shit," Peter said, his mind connecting to what Sam Becker Sr. had told him about the family that used to own the shoe store. "Oh, no."

"A few months later," Callum said, "Collin Rockwell's lung cancer got worse. Short time later: dead. A few months after that, colon cancer came for Stacy Rockwell. It was extremely aggressive. Dead. Pam lost control of her car near the northern tunnel and crashed into Skarsgard's Teeth—a rock spike went through her windshield and through her face. Dead. Finally, Stan Rockwell, who *allegedly* fell asleep behind the wheel of his SUV and drove his family into a truck. All dead. An entire bloodline wiped off the face of the Earth because Pam bumped into your mom in a hospital hallway."

Peter gulped, looked away, like he wanted to run away from the conversation. He glanced under the table. Would it be okay to hide there until everyone went home?

Callum's voice called his attention back. "Remember I told you I knew of another family that belonged to the Circle? I wasn't counting the Rockwells because it seems Stacy and Collin quit the Circle before Pam was even brought into it. That was the reason your mother hated them. So, between that and the whole family being dead, they're technically not members anymore."

"Nah." Peter shook his head. "Nuh-uh. That's crazy. It's just a gigantic coincidence. Series of unfortunate events. Some Lemony Snicket shit. That doesn't prove anything supernatural."

"I wish my phone was working so I could show you."

"Show me what?"

"I think it's better if you see it for yourself. So, tomorrow, when you come to my place, I'll show you the video." He stopped, looked around, gave him a dorky smirk. "That is, if this isn't the end of the world, and the power and Wi-Fi come back."

Peter stared back at him, eyes wide with apprehension.

"Don't overthink it tonight," Callum said with a dismissive flick of the wrist. "Look. Can all of this be disproved as a series of coincidences? Yes. But put that together with everything we've *seen* and *known* while living in this town. Does the existence of Blight Harbor and a supernatural blackout sound like such a stretch?"

Before he could answer, the sound of a car engine turning and someone revving the pedal blared into the bar. Royce's voice cheered from outside. A minute later, a gas lantern peeked through the door. Royce was holding it as he approached the group.

"Guys!" he said, brimming with excitement. "We got Peter's car started! We're giving it a few minutes with Barry on the pedal to fully charge. He thinks if we crank the charger a bit more, we can get his car started, too."

"That's great news, man!" Bobby said, sitting next to Angie, holding his jacket over her shoulders.

"Well, I'll be fucked!" Jess said, from where she was sitting with Nadine. "It worked!"

Jess and Nadine have been talking under their breath for a while, Peter thought in a flash. *What's with all the whispering?*

"I swear it was just a shot in the dark. How long do you think Barry's car will take?" Jess asked.

Royce looked up, did some quick mental estimates. "I think we can have the charger at full capacity again in like fifteen minutes. Then, maybe like five or ten to charge his battery."

"Thanks, hun!" Jess said with a big grin. "That's such a relief!"

The spot where Chuck Cunningham's car had come to a stop was a small industrial area adjacent to Seaside Park. The surrounding warehouses and businesses were all closed. No one was there to light a fire or start up a fuel lantern. In the distance, he could see windows with flickering lights from candles, fireplaces, or perhaps gas lamps, but his immediate surroundings were completely covered in darkness. To his left lay a marshy, sparsely wooded area that gave him the creeps. Beyond the trees and the marsh, the land broke into the gravelly riverbank where they had pulled out the corpses of Mikayla and Laurie Parham thirty years back.

It wasn't fear that prevented him from leaving his car.

It was the sheer grief, the insurmountable pain of knowing his dear Maddie had probably suffered a death not even the worst of humans deserved, much less such a wonderful woman.

Chuck sat hunched over, his arms resting on the wheel and his head buried in the space they formed. In this pervasive dark, tears fell from his eyes onto his thighs, unseen, but with the slightest sound as they hit the denim of his jeans with a soft *dap!* Lamentable, keening sobs and whimpers left his lips, which produced a bassy reverb in the closed space. The sound made him feel as if he were trapped inside a submarine beneath the ocean.

"Coward," he whispered. "You damn coward. You left her to die." He raised a fist from the wheel and slammed it into his thigh, wincing at the pain, then punched his thigh once more. He needed to punish himself for failing his family again.

"You *are* a coward, Charles," a woman's voice said from his right.

With a loud gasp, he raised his head and peered in that direction. He couldn't see much, save for a silhouette cast against the dim blue moonlight coming in through the passenger window. The person sitting there had a pale complexion that contrasted with the darkness, but her eyes were deep voids in her slightly pale face, which, upon closer inspection, shifted and moved, as if composed of living, writhing mass.

"You're fleeing from your responsibilities again," the

woman said, and he knew right away this was Martha Lange, or some abominable manifestation of her. "Wasn't losing your son enough?"

He gathered himself enough to respond in a disgusted tone. "Keep killing your own followers and soon you'll be completely alone, Martha. Wasn't losing *your* son enough?"

"You will address me as Mother, Charles. It's my title. You owe me respect."

"Anyone who needs to remind others to respect them doesn't deserve respect." The bile in his voice soaked every word.

"Look at you, playing brave," she said, and he thought he saw a repulsive grin form in that writhing mass of a face. "I remember you on your knees, pleading for me to allow you to abandon your God and condemn your family."

"I remember you in cuffs, raving like a lunatic," he said with a quavering upper lip, "foaming at the mouth like a rabid bitch, as the police took your son away. It was my girl that saved him from you. He's only alive because she found him. You should thank her."

"And you should thank me for not allowing you to abandon the Circle."

"Thank you?" Chuck's face was obscured, but the faint crease between his eyebrows made his bewilderment plain to see. "You killed my boy!"

"A small price to pay for your eternal soul."

"You killed my wife."

"I'll kill your daughter," she said plainly, and for a moment he thought he saw the faint blue light from the window pass through her, as if her body had become transparent, but the shadowy line that formed a smile on her face widened and became more visible. "Not you, though. You will stay behind to grieve them all. After the Lord remakes the world, I will make sure you linger here to mourn them."

"If you come close to Jess, I'll kill your son. I don't care about your fucking ritual or your ridiculous god. If you come close to my daughter. I will kill Peter."

That shadowy line was still there: a big smile.

"If you think that will stop God's design, do it," she said. "God promised he'd bring my son back to me from the wasteland of debauchery and sin this world has become. And you, Chuck Cunningham, a coward, think you can stop God from fulfilling His promise to me?" She now laughed, but it was more like a brisk cackle. "I would like to see you try, but you're not relevant enough."

Convinced she could see him, even in this darkness, he returned a scowl that transformed into a malicious smile. "You sound so lucid tonight, Martha," he said, highlighting just how much he refused to call her Mother. "God was lucky tonight wasn't one of those times in which you think the hospital reception is the restroom and shit yourself on the floor."

(*"That Lange woman is nothing if not spiteful."*)

"I will make you pay for those words," she said. "You will watch your daughter die screaming, Charles. You will want to die, but I won't let you. I will never let you."

"Fuck you," he said, putting on a brave face, though his heart shrank in fear.

Martha's shape vanished.

A second later, something hit the driver's side window with a *thump*. He almost jumped out of his skin. He noticed the light from a gas lantern being raised up to the window by someone's hand. The other hand pointed a gun at him. The barrel drew two circles in the air, signaling him to roll the window down.

Chuck obeyed. The face of a man he didn't recognize peered inside. The man was young and had big buggy eyes. He was wearing a jacket over a security guard's uniform.

"I need you to pop open the hood," the man said.

Chuck moved his lips to say something, but the man spoke quicker than he could.

"Now, Mr. Cunningham," he said, "or I'll shoot you with your wife's gun."

Chuck gasped. He recognized the gun, and the thought of what must have already happened in his marital bedroom made him choke. Still, he stretched his hand toward the small lever near the pedals and pulled it. The car's hood jumped up with a metallic *tunk!*

"Stay in the car. Don't move."

The man strode toward the front of the car, engaged the hood's lock, and raised it. Chuck heard the man doing something under the hood, then heard him say, "Start the car."

Chuck thought the man was insane. This was the First Night. All electrical instruments and batteries had been killed and would stay dead until the ritual was completed.

"Mr. Cunningham. Start the car. Now."

Expecting nothing to come from it, Chuck reached a clumsy hand toward the key and turned it. The engine struggled for two seconds, then, to his shock, it turned over. The headlights turned on. His car was alive—perhaps the only car in town currently working, he thought—the notion crossed his mind to put it in Drive, hit the accelerator, and run over the man with the gun

(*My wife's gun*)

but he didn't. He was curious. How did this stranger have that gun? How had he gotten the battery working?

The sound of the hood dropping loudly made him jump, and he was now following the man with his gaze as he made his way to the passenger's side. The light from the lantern making him look like some ghostly apparition in a scary movie. The man opened the door, dropped onto the seat where the shape of Martha Lange had been just a moment ago. The gun he'd put on the side of his wife's nightstand was now pointed at him.

"How did you—"

The man looked down at the gun, then at him. "Found it on your bedroom floor. Two shots had been fired. Your wife was already gone."

Chuck felt his heart twist in his chest.

"If it makes any difference, the fact this was fired implies she fought Freddie Parham before finally succumbing."

Chuck sighed. He felt the onset of tears on his face.

"I have no sympathy for you or your family, Mr. Cunningham," the man said. "You joined that profane group a long time ago, with promises of a long life, health, and prosperity, not caring that *this* was waiting at the end. You don't get bonus points for trying and failing to back out."

Chuck's face filled with shame and regret. This man wasn't wrong. They had been selfish, and it had cost them their son, Jonah, and now his wife. Chuck turned his gaze toward the man. "Who are you?"

"John Hitch."

"No." Chuck shook his head. "Who *are* you?"

Hitch reached into the neck of his shirt and pulled out a chain from which hung a symbol he recognized immediately. It was steel and looked like an upside-down letter "A" encompassing a half-circle.

Chuck nodded in recognition. "Order of the Rising Sun," Chuck said. "I always thought that was a lame, pretentious name." He glanced at the man with the gun. "No offense."

277

"Drive," Hitch said.

"Where are we going?"

"Lumenwood. We're going to put a stop to this whole thing." He gave Chuck a serious stare. "Your wife tried to stop Freddie Parham. He killed her. I wasn't there on time. She had the right idea, though. If you want to avenge her, and maybe save your daughter, you'll drive me to Lumenwood as fast as possible."

"Why can't you just go by yourself? Take the car."

"I need Freddie to see *you*," the security guard said. "And not me."

Peter and Barry's cars were parked in front of the bar; their engines already running. They were all standing outside the entrance to Cunningham's, and all around, the town looked dead, especially because Cunningham's was on King Street, which was mostly populated by restaurants and stores; all closed at this hour. No lights could be seen in the surroundings, other than the lanterns they were holding. Barry was leaning back against his car, with Royce standing beside him. Nadine, Bobby, and Angie were huddled together, close to Peter's Malibu, with Jess standing beside them; Peter was already in the driver's seat, his window rolled down. Callum and Sylvia stood near the entrance, while Ray was still inside, using some duct tape to attach one of the Coleman lanterns to his bike's handlebars.

Jess found it unsettling that nobody in town showed curiosity or initiative to investigate the power outage. No one outside trying to find a solution. No authorities. Why were the police not patrolling, at least on bicycles? Shouldn't they be checking if people were safe? At least one police bike circling around the stores and businesses to ensure there were no looters—but then again, even would-be looters were missing from the picture. It was like the whole town except for them had subconsciously decided they'd be better off staying inside and letting this whole thing play out the way it was going to play out.

That's in Blight Harbor, she thought with cynicism. *Leave it there.*

"Damn, it's cold!" Royce said, adjusting his jacket. "Ain't it supposed to be summer?"

"Thank God you've gotten fat on chicken wings and onion rings," Jess said, sounding testy. "You have some healthy padding to help you."

"Stop calling me fat."

"I've only called you fat once tonight. I called you chubby earlier."

"Oh, well then, my mistake," he answered with an eyeroll.

"Hey, guys?" Angela said from her wheelchair. "I would like to go on record that I think this is a horrible idea. There's a crazy man out there who was threatening to kill four of us a couple hours ago, and we're going out in a completely dark town, trusting he won't come back to finish the job? Isn't this the kind of thing they assign police protection for?"

Jess shook her head and placed a hand on Angie's shoulder. "I don't think he's that crazy, if I'm honest." She motioned toward the blue moon. "That thing up there? The weird power outage? He believes this is some preordained event. So, no, I'd bet a year's salary he won't be coming for us again tonight, because it doesn't fit what he believes in."

"You don't have a salary," Angie said. "You have profits from the bar."

"Be that as it may, you smartass. Soon as the power comes back, we'll have the police look for him. For now, if we stick to the plan we discussed, we should be fine: we go home, we lock ourselves in, we don't spend the night alone." She turned a knowing glance at Nadine. "All clear?"

Nadine nodded in acknowledgment. "I'll go in Peter's car. We'll drop Angie and Bobby at our place. I'll stay with Peter."

"Cal's place is just two blocks from here," Sylvia said, still not sounding tipsy, despite having downed an additional half a bottle of wine since emptying the last one. "We'll just walk there."

"Are you sure?" Barry asked, standing by the open driver's side door of his burgundy 2017 Honda Civic. "I can just drive you."

She shook her head. "We're with Jess on this. I don't think we're in any danger from Mr. Crazy Security Guard anymore. Plus, how often do you get to go for a walk under a blue moon in an empty town? It will be romantic."

"Sure, Morticia, that sounds like something normal people do," Royce said and turned to Barry. "Jess and I will catch a ride with you, man. She's staying at my place. Tracy will love having Aunt Jess over for breakfast tomorrow."

Peter shook his head with uncertainty. "Jess, I'm still concerned we're taking this too casually, regardless of your guys' reasoning. We're putting our lives at risk."

"We're not being casual," Nadine said in a dry rebuttal. "We're taking precautions. At home, we're in familiar territory, and we're making sure we won't be alone. If anything, it's all of us being together in the same place that might be a bad idea. We'd be making it too easy for him by putting all his targets in one place if he decides to change his mind."

Jess cleared her throat.

"Which, he won't," Nadine added.

"Sure," said Peter, dripping with sarcasm. "Let's split up. That works wonders in horror movies."

"It's not splitting up!" Jess said. "Not in a stupid way, at least. Nobody will be alone. We're separating into smaller groups, so he doesn't have access to everyone at once."

Peter gave a defeated shrug.

"Um," Ray said, rolling his bicycle out of the bar. "About that, Jess."

Barry watched Ray stroll out the door, a glowing lantern hanging from his bike's handlebar. He stopped at the center of the group.

Between the two cars' headlights and the lanterns they'd gotten from Jess, it looked like a cocoon of light grew out of this portion of the street, protecting it from the cold, blue darkness that had swallowed the town.

"Um, about that Jess," Ray said. "I'm sorry. I'm gonna have to decline Royce's offer and I'm heading home. Alone."

Jess's hands went to her hips. She looked worried. "Are you sure? C'mon, hun, I know you're stressed out after"— her eyes inadvertently flitted toward Barry and back—"every-thing, but you shouldn't be alone."

"For real, man," Royce said, settling into the backseat of Barry's car. "Don't be so damn stubborn. We have a really cool fold-out bed, top-notch, very comfortable."

He responded with that kind and beautiful smile he always gave everyone—*Except me*, Barry thought. *He'll nev-*

er smile at me like that again—though, behind the smile, he looked exhausted. "Thanks, Jess. That's okay. I've just had a rough day and I want to sleep in my own bed. My house is very secure. I promise I'll lock myself in. I have neighbors on every side. My neighborhood is gated, and we have a security guard at the main entrance."

She gave him a severe stare.

"Not *that* security guard," he added with that beaming smile of his that broke through the fatigue in his eyes. "Don't be silly."

Jess gave him a reluctant nod.

"Alright, people," Ray said, mounting his bike. "If we get electricity and internet back tomorrow, I expect a text from everyone on the group chat. You better check in. Stay safe."

He kicked down on the pedal, and the bike rolled forward.

Barry watched him go for a few seconds, fidgeting unwittingly with the fingers of his left hand, but before the bike reached the corner, he ran after him. "Ray!" Knowing glances passed between his friends; but he didn't notice them. "Wait!"

Ray stopped pedaling, and the bike came to a stop just a few feet from the corner, the brake releasing a squeak that sounded loud and angry in the pervading silence. He placed a foot on the sidewalk without dismounting. He didn't turn to look at him.

Panting, Barry caught up and stood two steps behind

him. "Let me drive you home."

No answer.

As he watched the shorter man's back, he noticed how his shoulders rose slowly, then fell, as he let out an irritated exhalation, warning him to stop.

"C'mon," he insisted. "Besides Peter, you live the furthest away. I just want to make sure you're safe."

"Barry," Ray said, in a hiss, pinching the bridge of his nose, eyes closed, brow furrowed, letting out another exhausted sigh. "A man just pointed a gun at my head." Slowly, he turned and directed an angry glare toward him. "I don't know about you, but, personally, I'd like to get home, shower, and go to bed. My head is killing me."

"I just want to make sure you're safe. Is that so bad?"

"That's not all you want." His words flew out of his lips, their tone as sharp as a blade.

"Okay, you're right." Barry nodded. Perhaps if he was direct and honest, it might sway him. "I also want to talk. Not long. Just however long it takes to drive from here to your place. All I want is to—"

"Let me stop you right there." Ray's glare turned cold. Final. "Just because you saved my life, it doesn't mean I owe you anything besides a thank you. Is that clear? I owe you nothing."

Barry pushed on, desperation permeating his speech. "We could've died today! If I had died, or you had died, *this* is how things would've ended up between us. Don't you think—"

"Maybe this is how they should end up."

It was a knife in his heart, which Ray now proceeded to twist.

"Go home. Maryann and your kids are waiting for you. They're probably scared because of the blackout. Go be a family man. Get it in your head once and for all: there's nothing you can say that I will *ever* want to hear. Got it?"

Barry's eyes overflowed with sorrow as he peered at his friend. He looked down, nodded in defeat—a word he'd increasingly come to associate with himself for years. "Okay."

Without another word, Ray got back on his bike and pedaled away. The light from his lamp grew faint in the night, leaving him standing alone on the sidewalk, enveloped by darkness.

A different light now approached from behind, growing closer and closer, until he could see the details of Jess's face.

"Already locked up the place," she said. "We're ready to go."

Feeling small and irrelevant, Barry nodded, doing his best to conceal the hurt in his face. He breathed in and out, in and out, forcing back the buildup of tears. When he met her gaze, he gave her a strained smile, but knew nothing eluded her shrewd eyes. He hated the sympathetic expression she was giving him, as if he was a wretch to be pitied.

"Barr, look—"

"Don't, Jess. This is embarrassing enough as it is."

"Why is it embarrassing?" Jess said, her face looking annoyed.

"This is not how I wanted you all to find out"—he hesitated—"you know. About me."

The look of sympathy in her eyes only deepened, making him shrink.

"You have nothing to be embarrassed about, hun. We're like your second family here. We love you. We *love* you. None of us care if you're what? Gay? Bi?"

His blush was so red it could be seen even in lamplight. He'd never actually said "the word" when referring to himself, and here came Jess Cunningham and her big mouth, saying it as if it wasn't the heaviest, most world-crushing syllable in the English language to him.

"Alright," she said, reading his shaken expression. "Gay all the way, it seems. So, what if this wasn't how you wanted us to find out? Who the fuck cares? We would've eventually found out, and no matter how, you would've had nothing to be embarrassed about."

His answer was a lackluster nod.

"I should be the one apologizing," she said, causing him to raise a puzzled look in her direction. "I should've known. After that night in the cellar, I should've known. Ray was also going through a big depression at the time."

He winced at this.

(*All I do is hurt people*)

"That's when it happened, right? I never put two and two together. I thought Ray's depression was him still missing his mom after she died. I didn't get involved. I'm the nosiest bitch in the universe, and when it mattered most, I didn't try to find out more. I wasn't there for you."

"You didn't have to."

"I did!" She clenched her fists, emphasizing her indignation. "Gerardo was one of my closest childhood friends, and I lost him to the Vanek House. I let myself abandon Peter for two weeks, starving under his house, and *we* lost him."

"We all did that," he said, looking this way and that, regret tinging his voice. "Not just you."

"Well, I couldn't save Leroy at the Vanek House, when I was the one that brought us there to save him. I've barely been there for Angie during her cancer because I've convinced myself I'm too busy, instead of delegating to Louis and dad. And, that night in the cellar, I almost lost you—with my dad's rifle, in my own bar—and I didn't do anything to help."

He thought of something to refute this; he hated making others carry the burden of his mistakes. "You twisted my arm into going to therapy, and that helped a lot... At least until Maryann found out, and decided it was a waste of money."

"Listen, here, big guy." Her voice was emotional, heartfelt. "I don't want to lose you because I fumbled the ball again. Take it from me. I hear all the shit people keep dumping in Blight Harbor every day. You have nothing to be embarrassed about."

"You don't understand." He averted his gaze, his voice ashamed and tired. "There are rules."

"What the fuck are you talking about?"

"Our generation? We didn't have it as good as this one. We had all these rules forced on us. In some cases, like mine, *beaten* into us. Men don't cry. You don't show emotion in front of others. You don't air your dirty laundry in public. You don't cheat on your wife"—he let out a hysterical chuckle—"even if she makes you feel worthless and won't let you leave." He paused. Took a deep breath. Let his gaze fall. "Men don't sleep with other men."

"That's a load of bullshit! We're in the 2020s. No one but the Bible Belt cares about how many dicks you can fit in your mouth."

"Jess!" He gave her a horrified look, once more turning bright red.

"Sorry." She gave him an apologetic smirk. "My tongue runs faster than my brain sometimes, you know that. What I mean is, no one cares if you're gay, and for those who do care, you just have to learn not to give a shit. Take it from this shameless dyke who fucked you twenty years ago"—she snorted and chuckled—"in hindsight, wasn't *that* a sad picture?"

Despite his glum expression, he couldn't help but crack a smile. "It was pretty bad," he said, nodding, but his smile faded. "Even if that part were that simple, Jess. It's not just about me, what about my w—"

"You don't have a wife, Barr." There was no hesitation in her voice—her statement was laser-focused and unflinching. "What you have is a collections agent. She gave you two beautiful children, but now she's demanding you repay her with your life and soul, plus interest. That's not a marriage. That's taking out a loan for a used car, spending extra on all the upgrades, only to find out it was a piece of junk you're gonna be paying off for years."

He couldn't think of a retort. He looked down at the sidewalk, at his shoes illuminated by Jess's lantern, at anything but her face. There was an old candy wrapper stuck to the concrete. There was a crack where a growing plant had gotten stomped over by countless feet. *There's a little black spot on the sun today,* he thought, his mind too preoccupied to even remember if that came from a book or a song.

"Give Ray time, hun. I know it hurts, but give him time. I don't know the specifics of why he's that pissed off—I bet it was more than just keeping him a secret—but that won't last forever. He's been your best friend for thirty years. You gave it a shot tonight. Let him process it. You'll at least get your old friend back. I'm sure of that. But even if he doesn't come back, get your shit together at home, Barr. Get outta there. Live your life. Find someone who *loves* you. God knows you deserve it after all the shit you've put up with."

Barry considered for a moment. Part of him wanted to do everything she was telling him to do, but the second he let one little reality in, all the other ones that followed piled up on top of that one, until a mountain stood between him and his freedom.

"Hey!" he heard Royce call from the backseat of his Civic. They turned their heads toward him. "We going or what?"

He turned a sad gaze toward Jess and said, "Let's go," in a tone that conveyed the topic was now closed. "I gotta get back home."

In his mind, Barry was convinced there was nothing to be gained from lingering in old memories of happier moments. They wouldn't change all that had happened.

All I do is hurt people.

Chapter Fifteen

Torch Song Trilogy – Part 2: "Linger"

1993

What he was seeing in his best friend's hand seemed almost blurred out by disbelief. To Barry's mind, it looked pixelated, censored. His brain couldn't handle or process what he was seeing.

"So?" Ray said with a beaming smile.

They were in Ray's bedroom waiting for his dad to call them for dinner. Barry was sitting in a desk chair; the smaller boy was on the floor holding this thing his brain couldn't process up for him to see.

"I'm..." Full stop. He'd forgotten all language.

"C'mon! Say something!" Ray let out a quick chuckle that showed he was relishing his stupefied expression. "I'll ask again. Do you, Barry Giffen, want to go with me and my dad to the 1994 FIFA World Cup next year?"

The pixelation faded away, that little portion of the world regaining definition, until Barry could see the papers in Ray's hand. He could see logos and dates he recognized all over, but still couldn't react.

"You're looking at a paid trip. Hotel, meals, transportation, tickets to four games of our choice—we have to sit down and pick them, I know you're an Italy guy and I'm more of a Brazil guy—and finally, here's my Willy Wonka moment..."

Sneaking a finger through the folded papers, he pushed a colorful ticket with a purple top and the number 94 in red and blue with a player kicking a ball.

"No way," Barry said under his breath.

"Yes way." The smaller kid grinned with pride. "No matter what teams make it, we have tickets to the final."

Barry let out a slow, tremulous breath. "Oh, my god."

"So?"

He gazed at him again, still in disbelief. "Did your family win the lottery or somethin'?"

"No." There it was again. That bright, beautiful smile that made Barry tingle all over. "My dad and I have been saving for this for a while. I convinced him to pay for one more person, since my siblings are lame, so they don't like soccer."

"I… I want to. Me and my dad wanted—"

"I know, Big Bear."

Barry remembered his mom, and his smile vanished. "I'd love to go…so much…but my momma—"

"Dad already talked to her. She said no at first, but I told him to say he'd be happy to take you off her hands for a few weeks."

He felt it now, Barry realized. That warmth in his chest rising to his face, making his cheeks redden. "Why would you do this for me?"

"Don't you know already?" Ray asked with a pining gaze.

"Yeah," he answered, shuffling his feet. "But, I'm not—"

"I know," the smaller boy interjected. "*I* am, but I'm guessing you already knew that. It's not that, not really… You're my best friend. You're one of the most important people in my life."

Important. That was a word Barry had never heard anyone use to refer to him. "You're my best friend, too. There's no one in my life more important than you."

Ray beamed in response. "So, is that a yes?"

"Yes!" Barry dropped to the floor and gave his best friend a tight bear hug. He had never felt happier in his life. "Yes!"

Once the embrace ended, their gazes locked, lingered; they smiled, neither saying anything.

Barry gasped, as if remembering something. "Oh!"

"What?"

"Uh, never mind…" He forced a smile, looked away.

"Big Bear. Tell me."

"Well…" He grabbed his backpack, which was on the floor under the chair he'd been sitting in. He pulled it toward him, but changed his mind and pushed it back.

Ray squinted with confusion.

He let out an embarrassed exhalation. "I brought you a present, too," he said in a low, bashful voice. "But, next to"—he shot a glance at the itinerary with the ticket—"*that*, I'm… It's lame. It's, uh… It's stupid. Forget it."

"Dude, I made up this whole 'friendiversary' thing as an excuse to have my mom make a special dinner. You didn't need to get me anything."

"But you—"

"I planned the World Cup trip long before I thought of the friendiversary." He motioned toward the backpack Barry was trying so hard to hide. "Show me. C'mon, man."

Barry still felt what he had in his backpack was laughable and poor. He pulled it closer, and from the way it dragged on the carpet, it looked like whatever he had there was heavy. He unzipped it, put his hand inside, and pulled out a round rock about nine inches in diameter. It had a porous, gray exterior, and a chunk of it was broken, like someone had taken a huge bite off it.

"Um." He glanced at his best friend and handed him the rock. "See? It's lame."

"No, it's not." Ray regarded the rock, looking unsure of what he was looking at. "I just…think you have like a whole idea behind it? Like a meaning?"

Barry nodded, still feeling quite embarrassed. Words weren't his strong suit, but he breathed in and did his best to explain. "Well, The Pines were always a safe place for me, a place my momma couldn't hurt me. But that day you found me there, I didn't feel safe. I thought my life wasn't gonna get better. I thought I just wanted it all to be over. Then you showed." He eyed him bashfully, then pointed at the rock. "That rock, I found it a while back at The Pines. There was just this bunch of rocks lyin' around in the grass, and that one caught the light a bit and I noticed the broken part. Put it up to that lamp over there." He pointed at the bedside lamp.

Ray moved the rock closer to the lamp and turned it, so the broken part faced the cone of light. The inside was dark gray, almost black, but there were tiny crystals inside, which reflected the light. They gleamed a bright silver blue. He gasped. "Whoa. That's beautiful." He took a moment to move the rock around in the light and watch the reflections shift on the crystals, then gazed at him. "I'm gonna say something that's gonna sound cringy."

"Sure."

"That blue? It matches the color of your eyes."

He flashed him that big smile of his, and Barry couldn't help but blush again.

"Oh, shut up," he said, chuckling. "Anyway... um... I wanted to give that to you, 'coz you gave me another safe place; and I don't have to be alone there to feel safe. I just thought it'd be, like, symbolic or something, if the rock I got from The Pines was here, where you are."

Ray stared at him in dumbfounded silence.

He got self-conscious, noticing the seconds ticking away without a word from his friend. Had he said something dumb? "I mean, I told you, it was lame. I'll take it back if you don't want it."

Without answering, Ray turned, opened the drawer on his bedside table, and pulled out a Sharpie. He put both hands forward, handing him both the rock and the Sharpie. "Write something on it and sign it."

"W-what?"

"Write something on it and sign it. It's the only thing missing to make it perfect."

"Man, I'm not good at...words. You know that."

"Write anything! Then sign it."

Barry took the rock and the Sharpie and sat there for a moment, thinking. His mind went to the most accessible words he could think of, and that was lyrics from the British bands he enjoyed listening to. He removed the cap with his teeth and scribbled, "You make me live," then signed his name under it. "Here."

Nervous, he handed his friend the rock, expecting him not to get it. Instead, Ray smiled, and with just the glimmer in his eyes, he knew he'd understood which song it came from.

Ray placed it on top of his bedside table, in a position where the lamplight would hit the crystals inside at just the right angle. "There," he said. "Now I can look at those pretty little crystals looking back at me every time I turn on the lamp." He turned that bright smile toward him. "I love it. Thank you."

2019

Barry's Honda was parked in Ray's driveway after a wonderful night out, watching a crappy movie they could both make fun of, and having pizza at Esposito's. During the drive home, Ray had noticed this strange atmosphere in the car, some weird, invisible electricity in the air, like seconds before raindrops come down from the sky.

"Thanks for everything," he said, sitting in the passenger's seat. "Great pizza and shitty movies make the best nights out. And damn, did *Dark Phoenix* suck. Bobby was right. No wonder Jennifer Lawrence used her producer powers to demand to be killed off in the first ten minutes. She was like, 'Bitches, screw you! I'm an Oscar winner. This movie sucks. I want out as soon as possible!'"

Barry let out a hearty laugh.

"I needed this," Ray said. "I've been gathering mold in my house for six months. I really appreciate you dragging me outta there. Losing my mom during the holidays fucked me up. I'm usually good with death, even people close to me—working with the elderly will do that to you—but my mom..." His gaze wandered toward the street. "It's like I lost this chunk of myself I don't even know how to get back."

"I miss your mom too," Barry said. "I miss her food. That smile she always put on when she saw me just wolfing down everything she cooked."

The memory of Hyun-Jung Chang's kind, heavenly face made Ray's eyes moisten. "Nothing got past that woman." He gave Barry a glance that highlighted this sentence, changed its meaning. "She knew you didn't get much love at home, and her food was her way of showing love. I think she knew about me before I knew. Never made me feel bad about it." He shook his head. "Nope." He wiped at his eyes with a clumsy index finger. "No crying. Shitty movie nights shouldn't end in tears. Screw that!"

Barry laughed again, only this time, Ray caught sight

of something he hadn't expected. His friend's eyes—those beautiful powder-blue eyes—were fixed on his, and he was giving him a dorky, captivated smile.

"Is there something on my face? Do I have breadstick sauce on my chin or something?"

"You're beautiful, you know?" Barry's voice had a whimsical quality to it.

Ray fretted for a second. He had no doubt his best friend was joking. He tried to laugh, but it came out choked and weird. "That's cruel, man. I've been single for so long, I might even fall for that cheesy little line."

"I'm serious."

There was an uncomfortable pause, during which Barry did not take his eyes off him.

Ray felt himself blush. "Uh... Thanks? How much did you drink?"

"No alcohol. Just root beer." His tone was assertive.

He averted his gaze and let out an audible gulp. "Big Bear, if I didn't know better, I'd think you were seriously flirting with me." Before he said or did something staggeringly stupid, Ray decided it best to call it a night. He reached for the door handle, ready to step out.

Barry blurted, "Wait... No, no, don't go yet." He turned awkward all of a sudden, as if he'd reached for the doorknob before he was ready for something. "I have a surprise for you."

Ray arched both eyebrows. "A surprise?"

"Hold on." Barry turned around and stretched between the seats, reaching a hand toward the back. He was so close, Ray got a whiff of his cologne—which Barry only wore sparsely to not let it become overpowering—the familiar scent lingered in the air, and it danced deliciously into his nostrils. When Barry came back to the front, he was holding a small, red cardboard box sealed tightly in a plastic bag. He handed it to Ray, who examined it with curiosity, then looked up at him.

"A fancy cardboard box wrapped in an airtight bag." He stared at him, eyebrows raised. "Why the double wrapping?"

"You'll see."

Ray tentatively scratched a corner of the plastic with a fingernail.

"The plastic doesn't matter. It's what's inside the box. C'mon." Barry made a hurrying motion with both hands he found comical.

"Alright, alright, Mr. Pushy," he said with an amused chuckle. The moment he tore the plastic away, he was struck by a sweet, intoxicating smell, which was all too familiar. The stare he gave Barry spoke volumes. "Barry. What is this?"

"Go ahead," Barry said with a big smile framed by his neatly groomed beard. "Open it."

He undid the rest of the plastic and opened the lid.

He gasped as he saw a neat stack of shortbread cookies, almost identical to the ones his mom used to make, down to the little strawberry jam dot in the center. He gasped, covered his mouth. His head shook from side to side in disbelief. With a breaking voice, he asked, "Where did you get these?"

"I made them."

This elicited a stupefied stare from him. "What? How?"

"I cook all meals at home. So, me baking a batch of cookies isn't so unusual. But those are the only shortbread cookies I made."

"Not how did you make them, literally. I mean, how did you make these specific cookies?"

"One day, you and your dad were running late doing some shopping for the restaurant, so when I got there, you weren't home yet. Your mom was making a batch of these. So, while we waited for you, she asked me to help, and..." He paused for a moment, probably knowing what he was going to say next would surprise Ray even more. "She wrote down the recipe and gave it to me. She said, 'Take this, so you can make them when I'm not here anymore.'"

Ray stared at him in utter shock. "Why would she even—" He started the question, then stopped.

(*Nothing got past that woman*)

Barry reached a hand toward the glove compartment, opened it, and pulled out a small, laminated notepad page, in handwriting Ray recognized at once as his mom's. "I already know it by heart, so you can keep that."

"Barry," Ray said, feeling out of breath. He examined the page—paper his mom's hand had written on—doing his best not to just flat out bawl his eyes out.

The big guy nodded toward the box. "Try them. Took me a lot of practice. I didn't want to make them for you until I got them just right. They're obviously not as good as hers, but they're pretty close."

He took one of the cookies and looked at it, almost scared to taste it. The first bite left him speechless as the sweet and buttery flavor danced all over his tongue, causing his eyes to well up even more. He swallowed, almost wishing he didn't have to let the taste leave his mouth, but it lingered there like a tender caress. "I don't even know what to—"

"You don't have to say or do anything."

Ray put his hand over Barry's, took it in his; fingers clasped together.

A long silence passed between them.

Ray gazed up at Barry. His bright blue eyes, his brown beard, his smile. Those old feelings he'd pushed down long ago—when he told himself what he'd seen in Barry was not really there—now bubbled to the surface. Could he have been this wrong for so many years about this?

He looked down at their hands again.

(*What the fuck am I doing?*)

His eyes wandered toward the box of cookies—their aroma still flooding the car. He felt the tiny hairs on the back of Barry's fingers under his thumb.

(*I can't do this*)

He glanced up again at Barry and was once more caught in those eyes that looked so—

(*Beautiful*)

He lunged forward and planted his lips on Barry's. Behind that kiss was the force of twenty-seven years of longing and shared experiences. Barry kissed him back, and without hesitation, put his big arms around him and squeezed. Ray clasped a handful of his thick brown hair in his hand—he'd always wanted to just run his fingers through it.

The kiss deepened. Nothing else mattered. Nothing could stop this.

"Wait, no! We can't do this!" he heard himself say, pushing Barry away, watching his chest heave, and immediately wanted to bang his head against the windshield for being such a goddamn idiot.

(*Shut up, you stupid moron! We've wanted this for years!*)

Barry restrained a sad twitch in his face that wrung his heart like a rag.

"Tonight was amazing, and the fact you did this…" He motioned toward the box of cookies on his lap. "I'm so lucky you're in my life." He squeezed his hand. "I know things with Maryann have been… Jesus, 'bad' doesn't even begin to

303

describe them, but you have your son to think about." He looked down at their clasped hands. "If *this* is really you, if *this* is something you want to pursue, there's a lot of stuff you need to work out, lots of stuff that needs to happen, before *this* can happen. That can take months, sometimes years, before you can… Well…you know."

Barry peered at him, then nodded. "I know. I know. You're right."

Trying to cling to everything he'd been taught, Ray said. "This isn't right. This can't happen."

Barry sighed, nodded again, gaze downcast. "I know."

2020

Barry stumbled backward up the stairs. His back collided with the wall at the top of the landing, causing two hanging picture frames to come crashing down. "I'm sorry," he uttered in a husky moan, as he felt Ray's teeth bite on his chin, soft but hungry. He could feel Ray's hand under his shirt, caressing the hairs on his chest.

He felt so awkward, so bumbling. He'd wanted this so bad for so long, and now here he was, tripping through each step, and they were only halfway up the stairs. He half-expected Ray to just throw his hands up and decide someone this clumsy couldn't possibly be good at—

"Bedroom, now," Ray growled through bared teeth, interrupting his thoughts. He sidestepped and climbed up one step, so his lips were again at the same height as Barry's.

I'm too tall and bulky, he thought, intent on finding every flaw he could in himself. *He'll think this is too awkward. Too—*

Ray kissed him, and he melted on the spot. He kissed him back. The very thought of stopping was unbearable. Ray's fingers tickled his skin as they curled around the hem of his shirt and pulled it up his torso. In a commanding tone, he said, "This needs to come off. Hurry."

He was more than happy to obey. He raised his arms and Ray pulled up his T-shirt. It got stuck around his head. They tugged and struggled a little, trying to pull the shirt off, and once it slipped over his head, a sense of overexposure washed over him.

Ray had seen him shirtless a million times since school—at P.E., at soccer practice, at pools, at the Pargin River. This wasn't new. It had been well over a year now since they'd started this relationship. The very same night he'd given Ray the box of cookies, despite initial reservations, they'd ended up making out on his couch, and it had only grown from there. Ray had seen him naked in pictures and video calls throughout this year, but the physical aspect of the relationship had never reached this boiling point. It was so different face-to-face and knowing what was about to happen at long last. He felt self-conscious about his (*Shapeless!*) thick torso, his (*Cumbersome!*) wide shoulders, his (*Fat!*) burly frame, and his (*Gross!*) body hair.

"God, I love that big hairy chest," Ray said in a throaty growl, entranced and breathless, contradicting his every self-deprecating thought.

He stared at him in amazement.

Ray's eyes took on this look of greedy desire as he ran his hands across his bare chest, as if he were appraising the texture and consistency of some rare, exotic textile. "You're so perfect."

His breath quickened. He shot Ray a lustful look. "More," he pleaded in a submissive moan. He propelled himself forward to continue devouring his lover's lips, and in turn, he took his face in his hands, working his beard between his fingers.

Ray walked backward, climbing the steps, fully in charge, pulling Barry by the head—his lips fused into his. He'd forgotten how strong Ray was. Every step they climbed seemed to be just an obstacle between them and the bed. He felt ungainly as he stumbled upstairs, trying to keep up.

"Left, left, left," Ray muttered against his lips, turning him toward the bedroom as they reached the second floor. Once there, he spun Barry around and pushed him onto the bed.

His full weight bounced just slightly on the mattress, and he crawled backward on his elbows, his graceless mass feeling like he was maneuvering a tank, until he reached the pillow. He didn't know what to do with his body, how to position his limbs, much less how he would even *do* all the things his instinct and his brain were telling him were about to happen, but he knew he wanted them. All of them.

Ray took off his shirt to reveal a slick body, toned and athletic, already glistening with sweat. Every contour of his physique looked to him like lines on a map he couldn't wait to explore. He looked so graceful compared to how *he* felt.

Still standing at the foot of the bed, Ray grabbed his pant legs and gave them a firm tug. Barry felt his jeans slide down just a bit down his hips. Ray gave another tug and looked straight at him with a raised eyebrow.

Realizing he was asking him to do something, Barry looked down at his pants and saw he was still wearing a belt. *Fuck! Idiot!* Feeling like he had sausages for fingers, he scrambled to undo his belt, unbuttoned his jeans, unzipped, and had barely pulled down his pants halfway to his buttocks, when Ray pulled on them hard, and they slid, slid, slid down his legs. In a matter of seconds, Barry was in his purple boxer briefs, feeling now more exposed and unattractive than ever.

That gorgeous man at the foot of the bed, however, gave him a voracious look, like he was seconds away from wolfing him down until nothing remained. He tossed the jeans aside and hurried in removing his own, revealing tight black trunks, then climbed onto the bed, and, crawling toward him, kissed his feet, and worked his way up every inch of his right leg, caressing it, worshipping it. The touch of Ray's hands and lips on his skin as he slowly came up his leg made him clutch at the bedsheets.

A flash of a thought passed through Barry's mind, though—that inner saboteur again—wondering why someone as gorgeous as the man now making his way up his leg would be this turned on by someone like him, someone so—

"You're so beautiful, Big Bear," Ray said, his exquisite brown eyes looking up at him with utmost craving, halfway up his thigh, both interrupting his self-critical thoughts, and answering his question at once.

Ray inhaled deeply as he passed between his thighs, and again as he passed the contour of his cock on his briefs, as if just the very smell of him was the epitome of aphrodisiacs. He continued traveling up his body, kissing his navel. Higher, kissing every inch of his skin, causing Barry to emit low, hoarse moans and grunts, until he reached his chest. Ray inhaled again, his face buried in his chest hair. He looked up again, and their rapturous gazes met.

He couldn't help himself anymore and wrapped his legs around Ray's waist. He could feel the way he moved between them. He closed his eyes, allowing himself to revel in the heat their bodies produced together, the way they thrust against each other. The contact was so pleasurable, so unique. His eyes shot open as he felt Ray's teeth biting—soft but firm—on one of his nipples, and he let out a louder cry than he would normally allow himself. Instead of being painful, the sensation had been like electricity tingling through his entire body. He felt self-conscious again, realizing the overwhelming pleasure had stolen his self-control. *Was I too loud?*

It dawned on him at last: it was going to happen. For the first time in his life, it was going to happen.

Five seconds later, he had Ray's lips on his again, and his growls and grunts as Ray pressed his body against him were muffled by the ferocity of their kiss. He felt him move his hips between his legs, and the rubbing sensation was maddening, literally like nothing he had ever experienced. He ran his hands down Ray's back, down every contour of every muscle in that back, his hands sliding over beads of sweat. Never in his life had he wanted anything more than he wanted Ray to make love to him. There was *need* in Barry's kisses, an almost desperate, primal need. He *needed* him to make love to him.

He felt Ray's fingers run down his torso, their touch sending tingling sensations all over his body.

Don't stop!

He felt Ray's fingers crawl down his stomach, then past his belly button.

Don't stop!

His pinky finger played at the edge of the elastic of his boxer briefs, teasing him.

Don't stop!

He needed it. His life depended on it. But the moment he felt Ray's fingers making their way into his underwear

(*Don't let me ever find out you've gone queer*)

his hand moved, with a mind of its own, and clutched Ray's wrist.

"Stop," he whispered, pulling Ray's hand out of his underwear. "Please." Barry's hand trembled. His fingers wanted nothing more than to release their grip on his hand and let him do anything he wanted.

Ray's eyes gazed into his. He could see a turbulent mix of emotions in that handsome face: confusion, frustration, empathy, annoyance, understanding, then back to confusion. "I don't understand," Ray said, trying to force a smile.

Barry gave him a sad smile and trailed the line of his chin with his big hand before tenderly pressing his lips to his. "I'm sorry. I can't do it."

"Why?" Ray asked, and from the way he then controlled his expression, he could see the question had come out with more disappointment than he had intended it to.

Barry gave him another kiss. It overflowed with tenderness, yet an undeniable sadness permeated it. "I want this. More than anything. But I can't... I can't go any further than this. Not yet."

Ray let out a long, controlled exhalation, rolled over to lie beside him, then gave him a tender look and said, "If you say you're not ready, then you're not ready. I just need to understand." As if to reassure him, he lovingly ran his hand through the hairs on his chest and Barry reached out and took it in his. "Where is this heading, Barry? We've been seeing each other for a year and two months now, and tonight is the furthest we've ever come. And you want to stop?"

A look of embarrassment appeared on his face. "I'm sorry."

"No, no, no, Big Bear," Ray said, reacting to his expression turning gloomy. He squeezed his hand. "I don't want you to feel guilty that you need to stop. We already have to deal with enough guilt in this whole situation to dump more onto it."

"Guilt is the right word," Barry said in a deflated voice. "I don't think I can get home and see Maryann's face if we cross that line."

"Doesn't that seem arbitrary?" Ray once more flinched as if the question had come out wrong and immediately redirected. "What I'm trying to say is, objectively, this thing we're doing, *this alone* is already cheating on your wife, don't you think?"

Barry lowered his gaze again.

"No, no, I'm sorry. This is coming out all wrong. Shit. I don't want to make this more difficult for you. I just want to understand what my future is with you, Big Bear. I'm crazy about you, but I don't think I can live my life in celibacy, jerking off alone after every groping session. You know what I mean?"

Barry saw the way Ray studied his expression. He still felt exposed, but this was a worse kind of exposure. Nothing to do with his body being naked but the weakness that lived within him.

"If you're asking me to wait, I'll wait. I just need to know there's something real I'm waiting for."

Barry thought about it for a moment. He nodded with just the smallest hint of resolve. "Give me time. You know how my brain works—all square, straight lines, parallels, right angles—if I do anything spontaneous, I'm afraid I'll just fuck everything up. I have all these mental checkpoints I impose on myself. I need time to get my ideas in order. I promise, there's something real, but can you give me some time?"

Ray nodded.

"In the meantime," Barry said, giving him a playful look. "I think there's something I *can* do, so you don't have to 'live in celibacy, jerking off alone.'"

Ray raised an eyebrow, giving him an intrigued grin.

Moments later, Ray lay on his back, a smile of contentment on his face. "Well, that was unexpected," he said. He was sweating and his underwear was a mess. He was looking up at the big, bearded, hairy-chested man sitting on top of him, who was currently wiping sweat off his forehead.

With a laugh, Barry ran his hands over Ray's damp skin and gazed at him with adoration. "Did that help, sir?" Ray returned a smile as he ran his hands up and down his man's legs. "Sure did. Can't wait to do that without this on." He gave a quick tug at the fabric of his Big Bear's purple briefs.

Barry chuckled and let himself fall beside him with a happy groan. "Oh, so you didn't like it? Should I not do it again?"

"I did *not* say that." He gave him a wicked smile. "The way you circle those hips. My god! Someone tell Shakira there's this big burly man in White Harbor, Oregon, that can give her a run for her money."

A big grin formed on Barry's sweaty face. He blushed bright red and let out a giggle of pure joy.

The brisk sound of his laughter made Ray's heart swell. "You sure you don't want me to return the favor?" he said, running a finger over the outline that bulged from under Barry's boxer briefs.

Barry took his hand with gentle fingers and brought it up to his lips. Kissed it. "Not yet. Soon. This was a bigger step for me than I thought I could take. Watching you enjoy it was all I needed." He looked at him with those clear blue eyes of his. "This *is* heading somewhere. You have my word." Barry rested his head on his chest. "I know I'm being selfish, asking you to wait."

Ray ran a tender hand through his hair. "We're in this together, alright? I get it. I know how that square brain of yours works. It's part of your annoying-yet-adorable charm. When I agreed to start this, I knew it wouldn't be a quick turn-around." He thought if the right way to phrase his thoughts. "That said… fourteen months. You say this is heading some-where. Can I at least ask where?"

His boyfriend put his arms around him—and yes, Ray thought, he was his boyfriend—curled up into a ball, and pressed his head against Ray's chest, tucking it under his chin. A curious picture, considering how much bulkier he was. It felt right, though. This was where he belonged.

Ray hugged him back and kissed the top of his head.

"You know how, even after we finished school, I al-ways told you The Pines were my safe place?" Barry said.

"Yes?"

"The truth is, for years now, the only place I truly feel safe is where you are."

Ray planted another long kiss on the top of his head.

Barry hugged him tighter, tucking his head further under his chin, as if letting go of him was an impossible un-dertaking. "I'm divorcing Maryann." His voice sounded more determined than ever. There was a finality in it Ray hadn't heard from him. "I've always caved under her threats to take my son away from me, but I'm going to fight her on that. I'm an amazing dad. My marriage is a sham, but I've always been an amazing dad. She can't just take Daniel from me, that's all I care about. So, I'm divorcing her. Should have done it a long time ago, not make you wait this long. I just need a week or two to settle some last pending items, and I'll get the papers." He looked up from his chest, and again, those blue eyes glowed bright with resolve. "I love you." He gave Ray a long, passionate kiss.

Ray caressed his dense brown hair. He gazed deeply into his Big Bear's eyes. "I love you too."

Chapter Sixteen

Taken

1993

Leroy Howe didn't often set foot in Lumenwood, but his mom had ordered him to deliver a bag of clothes to the Bakers. Something he'd been assigned to do ever since Royce mentioned to his mom how he'd made fun of Callum Baker wearing his hand-me-down shirt. His brother had only been scolded for making fun of the Bakers' humble abode, but for some reason that extra bit of humiliation had been enough to appoint Leroy as the official "hand-downer" of hand-me-downs. Something he'd had to do every six months or so for the past two years.

He'd gotten on his bike—not much use for his skateboard on this errand—and made his way to the trailer park and now stood in front of the pretty blue-and-white mobile home, with the cute porch and the hanging plants, where Droopy Baker lived with his family. Other than looking rather small to fit a family of five, Leroy had to admit it appeared rather cozy in a quaint sort of way.

He knocked on the door, and a minute later, there was Droopy, standing at the door.

"Oh, hey." Droopy looked oddly confused to see him at the door with a large bag. He'd already come three times before, but it always caught him by surprise.

"Hey." Leroy gave a resigned grin. "Home delivery of used crap, right at your doorstep, fresh from the laundry machine. We accept tips, good sir." He plopped the bag down on the ground in front of him and quickly noticed his greeting hadn't been as funny to Callum as it had been in his head.

"Thanks." Droopy picked up the bag and smiled with sincere gratitude, which only made him feel more like crap.

A pang of guilt crossed his chest. "I'm being an asshole, ain't I?" He gave him a bashful smirk. "I'm sorry."

"That's okay." Callum cast a glance inside, then back at him. "My mom's making meatloaf. She makes it round, not loaf-shaped, that way it feels like everyone gets an end-piece. Want some?"

Leroy's eyes flew open, and a hungry grin stretched across his face.

The Baker's home felt more spacious than it looked, certainly more than he'd ever pictured a mobile home to be. It wasn't just the main hub; they had installed upgrades through the years. There was the porch, an additional bedroom, and even an additional bathroom attached to it, as well as a small but functional kitchen, with an actual oven and all.

As Mrs. Baker picked up the plates off the table with a pleasant smile of satisfaction, noticing he'd nearly licked his plate clean, Leroy realized, while this wasn't like their two-story home, with its individual rooms and spacious living room and long dining table, it wasn't all that bad, and they kept it spotless. It felt like a home, he thought, not a cramped space where five people and their body odors were pushed together because they had no other choice.

"Thank you, Mrs. Baker." He slapped his stomach twice with satisfaction. "That was most excellent!"

She gave him a chubby-cheeked smile. "Don't mention it, darling. Thank your mom for the clothes. Next time, bring your brother. I'll make my chicken taco lasagna."

"I have no clue what that looks like, but that's three of

my favorite things together."

She laughed with a jocular wave of the hand.

Royce stood up and went around the table. "Better head back. Don't want the parental units getting all worried."

"You be careful now, you hear me?" Janice Baker pointed a motherly finger at him—it seemed all mothers knew that warning forefinger technique like it was a requirement to graduate from mothering school. "Go straight home. You heard about the three Knox kids, right?"

"The Knox kids?" He was puzzled by this.

"Oh, my dear boy, yes. They were taken sometime last night. No one knows how. No signs of a break-in. They were there by bedtime; gone this morning. Maria Knox and her husband are beside themselves! That poor woman. She's never been my cup-o'-joe, but no mother deserves that."

Royce shot a glance at Callum, who returned a grave nod. The Knoxes lived next door to the Vanek House and Old Man Curling. That nod was Callum telling him they'd been right to pull all their stuff out of the house three days earlier. If Caesar, Randall, and Paula Knox had gone missing all at once, there was no doubt in their minds the police were going to bust open the Vanek House's front doors and start searching.

With a foreboding sense of apprehension, Leroy said his goodnights, got on his bike and pedaled away as the last rays of the sun said their own goodnights.

He'd never see his house again.

As Leroy pedaled along Mason street, he passed a red-brick house with a gray roof, which would've been utterly generic in White Harbor, if it weren't because the person who lived there—whose name currently escaped him—didn't take down their Christmas decorations all year round. They even turned them on sometimes, randomly, out of season. He and Royce would ride their bikes, or their skateboards through here, and there would be Santa and his reindeer glowing on the roof in October, when every other house was covered in pumpkins, skeletons, and witches.

He turned right on the first corner past the house, continued for roughly two blocks—"roughly" since the uneven web of streets and roads that made up White Harbor didn't form any discernible grid—then turned left onto Jacobs street, only to be greeted by something that made no sense. There was the house again: red bricks, gray roof, covered in Christmas decorations.

They were lit.

Lights of many colors drew the entire shape of the house—the walls, the doors, the windows, the roof—and on top of the house was Santa in his sleigh, drawn in lights, pulled by three reindeer, all red and white and orange.

Leroy did a double take as he passed the house. *Déjà*

vu? he thought. It couldn't be there if he'd passed it a moment earlier. The only conclusion he could draw was he hadn't really passed it before. He turned right once more at the next corner, then the sign for Jacobs street appeared ahead. *Yup, definitely imagined passing the house before. Maybe someone else forgot to take down their decorations last Christmas... But what about the Jacobs street sign?*

He turned left at the corner, as he thought he'd done before, and his jaw dropped. He stopped pedaling. His bike rolled forward as he stared, gobsmacked. The Mason street house with the Christmas decorations was, again, ahead of him.

Leroy stopped in front of the house and gawked at it, not just because this was the third time he'd passed it—which not only did away with any rationalization about déjà vu— but because of what he was seeing on the roof. Someone had rearranged the light decorations on top of the house. There was Santa Claus, wearing no pants, suspended in the air, plunging his gigantic candy-cane penis into Rudolph the red-nosed reindeer. They had somehow arranged the tiny lights on Rudolph to display an open mouth, upturned, pleasured eyes, and a hanging tongue. Nearby, behind Rudolph, was the sleigh, upturned, with one of the other reindeer (Dasher? Dancer? Prancer?) lying belly up, on top of it, tied with the string of lights that had previously acted as the reins; its neck stretched toward Santa, and a long obscene tongue licked at his huge candy cane, while the third reindeer (Comet? Blitzen? Vixen?) stood on its hind legs, holding the other one's legs open with its front hooves, as the blinking lights animated it into a back-and-forth fucking motion.

"What the fucking fuck?" His entire attention was absorbed by the inexplicable spectacle in front of his eyes.

"Do you like it?"

Leroy's skeleton nearly jumped out of his skin as he gasped and turned to see Freddie Parham standing there, next to his bike, giggling his signature "Hee-hee-hee!" giggle. "Freddie?" He examined the other boy up and down. In his current state of shock, Freddie "The Hyena" appearing next to him, giggling, after being missing for a month and a half was anything but a relief.

When Leroy turned his head, he noticed, other than the Christmas decorations, every light in the town was off, the whole town was in darkness, and every building around him gave off a sense of deterioration, extreme poverty, neglect, and abandonment. He thought he heard something from below when he reacted—a wet sound—and he looked down to see all the surroundings were flooded with about six inches of dirty water. "What the…" The foot he was supporting the bike on was soaked up to the ankle, and he hadn't even felt it.

"I'm still learning how to move around Blight Harbor, so doing *that*"—Freddie motioned toward the roof decorations—"was freakin' hard, man!"

"What the fuck are you talking about? Blight Harbor? Everyone's been worried sick! Why did you just disappear like that? What is all this?"

Freddie turned his face toward him and flashed a big, crooked grin. There was a baseball bat in his hand.

The swing came too fast for him to react. It got him on the top-right side of the head, knocking him off the bike and sending him splashing into the shallow water.

Leroy peered up, his sight spinning, his head throbbing. Freddie's silhouette was now cast against a full blue moon in the black sky. "What... What are you...doing?"

"I'm doing just what you'd expect a kid from a cursed family to do." Freddie's grinning face looked down at him, accompanied by that awful giggle. "I won the lottery."

He knocked his lights out with another swing of the bat.

Leroy could feel his heart thumping in his temples and the ache in his head was like having a tiny person in his skull trying to kick their way out.

"You should've seen it, old man!" It was Freddie's voice coming from...somewhere. "I could walk into that other side. I could change things! Make things! It was dope!"

When Leroy opened his eyes and focused them on one spot, Freddie was standing in front of an older man he quickly recognized as Old Man Curling, who was giving Freddie a scrutinizing look.

"That's not something you should be proud of, Freddie," Curling said. "The things I taught you to do are tools to achieve this one goal. They should never be used again, and you shouldn't be enjoying it so much."

"Why not? I never had much to begin with, and I lost what little I had in that river. I couldn't do anything to change that. Even my friends weren't really my friends. Why can't I enjoy this one thing that makes me feel like I have some control?"

Curling sighed, pointed to a corner of the room. "Because of that."

With apprehension, Leroy turned his gaze toward the spot Curling was pointing at. He had to suppress a scream as to not draw attention to himself. Whatever was happening, he wanted to have every single possible second to figure out a way to escape. Against the wall, close to him, there were five other kids. The two that had disappeared two weeks earlier, and the three Knox kids—including a little girl around four or five years old. They were all sitting on the floor, hands and feet tied with rope.

"You see that girl over there?" Curling kept his index finger pointed at her. "She's almost the same age as your sister was when she drowned because of your stupidity."

Freddie gave the man the most hateful look he'd ever seen.

"You piece of shit!" Freddie shouted, and charged at the man.

Before he got close enough to punch him, Curling gave him a single backhand slap to the face that made him stagger and fall to the floor, a hand pressed against his aching cheek.

"Do that again, and I'll kick you out of the house. You'll lose everything. You will never have another opportunity to rid yourself of the curse." Curling pointed at little Paula Knox again. "Look at that girl," he commanded. Freddie reluctantly obeyed. "Picture your little sister's face on her."

Freddie's face filled with anguish.

"Think of what you need to do. Tell me if you're still enjoying yourself."

He truly didn't want to hear what was being discussed. He was bound and gagged along with five other children in a place like a stone chapel. Their captors were standing on a circular altar of sorts, surrounded by seats. In his head, it was clear what was going to happen to the six of them. Leroy tried to move his fingers, wriggled his wrists to undo the knot tying his hands together, feeling the fibers of the rope scratching and chafing his skin. Then came a sound he never thought he'd hear in response to Ben Curling's prompt.

"Hee-hee-hee!"

Freddie's giggle.

Leroy's heart froze in his chest.

"You're so dumb, old man. I already got my sister and my mom killed. What makes you think that little girl means anything to me?" Freddie turned a wicked grin toward Curling. "That other side is amazing. Infinite. So many materials to make stuff with, things people have tossed there forever. I can make them into whatever I want. Now, that's worth killing for."

Curling stared at him briefly, and in that look, Leroy sensed restrained disgust. Then Curling turned his head and finally noticed him. "Your friend is awake." He turned around to leave. "I'll bring them food and water. We finish this whole mess tomorrow."

Freddie eyed him and grinned. He walked over to him.

Leroy squirmed in his bindings and screamed through the gag in his mouth, prompting the other kids to scream and cry as well. He was further startled as the door to this bizarre chapel slammed shut as Curling made his exit. He turned toward the closed door, then back toward Freddie, who was now crouching in front of him.

"I just wanted to say"—Freddie placed a hand on his chest—"this ain't personal, Tweedle Dee." Leroy shook, trying to get away from the hand, but couldn't. "I needed at least one person close to me, and well"—he gave a shrug and a smirk—"I've got no family anymore, beside my uncle, but he's already too old for this, so you guys were the closest I had. I was kinda hoping to kill that little pussy, Lange, but he belongs to the old man. You were just…sort of there. So, I guess you'll have to do."

Leroy tried to speak, but only muffled exclamations passed through the gag, to which Freddie responded by placing a finger to his lips in a dramatic shushing gesture.

"No words, darling. Don't ruin the moment."

He stood up and walked toward the other children, who cowered away from him. He raised his hands, making claws, bared his teeth, and uttered a cartoonish roar. Despite his playful demeanor, the other kids were startled by this, and shrieked in terror.

Freddie giggled again, and his giggles echoed in the domed ceiling of the stone chapel. He walked away from them, toward the seats. Behind the individual chairs surrounding the altar were long benches, or pews, also circling the altar, forming something like an octagon with walking spaces between the segments. He laid down on one of the pews, closed his eyes, and covered them with his forearm.

Minutes later, Leroy could hear him snoring.

Chapter Seventeen

Split

1993

Royce pushed past the crowd gathered around his house. During the past month and a half, similar crowds had gathered around Freddie's uncle's home, also around the Grants' place, around the mobile home where the Ingrams lived in Lumenwood; also around the Knoxes' house, which was separated by only a wall from the Vanek House. Now, it was his home's turn to be beset by onlookers and rubberneckers, watching, theorizing, commenting, gossiping.

Feeding Blight Harbor, he thought.

The police were inside, talking to his parents, and he'd snuck out before they could stop him. He could see his friends at the edge of the crowd, and he needed to reach them quickly. He had a one-track mind right now. He knew what they had to do, and they had to do it immediately, before the police made their own move.

The first face he sought as he reached them was Jess's.

"We have to go to the Vanek House!" His voice sounded pleading, as if afraid his friends would push back or question his logic.

"We know," Jess said. She turned slightly and poked her shoulder up, nodding toward her rucksack. "We're ready."

He gave her a surprised look, then shifted his sleep-deprived eyes toward the rest of his friends, who were looking at him with determination. "How did you—"

"It's the only place they can be. This is Gerardo, all over again, but on a larger scale. With Gerardo, the police waited too long to go to the Vanek House. We're not doing that. We're not letting Leroy die like that."

Royce nodded. "We were in the house until a couple days ago, and we didn't see anyone being brought in or anything. Where do we even check?"

"You know where." She gave him a knowing stare.

He knew.

They all did.

They rode their bikes from Royce's toward the Vanek House—Peter riding with Bobby, Nadine with Jess, Callum with Sylvia, Ray standing on Barry's footholds, and Royce by himself.

As they approached the old house, they were just about to turn right on Graham street so they could sneak in as usual from the northern side—where the hole in the floor was located—but as he was about to make the turn, Royce noticed—

"Stop!" he called out.

—the front doors were open.

He stopped, turned, and pedaled toward the front of the house.

"What are you doing?" Bobby called.

Everyone changed course and followed him.

Royce stood in front of the house, staring at those ominous doors standing ajar, and as his friends joined him, their surprised expressions matched his.

"Wh-why is it open?" Peter asked, climbing off Bobby's bike's top tube. He cast a furtive glance up the hill toward his house, then back at the open doors.

"Ain't it obvious?" Jess said. "It's waiting for us."

She hurried forward, followed by the others. No time to hide their bicycles behind the shed in the backyard. The house was letting them in, so they went in, bikes and all.

As they crossed the threshold into the Vanek House's main hall, an oppressive feeling came over the group, as if the air had grown in weight and density. No sooner had they all entered than the doors slammed shut behind them; making them all jump and turn.

Barry dropped his bike on the floor, grabbed the door's handles and pulled as hard as he could, but they were shut tight. He shook his head. "This ain't gonna open." Strangely enough, there hadn't been the noise of chains outside, which meant no one had put the padlock on the doors. It had to be the house itself, holding them closed.

The small cracks in the walls, and the tiny spaces between the boards on the windows, didn't let in enough light to truly illuminate the hall. It was as gloomy as if dusk had fallen already when it was barely noon.

Jess slid off the straps of her rucksack and put it on the floor, as the others either leaned their bikes against a wall or dropped them on the floor as she'd done. She unzipped the rucksack, brought out four small flashlights, and passed them around. "Here. Thank God my dad didn't raise no unprepared little bitch."

"We need to check if the back room is still open," Callum said, pushing up his glasses, which had fallen askew as he got off the bike. "If something happens, we need the hole in the floor as an emergency exit."

"Let's go." Sylvia turned on the flashlight she'd gotten from Jess and pointed it toward the dining room entrance. The cone of light was small, and it faded in the gloom a short distance away, as if eaten by the darkness.

They both hurried into the depths of the house.

"So, we all agree, right? Door on the second floor?" Ray eyed the others, who nodded in agreement. "How are we gonna open it, though? The whole deal with that door is it *doesn't* open."

"It'll open," Peter said. "I'm sure."

Royce wondered how in the world he could sound so sure about something he couldn't possibly know. Though he was eager to get the search going, he just now realized he hadn't even considered Peter was here, even after what had happened with his mom a few days ago. "Pete. Are you sure you should be here? Won't your mom go all psycho on you?"

"I don't care," the thin, pale boy said. "Leroy's my friend. Screw what she thinks. I'm helping."

Royce smiled at him. The sadness and worry in his eyes couldn't be ignored, but his smile was heartfelt. "What's the holdup, then?"

"Wait," Bobby said. "Shouldn't there be a lookout in case the police get here? Or worse, Curling?"

"I can be the lookout," Barry said.

"What are you, nuts? We're not going without you. That'd be like the Avengers telling the Hulk to sit one out."

"Oh…okay."

Callum and Sylvia appeared from the dining room, looking agitated.

"They boarded it up!" Sylvia said. "The hole in the floor is boarded up!"

"Shit!" Jess said. The light from the flashlights gleamed on the curved head of a crowbar sticking out of her rucksack. She pulled it out and handed it to Sylvia, then pulled out a hammer, and handed it to Callum. "Here. You guys are pulling double duty. You'll be the lookouts and you'll peel those fuckin' boards out, no matter what."

"Are you sure we're the most qualified people for that job?" Callum asked.

"You'll have to be. Figure it out. We're going up."

She headed upstairs, followed by the rest of the group, leaving Callum and Sylvia behind. Their collective weight made the stairs creak in protest, or in warning—some beast lying in rest, groaning to let them know it should not be awakened.

The group made their way upstairs, then turned into the hallway with the bedrooms. All four doors lay open. It was at this moment that the enormity of what they were doing hit them all at once. They, a bunch of twelve- and thirteen-year-old kids, were trying to rescue six missing kids from the innards of a house that had killed at least a hundred people.

Despite the urgency, their pace slowed.

As they walked through the confined space, the groaning of the boards under their feet became more intense, as well as that sense of oppression in the air. It was almost like the beast, which lay in wait, now stirred because of their insistence on walking deeper into its den—or was it its stomach? Were those four open doors its gaping mouths?

Fighting his own fear, Royce hurried ahead, despite not having a flashlight himself. "Leroy! Lee! Brother?" He peered into one of the rooms, seconds before Jess was right there with him, shining her flashlight into an empty space with boarded-up windows and newspaper over the outer wall—the same as every other space in the Vanek House. They repeated this in the other three bedrooms.

Nothing. Only emptiness and the tiny specks of dust dancing in the flashlight's beam.

Ray shone his flashlight on the enormous, dark brown, permanent bloodstain on the floor of the last bedroom.

(*Forty-four times, he stabbed each. They said the little baby looked like ground beef*)

He swallowed noisily.

They reached the corner and turned right, into the last stretch of hallway, the one ending in a single boarded-up window just past the only door there (*The fifth mouth*) on the left side—the reinforced door with the rusted metal frame.

Jess stopped just two steps past the corner, stretched her arm out, open palm, warning the others to stop. Her eyes were wide open, pointing the beam at the heavy door.

"What is it?" Peter asked and leaned to one side to look past her.

The rest did the same, looking over her shoulder.

"Holy shit," Royce said.

Jess licked her lips nervously and swallowed. "The door's open."

It was only a little, but it was undeniable. The door was slightly ajar, barely pushed into a room none of them had laid eyes on before.

"C'mon." Jess's voice was dripping with dread. "Be quiet."

This was impossible, as the floorboards continued to groan with each step of the seven sets of feet currently walking on them.

They stood in a half-circle, staring at the open door. Hearts pounding, breaths trembling, hands shaky, imaginations contemplating whatever might be on the other side of the doorway. All but Royce, who only had one thing in mind.

"What are ya'll waiting for?" He glared at the others, who had turned to statues. "We have to go in! Leroy's in there."

"Wait, man, we need to stop for a moment," Bobby said in a serious, almost adult voice. "In two years, that door has been impossible to open. Now, the front door closes behind us and someone boarded up the hole in the floor. Suddenly, the only door we haven't been able to open is"—he gestured toward it—"well…doesn't that strike you guys as the least bit suspicious?"

"Like it's a trap?" Peter asked.

"You got it, Admiral Ackbar." Bobby was making a clumsy attempt at lightening the mood using a Star Wars reference, but the tremor in his voice made it fail outright. "If this was a horror movie, we'd all be shouting, 'Don't go in there!' What if whatever took Leroy and Freddie actually *wants* us to go in there?"

There was silence all around.

Nadine raised a hand as if she were in class, only with a numb, scared expression on her face. "What if the door being open means whatever took Leroy got out, and we just can't see it?"

"Fuck," Jess said, under her breath.

Royce shook his head, undaunted. "I don't care! My brother's in there! If you don't come with me, I'm going alone. I ain't leaving my brother *in there!*" He pointed at the door. "If you're not gonna come with me, then fuck all y'all, I'm getting Leroy out!"

"Hey! Hey! Hey!" Jess put a calming hand on his shoulder. "Hun, no one here said we're not going. How can you even think that? We're just scared, that's all. I mean, look at Brickhouse, even he looks like he's about to literally shit bricks."

Royce noticed Barry's complexion had gone pale.

"I'm..." Barry started, then added. "Shit, yeah, I *am* shitting myself, but I'm going in there, no matter what."

Royce gave him an apologetic smile. "Thanks, man. Lee and I were wrong about you."

"That's okay." Barry shrugged. "I deserved that."

Royce smiled and nodded, then turned toward the door. "Can someone with a flashlight lead the way? I'm all talk, but I can't move to go in there with no light."

Peter took a step forward, holding the flashlight up, and stood right in front of the door. "I think I should go first. I think there's a reason Mo... uh... My mom doesn't want me to be in this house. It needs me for something, so it's safer if I go first."

"That's some wild guessing on your part, there, hun," Jess said.

"Well, if I'm wrong, please don't let it kill me." He put his hand forward and pushed the door in, then walked inside.

The others followed.

Peter was still, silent, mouth agape, the same as all of his friends who now stood around him, huddled together a few feet past the doorway. What they were seeing couldn't exist, at least not inside the Vanek house.

They were in a gloomy chapel made of stone. Other than the short aisle before them, the space was circular, with a high dome held up by stone pillars, and lit up by four torches in sconces, which left the corners flooded with quivering shadows. The dome had a circular opening at its center, through which they could see the sky above, where it was nighttime—although it had been noon mere minutes ago—and rain fell in through the open ceiling, down onto a circular altar, which stood about ten inches off the ground. The sound of raindrops echoed in the open space as water hit the stone, then ran down the sides, into a small gutter at the base.

Concentric to the altar there was a circle of chairs—sixteen total—and beyond that one, another circle made up of pews with space to walk in between.

Ray tried to utter some version of, "What the fuck?", but it only came out as a weird mumble.

Barry put a hand on his shoulder. Though he was as dumbfounded as his friend, he turned to him and asked, "You okay?"

Ray responded with a quick series of jittery, uncoordinated nods.

"This isn't the Vanek House," Nadine said.

She was interrupted by a creaking sound.

They all turned to see the door closing behind them.

By the time Nadine spun around to stop it, it had clicked shut. Almost because it felt like the logical thing to do, she walked toward it and jiggled the knob, knowing already it wouldn't open. "Shit." She turned toward her friends' expectant glances and shook her head. From their reaction, she surmised they also hadn't expected it to open.

"We're all seeing this, right?" Peter asked. "It isn't just me."

Without answering, Royce stepped forward and walked toward the altar. He didn't care they had crossed through some kind of portal into a strange chapel, somewhere where it was night. All he cared about was finding his twin brother. He walked a full circle around the altar with long, decisive strides, looking this way and that. "There's nothing here. No doors, no ladders, no nothing." He turned toward a random spot in the chapel. "Lee! Leroy! Can you hear me?" No answer, only his voice reverberating in the dark space. "Leroy!"

Jess approached him. "Let's look around. There might be some—what the fuck do you call it?—some trapdoor, or hidden entrance or something. This is nuts." She surveyed the surroundings, a creeping sense of dread visible in her face.

Peter stood on the opposite side of the altar, Nadine next to him. "I know this symbol." He was pointing his flashlight at the raised surface. There was a symbol he recognized embossed on it. *Vertical line, two shorter horizontal lines, curved sickle top to bottom,* he thought. "The Sickle of the Moon."

"The what?" Jess asked.

Peter realized with unease he'd been talking out loud to himself. "From the book!" he blurted. "My mother's book. Her religion. That's the symbol on the cover. The Sickle of the Moon, they call it. I think this is where they had their meetings."

There was a brief silence, framed only by the sound of the cascading rain.

"Guys?" Nadine said, looking up through the gap in the dome. "The moon?"

The other three by the altar turned their gazes up, and through the rain and the soaring clouds was a full moon, which was an unnatural dark shade of silver blue neither of them had seen before.

Bobby approached Jess and Royce. He peered up at the blue moon with fascination.

"I want to leave," Ray whimpered from the aisle. He hadn't actually moved from the spot he'd been in after entering, three steps from the door. Barry was there, too, refusing to leave his side. They could all see Ray's hands were shaking. He was having a panic attack. "I want to leave!"

"Hey!" Barry said.

"I want to leave!" Ray repeated. "Oh shit, I'm so, so

sorry, Royce. I should've never come here. I want to leave!"

Barry put an arm around his shoulder and pulled him close. "Ray, buddy, we're all here with you. Calm down. I'm here!"

Ray shook his head, pushed away from him, and he immediately turned toward the door. "I'm sorry! I want to leave!" He tried to turn the knob, he shook it as hard as he could, and screamed. "I WANT TO LEAVE! I WANT TO LEAVE!"

"Barry, do something!" Jess gestured toward the burly kid, who gave her a helpless look, like saying, "What am *I* supposed to do?"

He grabbed the panicking boy's hands and pried them from the doorknob. "Hey… Hey, hey, hey. Dude, look at me." Ray wouldn't. He kept shaking his head, muttering under his breath in terror. "Look at me." Ray still wouldn't. He placed both his large hands on his shoulders. "Ray! Look at me!" The shorter boy's brown eyes finally met his. Barry lowered his voice to a whisper so only Ray could hear him. "You said you'd be my safe place when I don't want the others to see me cryin', right?"

Ray hesitated, then gathered enough of his wits to give a quick nod.

"Well, I'm fuckin' terrified, Ray. I need you."

Ray's lips worked to say something. Nothing came out.

"I know you don't want 'em to see you like this, either. Right?"

He nodded again. This time he uttered a weak, "Yuh-yeah."

"Then I got you covered. And you got *me* covered, right?"

Another nod. "Yes. Yes, I do."

"Cool." Barry smiled. "Whatever happens, I got you covered. You got me covered. After we save Leroy, Freddie, and the others, we can go to your place and have some '*yum-yum*' chicken to celebrate, alright?"

Ray nodded yet again. Now appearing calmer. "It's *yangnyeom* chicken."

"Right. However the hell you say that."

Barry turned toward the others, and his face took on a surprised expression. "What the hell?"

They were alone in the chapel.

One blink. In one blink, Barry and Ray had disappeared from the chapel's entrance.

"Wait, what just happened?" Nadine said. She turned toward the opposite end of the altar to find Jess, Bobby, and Royce were also gone. She grabbed onto Peter's shirt and pointed at the emptiness.

He had the same stunned look on his face.

They walked around the altar, looking around in shocked silence. It was as if a trapdoor had opened, like in the movies, and all their friends had fallen through. He pointed the flashlight toward the dark corners of the chapel. They were alone.

Before they could process this, the reinforced door creaked, a loud groan like a yawning dragon.

"Hey, lovebirds." Even more than their friends disappearing, it was seeing Freddie standing there so casually at the doorway that unnerved Nadine in ways she couldn't explain. "Freddie? You're... You're okay."

He chuckled, a disinterested expression on his face. "Yeah, guess so." He took a step back into the dark hallway, as if he'd forgotten something, then he pointed to one side. "Not much time to explain, so you should probably come this way." He walked in that direction and disappeared into the darkness.

Peter started toward the door. "Wait!"

Nadine grabbed his hand. "Don't." She stared suspiciously at the door and the dark hallway outside. "This doesn't feel right. Freddie's been missing for six weeks, and suddenly, he's here? Just walking around as if nothing happened?"

Peter turned a mystified look toward her; a look undercut with annoyance, as if he couldn't understand how she could even suggest not running after their lost friend. "Look, I get what you're saying. But that's our friend right there. We need to figure out what happened."

She eyed him with apprehension, but responded with a nod.

They ran toward the door. The second they stepped into the hallway, the door slammed shut behind them.

This wasn't the same hallway they'd come from earlier.

"What just happened?" Royce said, turning on the spot. "Where did everybody go?"

"Peter!" Jess called. "Nadine?"

"Fuck!" Royce shouted with frustration. "So, it ain't enough my brother disappeared, now everyone else keeps disappearing around me. It's this fucking house!"

"I don't think this is the same chapel," Bobby said, looking around silently, his voice tinged with both dread and fascination. In his mind, a fleeting thought told him Freddie would've loved this. He pointed around at the chairs surrounding the altar. "Look. Twelve chairs. There were sixteen before."

Jess studied the surroundings, as if some dark, stalking creature were lurking in the shadows.

There was a creak from the entrance.

"Guys?" Royce gawked at the now open door.

Bobby and Jess turned. Despite the darkness near the entrance, they could see Freddie standing in the doorway, greeting them with a huge smile.

"You're alive," Bobby whispered, then the relief came bursting out. "You're alive! How are you alive? Were you trapped in this house? In this chapel? No. Wait. You came from outside the room. Were you there all along? How didn't we see you?"

"Jesus, Bobster, you wanna write down all those questions and fax them to me? I might be able to send you all the answers in like three weeks?"

Bobby laughed at this, oblivious joy in his voice. He missed the suspicious stares Jess and Royce were giving his friend. "I'm just glad you're okay, man. That's all. I was so worried."

Freddie gave him a cynical grin. "Well, buddy, as you can see, no need to worry about me."

"*How* are you okay?" Jess interjected, in a down-to-business tone. "There isn't even food in this house."

"You don't sound happy to see me, Pippi Longstocking. Shouldn't you be all jumping with joy from finding your friend?"

"Where's my brother, Freddie?" Royce asked. "You know where he is."

Freddie clicked his tongue, placed his hands on his hips, and nodded. "Shucks. You got me."

Bobby frowned with confusion. The room seemed to grow darker, as if the flames from the torches had diminished. "Wait, what is this? What's going on?"

"C'mon, you piece-of-shit hyena, where's my brother?"

Freddie stepped out into the hallway and gestured with both hands toward his left. "He's right over there. Follow me."

He walked off, out of sight, and for a second, the glow from the torches seemed to flash in his eyes and his crooked grin.

"What's going on with you two?" Bobby gave Jess and Royce a mesmerized stare.

"I don't know," Jess said. "But your buddy there just gave me the creeps, like few things in this world." She unzipped her rucksack and brought out her stun gun, then brought out another hammer and gave it to Royce. "He's been gone for over a month. Now he's in this chapel, acting like he owns the place. He's got somethin' to do with this."

"What are you doing?" Bobby asked, motioning toward the stun gun. "Please tell me that's not for Freddie."

"It's for whatever the house has in store for us. If one of those things is Freddie, then so be it."

"Wait, what?" Bobby was flabbergasted.

Royce started walking toward the hallway. "Let's go."

Bobby followed, reluctant, eyes scanning the surroundings.

When they stepped out of the chapel, it became clear what was outside wasn't the same version of the Vanek House they had come from. The darkness was so thick, the beam from Jess's flashlight dimmed after just a few feet.

The door slammed shut behind them. The sound echoing loudly, startling all three.

They had no choice now but to deal with whatever the Vanek house had in store for them.

Chapter Eighteen

Peace and Despair

2022

In a queen-sized bed, in a large bedroom, on the second floor of her home in Oakland, Constance Miller slept peacefully, wrapped in her covers. Her curtains were open, save for a sheer curtain that hung still and diffused the silver moonlight from the outside. The surrounding space had been drained of all color, save for tones of silver and gray. Even her peach-colored walls were now a monochrome shade of gray that just slightly betrayed a faint orange hue.

It had been so many years since her husband passed

away, but she still had the automatic sleeping habit of reaching a hand toward his side of the bed. Every night before bed, seventy-two-year-old Constance took his pillow—which she had refused to wash since his passing—and placed it lengthwise on his side, so when she reached for him in her sleep, there would be something for her hand to grasp, something that would still hold a bit of his smell—she had put the last shirt he'd worn inside the pillowcase for good measure.

Eyes closed, a hand clinging to her husband's pillow, her mind wandering in dreams she wouldn't remember.

As she slept, the silvery moon that shone over Oakland darkened and changed in hue, turning blue in a matter of seconds.

The shadow grew out of the carpet, beside the bed. Black tendrils formed feet, legs, hips, a torso with old sagging breasts, a neck, a head, and the hair on it, then clothes—a buttoned blouse and a long skirt—none of it belonging to a real person, but tangible as if it did. Once the mass settled, Martha Lange's shape looked down at the woman on the bed. Though she had no eyes, only two empty black holes, her expression conveyed her hatred and disgust toward the woman—her sister, the pathetic wretch who'd taken her son away from her.

Earlier that night, she'd gone to visit Peter's little spawn, the one he'd made with that bitch of his—how she'd enjoyed watching her burn; a fitting end for a worthless woman. Peter's son, however, served a purpose, regardless of her feelings on the matter. If it were up to her, she'd have crushed him like the worm he was, but she might need him later. Her visit to the boy had been her way to test how capable she was to reach him, should the need arise. The blood bond held strong beyond the boundaries of White Harbor, she found. It had been tenuous at best when she'd used it to reach Peter's bitch. It had taken her many tries over many weeks—she wasn't related by blood, which made the connection difficult. The boy, however, was related by blood. Manifesting herself in his room had been easy. She couldn't remember the experience completely, though. She couldn't remember much of what she'd said. All she had was a mental image of the boy screaming in terror upon seeing her and fainting at the end.

The blood bond—she now confirmed—had held with her sister all the way in California.

"Wake up, Constance," she said in a disapproving hiss. "Wake up, you godless whore."

Constance's eyes sprung open with a gasp. "Martha!" The word escaped her lips, as if she'd heard her in a dream. She was greeted by a blurry view of the pillow—the stand-in for her late husband. When she turned around, she was startled by the shape of her sister standing in the dark. Her silhouette was drawn against the silver blue light coming in from the window. She recoiled in her bed with a cry and pushed herself away, unwittingly knocking her husband's pillow off the bed.

"Martha! What? How?"

"You took my son," Martha said.

Constance could now see the empty caverns she had instead of eyes and the way her skin and clothes wriggled and pulsated as if creatures crawled beneath.

"It's long overdue that you paid for your sin."

Constance tried to crawl out of bed with as much agility as her septuagenary body allowed, but she lost her balance and fell to the floor. She felt one of her ribs crack as she hit the parquet and let out a painful cry.

"You took what didn't belong to you," Martha said. Constance heard her voice moving around the bed, toward her. "You interfered with God's plan."

"Get away from me!" She stood up the best she could, even if the pain was sharp and unforgiving. She staggered toward the door, grabbed the knob, then whimpered when it wouldn't turn. She turned her head toward her sister, or whatever this thing that looked like her sister was, and saw she was now only a few feet away. Constance continued to tug on the doorknob, but it was futile. The ungodly thing approached.

"You took the most important thing from me," Martha said, and Constance was struck by the eerie realization that the creature's lips didn't move. "Now that your judgment has come, you try to run from your punishment. How pathetic."

She kept trying to open the door, grunting with the effort, moaning with terror.

"Stop," Martha said.

Constance's body stiffened. She couldn't move. "Why are you doing this?"

"Turn around. Look at me."

She obeyed. She turned around and found the thing that looked like her sister standing very close to her, the hollows of her eye sockets staring.

"You always looked more like our father. You have his eyes. His nose. His permissive, meddling tendencies. I always thought you should've been a man."

She couldn't believe what she was seeing. With difficulty, she said, "Martha, this can't be you," in a fearful moan. "This can't be happening."

"Motherhood was never for you." Martha's tone was scornful, venomous. "It should've been made clear by that barren womb of yours. But instead of accepting it, you had to steal my son from me."

Constance felt her sanity escape her. She knew the

eyeless ghoul standing before her could not be her sister, but it *knew* her. It spoke with her voice, and the sneering way she addressed her could only belong to Martha. "I didn't steal your son." Why was she talking to this thing? Could it really be her? "You hurt Peter. What you did to him was appalling. I didn't steal him, Martha. You lost him."

She noticed a curl and a quiver in Martha's upper lip, a furious, snarling expression, compounded by the void in her cavernous eyes. "You lost that ridiculous man you called a husband. I can feel how much it hurts you, even today, but it still pales in comparison to the pain of losing my son."

Martha raised a hand.

At first, Constance could see the many individual strings or worms that made up the creature's palm and its fingers. She saw its flesh wriggle at first, losing shape, losing consistence, then it reconstituted. It looked like skin with bugs crawling underneath it. A second later, it turned solid. The hand approached her face. She tried to pull back, but she was paralyzed. Then she felt its icy fingers run down her cheek as the Martha thing studied her face.

Martha bared her teeth at her, that inhuman horror of a face gazing into hers, hatred almost dribbling from the corners of her mouth as black tendrils in place of saliva. "You're a waste of a woman. I will enjoy seeing the life leave your eyes."

A long, black tongue, like a thick slimy snail emerging from its shell, pushed its way out through Martha's lips and ran a full circle around her mouth, as if savoring the image in her mind.

Constance's eyes sprung open with a gasp. She saw her hand in front of her, caressing her husband's side of the bed. His pillow wasn't there. It was by the headboard—had she forgotten to put it lengthwise before going to sleep? The bedside lamps were on; warm incandescent bulbs shone under their lampshades. And her hand... It wasn't wrinkled. She turned the palm toward her. It looked so much younger than before.

"What's—"

"So sorry, darlin', I didn't mean to wake you," a familiar, low baritone voice said. That slight Texas twang, still there despite the years living in California, was unmistakable to her.

She raised her eyes to see Max standing by the open bathroom door. The bathroom light was on, and the sound of running water danced into the room. Maxwell Miller, her beloved husband, was taking off his jacket, which he then threw onto a chair in a corner. "Why are you in bed this early, darlin'? Busy day? Is Peter back already? I thought college was out for summer as of next week."

She gawked. She had no words to answer. Words were an alien concept.

"Sorry, darlin', I startled you awake, and I'm just piling questions on you." He grinned, and it was then she noticed he looked younger, in his forties, perhaps. He undid the buttons on his cuffs and rolled up his sleeves up to his elbows. It was then the delicious scent of jasmine wafted from the bathroom and made its way to her nostrils. Max noticed she was staring at the open door. He glanced back toward the bathroom, then back at her and grinned. "Was kinda hoping you wouldn't wake up before it was ready. I'm runnin' you a bath. Figured it would be a delightful surprise when you woke up. How does Chinese sound for dinner?"

Constance sat up. She cast another baffled glance toward Max, then at the window. The curtains were drawn—she never drew the curtains before bed—there was something odd about the quality of the moonlight on the other side, but she attributed it to it being filtered by the fabric. She looked back at him. None of the confusion had left her eyes. She was still trying to make sense of it all.

"This is a dream," she said, but questioned herself. If the nightmare of Martha appearing in her bedroom, with her empty eye sockets and that disgusting tongue had been a dream, then had it been a dream within another?

"Well, no," replied Max, with a tilt of the head and a smile. "It's more like I know you've been workin' like crazy preparing the house for Peter to come back home. I wanted to do something nice, but it's flatterin' you think your husband being nice is so rare it has to be a dream."

She stared. There was an awkward silence between them.

All of a sudden, he burst out laughing. "I'm joking, darlin'." He approached the bed, put a hand out toward her, and she took it, then felt a very real but gentle pull as he helped her off the bed.

A second later, she was standing face-to-face with her late husband, who grinned as he studied her eyes with that fascination that always gleamed in his when he looked at her. He leaned in for a kiss, but she gasped and pulled her head back.

He frowned with puzzlement. "Are you okay?" He took both her hands in his and glanced down at them. "You're tremblin'."

Constance put her arms around him and rested her head against his chest, and immediately she was hit by the smell of his cologne, and it was so real it brought tears to her eyes. He was warm. She could even get the smell of his body *through* the cologne itself. *I'm not dreaming,* she thought. *I'm not dreaming! How is this possible?*

She felt his arms wrap around her. She even felt the muscles under his shirt move and tense up as he squeezed her close to his body. There was a soft kiss on her head and the sensation of him sniffing her hair.

"I had a nightmare," she said. "I had a horrible nightmare."

Max held her tighter for a while and covered her head with kisses. "I'm here. Come with me." With one more quick kiss, he took her hand and led her to the bathroom.

As she followed him, she surveyed the room to catch anything that might break the illusion, anything that didn't fit. But, to her astonishment, everything was accurate for the time period when they were both in their forties and Peter was in college. Their old blue curtains were hanging over the windows; the walls were not the current peach color, but yellow, as they had been before she'd asked Max to repaint them years ago. The frames and pictures were the ones they'd had back then—Peter's college graduation picture was gone, as was the last picture she and Max took together when they traveled to Cancun. It was impossible that this was real. It was utterly impossible that twenty-something years of memories could've been deleted, and yet, this felt *real.*

She felt the light of the bathroom wash over her and she turned to look at Max.

"Turn around," he said, giving her a soft pat on the shoulder. "Let me help you out of those clothes."

She turned her back to him and raised her arms to allow him to slip her silk top off over her head. As the fabric slid off, she opened her eyes and finally got a good look at herself in the mirror. Her skin looked so much tighter. Most of her wrinkles were gone. Her hair was the short length she used to wear at the end of the nineties and a more natural auburn than the darker dye she'd later wear. Her breasts still looked full and high.

She noticed the look Max was giving her in the mirror now that her sleeping trousers were lying at her feet. That crooked smile and lustful stare he gave her when he was feeling playful was in full display.

"I reckon," he said, "we might just skip dinner after your bath. What do you say?"

She turned around and kissed him passionately, as if she would never have another chance to kiss him, because— being honest with herself—she might wake up from this dream at any moment and never kiss him again. By the time she began pulling off his clothes, it was clear they would skip the bath altogether.

She was so convinced she'd wake up an old woman again after making love.

In the throes of passion and through her earth-shaking orgasm, she let herself be as unbridled as she could, certain that any second she would open her eyes as an old widow in her dark, lonesome room, accompanied by nothing but a pillow. But here she was, resting her head on Max's arm, gazing into his eyes.

"Well, that was better than a bath," he said.

She made a silly face, as if giving it some thought. "Are you sure?"

"Oh," he said, feigning offense. "So that's how it is, huh?"

"Well," she said, grinning widely, feeling a sense of childish glee. "It was *good.* Like *really* good! But a scented bath..." She looked deep into his pale blue eyes with a mischievous glint in her gaze. "I mean, a scented bath might be worth two of those."

Max laughed. "I see. So, this is your way of sayin' you want to go again?"

She answered with a playful shrug, then ran her fingernails over his chest hair and added, "I'm just saying. If you feel you want to prove a point, why risk me wondering how good that scented bath might have been, when you can just make your victory indisputable?"

He gave her a soft, throaty growl and kissed her. They were close enough for Constance to feel he was more than ready for another round.

She felt one of his hands playing between her legs for a minute, then felt it softly slide up toward her navel, then continue up until it was cupping one of her breasts. She felt herself about to release a soft moan. Then—

His hand was at her throat. It squeezed hard.

Her eyelids flew open, and she tried to scream. The

thing before her eyes was now a caricature of her husband, his eyeballs black like two small globes made of rubber. His skin now resembled the writhing, wriggling texture she'd seen on her sister in her nightmare

(*Was it a nightmare?*)

and he grinned like some hungry predator. He still looked like a disgusting facsimile of her husband in his forties, and they were still in their late-nineties bedroom. She hadn't gone back to Martha's nightmare. She was still here, but this was not her husband, with his hand around her throat.

Max stood up from the bed and pulled her with him as if she weighed nothing. She could feel him choking her but ensuring to release the pressure at times for air to pass. He wasn't trying to strangle her, but he wanted to hurt her; to make her feel like she was dying. She tried to scream, but he pressed harder, killing the scream in her throat before it came out—the ball of air pushing out, stuck in her trachea, burning like she'd swallowed a pool ball, stretching the delicate tissue within her throat. He held her up with impressive strength not even the real Max had ever had.

Constance could see his full naked body now, the way threads and worms appeared and disappeared over the surface of his skin, coloring and shaping themselves into muscles, and pores, and hairs. That grin looked like it would rip the sides of his mouth apart.

She struggled, punched, kicked, and scratched, but

Max laughed it off. The worms that made up his body spread and rearranged in place, leaving no mark.

"Look at you!" he said, a condescending chuckle emerging from the depths of his chest. "Never thought a thievin' cunt like you would have that much fight in her. Keep hittin' me, darlin'"—she found the mockery of Max's accent by this creature revolting—"ain't gonna do much for you!"

One of her fingernails scratched his chest, and she saw it bleed a black substance, but the writhing tendrils came from his skin and intertwined, healing the scratch.

He pulled her face close to his.

That grin! Jesus!

"That scared look on your face makes me so hard," the revolting monster said, his eyes shifting down, signaling her to look at his erection, but she forced her eyes shut. She refused to look, but she could feel it grazing her leg as she kicked and swayed.

"You're not him," she uttered through her narrowed windpipe and clenched teeth.

He spoke in her ear. "Yes, I am…and you know what I loved most about you?"

Shut up! Shut up! Not using his face! I don't want to hear whatever it is while you're wearing his face!

"I could cum in that pussy as much as I wanted, and that dried-up wasteland of a womb you've got in there would never get pregnant." He put his lips to her ear. "That was your one win over all the women I fucked behind your back."

Not Max! You're not Max! He'd never say that! Shut up!

She slapped him as hard as she could. The slap barely registered.

Max—the thing posing as Max—chuckled with pleasure. "Ooh, I wish you could give me more of that, darlin', but we gotta wrap this up."

"No!" she growled, but she couldn't say more, as air was scarce, and the effort was making her body weak. Her heart raced with fear as he carried her toward the bathroom like she was nothing. The second she saw the bathtub, full and brimming, with the faucet still dripping, she understood what was going to happen. She resisted, but her head was still swimming. She kicked him and clawed his face, but he didn't react.

The second they reached the bathtub, Constance felt herself pulled into the air, then pushed down into the tub. The bathwater was still warm as it enveloped her entire body and face.

She was underwater, and the person—the thing—holding her under was her revived husband. She clawed at him. It was all futile. Her feet kicked. She felt the water splashing around, as the strange blob in the vague shape of Max she saw through the water surface held her under with as much ease as if she were lying still.

She reached a hand up, looking for the lever that would open the drain and let the water out, but she saw Max's shape move his hand toward hers, grab it and hold it down under the water.

She had already been feeling the effects of oxygen deprivation by the time they'd reached the bathtub, so it didn't take long for her body to activate all alarms at once. She kicked more violently, she struggled with all her strength, which only spent more oxygen her lungs couldn't spare. Then, little by little, she stopped. Years earlier, a friend of hers who'd almost drowned in a pool had told her there was a point during drowning when the brain gives up on survival, and you're overcome by an enveloping moment of complete lucidity, of complete peace. Your body tells you it's time to give up, to let go, to let yourself be carried away. It's the way your brain prepares you for a peaceful death amidst one of the most despair-filled demises possible.

I'm dying, she thought, with no emotion. A simple fact. *Max is killing me. No. This is not Max. This is something Martha did. Something she created, somehow. She's doing this because I took Peter. Martha is killing me. Not Max. Not Max. Not Max.*

A voice rang in her mind. *"Is that what you really think?"* It was Martha's voice. *"You're so wrong, sister. So, so wrong."*

The image before her eyes cleared, as if there weren't a layer of agitated water between her and the thing that looked like Max. What she saw chilled her blood. She saw her Max, the real Max, not the strange, grinning creature with the blackened eyes, but her husband, his adoring eyes and his beautiful smile looking down at her, as he kept holding her down. He smiled pleasantly as he watched her drown—as *he* drowned her.

"*You stole everything that mattered to me,*" Martha's voice said, as Martha's eyeless image appeared in her field of vision, behind Max. "*I want you to know what a betrayal like that feels like.*"

Those last seconds of peace her brain had allowed her were now being stolen by the horror of watching the man she loved smile down at her as he drowned her. She couldn't move, but there was no peace. She couldn't move, and he only watched her die.

In her mind, she screamed in horror as her sight darkened.

The last thing she saw was that smile.

The last thing she felt was the purest despair.

Chapter Nineteen

Candlelight

The mobile home's door opened into an unusual world. Stephanie Bilson took off her glasses, standing at the door, and wiped them with a tiny cloth she carried in her shorts pocket and squinted at the blue-tinted darkness around. She had spent the entirety of her fourteen years on Earth living in Lumenwood, and she'd seen it become a pleasant place to live, considering it was nothing more than a trailer park surrounded by trees. As a kid, all she'd known had been dirt, mobile homes, and trees, but with time, people had made an effort to pretty up the place. Now there were plenty of gardens, lawns, fences, posts with hanging lights, Wi-Fi. Lumenwood had reached the unofficial status of a proper neighborhood.

Tonight, though, Steph wouldn't have been able to tell the difference between the Lumenwood of now, and the one from her childhood. No light, no colors, other than that bizarre dark blue that made all their pretty homes look the same: ghostly blue outlines in a sea of black. The lawns and gardens looked awash in blackness. Through curtained windows, she could see the flicker of candles and gas lamps. They made each home appear like a giant jack-o-lantern. Her home, though, was in darkness. Even the purple highlights in her hair, which she'd gotten just the day before, looked black in this merciless light.

"Stephie," her mom said from inside. "Ask if they got sugar, too."

"Sure, mom," she said over her shoulder, enthusiasm completely lacking from her voice.

She stepped out and closed the door behind her. Grass rustled under her shoes, gravel crackled as she stepped onto the center lane. As she strolled down the neighborhood, she looked up at that weird-looking moon. Every one of her neighbors acted as if there was nothing weird about it, but Steph knew better. Even though she didn't yet have money to buy a proper camera, she wanted to be a photographer. She'd studied lots about light and color. There were plenty of tutorials on Google and YouTube if you knew how to pick them—she did wonders with just her cheap cell phone camera—and it wasn't just that the moon *looked* blue, because of clouds or some atmospheric condition. It *was* blue. And blue light in this particular hue had the property of sucking out all color and detail from the world. It made things feel darker than if there was no moonlight at all. As she looked around, it seemed the darkness was alive with monsters prowling just out of sight. The flickering candlelight created a dance of shadows behind the curtains of the mobile homes, making it seem like ghosts were lurking behind each window, watching and plotting.

She reached the Ingram home, turned left into the intersecting lane, and reached the trailer next door. She turned and walked up to a door she knew was painted green but looked the same color as all the surrounding ones in this non-light. She let out a sigh, preparing for an interaction she did *not* want to have. She knocked half-heartedly, hoping no one would answer. She heard someone walk toward the door. Heavy footsteps.

The door opened, and there stood Zak Hopper's shape, silhouetted against a candlelit background.

"Oh, hey," the other teenager said, almost as half-heartedly as she'd knocked on the door. He looked her up and down with derision. "'Sup."

"Hi. Is your mom home?" She rolled her eyes, realizing of course she was, because where the fuck else was Zak's unemployed mom going to be at this hour when the power was out? "I mean, can you get your mom?"

"She's sleeping already." He crossed his arms over his chest.

"Okay." From his body language, she could tell he was going to be an asshole about it. "You think you guys could spare a couple candles? Our battery lamps aren't working, and we ran out of gas for the fuel lanterns."

"Doesn't your brother work at the gas station? Can't he get you some?"

"Don't be a dick, Zak," she said. "You know Gunnar works the night shift, so he won't be back until tomorrow."

He shrugged and shook his head. "I don't see how that's my problem."

You fucker! You mother-fucking-fucker! she thought. "Oh, so now you care if something's your problem or not?"

"I already said my piece, Steph. Paternity test, or it's not my business."

She gave him a hateful squint with a gasping mouth. "You piece of shit!" She lowered her voice. "I ain't going around fucking guys who aren't my boyfriend!"

"Oh, I was your boyfriend now?" He crossed his arms over her chest and gave her an arrogant expression. "See? You're a psycho. So, either get a paternity test, or leave me the fuck alone."

Her lips drew a thin, tense line, holding in the hurt,

but her eyebrows curled inward, betraying how she felt. She clenched her teeth, stopping short from cussing him out. Zak had been the perfect boyfriend for a few months: hot, popular, athletic; it made all the other girls in school envy her, but once he got her in bed—more accurately, on the grass in the woods—he'd changed, become more distant. That distance had become a chasm the moment that little pee stick flashed a plus sign at her like a portent of doom. Her already distant boyfriend had turned downright hateful and verbally abusive.

"You could always just get rid of it. Your body, your choice, and all that shit? You can just *choose* not to fuck up your life."

Steph had considered it. She definitely had, especially after seeing she was going to be on her own, and Zak would not be in the baby's life. She didn't want to deal with that whole mess on her own; she had plans for her life, for God's sake. That notion, however, disappeared completely when her dad found out about the pregnancy through rumors—Blight Harbor had carried the entire story to her dad like a messenger pigeon from hell—and he'd put his foot down.

"What you're carrying in there"—her dad had pointed a stiff index finger at her stomach as if it were some container, or a duffel bag, even if she wasn't showing yet—"that's my grandchild, and I won't have no baby killer in my home. You do anything to my grandchild, and you leave this house. You ain't taking anything with you. Everything you have, I paid for. You ain't taking your phone, you ain't taking your shoes, you ain't taking your clothes, 'coz I paid for that. You touch my grandchild, you leave this home broke and naked."

Her choice had been taken away from her, and she'd made her peace with the notion. Her mom, at least, had been excited. She'd told her she'd help her with everything she needed, so the baby wouldn't affect her studies. In a way, she figured it was the best outcome from a shitty situation, even if she wasn't exactly thrilled about it.

It didn't make it easy to deal with Zak fucking Hopper, though. "Are you gonna let me have the candles or not?" she said, done with Zak.

"Sure," he said. "Be right back."

He returned a minute later and handed her four candles. "Will that do?"

She nodded. "Tell your mom thanks. We'll pay you back." She turned around to leave.

"H-hey," Zak called. When she turned to look at him, his posture had changed and now he had his hands on his hips, fingers playing with the belt loops on his jeans. "Have you thought of what you're gonna name it?"

She gave him a frosty glare, taking advantage of the fact she was still standing in the dim rectangle of candlelight coming from the open door. "I don't see why that's your problem."

She walked away.

Steph heard the door of his mobile home close behind her as she turned the corner right at Ingram's. *Shit, I was so pissed off I forgot to ask him about the sugar.* She halted, her heart racing as she saw a figure standing before her. "The fuck?"

The stocky figure of an older man took a couple of steps toward her. "I'm sorry I startled you," the man said. "I'm not a creep. I swear. Are you Stephanie Bilson?"

"Who the hell are you?"

"My name's Chuck Cunningham," he said, and she saw a kind of awkward smile draw itself on his face—the kind worn by a person trying to seem casual and friendly and failing at it. He raised a palm in an even more awkward greeting.

"From the bar?"

"Yeah. From the bar."

She was about to ask him what he wanted when he pulled out a gun and pointed it at her.

"I'm so sorry about this," he said.

Chapter Twenty

Driveways

1993

"Who would've thought there was such a beautiful garden at the back of your house?" Nadine asked, sitting beside Peter on the top step of his back porch.

Peter gave her a proud smile. "You're the first person to see it——I mean, aside from my mother and I."

She blushed. "Thank you for bringing me." She looked over her shoulder at the open kitchen door. "But are you sure I should be here?"

"She won't be here for two more hours at least. She's doing her deliveries."

"Alright." She gave him a blushing glance and looked away, then pointed at one of the plants, one with flowers with pink, orange, and white petals. "I like those."

"The, uh... Lewisia, I think my mother calls it."

"They're really pretty."

Peter stood up all of a sudden, ran across the backyard to pluck one of the tiny flowers, ran back, and sat next to her again. "Here."

She took it with a big grin. "You're so corny," she said, spinning the orange flower by the stem back and forth. "I love it. It's so cute."

They stared into each other's eyes, the moment stretching for what seemed like an hour, with the nearby sound of cicadas coming from the wooded area beyond the back fence.

Nadine leaned halfway toward Peter. He reacted with a nervous flinch; his face turned beet red. He had to turn his head up a little on account of her being taller, even sitting down. His heart was beating a hole in his chest, but his eyes wouldn't leave hers. Nadine moved all the way forward and kissed him. His trembling lips bumbled against hers. His first kiss—the most beautiful girl in school, and his dear friend. He finally found the courage to kiss her back.

Once the kiss ended, they stared into each other's eyes with a bashful but complicit smile.

"Get away from him!"

They both turned to see Martha Lange, crazed,

charging toward them, wielding a pair of scissors.

"Whore! Get away from him!"

Nadine raised her arm to shield herself just in time for the scissors to come down, slashing a red line in her forearm. She shrieked in terror. The tiny orange flower fell to the floor to be stepped on by one of Martha's shoes.

"Mother, no!" Peter sprung to his feet and grabbed his mother's attacking arm and put his other arm around her, holding her back.

"You will not corrupt him with your sin!" Martha Lange said, her voice roaring with anger. "You will not sully him! I swear I'll drag these scissors across your face and men will cringe away from your whore face!"

"Nadine, go!" Peter shouted. "Go! Get out! Now!"

In panic and tears, blood running down her arm, Nadine ran past the two of them and disappeared into the house, leaving Peter and his raving, insane mother behind.

Two days later, speaking at The Pines, Nadine told him, despite how much she cared about him, they couldn't continue dating. She promised she would always be there for him as a friend, but she couldn't put herself at risk by having his mother see her as "the girl trying to take her son away". She couldn't be the face his mother would come after during one of her rages.

Peter had been very hurt, but knowing his mother, he was forced to agree.

2022

Peter's Chevy Malibu was now parked in the driveway in front of his house in the mountains. The two-story home was huge and was, at this moment, completely dark, save for the very faint blue outlines on walls and roofs, which made it look like a vampire's castle in some haunted mountain in the dark ages, looming over the small town below.

Absentminded and nervous, Nadine ran a finger over the scar on her left forearm. She was looking up in awe from the passenger's seat. "I keep forgetting you own a mansion."

"It's not a mansion," Peter said. "Stop exaggerating."

"Well, it's big," she said. "I'd say, unnecessarily big for a house you only visit once a year, in a town where pretty much no one could afford a property like this."

He turned a raised eyebrow at her, illuminated by the dashboard lights. "Should I feel bad that I can afford it?"

She returned an eyeroll and said, "No. You've earned it. Also, you're kind of letting Doris live her best mansion life, since she's the only one that actually lives here."

"She works here, she doesn't *live* here…and it's not a mansion."

"Fine. My point is, you didn't have to go that big

when it's just you, William, and…" She stopped talking, realizing she hadn't just put her foot in her mouth, but her foot, her shin, her knee, her thigh, all the way up until she had her whole ass in her mouth. *Shit!*

"Jenny?" Peter finished the sentence, and she wanted to die.

She sighed. "I'll see myself out and walk all the way down the mountain. I'm so sorry."

"That's okay," Peter said with a strange sense of peace in his voice. "Sometimes I forget she's gone, too. It's like phantom limb syndrome, but it's a whole person. I can still feel her, sometimes, sitting right there where you're sitting right now."

This made her wince a little, but she understood.

"When I walk around, I can still feel her hand in mine. When I'm in bed, and I wake up or turn around, sometimes it feels like she's still lying there next to me." He turned a sad face at Nadine. "It's only been a month…"

(*Hey, Peter, my stupid sister wanted me to tell you I still have feelings for you, and well, we're alone, at your mountain mansion, parked under the moonlight, and I was wondering if it wouldn't be totally, totally inappropriate for me to tell you I'm still in love with you, and I want to kiss you, even though you're clearly still grieving, and a man was about to shoot us dead, but we're both alone, the night is young, let's do something crazy! Let's go nuts! Hell, even borderline psychotic!*)

His last phrase drove it home for her. She'd had this

stupid moment of insane fancy when Angie had pushed this idea of professing her love for Peter. A moment in which it sounded possible, rather than certifiable. It was only a month since the love of Peter's life had died in the most traumatic, horrifying way possible.

(Nadine, my wife is dead! Jenny's dead! William saw her! We both saw her burning! Oh, my god! Oh, my god! We saw her burning!)

How lonely, sad, and pathetic had she become that the notion even peeked through a tiny crack in her brain? Peter was her friend. Her best friend. There would be nothing more harmful and selfish that she could say right now than, "I'm in love with you."

"A month," Peter continued. "It's not even enough for me to wrap my head around the concept of her death, much less around the concept of her absence."

Nadine felt like the bottom feeder that fed on the leftovers of the other bottom feeders. *Did I just refer to Jenny as a "bottom feeder"?* she thought. *I'm the worst human being ever.* She looked at the dashboard lights as they glowed in their faces. "I haven't been able to go in my mother's bedroom since a few days after she died."

Peter turned to look at her.

"That room feels like a hole in the house. Like a concrete and plaster monument to her absence."

He nodded. "Can I tell you something that will make

me sound like the worst human being ever?"

How dare you? she thought. *I'm the worst human being ever. Don't steal my title.* "What is it?" she asked.

"My son is the monument to Jenny's absence," he said, averting his gaze. "Every time I look into William's face, I can map out every part of that face that is Jenny's. It's like it's made of pieces of two separate puzzles, and I can pick apart which belonged to her. She's in every mannerism. I know every inflection he picked up from her. She's gone, but every time my six-year-old comes into view, I wince, because I hate how much he reminds me of her. That's why I needed this time away from him." She saw the shame in his face as he turned to look at her. "I wanted to *not* look at him for a few days."

Nadine stared at him, her jaw hanging slack.

"Am I a bad person?"

"No." She shook her head and took his hand in hers. "You're human, and you miss her very much, and you have to deal with him missing her as well. It can't be easy to juggle both things without a break."

He nodded.

"Don't move back to White Harbor." The words came out of her in a sudden burst. "Leave after this weekend and never come back here."

"Nadine, wh—"

"Shut up." She couldn't believe how effortlessly the words were flowing from her lips. "Ray is looking after your mom. If at some point she's close to dying, he'll call you. You can be here in no time, but for now, stay the hell away. This town is toxic. This town kills everything good, and even when good survives, it dies too soon. William is the sweetest kid I've ever met. I've always thought William is the boy *you* would've been if your mother hadn't done the things she did to you. You can't—listen—you *can't* let this town destroy that innocence. We're your friends, and I promise, I'll make sure we visit you at your new place, wherever it is, even if I have to bring them all at gunpoint, but please, sell this house, pay off Doris, and never, *never* come back here!"

Peter looked like his brain was working to drop words down to his mouth in an order that made sense, but nothing came out.

"Don't give me any stupid fucking excuse," she said. After her conversation with Jess, all she had in mind was getting Peter and his son as far away from White Harbor as she could—far away from Martha Lange, especially. "Just finish whatever business you have here this weekend, get out, and never come back."

He gawked at her, as if his brain had short-circuited. Seconds ticked away. "Okay?" he finally said.

"Promise me!"

His mouth opened and closed twice. "I promise."

"Good."

"I, uh… I was thinking we didn't really have much

chance to eat and all. Want me to make you a sandwich?" He stared as if he'd only said that to break the tense moment.

"Uh…" She stared back. Having finally gotten the words out there, it was like her brain had stepped out for a break. She nodded. "I could eat a sandwich."

On the north side of town, Royce was in the process of preparing the guest bedroom for Jess to spend the night, and his wife, Lillian, made sure all doors were locked before they went to bed. At the same time, on the east side of town, Barry was already parked in his driveway. He'd kept his headlights off, coming into his street, as to not call attention to himself this late. Without electricity, he was forced to get out of the car and manually open the garage door; however, when he used his key on the little knob, no matter how hard he pulled up on it, it wouldn't judge.

Thinking there might be an obstruction, he returned to the car, turned the headlights on. There was nothing blocking the door. He tried the key again. The knob shook left and right, letting out pathetic clicks, but wouldn't turn. He closed his eyes and brought a hand to his face, rubbing his eyes tiredly. "No, Maryann," he mumbled to himself. "Not tonight. Not tonight."

380

The sound of one, two, three locks opening, coming from the front door, reached his ear. He turned his head toward it just as the front door swung open, and there was Maryann, hair down, wearing a pink robe and pink slippers, one hand on her hip, the other, holding a lantern. He regarded her, expectant. He already knew it would do him no good to ask. If he was coming into the house, it had to come from her.

"You're not coming in," she said and nodded toward the garage. "I locked it from the inside."

He let his shoulders fall in surrender and readied himself. This wasn't the first time she'd done this.

"It's almost midnight," she said, looking at her wrist as if she were wearing a watch. "I had to cook, I had to play with the kids, I had to change them, I had to tell them their bedtime story, and on top of it all, just as they were falling asleep, the power goes out. Daniel got scared and started crying, which got Gabe crying too. I haven't had a second to unwind all night, and where were you? Drinking with your buddies. I can smell the alcohol from here."

"Hon', I barely drank, you have no idea the night I've—"

"Oh, you're going to tell me how bad your night was?"

He cast his eyes downward in a gesture of subservience. "No."

"Good."

"Can I please come in?" He put on his most earnest, pleading face, even knowing it wouldn't work. "I'll explain what happened. You won't believe—"

"No." She shook her head. "As far as I'm concerned, you're out with your friends all night. So, go be out with your friends all night."

"This is ridiculous, Maryann. This is my house, too!" He burst out in anger. *Stupid! Stupid! Shut up! Don't make it worse!*

"Oh, is that a fact?" she said with a mocking grin. "Do I need to remind you again the house is in my mother's name? You set one foot in this house tonight and she'll call the police for trespassing."

"The phones aren't even working!" he said, and regretted it at once. *Shut up! Shut up! Small! Be small! Be quiet!*

Maryann looked taken aback by this. She stuttered for a second and said, "She can call them as soon as the power comes back. I don't care about what time, but they will drag you out of here and lock you up for a while to think about what a lousy father you've been."

"Lousy father?" He'd heard her call him this a million times, but after everything that had transpired that night, something in him refused to stay quiet, to be small. "Are you fucking kidding me?"

"What did you say?"

"I work all day, I get home and have, at most, ten

minutes to shower before I have to cook dinner, do laundry, play with the kids, feed them, tuck them in—maybe get an hour to catch a TV show when everyone's asleep—I get four or five hours of sleep at most, then it starts all over again, and that's not all!"

"You keep quiet, Barry Giffen! The neighbors don't need to hear how shameless you are!"

"Shameless?" he said. "What do *I* have to be ashamed of? I give nearly my entire salary to you, to the family, to the house! I pay for a nanny to watch over Daniel and Gabe while I'm at work because you're too busy watching videos on your phone! Too busy taking your mom, or your friends out to lunch or shopping with the money *I* make! Meanwhile, I buy my clothes second-hand, so I can bring more to the house. You bought yourself a fucking SUV—"

"Watch your language—"

"A FUCKING SUV claiming the family needed it for emergencies. We already have a car that fits five!" He motioned toward his Honda. "You just wanted one for yourself and your friends, which would be cool if you'd actually fucking paid for it!"

Maryann gasped. Her eyes gave a baffled twitch.

A window on the second floor opened and Maryann's mother, Therese, poked her head out, accompanied by the sound of a baby wailing. "Maryann, tell your husband to stop shouting! He's upsetting Gabe!"

Barry turned a furious gaze toward her. "Maybe you can go back in and pick him up, be a grandma for a change, not just a meddling freeloader!"

"How dare—"

"Mom?" Maryann said, now grinning at him. "Stay there. I want you to hear this, while I tell this mockery of a man what's gonna happen."

"Let me in, so I can go tend to my son, Maryann."

"No. I think I'm going to let him cry for a few minutes. I'm going to let mom be a witness of my husband coming home drunk and upsetting our baby with his verbal abuse, forcing me to keep him out for our safety."

"What?"

"You heard me," she said, the left corner of her mouth pulled up in an evil smirk. "The moment the phones come back, I'm calling my brother. Remember my brother? Big-time lawyer? I'm gonna sue for divorce, and I'm gonna take Daniel and Gabe from you, and you're never going to see them again."

"You've said that before. You can't do that."

"Even if I can't stop you from seeing them, I'll ask for you to only get supervised visits."

This made Barry stammer. "You... You have no grounds to—"

"Chandler's a shark in court." She lowered her voice so only Barry and Therese could hear. "This little tantrum?

Verbal and psychological abuse. He'll say you have a history of violence in your youth because of what you did to Freddie Parham after the fire. He'll bring up your mom's alcoholism, and your dad's suicide as reasons for your violent tendencies. He'll even bring an examiner to confirm this. Mom and I will say you're an absent father, who only throws money at us, but we take care of the kids and the home."

He shook his head. "You can't prove that. I'll fight you on that."

She walked up to him until they were standing face-to-face. "Yes, but now we have the neighbors as witnesses with the little shouting spectacle you just made. All they saw and heard tonight was that during the night of a town-wide blackout, you came home drunk—"

"I'm not dr—"

"You came home drunk. Tried to force your way into my mom's house after I warned you not to come in, then, in your drunkenness, you verbally abused and threatened both of us as your baby cried his poor little throat raw from his crib."

"You can't do this."

"Oh, I can. And, if I feel for a second, I might not get everything I want. I'll throw in Raymond Chang for good measure."

Barry's jaw shook as he tried to work his mouth into producing words. "You wouldn't."

"Oh, you have no idea." She flashed him a full-toothed grin. "Mom and I sometimes think up stories of what we saw, what we heard. Dirty, tawdry details of everything you two might have done. And, hey"—she leaned in and spoke in his ear—"I have evidence, remember?"

She stared into his eyes with that sickening smirk of self-satisfaction.

He shook his head, tried to get a word out, couldn't.

"Go!" she said in a raised voice. "You scared our baby and I have to go take care of him. I don't want you here! I don't have to put up with you insulting me and my mother! Go look for one of your drinking buddies to let you sleep at their place!" She lowered her voice again. "Maybe Raymond Chang has a bed he can spare. Come back in the morning, and we'll see if after a good night's sleep, I decide *again* not to kick you out and take everything you have."

She turned around and headed back inside. Therese closed the second-floor window.

Before he could respond, the door closed, immediately followed by one, two, three locks.

Chapter Twenty-One

Ambush

The silent glow from the gas lantern on the ground between Chuck Cunningham and Stephanie Bilson made Chuck wish it was a small fire. At least the popping and crackling of the flames would've made the situation feel only a little less uncomfortable. He was sitting in the middle of the woods, holding back tears of grief for his dead wife as he pointed a gun at a pregnant, fourteen-year-old girl, marked as the last sacrifice of the night to the town's cruel deity.

The girl stared at him with fearful eyes but kept silent. He avoided meeting her gaze because he was consumed by guilt, but why should he be ashamed? He was doing this to save the girl's life. To save everyone's lives.

Who am I kidding? I was part of this by not stopping Martha Lange years ago. I wouldn't need to save her if I had put a stop to this craziness.

"Mr. Cunningham?" she said in a timid but warm voice.

He couldn't look at her.

"Mr. Cunningham?"

This time, with hesitation, he turned his eyes toward her. In the lantern's light, he saw a hint of color in her thick-rimmed glasses and her hair—a purple hue that made her look undeniably young. A pang of guilt wormed its way through his heart.

"Are you going to hurt me?" she asked.

"No." The answer came out fast. "I'm not. I just need you to stay here and be quiet. There's something that needs to happen before I let you go home." He noticed the way she wrapped her arms around herself, and he cringed, realizing what she must have understood from that. "No one's going to touch you." He tried to sound reassuring. "I just need you to sit right there. Don't leave the circle, alright?"

She turned her head to look at the wide circle drawn over the dirt and grass around them. She then glanced at a half-empty box of salt he'd thrown away after using about two and a half boxes to draw it and the strange shapes drawn inside it. She was sitting with her back against a tree, about a third of the way inside the circle. He sat near the opposite edge.

"I'm pregnant," she said, then paused. "I want to keep it." The way she'd added that last phrase seemed to be just a different way for her to say, "Please don't rape and kill me."

He could tell, despite his reassurances, she still thought he'd hurt her, which made him feel even more guilty. He looked down at the gun—his dead wife's gun—then back at the girl. "Stay within the circle and you'll be fine."

"Now, isn't this pathetic?" the voice was full of pride and mockery as it approached.

He saw the girl jump, startled, reacting to the voice. They both turned to see Freddie Parham's figure emerge from the darkness.

"A circle of salt," Freddie said with an arrogant grin. "What's next, Chuck? Are you going to press a silver cross to my forehead and shove a bunch of garlic in my mouth?" He then seemed to notice the other markings and runes Chuck had drawn inside the circle. Recognition appeared in Freddie's eyes. "Oh... I see." Freddie nodded. "Jeez, man, you've sunken low enough to use protective glyphs from the Order of the Rising Sun. This here is blasphemy, Chuck."

"I couldn't care less what you think," Chuck growled, feeling rage bubbling up inside him. "You killed my wife."

"Oh, no, no, no, old chump. I didn't kill your wife. She sacrificed herself to the Lord. You should've seen it. It was

389

glorious!" His lips curled into a sadistic grin. "You should've been there. Having you by her side might have made her sacrifice easier to bear."

Chuck had to restrain himself from running over and strangling him. He was baiting him, but he had to stop himself from reacting. He noticed how Freddie turned his gaze to the Bilson girl, who was confused and scared with all this talk of blasphemy, wife killing, and sacrifices.

"I promised Mrs. Cunningham I would do everything I could to ensure you and your daughter made it past the ritual alive, Chuck. But this…" Freddie gestured toward the circle. "You're not making it easy for me to keep that promise."

"This stops here, Freddie." Chuck was still pointing the gun at the girl. He didn't mean to harm her, but Freddie Parham didn't know that. "You're not coming any closer."

Freddie giggled. "And why is that, Chuckie, my buddy, my pal?" He looked down at the circle, acting as if he'd forgotten about it. "Oh, this? Interesting! I have bad news for you, Chuckles. You see. I don't know where you got the glyphs for this adorable little circle, but"—he took a very casual step forward, until he was standing inside its boundary—"these won't stop me from coming close."

Chuck aimed the gun at him and immediately cocked it. "Stop right there!"

Freddie's expression was of pure amusement. "I think you forgot an important fact about the First Night, Chuck

E. Cheese"—he spread his arms to either side, palms toward him, dramatic and boastful—"you can't touch me. Go ahead! Try it! Shoot!"

He felt tempted to take him up on his offer, but he knew Freddie was right. He knew he could empty the entire gun into him, and it wouldn't even scratch him; the bullets would just fly through him and get lost in the woods.

Freddie simply smirked at him. "See? Even you kn—"

He let out a surprised grunt as John Hitch plunged a knife into his lower back.

Hitch had been hiding behind a tree and had swiftly snuck behind Freddie as he'd been grandstanding for Chuck.

"Surprise, Freddie," Hitch said, pulled the knife out, then plunged it again into his back. In a swift motion, he kicked the back of his knee, causing it to bend, then pushed him forward, dropping him to the ground, and sat on his back, the knife still stuck in him.

Freddie bellowed in pain and anger. His eyes showed sudden fear in the realization that he'd become tangible, that he'd been tricked.

Stephanie screamed, covering her mouth with her hands. The eyes behind her glasses looked wide, terrified, shocked at the violence that had suddenly exploded before her.

"C'mon!" Hitch called out to Chuck. "Don't just sit there! Help me hold him down!"

Chuck scrambled to tuck the gun in the back of his pants and crawled toward him, kicking dirt in the air as he did. He grabbed Freddie's hands and held them down against the ground, then put his weight over his head while Hitch straddled Freddie's back and continued stabbing him. Spurts of blood flew into the air every time he extracted the knife.

"Stop!" Stephanie screamed. "What are you doing?"

"You don't understand!" Chuck cried. "He killed my wife. He was here to kill you!"

She seemed taken aback by this. He could picture the myriad thoughts clashing in her mind—her eyes flitted this way and that, to Hitch, to Freddie, to him.

Hitch kept stabbing, counting under his breath. "Nine, ten, eleven, twelve..."

"Then take him to the police!" she cried. "Stop this! You're killing him!"

Freddie's scream was a roar, interrupted by grunts and bloody gurgles each time Hitch plunged the knife in his back.

"Eighteen, nineteen, twenty, twenty-one, twenty-two..."

It needed to reach forty-four, Chuck knew. It was always forty-four, for some unknown reason. The circle made Freddie tangible, but because of the First Night's rules, he could only be killed by forty-four stab wounds.

"...twenty-five, twenty-six, twenty-seven, twenty-eight..."

Freddie was feeling every bit of pain, but he continued to struggle with the same strength he would've had if he hadn't even been stabbed once. His body wasn't showing signs of weakening, despite the many wounds that now riddled his back and soaked his shirt with blood.

"...thirty, thirty-one, thirty-two, thirty-three, thirty-f—"

Chuck gawked in bafflement as Stephanie Bilson tossed the remaining contents of the box of salt in John Hitch's eyes. A cloud of white crystal dust exploded in his face.

"Stop!" she said with a furious cry.

Hitch brought his bloodied hands up to his eyes and screamed. She took this opportunity to charge at him and push him off Freddie. Hitch fell to the floor and rolled in the dirt, covering his eyes. His knife fell several feet away.

"No!" Chuck cried. "What are you d—"

The girl's shoe came crashing against the side of his face, knocking him off Freddie. He fell down, and, still dazed, brought himself up on hands and feet as fast as he could, to see Freddie crawling with impressive speed toward the edge of the circle.

"STOP HIM!" Chuck shouted.

He heard Freddie's angry, triumphant grunt as his hand touched the ground outside the circle.

The world around them changed in the blink of an eye.

The gas lantern on the ground now illuminated a world that was made of moist flesh, veiny and sticky—an uneven, pulsing surface where indentations formed puddles filled with a viscous liquid. One of Chuck's hands was inside one of these puddles. He raised it and saw the liquid slide off, and he let out a disgusted noise. The substance was translucent white and smelled of chlorine. He was sure he knew what it was, but its very existence in this place, and in such quantities, was both inexplicable and unnerving.

Stephanie's horrified scream hit him next.

Chuck saw what she was looking at and gasped in disbelief. Where a tree used to be now emerged an obscene shape, like a bizarre sculpture made of flesh. The tree had become a trunk covered in skin and veins, ending in a hand, the fingers elongated, curled inward, and fused together like a cage that contained a mass resembling an unborn fetus the size of an adult human head.

"What the fuck?" Stephanie screamed, looking around in desperation and shock, like someone who's just entered their home to find their entire family butchered on the floor. "What's going on? What's going on? *What is going on?*"

Chuck surveyed the surroundings, everything the lantern's glow touched. All trees had become these strange, arm-like sculptures, every one of them holding fetus-like shapes of varying sizes, some cradling them, some caging them, some crushing them in the hands' grip. An entire forest of fleshy arms, holding these horrifying abominations. Multiple umbilical cords came from each fetus, and they formed a web of sorts that enclosed the four of them in this limited space.

Just then, John Hitch stopped screaming in pain, and opened his eyes, still rubbing them with the back of his hand, and he looked around with befuddlement. While Chuck could see the alarm in his expression, it didn't look like this was the first time he'd seen a place like this; his countenance was more like dreadful recognition than anything else.

Stephanie stumbled backward and fell down on her butt, still screaming in horror. "What's going on? What's going on? Jesus! What's going on? Fuck! What the fuck?"

John looked up; Chuck followed his gaze. There was the blue moon in the starless sky, just like on the other face of White Harbor.

He heard a squelching noise from his right. He swiveled his head in that direction and saw Freddie was back on his feet. The wounds were gone. Even the blood and the holes in his shirt were gone. "Oh, shit!"

Freddie raised his arms. "Thank you, Lord!" he cried, his voice passionate and insane, overflowing with fanatical fervor. "Thank you, Lord! Your mercy is never-ending for someone as filthy and unworthy as me!"

We're dead, Chuck thought as he felt his breathing come out in shaky rasps. *We failed. The sacrifice will happen. Close up shop. We're all dead! Jess. My baby, I failed you!*

Freddie turned to face them, his expression as arrogant as when he'd arrived, except there was anger in his eyes now. He regarded the screaming girl but ignored her for now and directed his gaze toward John Hitch. "Well played, New Guy," he said. "Blight Harbor has a place for you, and it's not here. Let's send you there, shall we?" Freddie waved a hand, and in a blink, John Hitch disappeared.

Stephanie screamed louder. Chuck could see the girl's mind unravel in terror.

Freddie turned his attention to him now.

He recoiled under his gaze, which blazed with insanity.

"I promised your wife I would do my best to ensure you survived," Freddie said. "This is me doing my best. Consider this the only warning you'll get from me. Go now."

Freddie waved a hand, and Chuck found himself suddenly in the woods near the trailer park, sitting in the circle of salt he'd drawn. The gas lantern was in front of him, but he was alone. The Bilson girl had remained in *her* version of Blight Harbor with Freddie, awaiting a horrifying fate, no doubt.

They had failed.

Chapter Twenty-Two

Rebirth

It was the same feeling on a different scale.

The moment that unspeakable piece of trash, Zak, had shrugged away the news of her pregnancy as if he'd had nothing to do with it, it felt like she'd been enveloped in a soundproof bubble of disbelief. She'd stared at Zak, dumbfounded, certain it was a horrible nightmare she'd soon wake up from. He couldn't, she'd thought—he couldn't really be saying what she'd heard him say. Her gorgeous, perfect boyfriend wouldn't reject her because she was pregnant. He wouldn't just shirk his responsibility like that, but there he was, doing just that.

It didn't make sense. The world itself didn't make sense. It had to be a nightmare.

In that instance, the result had been tears of anger. In this instance, the result was uncontrollable, mind rending screams of terror. Same feeling of dreamlike disbelief. Different scale.

There was something so real about the sensation of the moist flesh the ground had become. It felt like touching raw steak. Steph's foot was in one of those slimy puddles. The moment she realized this, she pulled her foot away and saw the substance dribble down from her shoe. This made her cry out again in disgust. She scuttled back on arms and legs until her back hit one of those repulsive, skin-covered pillars. A shudder coursed through her entire body when she sensed it was warm, and she saw the enormous veins pulsing along its length. She crawled away from it, and now her eyes once more focused on that thing—that impossible thing—at the top, an enormous fetus being squeezed by an enormous human hand to the point the only facial feature it had, an eye, looked like it was bulging out from the pressure inflicted by those fingers.

Then there was that man. She eyed the man the other two had been stabbing just a minute ago. He was standing.

It's a nightmare!

He wasn't bleeding. He was only watching her, a satisfied grin on his face. He'd brought them all here and made the other ones disappear.

This is a nightmare!

It could not be real. All sounds were gone. She didn't hear herself scream.

"This is a nightmare!" she heard herself declare unto the world but that feeling in her fingers as she touched the ground, that smell of blood, and cum, and exposed flesh, all of it was too real—it couldn't be a dream when it felt this real.

She saw the man's lips move, but she didn't hear him.

She stood up and ran until she reached the edge of the enclosure, delimited by those disgusting umbilical cords. She continued to scream as she pulled and tore them away, causing a disgusting black ooze to drip from the tips, but for every cord she ripped away, four more took its place. She was trapped. She was

(*I won't have a baby killer in my home!*)

trapped!

Sound came back to her, and she heard the man's voice so close to her ear it made the hairs on the back of her neck stand on end.

"Enough of that, Purple Rims," he said.

The umbilical cords continued to multiply, then whipped toward and wrapped around her. She felt them in her arms, her legs, her neck. She couldn't move. She was

(*What about what I want, dad? What about my plans? What about my dreams?*)

trapped.

"Let me go!" she screamed. "Please, let me go!"

She was

(*I said, I WON'T have a baby killer in my home!*)

trapped.

The umbilical cords turned her around to face the man who had brought her here.

"I said that was enough," he said. "We've wasted enough time. I was expecting to find you at the trailer park. This should've been over quickly. Hell, you weren't even supposed to see me; but we were interrupted. So, here I am."

"Why me?" she asked, weeping. "Why are you doing this to me?"

He looked down toward the general area of her belly. "You have a little bun in the oven. Well, more like a tiny ball of dough. Not quite baked yet. That's why."

"Don't do this," she cried, tears running down her cheeks.

"Sorry," he said with a smile and a shrug.

"I saved your life."

"And I thank you for it." There was that smile again.

She felt something crawling on the skin of her stomach. When she looked down, she saw black tendrils coming from the open end of one of the umbilical cords. They crawled toward her belly button and burrowed inside. She felt pressure, then pain. Nothing unbearable at this point, more akin to a needle like the ones used to draw blood. She grunted.

Her lips quivered in fear. She was paralyzed with terror. A few seconds later, there was movement inside her belly. Something stirred inside her. She felt it grow and swell. "What's going on?" she said, giving him a pleading look. "What the hell's going on?"

The man walked a few steps away from her, then turned to regard her as she squirmed, grunted, and let out pained moans.

"It hurts!" she cried, feeling the thing inside her move. She shouldn't have been able to feel the fetus move or kick or literally do *anything* this early in her pregnancy. "What the fuck is this?"

It was wriggling, moving, kicking, growing. She felt her belly expand from the size of the thing. The pain of the expansion became unbearable, and she let out the first scream of many. She felt her insides stretch, as well as her skin rupture. Something was making the fetus grow unnaturally fast.

It was then she felt something even more unexpected. Something—

Sharp!

—something like a sharp fingernail or a talon—something no unborn baby should ever have—was scratching her insides. There was a pop, more felt than heard, a sensation of something bursting within her. She screamed as amniotic fluid and blood flooded her shorts and ran down her legs as the scratching continued. There were now more sharp talons scraping at the tender tissue inside her body. She couldn't tell how many, but she was certain they were multiple.

This was not a baby.

She howled in pain. There was a strange creature growing inside her. She felt it unfurl within her. It was long. It had dozens of talons, clawing, tearing, breaking. Blood erupted from her mouth in a sudden cough that interrupted her chest-rending screams.

It's climbing! she thought with atrocious clarity. *It broke through! It's near my stomach!*

Then she felt her stomach burst inside her. Stephanie let out one last gurgling scream a second before she felt many talons scraping against the inner side of her ribs, and her pleural membrane was punctured. She felt her insides collapse and implode.

Her eyes rolled up into her skull the moment she gave into the madness of pain as the talons reached her esophagus and continued up her throat; her neck swelled, then the sharp, black tips of pointed insectile legs pierced the skin from the inside as the thing continued to climb, then it was crawling out of her mouth—a long, slime-covered caterpillar-like creature with the still-unformed face of a fetus, and legs like black daggers that stabbed and pierced every place they touched.

Stephanie still had enough life and sight in her to see the creature take bites off her body as a caterpillar would bite and consume a leaf, leaving round, ragged holes.

She once more heard her dad's voice in her head as he took the choice away from her.

"I won't have a baby killer in my home!"

Why didn't I...

Life had left her before she could finish the thought.

His eyes still burned from the salt, and he felt as if he'd been swallowed up by a whirlpool and come out the end of a meat grinder. Freddie had made sure the transition was as unpleasant as he could make it.

The ground was no longer wet. It felt dry and rough. *Wood. A wooden floor.*

John reached into his pocket and found his smartphone. He turned it on, found the flashlight icon, and tapped it. A beam of light broke through the oppressive shadows that flooded the place. He blinked twice, letting his eyes adjust to his newly illuminated surroundings.

His jaw dropped.

The boarded-up windows. The wooden stairs with no railing leading from the main hall to the second floor. The enormous stone fireplace. The walls he'd covered in newspapers, so curious eyes wouldn't peer inside through the cracks.

He was in the Vanek House.

Freddie reappeared in the woods, standing inside the circle Chuck Cunningham and John Hitch had drawn. He regarded the attempt with some level of respect. They had gotten close, but nothing could oppose the will of God. The woods were quiet and the only illumination in the area was Cunningham's lamp, sitting on the dirt, undisturbed. Cunningham was gone, most likely hurrying to find his daughter.

A tiny mass of flesh lay at his feet. It was barely over an inch in length, vaguely human-shaped. Minutes earlier, in the Moonlit World, he'd watched it emerge from its mother like a ravenous caterpillar and devour her down to her very bones, until there was nothing left. In the end, it had looked swollen and grotesque, full of the chunks of its consumed mother. Here, however, it looked tiny, defenseless, and dead.

Feeling like he had to pay some kind of respect, after how well its alternate self had performed God's work on the other side, Freddie crouched down. He dug out two tiny scoops of dirt with his hand, grabbed the fetus between his fingers, put it in the hole, then covered up the hole with dirt.

He remained there for a while, regarding the only sign of his work that would remain on this side, when he felt a sensation like a velvet-gloved hand caressing the back of his neck.

"Mother!" he said without looking back. "Is that you?"

"Yes."

He turned around to see the form of the Mother standing behind him. She didn't look as solid as she had in his cell at Lighthouse Rock. She faded in and out of reality, at times becoming translucent, and he could see the trees behind her.

"Are you okay, Mother?"

"I'm fine," she said in a stern voice. "I had to make two visits tonight that drained me. I've spent most of my strength for tonight, but I'll be fine."

Freddie nodded, but gave her a look of concern. He hoped she was not overexerting herself when there was still so much to do. "The four offerings have been completed, Mother."

"I can see that," she said, not showing any emotion about the fact.

"Did I do well?" Eagerness permeated his voice. He felt like a student showing his parent his report card.

"You were careless," she said, sounding displeased. "You were almost killed twice. If they had stopped you, you would have ruined an event that has been in preparation for over a hundred years." Her shape stabilized. She looked solid, angry, and terrible, even if she kept her voice under control. "You almost failed God when he appointed His mission upon you. One of the most unforgivable of offenses."

Emitting a sudden, whimpering gasp, Freddie dropped

to his knees and lowered his head until his forehead touched the dirt, and groveled. "I'm sorry, Mother! I failed you! I failed God! Please forgive me!"

"Do I need to remind you what's at stake?" she asked, disdain in her voice. "Was your adolescent arrogance worth risking God's new world?"

"No, Mother!" His entire body trembled in terror. "I was stupid! I got carried away!"

"Maybe I do need to remind you what's at stake for you?"

"No! Mother, please!"

In a flash, he saw a girl. He saw a little girl in the water. She was being carried away by the current. She couldn't swim. She struggled to keep her tiny face above water as her little, frantic hands moved, legs kicked, not touching the bottom most of the time, and when they did, the rocks in the bottom scraped her skin and the soles of her feet. Blood swirled in the current. She tried to scream, but merciless water flooded her mouth. The current became faster. She spun, tumbled, banged her arm on a rock—the bone shattered.

She kicked.

He could feel her terror. He could feel her drowning. Another spin. Her other arm was wedged between two rocks, and she spun yet again with her arm trapped. It broke in three places. He felt her lungs fill with water. He felt her hopeless-ness. Her stillness. Her death. Then, she woke up, and it started again. In Freddie's mind, this went on in a loop, over and over. He was watching her drown and die—feeling himself drown and die—for an eternity in only the second the images filled his mind.

Freddie clawed at the dirt. His eyes were wide open and flooding with tears. Solid horror got stuck in his throat and choked him, like a stale piece of bread.

"While you were prancing around feeling invulnerable, your family was suffering in the limbo that awaits all of you cursed Parhams." Her words carried an unmistakable threat. There would be no second chances. "You will take your mission seriously from now on."

"Yes, Mother!" His voice filled with dread and regret.

"You will avoid distractions."

"Yes, Mother!"

He looked up and saw her wave her hand. They were back in his cell at Lighthouse Rock, surrounded by all his paintings and doodles, which were almost indiscernible in the darkness. A small square of dim blue light from the barred window shone on the spot where he now kneeled.

"Stay here," the Mother commanded. "You are not to leave this room, and you are not to say a word to anyone about the ritual."

"Yes, Mother!" He couldn't even look up. He was in awe and terror of the figure before him.

"John Hitch," she said, and now he had to look up

at her. "He's not in the Moonlit World. Where did you send him?"

He grinned at first, feeling a surge of pride in having sent Hitch somewhere not even the Mother could see him. "I…" He stopped the grin from emerging. He couldn't let himself be arrogant again. "He *is* in the Moonlit World, Mother," he said, trying to sound as humble as he could. "I… God helped me create a separate space for him. It's like an open parenthesis in a specific area within Blight Har… uh… The Moonlit World. He's isolated until the parenthesis is closed. Only then can he come back."

She regarded him with the empty eye sockets this manifestation of her always had. She appeared intrigued. "Can he close it himself?"

Freddie's voice shook as he spoke. "He…might?" He tried to read her expression, but the only indication of her feelings was a small squint of the eyes. "It shouldn't be easy for him to do it, but he has a lot of knowledge from the Order. He might figure a way out, but it would take time."

Mother stared at him for a moment longer, gave him a single nod, and turned her back on him. "Well done, Peter," she said. "Do not leave your room. I'll have your father bring you dinner."

She vanished before his confused eyes.

He stared at the space where she'd stood, and thought of only one word: *Peter?*

Chapter Twenty-Three

Torch Song Trilogy – Part 3: Gravity

*A*ll I do is hurt people, Barry thought.

It was the night of the strange blackout, the night he and his friends had almost been shot and killed. Another night Maryann had locked him out of his own house. Barry was in The Pines, sitting on the rock Bobby had claimed as his own, back when they were children in school, his old tree had fallen down and rolled a short way down the slope many years earlier. He could hear the wind whispering through the surrounding trees. If he peered some distance to the right, he could still make out that old pile of rocks at the edge of the clearing—moldy and overgrown—where he'd found the broken rock with blue crystals when he was ten. The one he'd given Ray.

He sighed.

Regardless of what Jess said, he was convinced he'd lost Ray forever. Why was that surprising? After what he'd done, he was a fool to think there was any path to forgiveness.

He glanced down at his office keys. He planned on driving to his office and sleeping on one of the staff couches there, but he'd ended up taking a detour toward Garland Elementary and sneaking into his little safe place no one knew of—no one that cared, anyway. Adults never came here. He appeared to be the only one, especially because when he came, it was usually at night, outside of school hours. Myrtle Thornton, the night security guard, saw him sometimes, but she didn't mind him. Junkies and horny teenagers never came here, afraid to incite the curse of The Pines. He'd snuck in, like he always did, through the open corner in the wire fence that students kept opening and reopening, since years before he was even born, then walked up the slope, surrounded by the trees, the scent of pine and earth floating all around him. Once he reached the clearing in the woods, the sky opened up before his eyes. Granted, this specific night, he was looking at a starless sky with a preternatural, blue moon, but just the fact of being surrounded by pines and gazing at the open sky made him feel safe.

He'd been sitting alone on Bobby's rock for about twenty minutes, remembering his father's words: "*Sometimes, all you can do is try to be better.*" To Barry, it seemed all he'd done for so many years was try to be better and always ending up worse. He was so distracted gazing at that blue moon he didn't even notice the footsteps approaching up the slope, crunching on dirt and pine needles, or the rustling of grass being flattened under a thin tire, or the *tick, tick, tick* sound of a bicycle being rolled toward him. He wouldn't have noticed it at all had he not heard the happy clinking of bottles as a six-pack of six cocktails was set on the rock, next to his hand.

He turned his head and saw Ray sitting beside him, silent as a stone, leaving him perplexed. He had something in his hand, a ridiculous, tiny fuel lantern without a bulb or a wick, about nine inches tall. In his other hand, he had something that looked like a zippo lighter, which he flicked on, and set in a small indentation inside the lantern, its light defused by the glass globe that covered it. There was light now. Minuscule, probably not visible from afar.

Not addressing his confused expression, Ray pulled a bottle from the pack of cocktails—one containing a greenish drink—opened the lid and took a long swig. He let out a refreshed "Ahh!" At first, he said nothing and sat there, gazing at the moon with the bottle in his hand. He pointed the mouth of the bottle at the moon. "Is it me, or does that thing shine brighter here?"

Barry didn't turn his head. He couldn't take his eyes off him. He thought he was hallucinating.

The shorter man glanced at him. His eyes shifted down toward the pack of bottles, then back at him. "What are you waiting for? I took them out of my fridge. Power was out. They're gonna get warm unless we drink them soon."

Barry couldn't read his expression or understand what was happening, but he forced himself to answer. "I don't like wine coolers."

"Why?" he scoffed. "Too gay?" Ray hadn't really said it to take a jab at Barry, but there was enough venom in the comment to make him feel a tiny twinge of shame in his chest.

Without a word, Barry pulled a bottle of red drink, uncapped it, and took a swig. He grimaced slightly, shook his head. "Nope," he said. "They taste too artificial."

Ray just nodded.

They sat in silence for a while, the rustling of the trees appearing to stretch time forever.

"How did you know I was here?" Barry asked.

Ray took another drink of his green, artificially-flavored alcoholic beverage. He looked ponderous. He made a face as if the words he was about to say would feel like vomiting glass. "I got home. I got worried"—he paused, took in a breath, then continued—"about you."

He frowned. This could not be happening, not after Ray had flat out shut him down all night. "What?"

"At night, you can see Royce's house from mine. I saw your headlights from my window when you were dropping him and Jess off. Kinda hard to miss when you're the only car driving around, and I live just a couple blocks from there. I got worried about you, because you were alone, so I got back on my bike and followed you home."

Barry gawked at him. "You did what?"

"Let me talk, or I'm leaving," Ray said, giving him a serious face. "I'm only staying as long as the fuel on that zippo lasts or the drinks run out."

"I can't believe you actually came prepared to sit down and talk."

"Barry," he said in a warning tone. "Let me finish."

"Okay, go on."

"I heard the argument with Maryann—congrats on that wife of yours, by the way, she's just a winning lottery ticket—and I followed you when you left. I knew you'd probably head for the docks and sleep in your office, but I also knew you wouldn't just go straight there. There's only one place you go when you need to be completely alone with your thoughts. You used to come here on nights when your mom beat you up, or made you feel like shit. You do the same when Maryann treats you like garbage and Cunningham's is closed. Your little safe place." He shot a sideways glance at him. "Alright, then. Talk."

"I don't know what to say."

413

"All night, you've been saying you want to talk to me, and now that you have me here, you don't know what to say." He gave him another sideways look and raised a severe eyebrow. "I'd say I'm surprised, but that's how you've always been. You and words…are not friends."

"Hang on a sec, let me gather my thoughts, alright?"

"Okay. While you gather them, I'm only going to ask you for one thing. If what you're going to say includes the words 'I'm sorry' or any variations, I'm going to get up and leave."

Barry nodded quickly, the anxious look of a scolded child in his eyes, and after a long pause said, "I'm sorry."

Ray gave him another displeased look. "Are you for real?"

"Uh…sorry."

"Wow." Ray shook his head in disbelief.

Barry downed the entire bottle of cocktail until there wasn't a drop left. It was something like strawberry, or cherry, or cola, or "No.5 red chemical". He put his tongue out, licking his lips with disgust. "Blegh! Tastes like beetles."

"How the hell can you know what beetles taste like?" Ray tilted his head to one side.

"I work in imports and exports. I see all sorts of stuff arrive on those ships, and once, one of the guys taking inventory told me they were bringing a cargo of carmine."

Ray thought for a second. "Food coloring?"

"Uh huh. He told me carmine is made with ground beetles. It's in everything: strawberry yogurt, ice cream, drinks—if it's red, it's probably loaded with ground-up beetles."

"That's disgusting!" Ray swallowed with difficulty. "But wait, if it's just coloring, it shouldn't have flavor."

"It doesn't, actually."

"So?" Ray raised his palms and gave a questioning shrug.

For a moment, it seemed to him Ray had forgotten he'd been avoiding talking to him all night—and for nearly two years now.

"Remember when we were kids," Barry said, "whenever we drank Cherry Coke?"

Ray laughed.

The realization of how much he'd missed hearing him laugh at something he'd said hit him straight in the chest.

"We said it tasted like roaches," Ray said, wistful.

"Right!" Barry chuckled. "And I don't think either of us has ever eaten roaches, but we were both *convinced* it tasted like roaches. Now, imagine *knowing* that this"—he raised the empty bottle in front of him—"does, in fact, contain beetles."

Ray rolled his eyes, still chuckling. Little by little, his laughter became less and less enthusiastic, until an awkward silence stretched between them like an open parenthesis that refused to close. He took another drink from his bottle, let out

415

a long, severe exhalation. "Why am I here, Barry?"

He dropped his gaze, again trying to find the right words, when mere seconds ago they seemed to flow so easily.

"Barry." Ray stared at him. "I followed you literally all the way across town on my bike and illegally broke into school property to be here." He glanced at the pack of bottles. "I even brought some artificially colored wine coolers that aren't actually cool anymore—more like room temperature. Don't make me regret my decision. Just talk."

Barry examined the empty bottle in his hand, turning it over as if searching for answers within it. Still avoiding Ray's gaze, he said, "I've always been a fool. You've always been right."

It hadn't been an easy road to get from where both had started to where they were right now, and most of that complication had been his fault. He'd had many chances to do the right thing, and he'd always failed to take them.

2020

Ray surveyed his kitchen and dining room with a sense of accomplishment. The table was set, dinner was ready, the house clean, the candles lit. Only the guest of honor was missing. It had been three weeks since the night Barry had told him he was going to divorce Maryann, the night they'd both finally said, "I love you."

Tonight was the night.

That morning, Barry had gotten the divorce papers. He had sent him a photo of them on his phone, with the message: "Today *I* close a chapter, and *WE* start a new one, together."

He was going to deliver the papers to Maryann that afternoon. As soon as it was all done, he would pack a suitcase and come stay at Ray's house. *Our house, from now on,* Ray thought.

He knew his partner (it felt so good to call him that and not feel like shit about it) was going to arrive feeling vulnerable after saying goodbye to his one-year-old baby. "It's temporary," Ray had assured him. "While we get the custody thing sorted out." He was going to have a lot of mixed feelings to deal with, of course. Ray wanted his Big Bear to feel like he was stepping into what would soon be his new home; so he had resolved to prepare a nice dinner for him—something he knew Barry never got at home unless he cooked it himself.

He'd been anxious all morning, imagining everything that could go wrong. But, just as his worry had peaked, the picture of the divorce papers had come in, along with that heartfelt message, and he'd let out a breath of relief. There was a second message immediately after that one. It said, "I want you to make love to me tonight. No more boxer briefs this time." Ray had chuckled upon reading it but had finally burst out laughing when Barry followed the message with a GIF animation of Shakira shaking her hips.

It was almost 7 p.m. now. Their house was ready.

Today *he* closed a chapter, and *they* started a new one, together.

Ray's phone rang. The sound of a piano cover of The Cure's *Friday I'm in Love* danced around the kitchen. A picture of a cartoon bear appeared on his screen with the contact name "Baloo". He picked up his phone off his breakfast counter, and with a beaming smile, said, "Hey, Big Bear. Everything's ready. Surprise! I cooked dinner! Disclaimer: I can't guarantee my cooking is safe for human consumption—you know I didn't inherit my parents' cooking skills—but, what the hell, I was feeling inspired. I'm sure it will at least be—"

"Raymond, I won't be able to go."

Ray was speechless for a moment. His smile refused to go away—he was sure he'd misheard, or his partner was joking. "Big Bear," he said, in a tentative voice, but still trying to smile. "I think I heard you wrong."

In the microsecond it took Barry to reply, he felt himself falling into a deep chasm, not knowing when he'd hit the ground.

"No, you didn't hear me wrong." Barry's voice was expressionless, the way Ray imagined souls in limbo must sound.

"I don't understand."

"Maryann is pregnant."

(*Falling. Falling through a hole. Falling through the world. Falling forever. It's Friday… I'm in love*)

"What?"

"Maryann is pregnant."

The fact he'd repeated it didn't make the phrase sound less ridiculous than the first time. The words did not make it through the filters between his ear and his brain that were desperately trying to protect his heart.

In the back of his mind, he knew that, surely, at some point in the last fourteen months, Maryann *might* have asked for sex from her husband, and Barry would have had to comply. It was a possibility he was prepared for. It was something he had filed away in a folder, in a drawer, in a cabinet, under B for Blight Harbor, taking solace in the fact—according to Barry—Maryann had shown no sexual interest in him for years. Barry had even guessed she had a lover somewhere to take care of her needs, and he was fine with that, especially since he knew she was on birth control, just in case. However, this implied not only that it *had* happened, but that it had happened recently, and the result was—

"I thank you so much for all the years of friendship," Barry said, in a voice so cold, so distant, he sounded nothing like the man he knew; the man he loved.

"Why are you talking to me like that?"

419

"I'm sorry," he continued, as if he hadn't heard him, "but now that I'm going to be a father for the second time, I have to think about what's best for my family."

"Barry." Desperation seeped into his voice, climbing up his throat like acid reflux.

"All my time must be devoted to them."

"Why are you talking to me like…" He stopped. He knew why. He *knew* why. "She's there. She's there with you."

"Our friendship will always be a beautiful memory," Barry continued.

"She's there!" Ray now shouted, losing all self-control. "Isn't she?"

"I have to protect my family from sinful behaviors."

"Sinful behaviors?" He felt as if he'd been slapped through the phone.

Barry kept going, in that expressionless monotone, with careful, slow cadence, as if he were using text-to-speech. "As a family, we do not agree with the lifestyle you've chosen for yourself, and we prefer to stay away from it. We wish you the best in your life."

"SHE'S THE ONE TALKING!" Raymond shouted, feeling himself shatter at the sound of the pain in his own voice. "THOSE ARE NOT YOUR WORDS! THEY ARE HERS!"

"Goodbye, Raymond."

"Barry, you can't do this to me!" He was begging. Never in his life had he been reduced to begging, but here he was, regardless. "Please do not do this to me! This will destroy me!"

"You can take it however you want." The indifference in Barry's voice could hollow out a boulder. "Your feelings are not my responsibility."

The call ended.

Ray fumbled with his phone, his fingers moving fast and desperate to open the messaging app. Blocked.

Facebook. Blocked.

Instagram. Blocked.

Ray started hyperventilating. He took two steps back, stumbling, moving like a sailor on the deck of a ship, swaying side to side in the waves. In his dining room, he stood in stunned silence, noticing the table, fully set, with two candles still burning, casting their flickering light, which danced as if mocking him. Why had he lit them this early if Barry hadn't even arrived?

He stood there, staring at the candles for ten seconds, or a millennium. He blinked. Shook his head as if waking up from a daydream.

In a numb trance, he trudged toward the oven, grabbed his mitts, opened the door, and pulled out a tray of chicken breasts covered in a mushroom sauce, whose recipe he'd found on Google. He placed the tray on the stovetop, so hard the Pyrex clattered. He grabbed one of the two plates he'd left nearby, ready for serving. He helped himself to a piece of chicken and a couple of spoonfuls of sauce, then some roasted vegetables he had on a separate tray. A potato rolled off the edge of the plate and onto the floor. He didn't even pay attention to it.

He turned and walked away without closing the oven door, sat down at the table, dropped the plate in front of him—another potato rolled off on impact, printing two small spots of butter on the tablecloth before falling off completely.

Ray took the cloth napkin before him and placed it over his thigh. He looked around with a puzzled expression, as if he had woken up in a place he didn't recognize. Tears had been running down his face for a while, he realized, but he didn't know at what point he'd started crying.

He stood up. The chair made a scraping noise on the floor as he pushed it out and the napkin fell to the floor, unnoticed. He leaned over and blew out both candles; the flames dissipating into a thin, snaking plume of smoke. Without even looking at the plate, he turned and walked toward the living room, but he only went three steps before coming to a stop and letting himself crumble, like a tower in a controlled demolition, falling straight down, as his knees buckled, until he was sitting on the floor, leaning against the stairs.

No one knew of his relationship with Barry. No one *could* know of his relationship with Barry.

He couldn't call anyone.

He was all alone.

It's Friday...

2022

Barry had gotten through another wine cooler—this one, a facsimile of *piña* colada—that he'd forced down. While the artificial flavor of pineapple and coconut still tainted his palate, he put the bottle back in the cardboard pack, where it clinked when it touched another bottle.

He and Ray sat together under the blue moonlight, with the soft glow of the weird zippo lantern. He was still recounting the events of that fateful day—when he'd failed the love of his life in the worst way he could.

(*All I do is hurt people*)

"I got home so determined that day." He wrung his hands. The memory burned in his chest like fire. "I had the divorce papers in this neat manila envelope, and a thumb drive with recordings from the baby cameras showing my interactions with Daniel. I had voice recordings of Maryann and her mother insulting and threatening me. I had receipts, bank information, text messages. I was *so* ready!" He clenched his fists. "I texted her we had to discuss something important. I was terrified, but I was happy. I felt like a convict about to collect his things and leave prison."

He sighed.

Barry Giffen could point at many moments in his life where he could've ended up being a different person, a happier person, but hadn't. However, if there was one set of hours that encapsulated his life being ruined, it was that terrible Friday afternoon.

"When I came into the house, I saw Maryann's mother on the couch. She was stuffing her mouth with cookies and watching soap operas. When she noticed I was smiling, she gave me this horrendous grin full of yellow and gray smoker's teeth." He bared his own teeth, trying to emulate that face. "I knew that grin. It was the grin she always made when her daughter tore me to pieces. I walked by, and she said, 'Looks like someone's having a *fabulous* day', with this mocking tone I've always hated. I just ignored her and kept walking toward the bedroom. The plan was to give Maryann the papers, tell her about the USB drive and the other evidence, make her sign, and get the hell out of there."

He lowered his gaze and kicked the dirt at the foot of the rock they were sitting on. A tiny cloud of dust got carried away by the chilly wind.

"When I entered the room, what I found was *not* what I expected. Maryann wasn't all claws out and ready for a fight. She was sitting in bed with a smile from ear to ear. Beaming with joy. This was worse, so much worse. I couldn't figure out what in the world could be making her that happy, until she reached for the nightstand, and there, under the lamplight, was a pregnancy test." He shook his head, dejected. "I didn't need to see the result. That contented, evil smile on her was enough for me to know I wasn't collecting my things and leaving prison. My sentence had just become life."

He shot a furtive glance toward Ray. He was sitting there quietly, listening with a vague expression on his face.

"That's when she started ranting about raising our children away from 'negative influences.'" He made air quotes and scoffed cynically. Shook his head. "That she believed homosexuality was a choice and didn't want to expose the children to people who would 'influence them in that direction'. While she was saying all this, I was a statue, just standing there, motionless, speechless, with the damn manila envelope in my hand. I could've just folded it into an origami middle finger, for all the good it would do me. She ordered me to call you and say, uh"—he choked on his words, ran a hand over his lips—"all those awful things I said, and block you on everything, and like the biggest fucking coward in the world, I did."

He hadn't fully turned to look at Ray during the entire story. He couldn't face him without feeling like garbage, but now he forced himself to turn his head toward him and saw him nod in understanding.

"She knew," Ray said.

"Yes."

"All this time, I had a theory in my head." Ray's voice

was calm, almost serene, like this was a conversation he didn't know he'd needed. "There are a lot of stupid things you do while you're grieving, you know? One day, doing some mental math, I estimated Maryann must have learned of her pregnancy about three weeks from conception. Am I correct?"

A nervous croak escaped Barry's lips.

"Three weeks after the night you told me you loved me."

The way Ray looked at him was so intense he could feel its weight bearing down on him.

"You conceived Gabe that night, didn't you? You told me you loved me, then went home and impregnated your wife."

Barry's countenance took on an undeniable look of shame. He brought his palms up to his face and hunched over even more. "I…"

"Wow." Ray looked away and shook his head. Despite the peace he felt, confirming this one tidbit of information had stung.

Barry let his hands fall, still hunched over, resting his elbows on his thighs. "That night…when I said—"

"Don't say those words," Ray interrupted. "I don't want to hear *you* say them ever again. I swear I'll puke wine cooler all over you."

Barry acknowledged this with a regretful nod and continued. "*That* night, I got home, I took off my clothes and threw them in the laundry basket to take a shower. I made sure to put them under the other clothes, so Maryann wouldn't get curious and maybe smell them. I just wanted to keep them hidden until I did the laundry the next day. When I came out of the shower, the bedside lamps were on, and Maryann was waiting for me in bed, awake, naked, and she started kissing me, touching me, and—"

"I don't need details, thank you!"

"Right. I'm sorry."

"And stop apologizing, for god's sake. Just go on."

"When I said Maryann showed no interest in me sexually, I was telling the truth. We hadn't had sex in almost two years, and I was more than happy to keep it that way. I thought it was way too strange that she'd be that forthcoming all of a sudden, but I was still very"—he turned a regretful gaze toward him—"fired up by what we'd done that night; and this was a way to release the pressure. I know it's no excuse, but in my mind, I was…with you. You know what I mean?"

"Far more than I wish I knew," Ray said, his upper lip twisting in disgust.

"The next morning, I noticed my briefs from the night before were not under the other clothes like I had left them, but on top of the pile. When I examined them, I noticed a"—he cleared his throat, shifting in discomfort—"stain…in the backside of the… A stain from your… From when I did what I…"

427

"Are you kidding me?" Ray swiveled his eyes toward him in disbelief.

"She *wanted* me to see it. That was her saying, 'I know'. But I think she knew from long before. She had to have planned to stop taking her contraceptives with enough time, and I guess when she saw the stain in my underwear, she saw an opportunity to close my last avenue of escape. She still has them, you know? The briefs? Just tonight, she threatened to use them as evidence when she sues me for divorce."

"That woman is truly Machiavellian."

"Want to know just how much?" Barry looked at him, his eyes sad and puffy. "She spent years not showing any sexual interest in me, but since she made me break up with you, she does. She knows I don't enjoy it. She knows I don't want it. She knows it's literally one of the worst things she can do to me…and that's why she does it."

Barry looked up at the moon and thought Ray was right; here in The Pines, it glowed a much brighter blue.

"Barry, no…"

"She waits for days in which I'm happy." He sighed. "When Gabe said his first word, I was over the moon, because my baby's first word was 'Daddy'. He was toddling around shouting, 'Daddy, daddy, daddy, daddy—'" he turned a bright, proud smile at Ray—"I recorded him. I was going around showing the video to everyone at work. I was just so happy." He turned his eyes up at the moon again. "That day, she wanted to. I said 'No' more times than I could count, but she just flashed that little box of blue pills and said, 'Let's go.'"

"Jesus, Barry! That's horrible. That's—"

"I know what it is." He turned a deadened smile at him. "I've been experiencing it for years. Trust me, I know what it is."

"Why haven't you…" He stopped the moment he saw the telling look he was giving him. That wan, painful smile, with welled-up eyes. Ray let his shoulders drop. "Your kids."

"Every time I say I don't want to, she threatens to take my kids away from me. Says I didn't just cheat on her, but I cheated on her with a man, so with everything she and her mother will say, it would be an easy win." He shook his head, thinking wordless insults he went through in his mind to chastise himself for being such a coward. "So, I do it. I don't want to. I hate every minute of it. I know she's only doing it to hurt me and assert her dominance over me. But I do it, because I can't risk losing my boys. Not to her. Not knowing the way she'll poison them against me. Not knowing that monster will raise them without me."

He pulled in air through his nose; it sounded wet. He then wiped his eyes with his jacket.

"I didn't have a mom like yours, Ray. I can't help but think if my dad hadn't killed himself, things would've turned out very different for me." He struggled to say the next words as the onset of tears got in the way. "Maybe I wouldn't have been so afraid to be me…" He glanced at him with eyes that had already given up on holding back tears. "Maybe you and I would've been married for years now, living away from this town. Happy."

Ray swallowed hard.

"But I had the mother I had, and I lost my dad, and look at the piece of shit I've become." He sniffled, pinched his nose with his hand, and let go. Looked up at the moon again. "I can't let that happen to my children." He shrugged. He thought of whether to say the last thing he had to say. He swallowed hard and continued. "Little over a year ago, I would've killed myself if Jess hadn't reminded me I can't leave my children alone with that woman. I was ready to go. I wanted to. Still do, sometimes."

Barry's face twisted in an expression of regret and self-loathing, his back arched forward, and he wept into his hands.

Ray stared at this big, burly man he'd once loved so much, hunched over and destroyed, an empty shell of the kind-hearted man he knew him to be. He could see the regret, the self-hatred, and the way both of those emotions pulled at his chest from the inside, almost making his body collapse in on itself.

He remembered himself, many times, looking just like this, alone at home, hunched over on the couch, crying into a pillow to hold back his cries of anguish, unable to tell anyone because, no matter how unfair it all was, he was incapable of hurting Barry by outing him without his consent.

He thought of the damage Barry had done to him, pain so strong it consumed him. And yet, seeing him like this, broken, humiliated—something many jilted lovers would've derived pleasure from—made Ray feel a stab of pain in his chest. What Barry had done was unjustifiable, but he didn't deserve the hell he was describing.

Without saying a word, Ray moved the lantern out of the way, scooted closer, and put his arms around him. Barry hugged him back as quickly as a man hanging off a cliff takes a helping hand. He held him as he sobbed, and did his best not to get carried away, feeling his warmth, feeling that familiar scent.

"I miss you," Barry said, and he felt the vibration of his voice in his chest. "I've missed you every day since that call."

Ray wanted with all his heart to stay in that embrace forever, but he forced himself to be the first to release. *I can't go further. I can't go back. That time has already passed.* He carefully moved away from him. "Barry, I feel terrible about what you're going through, and I don't want to sound like an asshole, but you made your decision two years ago. You weren't powerless. You could've filed for divorce. I know you panicked, but I told you a million times: Maryann can't take your children just because you're gay."

Barry gave a regretful nod. His gaze downcast.

"It's taken me a lot of effort to recover a bit of normalcy in my life. When *us* happened, my mom had died just six months earlier. My siblings left White Harbor, and I was left to figure out how to balance my job and deciding what to do with that abandoned freaking restaurant. I was very lonely. So damn lonely. And you were always there, bringing me food, forcing me to leave the house, visiting me at work. You made me feel cared for... Loved. I knew how Maryann treated you and how lonely you felt, too... and, well... loneliness won. That night in your car, I thought, '*Why can't we both stop being lonely if we both need it?*' Maybe we both deserved a bit of happiness. Now I know it was just a different kind of loneliness."

Barry nodded again with resignation. "How about being friends, at least?"

Ray chuckled. "Do you know what synesthesia is?"

Barry made a confused face. "No."

"It's like when you smell something, and it evokes a visual memory, even though you're not really seeing it. Or you hear a song and remember what the blanket you used as a child felt like. Things like that."

Barry frowned, apparently not grasping what he was getting at.

"Do you know what it's like to see someone from across a room and immediately sense the smell of their hair? Or listen to someone's voice and remember the taste of their lips?"

From the pained look on his face, Ray could tell he knew the feeling firsthand.

"You must have crossed a certain threshold of intimacy for those specific connections to exist in your brain. Can you imagine being friends with that person?"

Barry didn't answer.

"It would be torture every time we saw or talked to each other. I'm not going to deny there's this pull... This... gravity when we're close. But..." He could see Barry trying to force himself to accept there was no going back, even to a friendship. "Give me time," Ray said with a faint smile.

Barry's blue eyes opened wide with shock. He'd clearly not expected those words.

"We already talked. That's something." He put what was left of the last cocktail bottle in the pack, took the handle, and stood up, lifting all the bottles together, just as the zippo flame died down and moonlight enveloped them again. "I have to go."

He caught just a glimpse of Barry's chest hair peeking from behind his collar. His fingertips tingled.

(*Synesthesia*)

"Can you drive me home?" he asked, and Barry's eyes

lit up. "I know it's all the way on the other side of town, but you can stay on my couch if you want, so you don't have to sleep at the office."

"Of course!" he answered with an eager smile, and looking like he was struggling not to cry again.

Just then, the night lights in the school building up the slope came on. They both turned around and, in the distance, saw the entire town coming back from the darkness, in sections, and the streetlights once more cast a warm glow over the sidewalks. He pulled out his cell phone and not only was it on, it had full bars. Messages sent right before the blackout started pouring in.

Not knowing why, he looked up, and what he saw was just a regular silvery moon, not full but waning, unlike the one that had been there for the entire blackout. "If we hadn't seen weirder things before, I'd say that's insane," he said. "But that *is* absolutely insane." He turned to Barry, who was also staring at the moon. "C'mon. I want to get home and turn on the heat before I go to bed. The power might be back, but the night's still cold."

Barry gazed at him, grinning, still in disbelief. "Sure."

Barry stood in the middle of Ray's living room for the first time in nearly two years. As he folded his jacket and placed it on an armchair, he observed the room hadn't changed at all since he'd last been there. He stood by the coffee table, turning on the spot. He'd missed this place so much.

He ran a hand over the couch's fabric, and remembered when they'd watched movies together on it, hand in hand, or resting one's head on the other's shoulder. They'd kissed so many times on this couch. Now, he'd have to settle for sleeping on it alone. One night only, like a traveling act about to be retired. Still, there was happiness in just being here now, when he thought Ray would never allow him to set foot in his house again.

Even if it wasn't everything his heart wanted—that bridge having been burned by one fatal phone call—it was something. Just listening to Ray speak to him as he had this night was more than he thought he'd ever have again—certainly more than he deserved.

As he turned, looking at the pictures on the walls, the decorations, the furniture, Barry's gaze stopped on a tall cabinet with glass doors containing glass shelves with different mementos and items from Ray's life. He saw pictures, trophies, souvenirs, trinkets of all kinds. He remembered it from Ray's parents' home. It had belonged to his mother. What caught his attention, though, wasn't the cabinet itself. He walked up to it and looked at the contents on the second shelf from the top.

435

"Here you go!" he heard Ray say as he walked down the stairs. He was holding some blankets, a pillow, and what looked like a shirt and pajama bottoms. Ray noticed him standing in front of the cabinet.

Barry pointed at something inside. "You kept it."

Ray stood by the couch and set what he was carrying down on it, then turned to look at the cabinet. His face didn't seem to react to what Barry was pointing at. He uttered a flat "Oh," displaying a deliberate lack of emotion, then walked closer to the cabinet, while keeping some distance from him.

They were both looking at the rock Barry had given him so many years earlier. Positioned discreetly in the back corner of the shelf, the rock was obscured by four matryoshka dolls, each one smaller than the last. But despite its understated position, the Sharpie-written note: *You make me live —Barry* was readable.

"I guess I forgot it was there." Ray dismissed it with a wave, then turned around toward the couch. "I left you some blankets and some clothes to sleep in. They should fit you."

Barry turned to look at the couch. The thought flashed through his mind. Why did he have pajamas his size when Ray was much smaller than him? "Sure. Thanks."

Ray nodded with an understated smile and strode toward the stairs as he approached the couch and picked up the clothes. He followed him with his eyes as he climbed each step, listening to the sound of his shoes on the wood. Just as he was reaching the landing, he said, "Ray?"

He stopped, turned around. "Yeah?"

"Thank you," he said, nodding toward the folded pajamas in his hands. "Thank you for letting me spend the night."

His old friend nodded, lips pressed together in a noncommittal expression. "Good night."

Barry ran a hand over the pajamas, unfolded them. They had never been used.

Chapter Twenty-Four

Lights On

There was an island with a steel top at the center of Peter's kitchen used for cutting and preparing meals, but which also had stools which could be pulled out and used for seating.

Peter had topped off the gas lantern's fuel and set it at the center of the island, so he and Nadine could sit down, have a sandwich, and talk some more. He'd cracked two windows open so the smell from the lantern wouldn't ruin their meal. The light reflected off the surrounding appliances and glassware, as well as the pots and pans that hung over the island from a decorative steel grating attached to the ceiling.

The many tiny spots of light looked like stars floating around a great central light—a miniature galaxy in Peter's kitchen.

A small piece of uneaten sandwich sat on Nadine's plate. Peter still hadn't eaten half of his. Two mostly empty glasses and a bottle of 7-Up sat on the island as well.

"That was one hell of a midnight sandwich," Nadine said. "Was never a tuna salad fan, but damn, Doris might turn me into one."

Peter wiped his lips with a napkin and smiled, glancing at Nadine's plate. "Doris is an amazing cook. Though, technically, tuna salad isn't *cooked*. Well, you know what I mean."

"She's good at putting stuff together that tastes good when you put it in your mouth? Is that the gist of it?"

Peter gave her a smile. "Something like that, I guess."

Nadine surveyed the large kitchen, with its top-of-the-line appliances, fixtures for hanging kitchenware, and its huge fridge, not to mention the door to a walk-in pantry, which was open, after Peter went in to get a jar of pickles. Everything was covered in shadows, lit up by only the lantern on the center island. Doris slept soundly in her room, and the unyielding quiet made the kitchen feel immense. *Frankly*, she thought, *it really is immense.* She glanced around some more, as if she needed extra time to take in the entire space. "And you insist this isn't a mansion. When are you planning on having cotillion balls and lavish orgies? Place in the mountains like this? Screams decadence and hedonism."

439

"Oh, shut up."

Nadine studied the bashful expression on his face. "Why are you so intent on trying to act like you don't have money? You've earned it. Having more money than your friends doesn't make you any less of a good person."

He gave her a slight lip-twitch of an unenthusiastic smile.

"What?"

"I'm not a good person, Nadine."

She rolled her eyes. "Well, then, I guess I'm just the worst friend ever, 'coz I hadn't noticed what a horrible human being you are."

Once more, he attempted a smile just two clicks under enthusiastic. "Did I ever tell you what I did with the first big paycheck I got for a novel?"

"Based on how crazy you're talking, you'd think you used it to buy an endangered tiger, then kidnapped a baby orphan from a war-torn country, then fed the orphan to the tiger, little by little, starting with its toes, *while* you pointed at other captive orphans going, 'Eeny, meeny, miny, moe', to pick which one's next. Am I close?"

He stared at her with an eyebrow raised so high half his forehead creased. "Jesus, lady! That mind of yours!"

She chortled. "Go on, tell me. You were getting way too serious, so I panicked, but I want you to tell me."

His gaze wandered toward the shadows of the kitchen.

He appeared to be stringing together a series of memories, most of them unpleasant. "I was in Seattle for a week—this was a couple years before Jenny and I got married, and I felt like I wanted to treat myself to an expensive dinner. I thought of getting an obscenely large steak, and my agent recommended this place downtown: the Metropolitan Grill. I didn't know if it was the best steak in town, but I was sure it was a fancy place—like super fancy-looking. So, I buy myself this expensive jacket, get all dressed up, and walk into this lavish monstrosity of a place you would expect to find in a 'coked-up businessman movie' from the 90s. And let me tell you, the food totally lived up to the hype.

"I ordered the Ossetra caviar as a starter, then followed it with the tenderest, most perfect Wagyu steak I've ever had in my life, a salad, and this unbelievable Château La Fleur. All amazing. Then, the dessert…" He let out a lascivious moan and swiveled his eyes toward her. "It was this nine-layer chocolate cake. To use your own words: decadent and hedonistic."

Nadine let out a brisk laugh.

"Tip and all, I paid something like six hundred bucks. Even now, I don't think I've ever paid that much for a meal for myself alone since then. Totally worth it, though."

He stopped and grabbed his glass, placing his fingers over the mouth, and turned it on the spot, emitting a soft clatter on the metal top of the island, and his expression turned reflective.

"Anyway, I come out of there, and I'm on top of the world. So, I'm waiting outside for my cab to arrive, and out of nowhere, there's this homeless woman standing next to me. Literally one foot from my face before I could even see her. It's the end of November, and it's freezing cold. She's only wearing this flimsy sweater and a skirt over torn leggings, and she's shivering. She's all dirty and stinks of garbage and sweat and shit." He pauses for a second, considering. "She's also Black—"

Nadine's face twitched at this. He noticed it.

"It might be important later," he added. "I can see she's quite *beautiful* behind all the dirt caked on her face. She had these gorgeous high cheekbones—but her hair is this"—he spun his hands wildly around his head—"colossal chaos of tangled, matted, sticky hair, as if she'd slept on her side, lying in God-knows-what. She's sobbing, and there's"—he made a disgusted expression as he ran his fingers down his face, as if indicating something pouring down—"there's snot running from her nose. Thick, lime-colored snot. So damn much of it. Running over her lips, all the way to her chin. I don't know if it's because she's crying or because she's sick with something, but the sight of it made me recoil. Then, she starts pleading, Nadine, pleading! 'Please, mister! A dollar or two! I'm hungry! Please! I'm hungry!'"

Nadine shot him an uncomfortable glance, then pushed the impulse to comment away.

"I'm suddenly panicking," he said. "I just scramble and dig into my pockets like a clumsy moron and pull the first bill I can get a grip on, and it's a ten. I just shove it in her face and take a step back, trying to keep my distance. She takes the bill, and I'm thinking that will be it, but suddenly..."

He stopped, palms raised and flared, as if he were about to do jazz hands and say he was just making stuff up.

"She suddenly goes, 'Oh, my god, mister, thank you!' and she *throws* her arms around me! A close, tight hug! Her chin's on my shoulder and I picture the lime-colored snot so close to my face, and I sort of turn my eyes, and see it's actually getting on my jacket, and my brain flashes the word 'DISEASE' at me, while she's still crying, 'Thank you! Thank you! Thank you!' and I'm keeping my hands raised because I don't want to hug her back, I don't want anybody to think I'm touching her, and I look to the left and at the restaurant entrance there's this group of people—people in suits—staring at the whole scene in horror, as if they were witnessing a man being infected with leprosy. Finally, she lets go of me, and she takes off down the sidewalk just repeating, 'Thank you! Thank you! Thank you!' and I could only feel disgust at the image of her hugging me."

Nadine studied Peter's expression. He averted his gaze. "Why do you think that makes you a bad person? I think most people caught off-guard like that would have had a similar reaction."

Peter chuckled with sarcasm, shook his head. "I think what you have to wonder is this: Was I repulsed by her because she was homeless? Was it because she was dirty and smelled bad? Was it because of the snot, which might mean I could catch some disease? Hell, could it be because she was Black, and I was raised by a woman who wasn't aware of how racist she was? Maybe it rubbed off on me. Who knows?"

"Don't you fucking say that," Nadine spat. "You're not racist. You've never been, and you never will."

"Why? Because I have a friend who's Black?"

She stared, mouth agape, caught off-guard. "That's in terrible taste. Listen to me. You're not racist."

"I sincerely hope not." He tilted his head, considering. "Cynicism aside, here's what I think was the *actual* reason. I think it was because that night was the first time in my life I felt better than someone." He gave a brief pause, waiting for this to process in Nadine's mind. "That night, I had money, I was well dressed, I had just come out of a six hundred dollar dinner, I was an up-and-coming author with a paid contract, looking to take the world by storm. In my mind—just for that brief minute—that woman was beneath me. How dare she ruin my perfect night? How dare she touch me when, at that moment, I was better than her?"

Nadine stared at him in silence.

"I'm not a good person. Not all the time. Not as much as I wish I were. When we talked on the phone earlier today, you said I kept making excuses for Mother. Well, that's part of the reason. Every time Mother does or says something reprehensible, and I feel like I should go off on her, I remember"—he touched his index finger to his head—"I remember that homeless girl, with a face that could've been on the cover of magazines if it hadn't been covered in dirt and mucus. I remember she let go of me a fraction of a second before I had the chance to push her off me. She would've fallen to the sidewalk, and the Martha Lange in me would've shouted some disgusting words at her, so the group at the entrance saw I was one of *them*. That's why I make excuses for Mother—because if there's a little of that nastiness in me, if I inherited even an iota of the way she sees others as inferior, then how can I judge her and abandon her for being the way she is?"

Peter fixed his eyes on Nadine, waiting for a reply, knowing there was nothing she could say to soothe the horridness that bubbled up along with that memory. He felt so disgusted with himself, he didn't even realize he'd called his mom "Mother". Everyone who knew him knew it meant something different from "my mother" or "my mom".

"It's not the same. You know that. You're not your mom."

"I guess." Peter shrugged, and became quiet for a few minutes, looking pensive. "Do you mean it? You guys don't want me to come back here?"

Nadine gave him a nod with zero hesitation.

"Fine."

The way he said this made her stare. "Fine?" she asked. "Just fine?"

"Fine," he said, then added, "I do still plan to visit my mother at Clarendon every day this weekend."

Nadine's body tightened at this, and she opened her mouth to say something, but he stopped her by raising a palm.

"I owe it to myself to see that through, but regardless of what happens, I'll leave." He glanced at her with a serene but sober look. "I'll sell the house, give Doris a good payout, and I'll leave."

"Are you just doing this because I'm telling you to?"

He pondered on this. "No. I keep going back and forth on that decision so much, it should be obvious what the correct answer should be. Even tonight, after telling you what I planned to do, there was like…an aftertaste. Your guys' reaction was one more weight on that side of the scale. So, I'll leave. I'll leave and stay gone."

She sighed, satisfied with that decision.

"I'm sorry about what happened tonight," he said. "The guy with the gun? I don't know what he was going on about, but you heard him: it has to do with my mother. A part of me feels like I'm the one putting you all in danger."

"That's enough." She waved a hand at him. "Not your fault. Is it the fault of dear old Martha Lange? Well, we could argue about it all night and get nowhere. But I know it's not your fault, so stop it."

The kitchen lights came on. The sudden reflection on the white walls, the glassware and the metal surfaces blinded them for a moment.

"Oh, thank god," Nadine said once her eyes adjusted. "Does this mean it's over?"

Peter didn't look convinced "over" was the right word for it. "I'll try to get some info out of my mom tomorrow. Even in her mental state, she might let something out."

She gave another nod and a tiny sigh, but this one didn't sound as relieved as the previous one.

The bathroom lights came on as Callum brushed his teeth before bed. He was dazzled by the lights reflecting off the tiles and mirrors. He cursed at himself for having flicked the light switch as he came in by pure force of habit.

From the bedroom came Sylvia's voice, cursing loudly, and he knew she'd also made the same mistake as she walked in the room. He spat the toothpaste out, rinsed his mouth, then the toothbrush, and went out into the bedroom. As he passed the light switch, he gave it a casual flick and turned it off.

He stood in front of the bed, where Sylvia was still

447

shielding her eyes. He adjusted his glasses and smiled. "The wine?"

"I'm not drunk."

"If you say so."

Sylvia moved her hand away from her eyes and squinted at him. "Do you think Peter will come tomorrow?" She reached for the bedside lamp on her side and turned it off. Half of the room returned to darkness, leaving only Callum's nightstand lamp on.

"If he said he'll come, he'll come."

"Do you want me to be here?" She settled down on her pillow and pulled up the covers. "You might need help translating that weird language."

"That's okay. Peter hates talking about the Vanek House. The two of us together might feel like an interrogation. Also, don't you have to work on the school budget tomorrow?"

She gave him a playful grin. "I do, but what about you, Mr. Baker? Tomorrow's still a school day. Shouldn't the school librarian be there?"

He gave her a deer-in-the-headlights look. "Um... Well, I thought, maybe..."

"You know, Mr. Baker? You look a bit under the weather, might be the flu. I can't have you be around the kids if what you have is infectious. Can you imagine? You pass it to one kid, then there are two sick kids, then there are four, and so on. I will not have one of my employees be the source of the first pandemic of the twenty-first century. Millions of people might die."

Callum frowned at this. "Um, actually, the last influenza-based pandemic was the swine-flu in 2009, the last before that was in 1968. Of course, even if we factor in multiversal theory, and there's another reality in which a pandemic killed millions in the 2020s, I'd still be willing to bet *I'm* not the source of it. Most likely, it would be caused by—"

"Cal…"

It took him longer than usual to realize she was being sarcastic. "Oh!" he reacted. "Oh, I see! You're giving me the day off?"

She rolled her eyes. "You're so adorably dumb sometimes." She patted the space next to her. "Come to bed."

"I… was going to check something in my office before—"

"Cal! Your papers will still be there in the morning. Come to bed!"

He shot an awkward glance toward the bedroom door, then back to the bed. He was exhausted. Dragging his feet, he walked around to his side, put his glasses on the nightstand, and slid under the covers. The moment he felt the soft sheets, he realized coming to bed was the right choice. He reached to turn off the lamp, then stopped, looked over his shoulder. "I've been wanting to say something to you for a while."

"Oh?" Sylvia peered at him through sleepy eyelids.

"People have this concept of you." He paused, hesitated. "They think you're this cynical bitch that takes nothing seriously because she's never had it rough."

Sylvia looked perplexed; clueless about where this had come from or where it was heading. "Cal, what the—"

"I'm sorry, I didn't start that right."

"You think?"

"I meant people think that, but they're wrong. You care. It's not your fault you didn't have it as tough as the rest of us. You do take things seriously and you do care about others. I'm lucky I get to see what others can't. I wouldn't be even halfway through my research without all your help and that wonderful mind of yours."

She stared at him, mystified, her mouth half-open, almost smiling.

Before she could answer, he rolled over to her side and planted a kiss on her lips. "I love you."

She stared at him, blushing, smiling, then gave him a proud smirk. "Of course, you do."

He winked at her and turned off his lamp.

Chuck Cunningham took advantage of the streets being empty to park his car facing the bar's sandblasted windows, creating an eerie diffused light effect inside. An upturned chair was all he'd found out of the ordinary, which could mean anything—drunks had upended chairs and tables many a time in his bar.

All at once, the lights in his establishment came on. The bar's lighting wasn't intense or blinding, but having all of them come on simultaneously, accompanied by the sudden *thunk!* of the refrigerators kicking into function, was enough to give him a start.

The first thing he did when the electricity returned was check his phone. Where the battery had been dead seconds ago, now there was 70% charge and a signal. Not even questioning whether this made sense, he dialed Jess's number.

The phone rang three times before her groggy voice came on. "Hey."

Hearing her brought him immediate relief.

"What's up?" she asked.

(*Your mom is dead. She's dead because I failed her like I failed your brother, because I'm a failed husband and father*)

"I'm doing okay," he said, trying to bring his emotions under control. "I'm at the bar, Pum'kin."

"Dad, please don't call me that. I'm not five. How was it for you during the blackout? How's mom?"

(*Your mom's dead*)

"Uh…" He stammered. Panic rose in his chest.

"Dad? How's Mom?"

(*She's quite dead*)

"She's at your aunt's… uh… She asked me to drive her there, and I was just getting back to town when all the lights went out. My car stalled near Seaside Park. I sat there for a while and then… uh… I walked to the bar to find you. Are you at your place? How was it at the bar?"

"I'm at Royce and Lillian's. Long story short, there was a thing at the bar; some nut job came in waving a gun at us."

"What?" He was sure he'd heard her wrong. "Jess, what the hell? Who? Why?"

"Some guy in a Lighthouse Rock uniform. I'll tell you tomorrow. I have to go to the police and stuff, but we're all fine." She yawned.

Chuck stayed in dumbfounded silence with the phone to his ear, realizing he'd been driving around with a man who'd pulled a gun on his daughter. As far as he knew, that man was dead now—most likely, given Freddie Parham hadn't brought him back from Blight Harbor along with him.

"Dad?"

Her voice called him back from his thoughts.

"Yeah. Tell you what, I'll pick you up tomorrow at Royce's and take you to the police station myself. Sounds alright?"

"Nah, I'm okay, dad. I gotta go with Royce somewhere at noon. Will *you* be alright?"

He took another perfunctory look around. His eyes rested on the cellar door. "Sure, Pum'kin. Why wouldn't I?"

Satisfied, Jess said goodnight—not without reminding him not to call her Pum'kin.

Chuck went back outside. He parked his car properly, turned off the engine and the lights. As he stood alone on the sidewalk, in the glow of streetlights and the comfort of electricity, he thought White Harbor had never looked darker. He then went back inside the bar and headed straight into the cellar.

He had preparations to make.

Chapter Twenty-Five

Kindred Victims

1993

"They vanished!" Ray approached the altar, his steps hesitant and his shoulders tense, struggling to regain his composure. "They're gone! Barry, what's going on?" He took a full turn around the platform, shaking his head in disbelief. "This is real. This whole thing is real."

Barry tried the door one more time. It wouldn't budge. He surveyed the surroundings for anything he could use to open the door, but subconsciously, he was aware he'd be unable to.

"One thing is sound not leaving the house, or a door

that can't be opened… That's weird and creepy. This is—"

"Bliiiiight Harboooor!" a booming, dramatic, spooky voice said from above, startling both of them.

Barry hurried beside his friend, who was already gawking at the opening in the domed ceiling. No more rain poured in since the others disappeared. There was Freddie Parham's smiling face peering over the rim—the ominous blue moon behind his head looked like a halo in some medieval religious artwork. Freddie looked amused, as if spooking them was the most entertainment he'd had in years.

"The fuck?" Barry said.

"Hey, Brickhouse." He then eyed Ray. "Plus-One."

"Freddie?" Ray said. "What is this? What's going on? What is this place?"

"You know? At this moment, Bobby is also asking me a bunch of questions in a row. Not sure you guys understand how annoying that is."

With a quizzical look, Ray asked, "What do you mean, 'at this moment'? Are the others okay?"

"Man, you're irritating," Freddie said. "I'd tell you all the things I don't like about you, Plus-One, but I don't know you enough to care."

"Hey!" Barry clenched his fists, looking up at him. "Stop that shit!"

"Or what?" Freddie giggled. "You'll rip out my ribs and shove them one by one into my peen-hole until I cum enamel, or some stupid fucking threat like that?" He scoffed. "Dude, look around. Get some perspective!"

Ray felt panic creep back in. "Freddie. Are *you* doing this?"

"Perceptive, Plus-One. I'm just enjoying the ride. A little pick-me-up after losing everything I had." He shrugged. "Also, maybe getting rid of that pesky family curse in the process."

"That curse is bullshit, Freddie," Ray said. "You're not cursed."

"What do *you* know, Plus-One?" He flashed a scowl at him. "You move into town a year ago, and you already think you know how it is? You and your perfect little family. Never knowing what getting your ass kicked by your drunk dad is. The fuck do you know? If, on top of everything I've done to make my dad cringe, I'd turned out queer, too, he'd have demolished me. Not you, though. Even if you grow into the biggest fag in the world, all you'll see is love and support from your folks. Me? I'd have been hospitalized during one of my dad's binges."

"Hey, shut the fuck up!" Barry said. "Leave him alone!"

"And *you*." There was a raspy, vile inflection in the way he said those words. "We should've been good friends, Brickhouse. After all, your mom was my dad's drinking buddy. They were so close. Who knows, man? If the truck hadn't gotten my dad, you might have ended up with a cursed little half-brother of your own! You gotta wonder how many times Chuck Cunningham kicked them out at closing time, and they drunk-fucked in an alley, then came home to beat both our asses to a pulp? That should've been something in common for us, man. What would you call that? Bruise buddies? Kindred victims? But, no, you and I were *never* friends. The rest of these fuckers might have forgotten what you were, but I haven't. I haven't forgotten how many times I came to school, fresh off a beating, to have you and your buddies dunk my head in a toilet or toss my sketches in a gutter. *You*, I fucking hate, Barry Giffen."

Their eyes widened in disbelief, shocked by the sudden viciousness from someone they had considered a friend until now.

Freddie composed himself, cleared his throat. "I was thinking of letting you out into the house, like I did with the others, but I think I'll leave you both locked up in here. I got a bunch of stuff to do, and I don't want the two sports jocks of the group getting in the way." He flashed a malicious, crooked grin at Barry. "But I got a gift for you, Brickhouse! A playmate so you don't get bored while you're here, since Plus-One is so goddamn dull! Let me call him over!"

Freddie disappeared from the hole in the dome. The only thing left of him was the sound of his "Hee-hee-hee!" giggles echoing through the chapel, coming from everywhere, sounding malevolent.

"Freddie!" Barry said. "What's going—"

A body dropped from the hole in the ceiling. There was a sickening *crack!* when its fall was stopped by a belt tied around its neck. It was a man's body, but it was the color of dull, black rubber, and all over, there were shapes like liquid strands moving over its surface, as if its flesh were alive. Its legs were bound together tight by many black belts with black buckles.

Barry let out a single short gasp, then another, as if his chest were failing at pulling in air from the sheer horror. The thing up there, the build of its body, the slight sideways tilt of the head, the visible shape of the belt's buckle, the protruding tongue. This revolting thing, he realized, was supposed to be his dad.

It opened its eyes. They were the same blue as the moon. Both Ray and Barry took a step back. The belt snapped, and the creature fell to the floor with several louder, wet cracks as its bones broke on impact.

Barry and Ray seemed to be rooted to the floor; that was until the monster made its first move toward them, crawling, pulling itself along the stone floor, wriggling, broken; the belt, up in the air, one end snaking loosely, the other end around its neck. It looked like it was on a leash.

"No way, no fucking way!" Ray panicked and tried to walk away, pulling at Barry's arm, but he was paralyzed, as if he were some monolithic sculpture, too heavy to move.

"Barry, run!"

He didn't move. He stood frozen, mouth wide open, eyes popping out, filled with terror.

"Barry!"

Closer. Closer. Closer. It crawled, leaving a slimy black trail behind it, from which flat tentacles emerged.

Belts! Barry thought. *Not tentacles. Belts!*

The inexplicable black belts shot in all directions, attaching themselves to pillars, furniture, to the sconces, to the ceiling, creating a black web.

"Barry!" Putting all of his weight behind it, Ray gave a powerful pull on his arm, and it made him stagger backward and almost fall. He finally reacted, turning a terrified gaze in his direction. "Run! Run!"

Barry nodded, still in a state of confusion. He tried to get away from the monster, but as he turned, the creature opened its mouth, and a belt-like tongue lashed out and wrapped itself around his calf, causing him to lose his balance and fall to the floor. The belt tied to the monster's neck struck like a whip and wrapped itself around Barry's other leg.

"No!" Ray shouted. He grabbed Barry's hand as the monster pulled its tongue taut as a guitar string, using it to pull itself toward the terrified boy. More and more of the belts rose from the creature's trail and continued to attach themselves to the walls and other items. It was closing them in, blocking their exit, leaving no path to run.

In the monster's face, Barry could see his dad's facial features, even with those unnatural, glowing blue eyes, its black teeth, and the black tongue attached to his leg. Its fingers stretched into long claws, which scraped against the floor as it continued its approach.

He sensed Ray's grip loosen. "Ray, help me!" he cried, but found, though Ray was still holding his hand, he was no longer pulling. Panic had taken over, and he was only staring, transfixed, at the abomination crawling toward them.

The light from Jess's flashlight was diminished by the suffocating darkness of the hallway. While the hallway itself looked like part of the Vanek House—wooden walls and floor, one end with a boarded-up window—it didn't lead to the bedrooms as it normally would. It continued on and on. They had now walked what felt like the length of two city blocks. No windows, no doors. Only an endless tunnel in the darkness.

Once he'd moved a touch past the initial shock of their surroundings, Bobby gathered himself and pressed the issue of what Jess and Royce had said about Freddie. "Jess…" he said in a hushed voice.

"What do you want me to say, Bobby?" While Jess maintained an air of composure, there was a slight tremor in her voice, and a shortness of breath letting her friends know she was as terrified as them. She held the flashlight in one hand and gripped the stun gun in the other, so hard it looked like it was fused to her hand.

"You're saying Freddie is involved in the disappearance of the other kids. That's crazy."

"I don't know, man. You tell me how your buddy's walking around the house like there's nothing weird going on, and he's been missing for over a month. Where's he getting food? If someone saw him at a store in town, they would've called the police."

"I mean, he couldn't have done *this*." Bobby gestured toward the hallway they were creeping through. "He's just a kid, like the rest of us."

Jess tilted her head left and right, letting out an audible crack. "Guess we'll ask him when we find him."

"Wait. Stop." Bobby halted, staring down at the floor. "Could you point the flashlight at the floorboards?"

Puzzled, Jess did as she was told. She couldn't see what had caught his attention.

"Look!" He pointed at the floorboards with both index fingers and drew a hexagon in the air with them. "Do you see it?"

"There's a…" Royce stopped speaking, then his eyebrows arched with surprise.

"Hicks' hexagons," Bobby said. "It's the same carpet.

461

Well, no, not a carpet. There's no carpet, but I mean, you see the pattern, right?"

"The fuck?" Jess muttered.

A pattern was painted onto the old floorboards, only it was more than that. The wood itself had sprouted that pattern somehow, as if it had been part of the tree the floorboards came from all along. It was a series of interlocking hexagons drawn in three shades, with a corner which opened to form other hexagons in the opposite direction. While they still retained the overall look of wood, the center of each hexagon was almost fully red.

"The Overlook Hotel?" Bobby saw no recognition on either of his friends' faces. "Stanley Kubrick's *The Shining*? 1980 movie? Little kid rolling his tricycle over the hotel? The carpet?"

"I never saw that," Jess said.

"Oh, shit," Royce said. "I see it!"

"It's my favorite horror movie." Bobby's voice was a stunned whisper. "Jesus Christ, Freddie *is* doing this. He and I have watched that movie together like a million times."

Bobby and Royce kept examining the pattern on the floor when Jess pointed the flashlight away from it and to the hallway ahead. "Guys?"

When the boys looked up, something had changed. There was a bend in the hallway a few feet ahead. It turned left. It hadn't been there seconds ago.

"He wanted me to notice the pattern," Bobby said, feeling his heart sink down to his stomach and dissolve in his gastric juices. "We had to notice the pattern before he'd let us continue. This is all a game to him. I think you better have those weapons ready."

Jess regarded him with dreadful understanding. "Should we go on?"

"I don't think we have a choice."

They turned left at the corner and stopped again. They were in an area resembling the bedroom hallway, with the bedroom doors on either side, but beyond the second pair of doors, the hallway ended abruptly on a windowed wall. This window wasn't boarded up, but looked out toward a starless sky with that same blue moon they'd seen in the chapel, but worst of all—

"Holy shit!" Jess cried. "What the fuck?"

—there were two children, or more like two creatures, standing almost at the end of the hallway. They were emaciated, almost skeleton-like, naked, shaped like little boys—their bodies soot-black, with glowing blue eyes. While they appeared to be holding hands, upon closer inspection, each arm hung down from one child's shoulder, formed a U-shape, like a bizarre black tentacle, then went into the other's mouth. The way the arms' texture moved made it look like they were endlessly being fed into the other kids' mouth.

"Back! B-back! T-turn back!" Royce's voice became a

screeching, terrified mess. The fact these creatures appeared to be twins, as he was searching for his twin brother, hadn't been lost on him. "Fuck this shit! We'll find another way! We're not going near those things!"

They spun around, turned right at the corner they'd come from, and had only gone a few steps when they halted again. The hallway—which they'd spent several minutes walking down—now ended just about ten feet away from the corner, once more at a window, once more looking out at the blue moon—*Wasn't the blue moon on the other side?* Bobby thought. Lying on the floor was a head. It was a human head, but the same charcoal black as the twins at the other end.

Jess let out a yelp. "Fuck! Bobby?"

Bobby was staring at the inert head resting on the floor. "What?"

"Is this from that movie, too?"

Bobby shook his head. "No. That's just a head." His tone was unwittingly deadpan.

The head opened its eyes. They glowed that unearthly blue. It rolled on its side. Out of nowhere, six black appendages broke through its skin and extended, finding footing on the wooden floor and lifting the head, which hung upside-down. The blue eyes retreated into the skull, then emerged atop antennae sticking up from the bottom of its jaw.

"Oh, you've got to be fucking kidding me!" Royce said.

"*The Thing*," Bobby said. "Freddie's doing *The Thing*!"

"Back! Back! Go!" Jess said. "We'll hide in one of the rooms back there!"

"Right!" Royce turned around and the twin creatures were standing right behind him. He let out a shrill cry. They jumped on top him and their conjoining tentacle arms stretched and looped once around his neck, choking him. They started scratching at him with the clawed fingers of their free hands. He let out a choked, terrified cry of pain.

Jess considered using the stun gun on the creatures, but she didn't know if it would electrocute Royce, too. She pocketed the stun gun, wrapped her flashlight arm around one of the twins' necks, and tried to pull its clawed hand away from Royce, so it couldn't scratch at him anymore. Its flesh wriggled and shifted like it was covered in living worms reacting to her grip.

Royce grappled with the other twin monster.

"Guys, the spider's coming!" Bobby cried, with his back to them. "I need a weapon!"

As fast as she could, Jess used her free arm to pass him the stun gun.

"Flashlight, too, Jess. It's moving fast!"

She passed the flashlight to her free arm and pointed it toward Bobby, who reached out and grabbed it. He turned, and the spider was gone. Then came the pat-pat-patter of its legs from above. He looked up and froze, seeing the creature clinging to the ceiling. It let out an angry hissing sound at him from that revolting mouth and leaped down toward him.

Bobby fell to the floor, with the spider creature on top of him—black teeth snapping at his face, glowing blue eyes radiating cold murder at him. Clumsy, hollering in terror, he got the stun gun between him and the spider's face, then pressed the button, releasing an audible electrical *tak-tak-tak-tak!* noise, and finally pushing its two contact spikes against its body. The spider shook. Its legs spasmed, and it sprang off from Bobby in an uncoordinated jump. It fell beside him, kicking and convulsing.

He scrambled away on the floor when the sound of something heavy falling down startled him. Royce's hammer was lying on the floor. As fast as his trembling body allowed, surrounded by his friends' screams and the disquieting choking sound coming from the twin creatures, he dropped the stun gun, crawled toward the hammer, grabbed it, and held it up. "Jess!"

She turned toward him, noticed the hammer, and reached for it with her free hand. Realizing she wouldn't be able to exert as much force while wrestling with the creature. She let go of it and shouted, "Royce, hold them still!"

"I can't!" he screamed. The creature scratched two red furrows into his arm. "It hurts!"

"Bobby!"

Adrenaline kicking in, Bobby got back on his feet and

grabbed the closest of the two monsters. He pulled its head back, eliciting a scream from Royce as its claws tore off a slice of skin. "Got him! Hurry!"

Jess raised the hammer with both hands and brought it down on the creature's head once, sending black blood flying everywhere, but only dazing it, then twice, crushing its skull and making it go limp. Since the creatures were still linked to each other, the dead weight of this one pulled Royce down into an awkward crouching position. "Bobby! The other one!"

He ran around Jess and grabbed the other creature. Its clawed fingers were leaving furrows in Royce's side, cutting through his shirt. The best Bobby could do was hold its head as Royce tried to hold its body still.

Jess raised the hammer over her head and brought it down once. It made Royce scream, as the blow had caused the creature to dig its claw further into his skin. The second blow made it go limp.

Royce pulled the weird looping tentacle over his head and, with a scream, let both creatures fall to the floor, dead, in a pool of black blood. He screamed in pain. "The scratches! Shit, it hurts!"

Shining the flashlight on him, Bobby could see deep scratch marks all over his arms and side. Some only bled a little, but the one on his side bled a lot more.

Jess reached into her rucksack and pulled out bandages, alcohol, and surgical tape she'd bought at Mr. Yates's phar-

467

macy on the way to Royce's house. "Lift your shirt. Let me patch you up. Then we'll go into one of those rooms past the corner, if they're still there."

A few minutes later, as she finished disinfecting and patching up Royce's wounds, there was a shuffling sound coming from the left.

They all turned to see the spider was moving again.

"We need to go," Bobby said, pocketing the stun gun. At the same time, he noticed how the caved in head from the first child creature was knitting itself back together. It was gruesome to see the black threads intertwine and harden. "We really need to go."

Jess took the flashlight back.

They turned left at the corner, and the room doors were still there. The sound of the spider already scurrying toward them, and the hissing noises of the twin creatures coming back to life, sent renewed fear up their spines.

"Which one?" Royce said, baring his teeth in pain.

"Either." Jess headed to the first door to her right and walked in, followed by her two friends.

Bobby locked the door behind them, not realizing both Jess and Royce were staring in terror at what the room contained. The sound of strange moans, hisses, and growls violated his ears before he even had the chance to turn around. He hesitated before turning, took a breath, and spun around to witness an ineffable sight.

Instead of a bedroom, the three of them were standing on a broken outcrop of the second-floor landing, no more than six-by-six feet in diameter. They were looking down at the Vanek House's main hall. In the light of Jess's flashlight, they could see a mass of black flooding the entire hall, and within it, writhed dozens of human figures, distorted and perverted, glowing blue eyes staring back at them. Greedy hands and tentacles, and appendages for which there was still not a name, reached up to them from below.

As the main hall continued to flood slowly, the creatures rose with the tar-like substance, as if they weren't swimming in it, but were growing from it. There were men, women, children—their bodies disfigured, melted together, and through it all, moans and hisses, moans and hisses, incessant. They sounded sad, yearning, and pleading. Bobby thought this could've been a scene in any of Romero's films—except the zombies in those never coalesced into a writhing, almost liquid mass.

"Oh, my god!" Jess said, and for the first time, her voice cracked with despair. She pointed her flashlight at a spot in the crowd. "That's Gerardo!"

Bobby and Royce peered in the direction she was pointing and noticed, in fact, one of the creatures rising from the central mass, despite being black as charcoal and having an appendage like a mixture of a claw and a giant earthworm, was indeed Gerardo Valencia.

"Why?" Jess's voice sounded like a sob, but no tears were coming from her eyes. "Why is Gerardo there?"

The realization hit Bobby. "The people that died in the house." He felt his voice fail him. "Freddie's using them like Lego pieces. He's using the power in the house to shape them however he wants and sending them out to kill us."

"But why? Most of those people were found," Royce said, eyes bulging with dread. "They didn't stay in the house."

"Maybe they're like a memory of them, a stored memory." He let out a long, dreadful exhalation, then breathed in. "Jesus. How's Freddie doing this?"

"I don't care how!" Jess spat with rage. "You have to be a real piece of shit to do something like this. Using memories of dead people like toys? Use them to hurt your friends?"

"That asshole isn't our friend." Royce grunted with pain from his scratch wounds.

The remark made Bobby's heart twitch. He did still think of Freddie as his friend. He only wanted to understand why he was doing what he was doing…and how.

"We have to get outta here," Jess said.

They were huddled together, pressed as close as possible to the door. It gave a sudden shake, startling them, followed by the constant slamming of what they assumed were the arms, legs, and heads of the creatures out in the hallway.

They were trapped.

There was something crawling under the wooden walls. Peter could make out tiny scuttering lumps under the yellowed and stained newspaper that covered them—which, now that he thought of it, should only be present on the outer walls of the house, but here, the entire hallway was wallpapered with it. It looked as if ticks had burrowed under the house's "skin" and now crawled trying to find the right place to feed. There also seemed to be faces, body parts pushing from beneath the newspaper at random spots in the wall.

"Please tell me I'm not the only one seeing this." Nadine had a stupefied look on her face as she stared at the illogical thing this hallway had become. "It'd be nice to not be crazy."

"You're not." He shone the flashlight on the walls and the ceiling; the shapes beneath it let out barely audible but disgusting wet sounds. "Nadine, I can't move."

"What?" She turned a worried gaze in his direction.

"Th-the bugs. This... This is like The Hole. The space under my house where Mother locks me up."

She grabbed his hand, but he pulled it away, then flinched, as if realizing he'd done something on instinct he shouldn't have done. They'd broken up. He probably shouldn't—

"I'm... I'm sorry.... I didn't know if I—"

She took his hand again. "You're still my friend. I'm not going anywhere. C'mon. Don't be stupid."

He nodded. Still frozen with fear.

"Give me the flashlight. I'll lead the way. Don't let go of my hand, alright?"

She pointed the flashlight forward, doing her best to ignore the moving walls. Almost as if the wall had arranged itself to put it in the exact spot, the light passed over a newspaper article about Gerardo Valencia's death. One of the insect-like lumps passed right under Gerardo's picture, distorting his smiling face into an inhuman mask. She let out a disturbed whimper.

They turned the corner and were flabbergasted to find themselves in the dining room, on the first floor, even though they'd been on the second floor only seconds ago. All the things they'd brought in for their clubhouse—the picnic table, the cushions, the cooler, the TV, even the video game console—were back where they'd been before they'd taken them out, but they were wrapped in newspapers that grew out of the floorboards like skin, like the most unpleasant Christmas presents they'd ever gotten.

Peter turned his face left toward the wall where Freddie's mural had been. It had taken a long time to erase it from the wall, but it was back: an inexplicable moving picture that rose all the way to the ceiling—a writhing mass of tentacles, claws, eyes, limbs, faces, mouths, and teeth, surrounding a tiny yellow house with colorful flowers, making it look as if the monsters were about to devour it.

Both teenagers took a horrified step back, gawking at the moving image, which at times appeared to emerge from the wall like in a 3D movie.

"I can't..." Nadine said in a weird babble, then stopped. Her knees buckled, and she fell to the floor, her hand over her mouth.

"I shouldn't have come in here," Peter said in a vacuous voice. "Mother told me not to. What if the house really wanted me? What if *I* made it come alive? What if the others are dead and it's my fault?"

"Stop." Despite her eyes being fixed on the moving mural, she squeezed his hand. "If it were you, the house would have singled you out." She turned a pale face toward him. "If it wanted you, it would've taken only you. So, either it doesn't want just you, or the one that separated us was Freddie and not the house."

Peter shook his head, looking anguished. "You don't know that."

"You don't either." She cast a terrified glance at the mural as she stood up. "This is bad enough without you falling apart, so please work with me, alright?"

He hesitated, peered at the ominous mural again, which loomed over both of them, then nodded.

She led him across the dining room and into the main hall, where the staircase, instead of leading to the second floor, now led down into a basement that couldn't exist—the stairs disappearing into the thick darkness below.

"No." He shook his head, eyes bulging open. "I'm not going down there, Nadine."

"Let's, uh… Let's just get out of the house." She peered at the front doors. "Shit!"

Peter followed her gaze. The doors were only a chalk drawing on the newspaper-covered wall. The windows, too.

Nadine shook her head. "We can find another way. Let's go back."

They spun around, and at once noticed, coming out of the dark, were two sets of blue, gleaming eyes. The flashlight revealed a pair of huge black Mastiffs standing in the doorway between the hall and the dining room.

"No, no, no," Nadine said. "Oh, shit."

"Curling's dogs."

"Run!"

She pulled him by the hand toward the stairs, and despite his protests, they ran down into the darkness, followed by the clicking sounds of dog paws on the floor.

Despite their haste, they noticed they were running on the bottom part of the stairs as if they had been reversed, and pointing the flashlight down, they could see the main hall's ceiling an impossible distance below—like the steps had doubled or tripled in number—vertigo disorienting them, almost causing them to stumble. They reached the landing, turned right, and kept running on the bottom part of the stairs until they reached the second floor—or the first basement depending on how they looked at it—however, instead of reaching the hallway leading to the bedrooms, the stairs only led to a wall with a single door. They could hear the dogs huffing behind them, and their paws clicking on the wood as they chased them down the stairs.

Nadine threw the door open, and they ran in. She closed the door behind them, and shortly after, the dogs smashed into it. They barked and scratched and slammed their paws on the wood.

"Peter?" Nadine had already turned around while Peter still faced the door. "Peter!"

He turned and gasped so loud it echoed in the space.

There was a man standing in front of them, a man of similar age to their parents, giving them a bewildered look. He stared at them, then at the door, clearly scared by the dog noises outside. His hands and knees were covered in dirt. He was holding a gun.

"You're that Lange kid," the man said. "What's going on? What are you kids doing here?"

Peter stared, mesmerized, panting. The part of his brain that processed logic short-circuited.

"You're Elijah Knox." Nadine tried to catch her breath,

but she wasn't as winded as Peter—playing basketball and running had their benefits.

"Were you taken too? Have you seen my kids? I don't care what the police say, I don't need proof. I know Curling took them!"

The dogs continued to bark and growl outside.

"We haven't seen them, Mr. Knox," Nadine said. "Our friend Leroy was taken. We came here to look for him."

Even though the man was clearly distraught, he took a quick look around, trying to gather his thoughts. "Are you okay? Have you been hurt?"

They both shook their heads, then were startled by the sound of the dogs once more crashing against the door and continuing to bark in a rage.

"Look, I can't leave this house until I find my children. Why don't you wait for me in this bedroom, and I'll come back for you once I find them."

Nadine nodded toward the door. "What about the dogs?"

"Curling's dogs, right?"

They nodded.

"Fuck, I hate those fucking things." He gave them an awkward look. "I'm sorry. I didn't mean to curse."

"That's okay." Nadine's voice teetered between collect-edness and terror. "We curse all the time."

He paid no heed to what she'd said, motioned with his

gun. "I guess I'll have to put them down, right?"

Peter and Nadine moved aside.

"Wait," Nadine said. "Did you say bedroom?"

Peter had also caught this, but he was too afraid to even speak, exactly because he wasn't seeing a bedroom.

"Yes." There was a puzzled look drawn on Mr. Knox's face. "Why?"

Standing near the door, looking toward Mr. Knox, Peter was seeing the dining room from above. They were up-side-down, standing on the ceiling; their newspaper-wrapped belongings down below. At the further end, past the man, Peter could see Freddie's mural still moving and writhing in its inexorable tentacled monstrosity. This was clearly not what Mr. Knox was seeing. Peter turned to Nadine, realization on his face. "He didn't go through the door."

"What door?" the man asked.

"Uh..."

The dogs went quiet. They all regarded the door for a minute, waiting to see if there was any more noise.

"How did you get here, Mr. Knox?" Nadine asked.

"Since I couldn't come in through the front door, I figured some of the floorboards might be rotten and easy to break. That's when I found the hole in the service room floor. I came through it like fifteen minutes ago."

"You weren't the one who nailed it shut?"

He made a face as if no word coming out of the kids'

mouths made any sense. "No. Why would I? That's my only way out."

Nadine and Peter exchanged a knowing look.

"What is it?" the increasingly confused man asked.

"Um, Mr. Knox," Nadine said. "I'm going to ask you a question that's going to sound really weird."

He squinted at them.

"When you turn around, what do you see?"

He squinted again, looked over his shoulder, then turned a confused stare toward them. "A bedroom wall with a window."

"You don't see a mural full of monsters? A moving mural?" Peter asked.

He canted his head to one side. "Are you kids on drugs?"

Peter shook his head. He was about to give some lame explanation when the sound of clicking paws reached his ears, coming fast from the other end of the room. For Peter and Nadine, the sound was coming from the further end of the dining room ceiling, but for this man there was a wall blocking his view. "Watch out!"

It was too late.

Nadine's flashlight was pointed in the wrong direction and the dogs were coming from the pitch darkness at the other end. By the time they both screamed, one of the dogs was mid-leap toward the man.

Elijah Knox turned around just in time to have one of the dogs sink its teeth into his neck, while the other one bit into his calf. He let out a gurgling scream as blood sprayed forth from his carotid artery, fat globs of the vital liquid falling on the kid's clothes. He fell to the floor.

The kids shrieked in horror, watching the dog's teeth tear muscle and skin as a pool of blood spread around the struggling man.

Peter turned to grab the doorknob.

"Wait!" Nadine shouted through the hand covering her mouth. "The gun!"

"Nadine, no!"

She hurried forward and picked up the gun off the floor. By the time she stood up, one of the dogs—the one biting into Mr. Knox's leg—turned its blue eyes toward her and growled, its head tense and motionless as it prepared to attack. Without hesitating, Nadine pointed the gun the best she could and pulled the trigger. The recoil pushed her backward against Peter, but the dog flew backward with a sudden yelp. Somehow, by some miracle, she'd gotten it dead in the head.

The remaining Mastiff reacted fast. Nadine turned and pulled the door open. The dog left Elijah Knox's body and spun toward them. They slammed the door shut, and the large animal crashed into it.

They ran up the reversed stairs, emerging once more in the main hall with its chalk-drawn doors and windows.

"Let's try to go back to the chapel," Nadine said.

They ran into the dining room. Peter couldn't help look up, expecting to see an upside-down black dog standing on the ceiling in front of a non-existent door, but there was nothing. No sign of Elijah Knox's corpse either—they were both probably in a different version of the dining room. As they passed the living mural, one enormous tentacle shifted and made them flinch, looking like it was about to emerge from the wall and grab one of them.

They continued around the corner, but now, instead of the hallway with insects crawling under the newspaper, leading to the chapel, they came to a sudden stop. They were in a bedroom; Elijah Knox's bloody corpse and the dead dog were lying on the floor before them. The other dog was in front of the door they'd just come from, up on its hind legs, scratching at the wood. It turned around in a swift motion, reacting to their noisy footsteps.

Nadine tried to point the gun at the dog, but her hands were shaking too much. "Back! Back!" she shouted.

They turned around, double-backed as fast as they could, screaming in panic, hearing the enraged Mastiff chasing them across the house. They reached the main hall, once more descended the inverted stairs—seeing the roof far down once more made their heads spin—they reached the door, and ran through it, once more, barely in time for the dog to crash into it and start barking and scratching at the wood.

"What do we do?" Nadine said. "If it doesn't hold still, I can't shoot it. I'm not good at using these things."

"It's a loop." Peter was sweating, panting. "It's an endless loop. We're just going to go back and forth. There's no escape unless we..."

(It's no use, Mr. James, it's turtles all the way down)

A thought crossed his mind. It was something he'd read in a book a long time ago. He couldn't remember the name of the book, but this idea of endless repetition reminded him of it. Four years earlier, when his mother had first locked him in The Hole for having gone into the Vanek House, for having lied to her about reading books. This book had been one of the three that had been under the trapdoor in the pantry. They were *The Tell-Tale Heart*, by Edgar Allan Poe, *And Then There Were None* by Agatha Christie, and... No, the other one wasn't really a book. It was this sort of digest of interesting anecdotes whose name he couldn't remember. Why was he thinking of that now?

Because that was the day Mother told me I should never go into this house, he thought, answering his own question. He turned to Nadine as soon as the dog stopped attacking the door. "I have a stupid idea. What if... What if I'm right and the reason Mother didn't want me to come here was the house needs me for something?"

"That makes no sense, Peter!"

"No, listen, because I think the dog's coming back

around, like it did with"—he shot a glance at Elijah Knox's bloodied corpse—"um… I've always felt drawn to this house, like it's calling me. It's how I found the hole in the floor. I didn't have to search much. I just kinda *knew* where it was. Before we entered the chapel, there was this thing in my head, telling me I had to be the one to open the door. I think if anyone else had pushed it open, we would've only found an empty room. I know it sounds dumb, but it's like a part of me knows the way around this house, even when the house changes."

Nadine stared at him as if he was off his rocker. "Okay, fine. So, what do we do?"

"Wait for the dog to appear on the other side, then follow me."

The seconds passed. One. Two. Three. Four…

"Tuck the gun in the back of your pants."

Nadine obeyed.

"Hold the flashlight. You light the way for me, alright?"

Eight… Twelve… Sixteen.

The huge black Mastiff appeared on the other end of the upside-down dining room, passing through the opposite wall as if it didn't even exist and dashing toward them.

"Go! Now!" Peter opened the door, they went through it, closed it. He took Nadine's hand, and they ran up the reversed stairs, once more coming out into the main hall. Peter turned to the left, covered the four strides it took him to reach the papered wall with the chalked-on double doors, and without hesitating, or thinking about how senseless it was, he put his hand forward and grabbed the area where the doorknob was drawn. There was a jolt of shock in his brain as his fingers gripped—even though he couldn't see it—an actual doorknob. He gripped it, turned it, pulled the door open without even looking, and he pulled Nadine through the threshold.

As the door closed at their backs, Peter and Nadine now stared into an unfathomable horror. There was a mass of bodies, black as tar, fused together into a writhing mass of heads, eyes, limbs, claws, and tentacles; moving, flowing, and dripping, as if covered in a black substance that flooded the floor they were standing on. Peter soon recognized this monstrosity as the embodiment of Freddie's mural.

They jumped when the dog once more began barking and scratching at the door. Some of the heads in the mass of bodies turned glowing blue eyes toward them, baring uneven teeth and fangs, all black. Some of the heads and limbs, however, remained turned toward an area on the second floor. An area where Jess, Royce, and Bobby stood, staring down at them.

"Peter?" Jess gawked at them from what looked like an isolated balcony upstairs. "Nadine?"

"I don't get it," Sylvia said as they walked from the service room where the hole was and into the kitchen. The entire space had a gloomy ambiance to it, despite the early-afternoon sun shining through the boards and casting a diffused light on the newspaper-covered walls. "It should've moved at least a little. We put both our weights into that crowbar and the hammer's claw at the same time! Didn't even shake. It's like it's welded to the floor."

"You can't weld wood," Callum said—unaware years down the line he'd be telling people the fun fact that, as of 2005, wood welding would be possible.

Sylvia gave him an unpleasant curl of the lip. "Oh, really? Thank you for that extremely obvious remark."

"What do we do?"

She let out an exhausted sigh. "We should go tell the others."

"What about the front door? What if someone comes?"

"I don't think they will. My grandpa was in the police. Leroy disappeared yesterday, the Knoxes the day before. Wanna bet they don't have a court order to search the Vanek House yet?"

Callum eyed her, intrigued. "They'd have a hard time showing reasonable evidence the missing kids might be here."

"Also, who gives a crap? If the police come, sure, we'll get in trouble, but they can also help with whatever's going on here."

"It *has* been a while, actually. It shouldn't take this long to check the second floor."

They exchanged a nod, crossed the dining room into the main hall, and let out a simultaneous gasp.

Sitting at the bottom of the staircase was Freddie.

"Oh, hi guys!" He flashed a wide crooked-toothed smile, raising a greeting hand.

"Freddie, what the—" Sylvia said.

"I wasn't counting on you guys not going upstairs, you know? The others are already having a great time, and you're here all bored. I've been such a shitty host. Sorry 'bout that."

"Host?" Callum adjusted his glasses.

Freddie stood up, dusted off his butt. "I've got some important stuff to do, but I ain't just gonna leave you guys here all alone." He pointed at the fireplace. "My buddy over there will keep you company."

Sylvia screamed. There was something in the fireplace. A man's body, charred from head to toe, lying face-down where the wood and the coals would be.

The man slowly rose to his feet, and as he did, Callum realized it wasn't that his entire body was charred. It was coal-black. This wasn't a man, it was something else. The upper part of its naked body looked skeletal, curled inward, arms turned to bent claws against its chest, skin like burned tree bark, resembling how scorched corpses looked when their muscle fibers burned and tightened, bending the limbs. The head had no features—nose, teeth, or cheekbones—only two vertical cracks in place of eye sockets.

"Sylvia," Callum cried. "The doors! Head for the doors!"

"What is that?" Sylvia cried. "What the hell is that?"

"The doors! We have to get to the front doors!"

"C'mon, don't disrespect my buddy like that, you guys!" Freddie was now halfway up the stairs. Every single step up to where he was had disappeared, and the other steps continued to disappear as he climbed. "Dude can really light up a party."

Tiny flickers of blue sprouted all over the creature's body, which glowed brighter and brighter until there were small flames emerging from several nooks and cracks in its head and torso. The fissures on its face lit up blue with flames as it shuffled in their direction.

By now, Callum was at the doors, trying to pull them open.

"Let me!" Despite her terror at the inexplicable creature coming toward them, Sylvia shoved the tip of the crowbar between both doors and tried to pry them open. They put both their weights into it, but the doors wouldn't move an inch. They could see the blue glow and feel the heat of the flames as the monster approached.

"Doesn't work!" Callum shouted. "It's like the boards in the service room. They're sealed shut!"

"Nice catch, Einstein!" Freddie was already on the second-floor landing. The stairs were gone. "This is payback, Droopy." His voice turned menacing, taking on a flinty, low tone. "What was it you said? I tossed my little sister into the deep part of The Eye and pushed my mom off the edge into the rocks?"

"What?" Callum was gobsmacked.

"That was a mistake. Totally uncool. Say whatever you want about me, but you never mess with my mom and my baby sister."

"I never said that!" Callum turned his head toward the monster. It was staggering closer. "Sylvia, get behind me." He stood firm, holding the crowbar in front of him with both hands.

"Oh, and Sylvia?" Freddie now ambled along the second-floor hallway, right to left. "You said we should let you know when someone actually important dies, right?"

"What? I never—"

"Well, you're both about to die in a big, flaming hug."

The monster opened its arms. Its charred skin crackled and its surface splintered as the arms moved apart, wide, readying for a deadly, burning embrace.

"Not that it matters to me, but I'm sure you care a

lot." He disappeared past the bend in the hallway, heading deeper into the house. The last thing he said was a casual, "Bye, bitches!"

"Cal!" Sylvia cried.

He raised the crowbar and swiftly brought it down on the creature's left arm, which broke off as if it were made of nothing but coal. The fire extinguished from the arm as it hit the ground. Then the monster swung its other arm and grabbed Callum's left forearm, which sizzled at the touch of the flames.

"Let him go, you piece of shit!" Sylvia shouted as she came swinging the hammer at it. She took two hard swings at the creature's right shoulder, which broke and extinguished— the arm first hung from Callum's burned forearm, then fell to the floor. She breathed in some of the hot coal dust that had flown off its arm as the hammer impacted it and coughed.

Even though he was screaming in pain, Callum raised the crowbar once more, breathed in, held his breath, and swung it, knocking the creature's head off, then swung it again at its mid-section, then again, then again, until its body broke in half, and it fell to the floor. A cloud of black dust spread through the air. He took Sylvia by the hand and pulled her along. They ran toward the dining room, both coughing.

They glanced at the main hall, where the parts of the monster partially melted into a black liquid and slid toward each other as it put itself back together, little by little.

Callum's glasses were crooked. He straightened them as he panted. "That's Milo Calhoun."

"Milo who?" Sylvia managed, trying to stop herself from coughing.

"Milo Calhoun. One of the people who died here. 1956. Allegedly, he wandered into the house, drunk, and passed out in the fireplace. Someone lit it while he was lying there. They found him like we saw him when he appeared; upper half carbonized. I saw the photo. Same position." He let out a pained grunt as he held up his burned forearm. "If that were just a visual manifestation made by the house, this burn would be impossible. That's—"

"Terrifying? Yeah, I know."

He shook his head. "Fascinating."

"We need to get out of here, Cal! There's no time to geek out over paranormal manifestations."

"Right. The door can't be opened, the windows are boarded up, the stairs are gone, the hole in the back room is closed. Only one way out." He turned his head. "The fireplace."

Sylvia stared at him as if he'd just let out a thundering fart.

"It's made of flat stones, stacked up," he continued, and mimicked climbing. "Hand and footholds. Technically, it's not a long way. It's not much more than rope climbing in gym class."

"You suck at rope climbing in gym class!"

"Well, then, I guess I'll die if I can't make it."

Without another word, they ran toward the enormous fireplace. They could hear the sounds of the creature putting itself back together on the other side.

"You first," Callum said. "I don't want to slow you down."

Sylvia went down on her knees and crawled into the fireplace. The opening being double-sided, she could actually see the monster—*Milo Calhoun?*—as its pieces reconstituted its body. She examined the shaft. "I can see light up there. No obstructions."

"Good. Can you climb it?"

"Plenty of protruding stones. I think I can." Quickly, Sylvia grabbed on to one side of the fireplace, then the other. She put her sneaker on the edge of one of the stones and pushed herself up. Her footing was firm. "I got this. It's all sooty and dusty and filled with—"

She shrieked.

"What happened?"

"Spider!" she cried. "Spider crawled over my face. Gone now."

"Hurry! Something worse than a spider's coming!"

Sylvia continued climbing slowly but steadily. Then came Callum's turn. He realized she was now holding the flashlight with her mouth. She took it out with one hand, while holding herself up with both her feet and a hand. "See it as a ladder. Don't think of it as ropes in gym class. That's harder. It's a ladder and the rungs are on different sides, that's all."

He nodded nervously, grabbed one small crag between two stones, then another, placed one foot on a stone, then the other. He was terrified he wouldn't be able to pull himself up with his arms, then—

"Don't pull yourself up with your hands. Hands keep you steady. Legs push you up. C'mon."

He nodded, pushed up with his legs. Hands alternating from stone to stone.

"Careful with your burned forearm. Try not to have it touch the walls. You don't want it to get infected."

He nodded, yet again, not speaking, trying to keep his breathing in control to compensate for his questionable fitness. He was about four feet up when, from below, came a blue glow approaching the fireplace.

"Crap!" Sylvia shouted.

"Oh, shit!" Callum shouted too, as the monster's burning head entered the fireplace below.

Chapter Twenty-Six

The Vanek House

Nadine raised the gun, pointing it at the inexplicable mass of insanity rising before them. The horror was mind-breaking, overwhelming. Between the monstrosity looming before her, the sound of her friends crying out for help from above, and the rabid noises of the dog rushing the door and barking madly, at any moment she was sure her brain would simply shut down. If she was going to fire off a shot, she needed to do that before she fainted—one more worry on top of the pile.

Peter's fingers slid over hers, taking her hand, then pulling it down.

"Don't!" Peter said over the noise of the creature's moans and hisses, and the barking dog. "It won't do any good! We don't know where to shoot it!"

"You shitheads, get out of there!" Jess shouted from upstairs. "We'll call its attention from up here so you can escape!"

"No way!" Nadine shouted, though every fiber of her being wanted her to open the door and hightail it out of there. Even if there was the dog to contend with, it was a lesser evil than this thing, which occupied almost the entire main hall.

The creature's movements were hypnotic. No matter where she looked, there was a new face, a new inexplicable appendage, a new deformity, and all over, there were those blue eyes, watching them and their friends, like blue fireflies in the darkest forest.

Another slam at the door.

"Nadine!" Peter shouted over all the noise Jess, Bobby and Royce were making to call the creature's attention to them. "We're opening the doors. When I tell you to run, run!"

"What? But the dog—"

"Trust me!" He gave her a reassuring glance.

With a shaky hand, Nadine grabbed the doorknob, which *was* present in this version of the main hall.

"On three! One. Two. THREE!"

Peter and Nadine pulled the two doors open, and a second later, in flew the black dog. One of Ben Curling's two vicious creatures. It landed smack in the monster's body. The Mastiff whined as hungry hands clawed at its fur.

The opportunity Peter was hoping for came. As the creatures making up the main body lunged to grab the dog, a narrow path opened toward the stairs. "The stairs! Run! Now!"

"But the stairs are broken!" Nadine said.

"I know!" Peter shouted with determination. "C'mon!"

They rushed toward the stairs, their feet splashing in the black viscous liquid sloughing off the creature. They climbed the stairs up to the landing, from which there were no more steps, making the second floor unreachable.

"Now what?" Nadine sounded exasperated and terrified. "Now motherfucking what?"

They turned to look at the monster.

Peter's eyes searched for the dog, and, at first, he couldn't find any trace of it, no blood, no fur, until he saw the hint of a skeleton, dog bones, cleaned off, nearly bleached white. He was horrified—though not surprised—to see two more heads emerge from the main body, two deformed dog heads with glowing blue eyes, a strange, twisted paw coming out between them, their black jaws biting toward them.

The second time they'd seen the corpse of the Mastiff Nadine shot, it had looked strange. Its fur and flesh were melting into black goo where it touched the floorboards, but left behind a skeleton, as if its flesh were being absorbed by the house. Everyone had always theorized Curling's dogs weren't normal animals, and this, Peter thought, proved it. They were an extension of the Vanek House, able to go outside for some reason. *But according to stories, they were regular dogs,* he thought. *They even went to the vet and all.*

He had little time to continue with his musings when the entire mass spun around to look at him and Nadine. The way it turned, it looked like a whirlwind made of tar, with blue glowing lights inside it.

"Peter! What now?"

Without saying another word, Peter grabbed her hand. If he was going to do this stupid thing, he'd do it right away. If he was wrong, Nadine would catch him—*Maybe*—if he felt he was pulling her down with him, he'd simply let go. He put a foot forward, roughly measuring where a step would be if the staircase weren't in splinters.

"Wait!" Nadine said. "No, what the fuck! Don't!"

His other friends shouted from above, telling him to stop.

Then, dead silence from everyone, only broken by the disturbing sounds coming from the amorphous blob inching its way toward them, as his foot rested firmly in the air, on a step none of them could see.

He huffed twice, finding bravery within, and he moved his other foot, placing it on another invisible stair. Now he was standing in the air.

He peered over his shoulder and there was Nadine, gawking at both his feet, supported by nothing. He turned toward the creature, which wasn't only extending a massive tentacle from its central mass, but had several clawed hands gripping the stairs below. "Nadine! Now!" he shouted, as the tentacle came down, directly where she was standing and the claws tore the stairs away.

With a loud scream, Nadine stepped up to the invisible stairs a second before the tentacle crashed onto the landing.

"Don't stop!" Peter continued to climb, pulling her along, focusing on his feet landing on the surface of each step and not hitting the side, which could make him stumble and fall, dragging Nadine down with him.

The creature hissed as he reached the top. He shot a glance at his friends, who were gawking—disbelief carved into their petrified faces—then shot a glance at the creature, who was changing, gathering the mass that was flooding the first floor into its body to make itself rise higher and higher.

"Hurry!" Royce shouted. "Pete, hurry!"

Without hesitating, he ran on air, pulling Nadine by the hand. They reached the platform the others were standing on, as the mass of faces and limbs reached the roof and branched out, crawling on it. It looked like it had stretched into a disturbing black tree covered in body parts and ominous blue fireflies.

As soon as he joined his friends, Peter could hear the banging on the other side of this door. He turned to Bobby. "What's that?"

"Things." Bobby motioned toward the enormous pillar of body parts, which was extending its branches over the roof toward them. "Like that one. Freddie's making them. He's using the house's memories. Don't ask me how. All I know is he wants to kill us. We're trapped here!"

Peter stared at the door, then at Nadine. "How many bullets are left in the gun?"

Nadine raised her shoulders, shook her head. "I… I don't know! I don't know anything about guns! I've never held one before!"

"Colt All American 2000," Jess said. "Fifteen shots. How many have you fired?"

"One?"

"Give." Jess put a hand toward her.

Royce cast a glance toward the ceiling. The mass of bodies kept crawling closer and closer. "Jess, if you've got anything in mind, you better do it now!"

"Bobby," she said, checking the gun first with the flashlight, then pointing it at the door like police did on TV— one hand over the other, flashlight in her left hand, gun on her right. "Grab the knob, unlock the door. When I tell you, open it quick!"

Bobby unlocked the door. Royce, Nadine, and Peter put their weight behind it to avoid having the creatures on the other side open it.

"Open!" she shouted.

The three against the door moved aside. Bobby opened it, and Jess's light illuminated the creatures outside. First, she put four shots into the twin creatures. One went into each torso, one went into each of their heads. They fell back, barely in time to reveal the spider head, gearing to leap on her, but Jess had a firm aim on it, and fired twice—one shot went into the floor, the other one hit its mark, and the head rolled backward, lifeless.

"Go!" They all poured into the hallway outside.

Peter went through last, and closed the door, as an avalanche of monsters fell from the ceiling.

"Where to now?" Royce asked, then pointed to the hallway that should've led them back to the chapel. "Past that corner, it's either an endless hallway or a hallway that ends shortly after. Should we try our luck with one of the rooms?"

Peter shook his head and took the flashlight from Nadine. "No, we should go back that way. The chapel will be there."

"How can you be so sure?" Bobby asked.

"Trust him." Nadine stepped over the corpses of the twin creatures, trying her hardest to stop shaking. "You saw the thing with the stairs…" She gagged. "Th-the sta—"

She puked on the floor, liters of bile and fluid spewing from her mouth. Bobby turned around and put a hand on her shoulder, holding her steady.

"About time someone did that," Jess said. "I've been barely holding it together."

"Are you freakin' kidding?" Royce said. "You're breezing through this!"

She gave him a grave look and shook her head.

"Sorry."

Something huge shook the door from the other side.

"We need to go find my brother and kick Freddie's ass, and we need to go now. That door's not gonna hold that thing."

Peter nodded.

They followed him a few feet down the hallway, then turned right to find—other than the abject darkness and the blue moon outside the window—it was the same hallway from the normal Vanek House. The door with the metal reinforcement was on the wall to the left.

"How are you doing this?" Bobby said.

Peter shook his head. "I… I'm not. I don't think I am."

They walked toward the door, following Peter. He reached out a hand, turned the knob, and pushed it in with ease.

Ray was cowering with his back against a stone pillar, every muscle in his body refusing to react, despite watching his best friend in the clutches of the abominable creature that had fallen from the ceiling.

Once it got one of its claws on Barry's leg, it unwrapped its belt-like tongue from his calf and spat it back out, wrapping it around his neck. It then sent out several more belt tentacles from the slug trail behind it, wrapping them around his every limb. The creature had him nearly immobilized, strangling him with the belt from its mouth.

"R-Ray!" Barry's terrified eyes were fixed on him, his voice came more like a gargled, pleading utterance than actual words. "H-help me!"

I'm sorry! Ray's panicking mind replied since his mouth couldn't form words. *I want to help, but I can't! I can't move! I can't help! I'm scared! I'm so scared!*

Barry let out a raspy sound out of his throat. He shook his head left and right, his face went red with effort; he shook his body, every muscle tensing up at full capacity, but was still impotent to free himself. The creature climbed up his body, little by little, clinging to his clothes with its clawed hands.

"Hel-lp! Ray! Pl-gh-leeeaass-se!"

I can't! I can't! I can't!

Ray's eyes were open wide, pupils dilated, a shaky hand covering his mouth. He glimpsed the creature's hand clinging to Barry's collar, its open mouth full of crooked teeth now mere inches from his neck, which was tightly constricted by the belt. Ray's ears were pierced by the choking sounds coming from his lips. Amidst the terrified haze overwhelming his brain, he caught sight of one of Barry's eyes—teary, capillaries close to bursting, overwhelmed with terror—and could almost see the light beginning to diminish from their bright blue. It was then the words passed through his mind in an instant, in his own voice; calm and factual: *Barry is going to die.*

The despair and hopelessness in that one blue eye stirred something deep within him.

The thought ran through his head again: *Barry is going to die.* This time, though, it didn't come as a factual statement. It was a call to action.

Before he knew it, he was on his feet. He stretched and took a torch from the sconce atop the column he'd been leaning against. With a scream, he swung the torch and hit the creature across the face. It didn't react. It remained on top of Barry, advancing toward his face. He hit it again.

Nothing happened.

For a moment, panic crept back up. This seemed futile, until he noticed the creature couldn't close its mouth, having its tongue around his friend's neck. He shoved the blazing torch into its maw. Flames spread all over its head, as if it were covered in oil, and it was then Ray realized his mistake: there was a creature, whose head was in flames, clinging to Barry's body. If it didn't let go, Barry's clothes would catch on fire.

(*Barry is going to die*)

Ray pulled the torch out of the creature's mouth and began kicking its head, over and over. The head moved back with each kick, but mindlessly returned to its original position, showing no signs of pain. "Let him go! You piece of shit! Let him go!"

A tiny flickering flame appeared in Barry's shirt. He struggled, grunted; his limbs still bound by the belts.

"Let him go! Goddamn it!"

He raised his foot, ready to kick again, expecting it to be as useless as the previous kick, then out of nowhere, a mental image flashed in his brain: him kicking a soccer ball so hard it had knocked the lights out of the biggest kid in the soccer team, and it had led to him becoming his most beloved friend. He couldn't let that end here, not because of him suddenly starting to kick like a wimp.

(*One of these skinny legs kicked the ball that knocked you out a moment ago*)

He repositioned his leg—not kicking down with his heel but pulling his leg back—and he let his foot fly as if he were unleashing a tie-breaking penalty kick to win the game. It connected with such force and at such a perfect angle, the creature's head came partially off, swinging back on a strip of black flesh like a sling. The belt tentacles unwrapped from Barry's limbs all at once, and its body went limp. The belts from the slug trail retreated from the surroundings.

Barry took in a huge lungful of air, then went into a coughing fit. He pushed the burning creature off his body, and it fell inertly to one side. He slapped the tiny flames off his shirt, then crawled back on his elbows, staring at the burning effigy of his father with horror.

Ray went down on one knee beside him, putting his hands on his shoulders. "Barry, look at me. Are you okay?" He put a hand on his cheek to turn his gaze away from the burning monster, forcing him to look at him. "Big Bear, please, talk to me! Are you okay?"

He only managed a hurried nod.

"I'm so sorry! I froze! I couldn't... I..."

Barry, still unable to speak, threw his arms around his best friend, breathing deep, recovering from the ordeal.

"I'm so sorry," Ray said.

"S'okay." Barry's voice was coarse, his throat was still raw. "You got 'im. You got 'im. You..." He turned his head away from Ray and toward the spot where the burning creature had fallen. "What the…"

It was gone.

They both turned at once. There were still a couple of black, smoking pieces of the monster, but no monster. They spun their heads this way and that. Was it gone?

A belt came down, wrapped itself around Ray's neck.

"No!" Barry sprung to his feet.

The creature clung to the ceiling like some kind of lizard. Its reattached head and its upper torso were in flames, but it looked unbothered by them. Its belt tongue pulled Ray up toward it. The flaming belt around its neck lashed at him, forcing him to keep his distance.

Before he could make a move toward a torch or a chair, which appeared to be his only available weapons, a multitude of belt tentacles shot in all directions from the black trail on the ceiling, blocking his path. He tried to duck under, over, and past the web of crisscrossing tentacles, but as he did this, the belt from the creature's neck wrapped around his leg and pulled, making him topple over. Soon, there were more of the belt tentacles wrapping around his body, spinning him around, one wrapping around his neck yet again. He was immobilized, but noticed the tentacle around his neck wasn't squeezing. A crazy notion crossed his mind: whatever or whoever was controlling the house now wanted him to watch Ray die, and it wanted him to see him die at the hand of a monster crafted after his dead father—just like a moment ago, it had wanted Ray to watch him die.

"Ray!" he shouted, seeing him helpless, kicking in the air, hands clinging to the belt wrapped around his neck, face going red with strain. "RAAAAAAY!"

A loud *BANG!* rang and bounced off the walls of the chapel, and the creature's head flinched. The belt around Ray's neck loosened and let him fall to the ground.

Barry couldn't see where the shot had come from. He couldn't turn his head.

A second shot rang out, appearing to get the creature right in its upper spine. It turned its flaming head toward a spot behind Barry, and his father's burning face let out a loud, horrendous hiss.

Ray was on the floor, crawling away, coughing.

The monster's head reared back; its jaw clamped shut. *It's going to shoot out its tongue!* he thought. "Watch for the tongue!" he shouted at whomever was standing behind him, but the warning was unnecessary, as another shot blasted it in the face. The monster's tentacles retracted from the walls and the columns, releasing Barry as well. It fell to the ground with an unceremonious wet splat.

"Barry! Finish it off!" It was Jess's voice.

He turned an astounded stare toward her, especially seeing her with a gun in her hands.

"What, do you need a fuckin' permit? Go!"

Barry scrambled to his feet. Ran up to the creature on the floor and with one large Timberland, kicked its head in, as if he were putting out a campfire. By the second kick, the creature's head split like an egg, but he gave it two more stomps for good measure.

He ran up to Ray, who was sitting with his back to the wall, rubbing his neck and coughing. He went down on one knee next to him. "You okay to stand up?"

The smaller kid gave him an agitated nod, and he helped him to his feet.

"Can you talk? Are you okay?" Barry's own voice was still hoarse from almost being choked to death.

Ray again nodded. He'd halfway croaked the word "Yes" when he already had a pair of large arms around him, pulling him in for an almost suffocating embrace.

"Don't you fuckin' dare die on me, you hear me?"

Ray slapped his hand twice on his back. "I won't, as long as you don't crush me to death."

Barry let go of him. "Sorry." He turned to see Jess, Peter, Bobby, Royce, and Nadine. "We have to go." He glanced at the creature, could see the bullet holes and burns beginning to stitch themselves together. "That thing won't stay dead."

"We know," Peter said. "It's not alive in the first place. These things are made by the house."

Barry stood up and stomped on the creature's head twice more to delay it coming back. "Freddie... Freddie did this." By the looks on the other's faces, he realized they already knew this as well.

"I've only got five bullets left in this thing," Jess said to the others. "Something tells me that won't kill the huge thing from the main hall."

"Huge thing?" Ray asked in a rough voice, rubbing his sore neck.

"Pray you don't have to see it."

"Where'd you learn to shoot like that?" he asked.

"My dad taught me. He takes me to shooting practice on weekends. It's for self-defense only. He doesn't let me even come close to a gun unless he's there, so he'd probably throw a fit if he saw me holding one now."

"That was awesome shooting, though."

She gave him an awkward grin. "Well, thank pure fuckin' luck the creature was holding still. If it had been shaking its head around, I might have hit you instead."

"Oh... that's... lucky." Ray gave an uneasy smile.

Nadine turned to Peter. "Lead the way. We have to hurry. That thing will break down the bedroom door in no time and come after us."

Peter nodded and headed back toward the chapel door.

Everyone followed close behind, brandishing flashlights and whatever improvised weapons they could get. Barry picked up two torches from their sconces, extinguished them with his boot, handed one to Ray, and kept one himself.

"Why put them out?" Ray asked.

"The house is made of wood," Barry said.

Peter reached the door, turned an apprehensive look toward his friends, and pulled it open. As soon as they'd all set foot in the hallway, something exploded from beyond the corner that led to the bedrooms.

"The fuck was that?" Barry asked.

There was the sound of something enormous and slimy dragging itself over the floorboards, accompanied by a strange rumbling. Along with it came barks, and moans, and scratches, and cries, and hisses. Angry gurgling noises as some creature or creatures approached. Their flashlights shone on a black hand clinging to the corner wall, then another hand, then something like a tentacle. Then, there were many tentacles, many hands, clawing at walls and ceiling and floor, as an abomination filled the entire hallway, slowly turning the corner.

Everyone in the group cried in terror, seeing the many blue-eyed faces, human and inhuman, appearing and disappearing from the black blob crawling toward them. Whole human torsos emerged from the central mass, multiple hands reaching toward them, until mouths formed in their palms and writhing tentacles pushed out through from behind their black teeth, only to dissolve into screaming blue-eyed faces. It was an ineffable chaos, a rolling accumulation of madness, hungry for their flesh.

Nadine turned to Peter. "What now? It's blocking our only way out. You're the only one that knows."

Barry had no clue why everyone kept asking Peter—not having been there to see the invisible stair trick. What did he know that the rest didn't?

"Pete?" Royce asked. "What about the window? If we jump out, do you think we'll make it?"

"Peter, we have to hurry!" Jess shouted, panic now unbridled in her voice.

The monster crawled closer to them. It was only a few feet away.

Peter turned toward the chapel door. "We have to go back!"

"What?" Barry asked. "But what about the thing in the chapel? It's probably already coming this way!"

"It's not there," Peter said, then hesitated. "Um… I think… It's not the same chapel since we closed the door."

Without a second's pause, Peter pushed the reinforced door open. Not four feet from the group, a hand with only three fingers and a long claw for a thumb clung to the wall, and a dog's open maw let out a tongue with a baby's wailing head at its tip.

"Hurry!" Peter said.

Everyone rushed back inside amidst screams.

Peter went in last and closed the door behind him. They were back in the chapel, but as he'd predicted, something was different.

Freddie stood at the center of the altar. His clothes were soaked with blood, as well as both his hands, one of which held a knife. Fresh crimson threads hung from it and fell as long, thick globs. Blood streamed down the sides of the altar and ran down the concrete into the small gutter around it. At Freddie's feet were four bleeding corpses the group recognized as Wilfrid Ingram, Kayleigh Grant, Randall Knox, and his sister Paula—a four-year-old girl.

Screams came from the altar from the remaining two hostages. The group watched in disbelief as Freddie stood in front of fifteen-year-old Caesar Knox, who—having seen his younger brother and baby sister's throats slit—squealed in sharp terror as he realized it was his turn. Caesar was gagged, crying, shaking his head, pleading.

"What the hell are you doing?" Bobby shouted.

Freddie stopped. Peered at the group. His eyes opened with surprise, their whites contrasting with the crimson covering his face. There was a bizarre sort of glee in his gaze. "Oh, will you look at that?"

Vomit rose in Bobby's throat, seeing the pale, drained corpses on the concrete, breathing in the meaty iron smell of blood, but he continued. "What the hell, Freddie? Why are you doing this?"

"Who the fuck cares why?" Royce held the hammer tight in his fist, pushing his way from the back, striding decisively toward Freddie and the altar. "We're ending this shit now!"

"Dude, wait!"

"Quit it, Bobby! I don't care about his reasons. He's got my brother. He's going down!"

Freddie scoffed. "Can't let you do that, Tweedle Dum." Out of the shadows formed by the torches in the sconces came thick black tentacles that wrapped around each of The Vigilantes' feet, holding them in place. All except for Peter. "You all refused to die, so I guess you get to watch." He drove his eyes into Peter's, he pointed his knife at him. "Except you, Norman." He eyed a spot behind Peter. "You have an important appointment."

The entire group turned and gasped.

"Peter, watch out!" Nadine shouted, pointing at Ben Curling, who was standing behind him.

Among the screams and commotion, Curling hooked his arm around Peter's neck and dragged him, kicking and screaming, out of the chapel, ending with the loud, metallic slam of the door. None of The Vigilantes could move to help.

"Alright, where was I?" Freddie said.

"Stop!" Jess shouted from the back of the group. "Freddie, please, we'll do anything, just please don't do this!"

Freddie once more turned to face Caesar Knox, who resumed struggling and letting out wordless shrieks through his gag, pleading for his life. Freddie held the knife in front of his face, and the teenager pissed his pants, squealing in fear.

"Freddie, talk to me, man!" Bobby cried with desperation. "Talk to me! Why are you doing this?"

Freddie turned a sarcastic grin toward him. Giggled. "C'mon, Bobster. You and I have watched enough movies together for you to know I'm not gonna pause for a villain monologue." He grabbed Caesar's head, pulled it back and in one straight motion drew a deep straight line in his throat.

Blood sprayed all over Freddie's clothes, and screams of horror filled the room, echoing off the chapel walls, as blood sprayed all over his shirt, his pants, and splashed a fresh coat of crimson on his face. Caesar collapsed to the floor, convulsing, eyes wild as his lifeblood left his body to run down into the gutter with the others'.

Freddie grinned at his former friends. Thick lines of blood raced down his face to drip from his jaw. Red on red. "I'm not the villain here."

He now ambled toward Leroy, who was kneeling a few

steps from where Caesar lay dying among wet gasps. Like the Knox boy, Leroy screamed and struggled, trying to get out of his bindings before Freddie could slit his throat and end his life. Leroy let out angry and terrified screams through his gag.

"Leave my brother alone!" Royce shouted. "I'll kill you, you twisted piece of shit! You think just 'coz you lost your family, you get to hurt other people? Is that your excuse to finally show how fucked up you really are? You gonna prove everyone right?"

Freddie positioned himself behind Leroy and grinned back at him, as if he wanted him to get a clear view of the show. "I don't care what anyone thinks."

In Royce's mind, he could picture the knife slicing through his brother's flesh and the blood they both shared would pour over his shirt. The image itself was enough to drive him close to madness. This could not happen. This could not be allowed. Leroy was his brother. Leroy was—

Special? Who the fuck do you think you are? Look at the other five kids lying dead at his feet. They also had people who thought they were special. Why can't it happen to Leroy?

"I'm glad your baby sister is dead!" he shouted.

Freddie froze in place.

"I'm glad your mom died!"

"What?" Freddie's voice came out as a throaty growl.

Everyone else stared at Royce, jaws hanging open.

"They didn't need no curse to die. All they needed was

a stupid fuck-up like Freddie 'The Hyena' Parham to take his little sister to the deep end, no matter if it was irresponsible and stupid!"

"You're not gonna bait me, Tweedle Dumbass. I already know it's my fault my family's dead. That doesn't change a thing."

"Then why are you trying to stop your family curse?" Bobby's voice cut through the exchange like a scalpel. Freddie stared at him, shocked. "That's what you're doing, right? It's the only reason you'd do something this horrible!"

"Shut up," Freddie said with a flat voice.

"You always said it. You'd do anything to get rid of it. Anything. You wanted Laurie to live a full life. Now Laurie's gone. It's just you left for the Parham line to continue. You always wanted to grow up and be a better dad than the piece-of-shit you had to live with. You wanted Laurie to grow up and have her own family, and you'd all leave White Harbor, free of the curse. That's the part no one knew about you. You're not all zombies and tentacle monsters. You loved your family. You wanted your own family! You're brilliant and more mature than any of us! But is this what you meant, that you'd do *anything*? Killing six innocent kids? A four-year-old girl? For what, now that Laurie's gone? Just for you, you selfish piece of shit? You think you're gonna have a big happy family after you kill six kids? How fucking pathetic are you?"

Freddie stared at him, mouth hanging open, eye

twitching with rage, but there was also hurt in those eyes. "Y-you don't underst—"

Three shots rang in quick succession. All three got Freddie square in the chest. Three holes appeared in his shirt, and though it was drenched with blood, it poured fresh from the holes.

"Thanks, Bobby," Jess said, in a thin voice, so unlike her. Her voice quivered, but her gun arm remained steady. "I needed time to get my aim right."

Freddie gawked at her.

"Don't make me do it, Freddie!" A whine snuck into her usual firm voice. "Please!"

He shifted his gaze down toward Leroy. He reacted, as if realizing this would be his last chance. He moved the knife toward his hostage's throat, and there was another *bang!* His head whipped back, and he fell down.

A second later, the shadow tentacles binding them to the floor let go, and they all ran toward Leroy.

Royce untied his brother and removed the gag from his mouth. "I'm here, Lee. I got you!" The brothers embraced. "I got you!"

Leroy glanced at Bobby and Jess as his brother helped him to his feet. "Thank you!"

Bobby shambled, numb, past the twins and fell to his knees beside Freddie. He started sobbing his eyes out—the horror of his friend's open, dead eyes, and the bullet hole in his forehead burning itself in his memory.

Nadine kneeled next to him and put a hand on his back.

"He needed help." He cried fat, copious tears. "He went through something horrible. He needed help. Not this!"

"I get it, Bobby, but it's too late for that," Nadine said, pushing her own horror down. "We have to go. We have to help Peter."

Bobby returned a reluctant nod. Wasting no time, the entire group headed for the door, sparing a look back at the six corpses, including someone they'd called a friend.

"Jess," Ray asked. "Are you—"

"Not now." Her hand still clung to the gun, the space between her fingers corpse-white with how hard she was holding it. "This isn't over. I need to keep going. I can't lose my shit. Not yet."

He nodded.

"Wait." Nadine stood in front of the door. She turned around to face the others. "Peter opening the doors led us here. I don't think he's going to be right outside with Curling. I think he'll be somewhere else. How do we know we're not gonna open that door and walk into the huge monster outside?"

"Only one way to know," Royce said.

"Monster?" Leroy asked and peered at his brother.

Peter took one step back, then another. Curling stood in the hallway, regarding him. The hallway was like the one he and Nadine had seen, every wall covered in yellowed, stained newspapers, except there were no bugs or faces underneath. The window was behind Curling—it wasn't boarded up, but the strange blue moon wasn't there, only a black, starless night. Peter turned around, ready to run away, but there was a wall behind him, which hadn't been there mere seconds ago.

"There's no way out, Lange," Curling said, his tone measured. "The house isn't watching you anymore. That Parham boy has all its attention right now. It's just you and me."

Peter examined the man, who wasn't moving from where he stood. "What do you want from me?"

"Sit." The old man's voice was calm. He nodded toward a chair which materialized beside Peter.

He shook his head. "I'd rather stand, sir."

"Suit yourself." Curling sat down in another chair, which appeared out of nowhere.

He hesitated, looking from Curling to the chair inches from him. He sat and eyed the old man warily.

"You felt it, right? The house? In your head? Like you could talk to it without words?"

He nodded.

"Your mother didn't want you to come here, because this house has been waiting for you for a long time. Only it's not the house, but the entity controlling the house. It's what your mother calls 'God'. The more you come into the house, the more it awakens. Your mother and her group don't want that. Not yet. They have a timeline, they have plans, they want to control what can't be controlled. You're the son of the Circle's Mother, and there's a time coming up in which she will need you, so she can't let the house take you."

This didn't sound to Peter like the Ben Curling everyone talked about. The one that only communicated in grunts and two-word statements. This was a man who wanted to talk to him for whatever reason. "Why are you telling me all this?"

Curling sighed. "I've spent way too long doing too many questionable things. Things that dirty my soul. And, year after year, I keep shoveling more and more dirt on top of it. Alone, with no one to tell these things to, but a pair of dogs that haven't even been dogs for years. I know they came after you, and you kids killed them. So, please indulge me."

"The dogs. They came from the house, right?"

The old man gave him an impressed stare. "Yes. They used to be just regular dogs. One day, the house killed them. I was late to feed it that year, so next time I came in, it killed my dogs to punish me. Replaced their flesh with its own, left the bones. That way, it could follow me around, keep an eye on me, make sure I wouldn't be late again. They were just like normal dogs: ate, shat, got sick. They still obeyed me, but they were smarter, meaner. Thought of killing them a few times, but that would've been irresponsible. I didn't want the thing in the house getting too hungry and breaking out into the town."

The old man looked wistfully to one side, took a deep breath.

"You see, boy, I'm finding myself in an unpleasant position. I can't let your mother's group have you when their time comes, but I can't let the house have you either. I can't lay a hand on you outside of this house, because there are rules to this thing, but if I bring you in here, the house will try to take you. So, I had to give the house a large enough meal. Let your friend Parham distract it, doing what he's doing in there"—he nodded toward the reinforced door—"thinking that will take away his curse." He scoffed, rolled his eyes. "As if anything could do that. But he buys me time"—he turned a dark gaze in his direction—"to shovel more dirt on my soul."

Peter sprang up from the chair with a gasp.

"I'm sorry." Curling stood, bringing out a knife from his belt. "I felt you deserved to know why."

Peter moved to one side, then the other, trying to find an opportunity to run past the old man and hopefully make it back through the door to the chapel.

"The door's locked, Lange. There's no way out of this hallway." Curling feigned to move right, then immediately went left and with a single hand grabbed Peter by the neck and slammed him against the wall. He raised the knife. "I'll make it quick."

There was the sound of glass breaking, then two bodies hitting the floor. Both Peter and Curling turned with surprise toward the source of the noise. The window was broken.

Lying on top of a jacket on the floor, surrounded by shattered glass and small pieces of wood, were Callum and Sylvia.

"Did you cut yourself?" she asked.

"No. My elbows got banged up, though."

"Good idea with the jacket. Did you feel that? The way gravity shifted the moment we came through? That's crazy! How does a vertical chimney lead horizontally into a window?"

"I think I'll need a physics degree to figure that o—"

Sylvia shone the flashlight toward Peter and Curling. "Oh, shit."

Callum adjusted his crooked glasses. "Peter?" He pulled the crowbar from his belt and held it toward the old man. "Let him go, Mr. Curling!"

Sylvia, holding her hammer out toward the old man, elbowed Callum in the arm. "Why do you call him Mr. Curling? Stop being so polite. Look at what he's doing." She turned to Curling, brandishing the hammer, and in the toughest voice she could make, said, "Let our friend go, you motherfucker!"

Taking advantage of the distraction, Peter kicked the old man hard in the knee, causing him to drop the knife. As Curling winced, Peter grabbed the knife and ran toward his friends, then pointed the blade toward the old man. "Stay away!" he commanded, trying to sound tough. "Let us out of here!"

Curling shot him an angry glare. "That's not happening."

"Uh, Peter?" Callum whispered, looking nervously over his shoulder. "We need to get away from the window."

"Why?" he whispered back, then peered at the window. Beyond the broken pane, there was a square tunnel made of stones. Something was coming from it, something that glowed with flickering blue flames. It was then he noticed the stench of smoke, of charred meat. "What is that thing?"

"Milo Calhoun," Callum said, as if that explained everything.

Peter stared at him. "Okay?"

"Once that thing gets here," the old man said, having noticed the creature, "you'll be stuck between me and it. I can let your friends out, Lange. I only need *you*, but that thing will come for all of you. Even worse, soon as it sees you, the house will know you're here. It will send everything it's got into this hallway I made. None of you will make it out."

"Fine." Peter said, without hesitation. "You let them out first."

"No!" Sylvia said. "Are you crazy?"

Curling turned toward the reinforced door, and it cracked open. "Don't even try it. I control this hallway. You can't cross the doorway. Only they can."

Peter gave them a confident nod. "Go."

Sylvia shook her head. "We're not leaving you with him."

"Go," Peter repeated. "Just trust me, alright?"

"Out," Curling said. "Before I change my mind."

Reluctant, both his friends moved toward the door, sparing a worried glance back at him as they walked through, and it slammed shut behind them.

"Now," Curling said. "Come here."

Peter took small steps, inching toward him, hands raised above his head, Curling's knife held in one of them. He could already hear the creature shuffling and dragging its body through the tunnel, ever closer.

"Throw the knife on the floor. Over there." Curling pointed to a corner.

Peter grabbed the knife's handle, pulled it back, ready to toss it toward the corner, but instead, turned toward Curling and threw it at him. The knife's handle bounced off Curling's chest. Peter hadn't expected the knife to pierce the man's heart—he was nowhere near strong or skilled enough to do that—instead, he took advantage of the man flinching to grab the chair he'd been sitting on and smashing it over his head.

Having at least stunned him, he was able to strike him with the chair one more time, and another, until the old man fell to the floor.

Something hit the floorboards by the window with a disgusting, dry, bony clatter. Peter turned to see the creature lying on the floor and slowly bringing itself up. It was shaped like a man, but its arms were crooked, longer than normal, and ended in black claws—its entire upper body was burning with blue flames, which began licking at the walls nearby.

He started waving his hands in the air toward the creature. "Hey! I'm here! See me? You want me, right? I'm here!"

The creature let out a hiss like the sound of burning coals, the sound and sight of it sending chills down his back. He was only playing brave, after all, and if this little gambit didn't work, he was going to die.

He dashed toward the reinforced door. Curling had said he owned this hallway. He said the house's attention was on what Freddie was doing. He said if the creature saw him, the house would see him. If he was right, that meant the house had now seen him, which meant *he* could see the house, too.

He pulled the door open, and hurried through, ensuring to lock it, leaving Curling behind with the flaming creature. A second later, he was standing in the darkness of what he assumed was a hallway. He had no flashlight since he'd left it with Nadine. The only light was a sliver coming from his left. The window at the end of the hallway. He'd somehow both entered and come out of the same door into the same hallway, but Curling and the flaming monster weren't in this version of it. There was that corpse-blue moon glowing outside the window, casting non-light inside.

He had to hurry. If Curling got away from the creature, he'd soon be following him here. He wasn't sure locking the door would do anything to stop him.

All he had to work with was his orientation of where the hallways and rooms were in the regular house. If he walked to his right, he could follow the hallway, turn left at the corner, and reach the bedroom area. Another left at the end to reach the stairs. But what if the house shifted to confuse him? He had no choice but to figure out the right path, regardless.

He walked close to the wall, feeling it with his hands

(*What if there are bugs beneath the newspaper? Faces and bugs!*)

until he reached the corner, and turned, still following the wall. This version of the hallway didn't have bugs crawling under the newspaper. In fact, he sensed—like the normal version of the house—the inner walls weren't covered in paper. His fingers ran over rough wood. He reached the spot where his fingers touched what he recognized as a doorframe. *First bedroom on the right. One more door after this one.*

The door emitted a slight vibration. A sound coming from inside the room. Something was moving in there. He couldn't stay here long.

He continued forward, reached the second door on this side. The vibration grew, the rumbling got louder. He walked faster. He got only about three steps from the second door when there was a booming crash, as if the house had been struck by a wrecking ball. He instinctively went down to a crouching position, hands over his head, like in an earthquake drill, but he knew all four bedroom doors lining the hallway had burst open.

He turned his head toward the darkness that saturated the hallway and was met by dozens of glowing blue eyes, flowing from the doors, converging at the center of the hall, accompanied by growls, and moans, and barks, and he knew at once what was taking shape. The black mass, composed of all the memories of every dead person this house had known— plus two dogs. Some of the blue eyes merged into each other, forming large eyeballs the size of human heads, glowing blue, staring at him. Then came the unnerving sound of fingernails and claws, and the wet slapping of its slimy body as it shuffled toward him.

Peter stood and hurried toward the next corner of the hallway. His mind flashed warnings about what lay ahead. The wall would soon disappear to give way to an old balustrade filled with gaps, beyond which was a swift fall to the first floor, which, while not fatal, would at least result in broken bones and leaving him vulnerable to the approaching monster.

He reached the corner, the shuffling monstrosity

behind him closing in at surprising speed—the house was desperate to get him. He turned. The wall gave way to the balustrade. It was still dark, but the windows, which, in this version of the house, weren't boarded up, let in slight bars of blue light, which gave his surroundings some depth of field, though no useful illumination.

With his hand on the wooden handrail, he followed the edge, and was reminded of the gaps in the balustrade as his hand lost its grip. When he tried to grab it again, a sharp splinter drove itself into his palm. He cried out as he plucked it from his skin, which excited the concert of moans and grunts coming toward him.

He stepped sideways, letting go of the handrail to touch the opposite wall. He followed it until he reached another corner and turned. This would lead to the stairs, but since the stairs themselves had no handrail, he'd have to use what little light he had at his disposal to know when to take a step down.

He moved forward, hearing the creature's noises coming dangerously close—this maneuver of stopping and moving toward the wall had cost him precious seconds. He dragged his feet until the tip of his foot touched the edge of the stairs. A flash of panic struck his brain, thinking he would topple over and roll down in the dark. He carefully put a foot down, then another.

Panic hit him again when the sound of the balustrade

breaking echoed through the hall, followed by the sound of things falling down and crashing to the first floor. He could now see blue eyes close behind him, as well as in the main hall below. The enormous creature had split in two, trying to cut him off before he reached the first floor. He took a deep breath and—on feel alone—started running down the stairs, the creature close on his heels.

He was halfway down when his mind flashed a warning. *The landing!* But it was already too late. He wouldn't be able to stop. He ran past the edge of where the stairs changed direction and fell.

Peter crashed on the floorboards below, only hurting his elbow and his knee, not a serious injury, but enough to leave him groaning with pain for far longer than he could afford. He noticed the rumbling sound again, unnervingly close. His mind flashed another warning. He turned his head to see a cloud of blue eyes with three large blue eyeballs on the landing above him. As fast as he could, he stood up and ran two steps before the rumble and clatter of bodies filled the air as they crashed down on the spot he'd been lying in.

He raised his head and now there was the other mass of eyes, hissing and growling at him, coming from deeper in the main hall.

Peter scrambled to feel his way along the wall until his fingers touched a door—*The front doors!*—he was almost out. He turned the knob closest to him, but as he tried to open it, something heavy slammed against the upper part of the door and closed it again. The mass of creatures from the stairs was already two feet behind him and had extended a limb to hold the door closed. A horrible, cavernous moan came from above his head, and he pictured a gaping mouth opening to swallow him in one bite. He reached for the other knob and pulled the door open, as thin, bony fingers caressed his leg.

He kicked at them, ran out, and shut the door.

He now stood outside the reinforced door on the second floor but dim light shone from his left. Panting, recovering from the fear and panic, he turned his gaze to the left to see the boarded-up window on the Vanek House's hallway, through which thin bars of sunlight filtered in.

He smelled smoke.

A collective exhalation of relief escaped Jess's group as they realized they were in the hallway outside the reinforced door. It was gloomy, but there was light coming in between the boards nailed over the window. As far as Jess could see, they were back in the normal version of the Vanek House—if there was such a thing as a normal version of the Vanek House.

It would've felt like the ordeal was over if it weren't for two things: they didn't know where Curling had taken Peter, and there was the smell of smoke wafting in the hallway. She could even see the smoke drifting through the bars of light from between the boards and the glow from their flashlights.

She turned to the others. "We have to find Peter and get out. This house is going to burn quickly."

There were assenting responses all around. They ran down the hallway and reached the bedrooms.

"Check the bedrooms," Jess said.

They opened the four doors. Three bedrooms were empty. One wasn't. It elicited a startled cry from Bobby as soon as he opened the door. The group peered in and found Elijah Knox's corpse lying on the floor, his throat torn, a nasty bite on his calf. He lay in a pool of congealed blood, next to what looked like a dog's skeleton.

"Peter and I ran into him," Nadine said with a horrified expression on her face. "One of Curling's dogs killed him." She motioned toward Jess. "That's his gun."

Jess realized she really didn't want to answer any questions about why she had a dead man's gun in her hand, especially when she'd just used it to kill her friend; a teenager who had been missing for a month and a half. "Should I leave it with him?"

Nadine shook her head. "We're not out of the house yet. I'd feel safer with it. We wipe it down and toss it somewhere on the first floor after we've found Peter."

Jess agreed.

They hurried down the stairs and, when they reached the main hall, they stood together by the front doors.

"Where the fuck are Callum and Sylvia?" Jess asked. "Shouldn't they be down here?"

As if answering her question, the pair appeared from the dining room, running toward them.

"Oh, thank god!" Sylvia said. "Curling's got Peter! We appeared outside the service room after we crossed the door upstairs, then we couldn't go back. The door won't open, but there's smoke coming out of it! We don't know what to do."

"Is Peter back there?" Nadine asked.

"No." Callum shook his head. "We checked everywhere for another gateway leading back to where he and Curling were, but no luck. The only door that won't open is the service room. The smoke's coming from there."

"Show me," Jess said, and followed them all the way to the back of the house, joined by Nadine.

"Should we wait here?" Ray said, sounding drained from the entire ordeal. "Are the doors still shut? There's smoke. I'd like to get out of here now."

"You got it." Barry walked past the twins and Bobby. He reached the double doors, ready to crack one open.

As he turned the knob, there was a sound. A sudden sound. A human sound. A vacuous, echoing: "Ooh-augh!"

Horrified cries ensued as they all saw Freddie Parham, his knife deep inside Leroy's back. He took out the knife and got two more stabs in before Barry was on the move, trying to get him off Leroy, not even questioning how he was alive after a bullet to the head.

Bobby stood there, paralyzed, in disbelief. The world slowed down to one-quarter speed. From where he stood, he could see—in the sunlight coming in from the front door—the blood on Freddie's forehead, where Jess's bullet had gotten him, but no hole, no scar, only a tiny, clean, skin-colored circle amid a red stain. He was still alive, still fighting, still killing. There was something in those eyes he'd never seen, though—even back in that blood-soaked altar—a deranged, primal bloodlust. He gawked in abject incredulity as Freddie put his lips to one of the wounds he'd opened in Leroy's back, sucked out blood, turned his head, and spat it right into Barry's eyes before the big guy could reach him.

Barry brought his hands up to his face and screamed as his eyes stung.

In a sudden burst of speed, Ray leaped at Freddie and tackled him to the ground. Bobby watched as the knife slid across the floor.

"Lee!" Royce cried, at last reacting to the shock, grabbing his brother and pulling him against his chest, both their faces displaying the same expression of surprise, for entirely different reasons.

There was a ringing in Bobby's ears, as if this were a bad fever dream. He first regarded the knife on the floor, then Ray, who'd found his courage somewhere deep within and was now trying to wrestle Freddie into submission.

Barry wiped blood off his eyes with the back of his hand, his teeth bared in pain and rage.

Leroy—blood bubbling out of his mouth—threw the front doors fully open and staggered outside, as if in a trance, closely followed by Royce, who was shouting panicked words so fast it was hard to understand anything he was saying. A mixture of "Stop moving!", "Lie down!", and "Where are you going?"

Freddie punched Ray in the face twice, kicked him off, then crawled toward the knife, grabbed it, and lifted his gaze to find Bobby's stupefied stare fixed on him. "Oh, just the one I wanted!"

Bobby turned just as Freddie—with animalistic agility—tackled him to the floorboards. He barely snapped out of it in time to catch Freddie's arm in the air as the blade was coming down. "H-ho-how?" he asked. "How are you alive?"

Freddie's response was that high-pitched laugh of his, now louder, now crazier, from an unhinged grin that made his crooked teeth appear huge this close. Even his eyes appeared off-center, and there was that tiny circle, that clean circle in the middle of his bloody forehead, where not even a scar remained. "I'm disappointed, Bobsterrrrrr!" Freddie said in a shrill voice

(*This can't be you, Freddie! This isn't you!*)

which echoed in the hall's emptiness. "You should know the killer always comes back to life at the end!" He put his weight behind the knife. "I control the house right now! I made a deal for those kids in the chapel! You can't kill me while I'm in this house!"

"Oh, yeah?" A large fist flew toward Freddie's face, smashing into it like the truck that had killed his father. Freddie flew back, and he'd barely hit the floor when Barry took him by the neck, his face sticky with blood and fury. He lifted the shorter, skinnier kid in the air, as if he were weightless. "Let's do somethin' about that, bitch!"

Barry carried Freddie to the door, grabbed him with both hands, and hurled him out, throwing him as high as he could. He came down with an unbuffered crash on the front lawn. He stomped out the door. The last glimpse Bobby got of his eyes before walking outside showed murder in them, accentuated by the traces of blood still clinging to his brow and cheeks.

A second later, Ray was there, helping Bobby up. "Did he hurt you?"

He shook his head.

"Guys!"

They both turned to look at the second floor. Peter was running toward the stairs.

"Is everyone here? The house is on fire!"

"A group went in there to look for you." Bobby pointed at the dining room entrance as Peter reached the bottom of the stairs.

"We have to get them," he said. "Old Man Curling is here."

At first unsure of whether to go outside or follow Peter, Bobby shook his head, snapping out of his confusion. "It isn't safe to go alone. I'll come with you." He took one look over his shoulder, past the entrance, where he couldn't only see but hear Barry punching Freddie over and over in the front yard. He eyed Ray, who was already heading outside toward him, and prayed he was actually heading there to stop him from killing his old friend. If he didn't—he had a hard time digesting this last thought—Freddie had made his choices.

He and Peter ran toward the dining room, and there was a sudden change of light from the glare coming in through the front doors to the gloom in the deeper areas. There was a wedge of light coming through the two-sided fireplace, which caused a harsh contrast, making the areas closer to them look illuminated and the areas past the fireplace look darker than normal. This gave Bobby only a fraction-of-a-second glimpse of Ben Curling in the darker part before the man rushed him and knocked him into a wall with a punch to the face.

As soon as he reoriented himself, he saw Curling—his clothes and face covered in soot, as if he'd crawled a mile through a chimney. He had Peter against the stone fireplace, a knife raised, ready to be brought down into his friend's chest.

Bobby raised his hand. He was about to shout, but—

"Stop!" Jess and the others stood a few steps past the corner leading to the kitchen. Jess was pointing the gun at the old man, as dark fumes emerged from the doorway behind them, like an exhalation from a smoker, flowing out, folding over the upper part of the frame and accumulating in the tall ceiling, like an upside-down flood. "I'm not gonna ask twice, you ancient limp-dick asshole. We've been through enough shit. Don't make me fuck you up!"

Curling turned around and stared at her with those large, scary eyes of his. His mouth was a straight line of seething anger.

His lips moved. "You don't know—"

"Oh, please fuckin' tell me what I don't know, so I can cap you in the nose, you motherfucker! I swear, I'll put a second bullet in your corpse's bunghole, so you can carry that with you to hell."

Big talk, Bobby thought, *but she only has one bullet. If she shoots and misses...*

Curling appeared to buy it, though. He stood there, glowering at Jess, still holding Peter, still holding the knife.

Bobby carefully reached into his pocket until his fingers wrapped around something rectangular and plastic. Taking advantage of Curling's distraction, he went up on one knee, pushed himself forward, and pressed the stun gun's button. Curling reacted to its *tak-tak-tak!* noise too late, and the contact spikes got him in the thigh.

The old man shook and dropped to the floor, but he didn't let go of Peter, he didn't let go of the knife. He was still conscious as Peter went down with him, struggling to pry the dazed old man's hand off his shirt. Curling recovered, and in one swift motion, raised the knife faster than any of them could have expected. Peter screamed, just as Bobby grabbed him by the arm and tried to pull him away.

Too late! Bobby thought. *I was too late!*

The knife was coming down.

BANG!

The knife fell to the floor.

In the light of Jess's flashlight, Bobby could see the tiny hole in Curling's chest, and the first spurts of blood coming from it. She'd shot him straight through the heart.

Curling stared at her in astonishment. His stare filled with hatred, but above all things, bafflement that the thirteen year old, with the ginger braids and the freckles, had been able to hit home so perfectly. Curling's knife arm fell to his side, as if he could no longer use it, and through it all, the shock—the universal shock—in his face that this could've happened. Curling's lips trembled, shaping perplexed words. "How will

I... I won't be... Won't be back before the... How will I..."

He fell to the floor, dead.

There was another noise of something falling. Jess had dropped the gun and was now holding Nadine, and she was wailing like a child. She'd said she'd been barely holding it together, and as far as she knew, she'd killed Freddie and now Curling.

Peter and Bobby got up and joined the rest.

Jess sobbed in uncontrollable bursts. "I killed them!" she cried. "I'm a murderer! Oh, my god!"

"You're not, Jess," Peter said, as they all huddled together in a group hug they knew couldn't last long now that the fire was spreading. "You saved me."

Bobby noticed the flames beginning to come out of the kitchen area and licking at the doorway. "You guys get out. There's one thing I have to do." He crouched and took the gun in his hand.

"Are you nuts?" Nadine asked.

"They can't know Jess shot Curling. Get out of the house, now!" Bobby ran off toward the main hall. The others followed suit. He turned and ran upstairs. The smoke was building up. Downstairs, his friends crossed the hall and ran out the front doors.

At the back of the hallway, where it turned toward the reinforced door, the furious orange flames glowed like a furnace. He needed to be quick about this.

Bobby ran into the room where Elijah Knox's corpse lay. He went down to his knees next to the body and wiped the gun clean with his shirt the best he could. He knew the whole town talked about the Knoxes' feud with Ben Curling. Jess had told them, when Mr. Knox got drunk at the bar, all he did was complain about the old man. It was easier for everyone to think he'd broken into the house—believing Curling had kidnapped his children—shot him in the dining room, then continued through the house, searching for his kids, only to be killed by Curling's dogs. He knew close to nothing of real-world forensics, but he knew White Harbor. He knew the fire would cover any glaring evidence to contradict the story. Ultimately, it would become the local truth within Blight Harbor, and that would be the end.

"I'm so sorry, Mr. Knox," he said, and placed the gun on the floor, close to his hand. He pulled his shirt up to his nose and ran out. The flames were already reaching the adjoining bedrooms, and the smoke was thickening. Bobby turned and ran from the second floor. Running down the stairs. Running toward the doors. Running toward the light. A light dimmed by the horror that greeted him beyond the front porch.

Barry had stepped out of the Vanek House with a single

thought: *Freddie Parham has to die.*

Freddie had used the house to create a disgusting creature resembling his dead father, and used it to try to kill him, and even worse, to try to kill Ray.

The little shit was lying in the tall grass, rolling in pain. He'd apparently broken his arm upon landing, and he still kept giggling.

Freddie had tried to kill all of his other friends by splitting them up and using the Vanek House's twisted powers.

Barry stomped on the house's crooked porch. The floorboards creaked under his weight, and each step he took down the broken steps sounded as if he'd grown twelve feet tall and twice as heavy.

Freddie had murdered five innocent children in cold blood.

Leroy was lying in the grass. Blood all over. His mouth opening and closing like a fish out of water, his eyes lost, not looking at his twin brother, who was kneeling beside him screaming in a type of horror he could never put into words.

Freddie had stabbed Leroy in the back. He'd dared to hurt Ray, spit blood in his face, then tried to kill Bobby, who, for all intents and purposes, was Freddie's brother, laughing as he did it.

Barry stood over Freddie. He was still laughing. His annoying "HEE-HEE-HEE!" laugh louder than ever, despite his pain, or maybe even fueled by it.

Freddie Parham has to die.

Huffing, pushing through the pain of his broken arm, Freddie stared at him and grinned, his teeth red with blood. "Hey, Brickhouse," he said in a mocking whisper. "Is it true? What I heard in Blight Harbor? Do your lips taste like root beer?"

The rage overwhelmed Barry. It rose from his chest, nullifying what little self-control he could still retain.

"Wish I'd stabbed your boy instead of Leroy." Freddie pursed his lips, winked, and blew him a kiss.

Freddie Parham has to die.

There was a roar his ears, and it was his own raging voice.

The first punch knocked out a tooth. Blood stained the grass on the left side of Freddie. The second punch dislocated his jaw.

There was a third, a fourth, a fifth, a sixth. Little by little, Freddie's face became less and less recognizable and stained with blood.

Barry wasn't going to stop until there was no trace left of Freddie's face. No trace left of Freddie.

He didn't hear Ray calling his name. He only realized he was there when the image of the bloodied mess that used to be Freddie Parham moved further away in his vision. Ray had him on a headlock from behind. Barry kept struggling, swinging his fists toward Freddie, and missing every blow. He put all his weight forward, knowing in his fury there was no way someone as small as Ray could restrain him. It was laughable. Ray was wiry. Ray was strong. But it was ridiculous to even consider he'd be able to stop him from doing what he had to do. He moved toward Freddie again.

Freddie Parham has to die!

"Barry!" Ray's face was now in front of him, filling his entire field of vision, holding his face in his hands. "BE BETTER!"

(*Try to be better, son*)

That made him stop. Still not quite able to bring himself under control, but this gave the shorter boy enough of a chance to shove his head under his raised arm and wrap his arms around him. Ray put his entire weight into pushing Barry off Freddie, then to a standing position, and away from his unconscious body.

After the stunned moment passed, the anger came back, and Barry pushed again toward Freddie. "Let me go! He needs to die! You saw what he did! He needs to die!"

"Stop! He's unconscious! He's not worth it! He's not worth half as much as you!"

Barry's eyes shot toward Leroy. He'd stopped moving his mouth. He'd stopped breathing. Barry turned to Freddie and, in tears, shouted, "Leroy's dead! Leroy's dead, you fucking murderer! I hope you fucking die!"

Royce sprung to his feet, his hands covering his

mouth, eyes out of their orbits. Barry's words had made him realize something inconceivable. His appalled expression was as if he couldn't bear being close to his brother's dead body, like the proximity itself was poison, and breathing it would damage his lungs and taint his blood. He shook his head as tears drew slick lines on his face. A low mournful moan left his mouth, but crashed against the barrier of his cupped hands, like a wave against a seawall, breaking as he let out a continuous sob, which crescendoed into a dissonant, demented wail.

The fight left Barry's body when he heard him scream, realizing Royce wasn't just seeing his brother lying dead at his feet. He was seeing his own dead face on the lawn. The two feelings together must be what madness was made of.

The afternoon sun shone down on the crowd in front of the Vanek House. Four hours had gone by since they'd entered the place. It had felt like much less.

Once the fire had reached a certain point, it spread fast, as if something had been holding it back, then let go, causing the old wood and the newspaper on the walls to be consumed faster, and now the house was fully ablaze.

Bobby and Ray had pulled Leroy's body by the legs to the edge of the front lawn, to a safe distance from the fire, while Royce followed them with a vacant expression on his face.

Jess was now crying on Royce's shoulder, but he didn't appear to notice. Many years later, Bobby would learn he was at this time realizing the surrounding birds had gone completely quiet and no one else seemed to notice this.

Bobby stood with Peter and Nadine, all of them distraught beyond the capacity for words. Bobby himself wasn't only crying for Leroy's death, but also for losing his best friend, because regardless of the horrible things Freddie had done, he had to believe this had been part of some kind of crisis or breakdown that had overtaken the real Freddie.

Or was this the real Freddie? he thought.

Something had changed, not only between the Freddie he'd always known and the one they'd encountered at the altar, but between that one and the one that had attacked them in the main hall. For a second, he thought, even if the house had healed him from a bullet to the head, it had healed him wrong. Something had become dislodged or unhinged in his brain. He had to believe this creature couldn't be Freddie.

Callum and Sylvia stood together with Ray and Barry, who kept having sudden outbursts of rage toward Freddie, getting riled up again by the tiniest provocation, yelling curses and insults at an unconscious kid, who couldn't hear him, as Ray tried to calm him down. Callum's forearm had been bandaged by Jess while the ambulances arrived.

The crowd got there faster than the police and the fire truck. They could already sense them begin to murmur and gossip and point and stare. The police line was set one foot from where they stood, so the firefighters could work without interrupting the police and the coroner when they arrived.

For most of The Vigilantes, it would take years of therapy—and no small dose of rationalizing and denial—to mostly overcome what had happened that day, not that they knew that at this point. And for all the horrors they'd been through, there was still one last indignity to come.

A murmur approached from the crowd.

Bobby turned to look over his shoulder to catch the nearby faces turning, brows furrowed. The whispering from the crowd became louder until the front line broke and out came Martha Lange.

No. Not this, not now.

She walked with silent purpose and stood in front of Peter. Her upper lip quavering with rage.

"Don't!" Nadine pleaded. "You have no idea what we've all been—"

"Quiet, whore," she said in a raspy, low voice.

Nadine's lips sealed shut. Puny moans sounded from her throat as air left through her nose and a terrified expression took over her face, the realization that she couldn't open her mouth.

"Mother, no!" Peter said with outrage.

"Stop! What are you doing to her?" Bobby's mouth clamped shut in the blink of an eye.

Martha turned to Peter, glaring quietly into his eyes. Her silences were even more terrifying than her rants and curses. "I am disappointed in you."

Peter stared back, terror in his eyes.

"You will learn to obey me, boy, even if I have to break you into submission."

Peter was trying to sound brave and stand his ground. He appeared determined not to backpedal on how much he'd grown these past years. "I'd rather have you punish me than abandon my friends, Mother."

She peered to one side, then the other, surveying all the terrified stares directed at her—Royce being the sole exception. He didn't even seem to notice she'd arrived. "They don't matter." Her voice was sibilant and filled with poison. "You could have died for irrelevant people."

"What?" Jess shouted, only to have her lips sealed and her body paralyzed the same as Nadine and Bobby.

She turned her gaze down to Leroy's corpse, then turned to Peter. "What if that had been you? A waste. Better let the plankton die than a blue whale."

"What the fuck did you say, you gross bitch?" Royce was now staring at her with eyes like blazing infernos.

"You'll pay for those words." She made his lips clamp shut, his body stiff, but he still glowered at her, his disgust not diminished by what Martha Lange was doing to his body. Royce's knees buckled, and he dropped next to Leroy's body.

Barry, who was at this point on a hair trigger, took a step forward. "That's enough! Stop that, you old hag, or I'll—"

She turned her gaze to him. He stopped, like the others, his lips sealed shut, his body stiff. "You'll what?" Martha Lange gave a venomous hiss. "You'll hang yourself, like that treacherous, cowardly father of yours? You'll drink yourself into liver failure like that alcoholic, useless mother of yours? Oh, yes. I know what will take her out. God has told me. Stay there and be humbled. You're nothing to me." She cast her gaze toward the other kids and, in a second, their bodies went stiff, unable to move their lips or their bodies. Only Peter remained free to move, but he didn't. He was stuck in place, a look of panic carved in his face.

She turned to Royce, who, even on his knees, stared daggers at her. "You do *not* look at me like that, you insolent nothing." She forced his head to turn toward Leroy's corpse. Forced his eyes to look into his brother's dead face, which still had its eyelids open, as none of them had dared touch them. She made Royce bring his face closer to those eyes and held him there, unable to blink even after his eyes turned red, until his anger faltered and turned to terror, and muddled moans sounded at his throat, and fresh tears rolled down his eyes.

"No! Mother, I'll go!" Peter shouted. "Don't do this, please! Not today!"

Martha shot him a withering stare and let go of Leroy, who recoiled back from his dead brother and fell back onto the lawn, sobbing and screaming into a cupped hand.

Soon, the rest of them could move, and they all ran to Royce's side. Jess helped him to his feet, and they all turned to watch helplessly as that horrible woman dragged Peter away, fingernails digging into his forearm, as they had so many times before.

Peter shot them an anguished look over his shoulder, before disappearing into the crowd, then reemerging on the other side, as stares followed him and his mother up the slope and across the street to their house, all visible from where they stood.

Once the door to the Lange house closed, none would see Peter for two weeks, until he was pulled from the crawlspace under the house, starved, dehydrated, and delirious.

The flames consumed the Vanek House, almost impervious to the water from the firefighter's hoses.

It burned until it collapsed.

Chapter Twenty-Seven

Who Will You Spend Your Last Day With?

2022

7:12 A.M.

Alberto Ruiz's red Kia Soul emerged from the tunnel near Skarsgard's Teeth and reached the Blue Overlook, where the road turned a sharp left, descending toward White Harbor. He could see the entire bay and the town from this point, and wondered how such a plain-looking place could be evil.

"*Mami.*" He glanced at his dashboard. "I'm pulling into town right now."

"*Qué* bueno, m'hijo," she said, rejoicing at the news. "Did anything else happen last night?"

"They completed the four sacrifices." Her ominous tone sent chills up his spine. "The news is saying only three people disappeared, but I called Father Erwin in Burley. He said all the brothers and sisters cast lots. They all confirmed the four were completed."

He let out a worried sigh. "What's coming on the Second Night?"

"For the Second Night, it's only one. What's wrong with you, Carlos Alberto? You should know that already."

It annoyed him she'd say this like he hadn't spent years away from this whole mess and had been pulled back in against his will.

"The problem is, it can be anyone. There's no stopping that. If anyone can find out who it will be, it's John Hitch, but no one in the Order can find him. It's like he vanished."

"John Hitch is..."

"Curling, Curling. Sorry. I forget you're not used to his name now."

"Oh." He cast his eyes toward the bay and the sea, which reflected the dim morning sunlight on an immense circle of deep blues and greens. "So, is he dead?"

"No. He's just gone. The Order would have started looking for the new vessel if he were dead, but he's not. He's just not here. Which means...he's probably over *there*."

He tried to shift topics. The whole "Curling succession" thing gave him a goddamn headache. "Should I come up to the house?"

"No, not yet, *m'hijo*. Peter is still sleeping, and he brought his friend with him. I don't want them to think we're doing anything shady. Go stay at the Callahan Inn downtown, find a room there, and I'll see you here later today. Look in the books for protective rituals, invoking Dalàbulu, Hshahshiel, Quetzalcoatl, Frigg, or Guanyin. Those would do for now, and studying what the combined sigils look like."

In his mind, Alberto worked hard to silence the voice repeating, "*Gobbledygook, gobbledygook, gobbledygook,*" and tried to listen to his mother in earnest.

"I'll call you when you can come."

"Sounds good, *mami*. Will you be okay?"

She made a pause at this. "Yes. I'm not in any danger."

"Okay." He wasn't satisfied with that answer. "Talk to you later, *mami*."

8:05 A.M.

Jess peered down at her mug of coffee, black as the depths of space minus all the stars, and steaming, letting out that addictive aroma that always made her soul feel warm and cozy, no matter what was shaking her world at any given time.

The smell wafting from the pancakes Royce was working on took "warm and cozy" and dialed it up to "self-indulgent and orgasmic".

She was still struggling to relax fully and revel in the moment. The events of the previous night had left their mark, especially when she considered the other things they'd gone through together as kids. *It piles on,* she thought. Kids in White Harbor grew fast, she knew—fast and inured to the town's bizarre events—but most not as fast as she and her friends were forced to. So many things she still struggled to explain from back then. Group hysteria, a hallucinogenic gas leak, they'd been drugged by Freddie Parham, none of it lined up in her head. It was like building a house but fucking up a measurement by an eighth of an inch, which throws the entire construction off. Now your window's crooked or there's a barely noticeable gap between walls that lets in moisture and allows mold to form. She'd also shot and killed a man and watched his house burn with him in it when she was thirteen. There was no easy way to rationalize that one.

Self-defense? Of course, no doubt about it. He would've killed Peter and then gone after them for being witnesses,

(*How will I... I won't be... Won't be back before the... How will I...*)

but despite that, her brain hadn't stopped pointing a

finger at her, reminding her, regardless of the reasons, she'd killed a person. *They would've been two if Freddie hadn't casually shrugged off the notion of a bullet to the head. Just like we shrugged off the notion of him* surviving *a bullet to the head.*

Why was she thinking about this? It made sense, she assured herself, when a family member of the man she'd killed pointed a gun at *her* head and the heads of all her friends.

The townspeople could rationalize and fictionalize all they wanted, but everyone knew the truth—the local truth—everyone and their cousins knew there was more to events like that in this town. It was never an accident or a coincidence. Denial could only go so deep. And yet, here they were, not completely insane despite having seen and lived insane things, about to have pancakes.

"I've been thinking," she said.

"Oh, no," Royce said, not taking his eyes away from the frying pan. "That's never good."

"Oh, shut up. Now I see why you're getting chubbier by the day. Chicken wings and pancakes, now that's a fuckin' diet!"

He sighed. He was still smiling, and spoke in a somewhat condescending tone, apparently deciding not to engage. "What were you thinking?"

"How are we not crazy?" she asked in an earnest voice. "We had a brush with death last night. We had a gun pointed at us. Barry and Ray nearly got shot. There was a weird-as-fuck blackout all over town. Three people were reported missing, including a goddamn baby. And we're all here, all hunky-dory, going on with our merry lives, like nothing's going on. I'm even questioning if I should bother going to the police about the man with the gun, because my mind is like, 'Nah, just let it go, you guys are fine!' Your wife just took your baby girl out to preschool, people are going to work, and you and I aren't bundles of stress and anxiety in the fetal position on the floor. How does that happen? How. Are we. Not. Crazy?"

He started plating the pancakes. "Who knows? Denial, casual sex, drugs, alcohol..." She could see him putting blueberries on them and doing something with the whipped cream can, then he turned around and placed the plate in front of her with a stack of pancakes, decorated with blueberries as eyes, half a strawberry as a nose, and a wide whipped-cream smile. "Or maybe, just pancakes."

Jess considered the smiling pancakes, then turned an annoyed look at Royce's grinning face. "This is so passive aggressive of you."

"Now, what do you say when you daddy gives you pancakes?" He flashed an ample grin.

Jess harrumphed with irritation, then forced a smile. "Thank you, Daddy."

"Atta girl." He sat down to eat with her.

The sound of forks and knives on plates was all that rang in the kitchen for a while until Royce broke the silence.

"You know why that is." A somberness settled in Royce's voice. "It's this town. It's a creature. It's swallowed us whole, and we're accustomed to getting digested."

Jess took a long swig of hot, bitter coffee.

8:43 A.M.

Ray descended the stairs, having been woken up by the smell of breakfast, which rose to his bedroom like something out of a dream. Confused, considering no breakfast was ever made in this house unless he actually made it—and given he often left for work in a rush, it often comprised cereal and coffee—he continued down, until he noticed the couch, a pair of folded blankets and a pillow neatly set against the armrest—jeans and a shirt on a nearby chair.

That's right, Barry spent the night.

The smell of bacon filled his nostrils with the underlying salty-sweet smell of scrambled eggs cooked with butter. And were those hash browns?

When he stepped into the kitchen, Barry's broad back was turned toward him as he faced the stove. He was still wearing the pajamas he'd handed him the previous night and some old socks.

"What are you doing?"

The large man turned around, holding the pan by the handle, and gave him a bashful smile. "Sit down, it's almost ready."

Ray regarded the table. There were already two places set. He hadn't even finished settling down when his unexpected breakfast chef put a plate in front of him with exactly what he'd been imagining: crispy bacon, golden scrambled eggs, hash browns. Before he could even ask, he was pouring coffee into his mug.

Ray was puzzled. Surprised, but pleasantly so. He raised an inquisitive eyebrow at the tall, bearded man standing in his kitchen.

Barry brought his own plate and sat across from him. "I wanted to thank you for letting me spend the night. Thought I'd make breakfast."

He considered for a moment, in silence, gave Barry a noncommittal smile and an approving nod, and went to town on his plate.

"Dig in," Barry said.

He did.

It was the best breakfast he'd had in years.

8:49 A.M.

Callum's doorbell rang once. His brain had been in overdrive the whole night, so it had been difficult for him to fall asleep. Now there was the damned doorbell waking him up when he'd barely gotten any shuteye.

He rolled in bed and peered to the right. Sylvia had already left for work. Peered to the left and there was his little notepad, where he'd jotted something like, *Two groups. Sun/ Moon. Complementary? Contentious? Look into.*

The doorbell rang again.

"Coming!" He took his glasses from the nightstand and put them on.

He got out of bed, put on his slippers.

The doorbell rang yet again.

"Coming! Jesus! It isn't even nine for this much ringing!"

He hurried out of the bedroom and toward the door. As soon as he pulled it open, sunlight stabbed his eyes, almost leaving two empty holes straight through his brain.

Once his eyes adjusted, the shape of a man appeared, standing outside. A man wearing glasses with a long beard and long hair, wearing a thick jacket.

"Hey there!" the man said. He blew out air and a bit of steam came out. He hugged himself and rubbed his arms. "Damn, cold for a summer morning, huh?"

"What do you want?" Callum squinted so hard his eyes were two thin lines behind glasses.

The man put his hands up in an appeasing gesture. "Dude, I promise I'm not selling anything, and I'm not associated with any religious groups akin to doorbell ringing. I'm—"

"I know who you are."

Xavier grinned. "Oh! A fan?"

Callum stared at him.

"Not a fan. Okay."

"What do you want?"

"So…one of my listeners told me you were doing some research on the town history, and you came upon a—"

"Goodbye," Callum moved to close the door.

"Wait, wait, wait, man! Please hear me out!"

Callum sighed, did an eyeroll. "I'm not interested in sharing my research, especially since what you do with your little show might tarnish any scientific credibility for anything I put out there. Also, I haven't had my morning coffee, and that means you're an obstacle between me and my brain functions. So, goodbye."

"I'll trade you!"

Callum stopped. Eyed him with mistrust.

"It's something I'm pretty sure you don't have, because if it took me—with all my contacts—a shitload of work, a small-town librarian wouldn't have a chance."

"You'd be surprised."

Xavier nodded with a stubborn expression on his face. He moved his rucksack from his back to the front, opened it, and pulled out a leather-bound book. Even though Callum had never actually seen the book itself, when he noticed the symbol on the cover, he knew what it was.

Xavier waited for an answer.

"If we're really going to talk about this," Callum said, "I'm going to need some coffee."

9:35 A.M.

Ray came out of the shower, putting on a plain light blue T-shirt over some cotton pants. He hung the wet towel and headed downstairs.

Barry was already dressed and ready to go, sitting on the couch, waiting—the pajamas neatly folded on top of the blankets. He glanced at him, awkwardly wringing his hands.

"Are you…leaving?" Ray asked.

He nodded. "Yeah. Probably should." He stood up to greet him. "Thanks again for letting me spend the night. I figured you'd want to get some rest before going to the hospital in the afternoon."

"I asked for the day off. I knew I was going to come home late, and I wanted to rest. Didn't expect such a hectic night, though." He let out an uncomfortable chuckle, glanced around, and realized he was trying to find a reason to keep talking. "Wh-why don't you stay a bit? Maybe we could, uh… Like go for a walk a bit later, when the wine cooler hangover has worn off a little?"

At first, Barry didn't respond. He studied his eyes, as if he were hearing words he'd never thought he'd hear, and was expecting him to say: "Kidding! Get the fuck out!"

"I mean…" Ray stumbled over his words. "I'm sorry. It just hit me, you're probably not feeling well after everything that happened last night, and you might want to go home and talk things out with Maryann, maybe try to patch—"

"No." The bashful, reserved look was gone from Barry's face, and he gave him a serious stare, his expression resolute. "No, I don't."

"Are you sure?"

"Did a lot of thinking last night. So, yeah." He maintained the determined stare. "Regardless of"—he pointed his finger back and forth between them—"this. I'm done with that. Done with her. Done being scared."

There was a moment of awkward silence. It was then, out of the corner of his eye, Ray caught sight of the oval-shaped rock in his glass cabinet. Despite being in the back, concealed behind four matryoshka dolls, a very tiny ray of light reflected off one of the tiny blue crystals within.

"Oh, fuck it," Ray took a sudden step forward, took Barry's face in his hands, and kissed him. Despite his words of the previous night, the haunting thought that they could've died lingered in his mind. He couldn't shake the feeling if anything had happened to Barry, he would never forgive himself for not giving this one last chance.

Almost as if by reflex, Barry kissed him back and wrapped his arms tight around his body.

9:36 A.M.

Xavier and Callum sat at the latter's small, round, glass dinner table. Callum had his second mug of coffee, already half-empty. In front of Xavier lay a folder containing a copy of the documents he'd come for, including a map of a probable location where the mysterious event would've allegedly happened three hundred years ago. Callum paged through the strange book— the Uolminar, Peter had called it—for a second, forgetting he had a guest right in front of him.

"This is really cool," Xavier said, holding the folder up.

Callum looked up from the book, as if pulled from a trance. "Sure. Just please *do not* call it a UFO crash, because if you look at the telling of the events, nothing ever crashed anywhere. And if you can't help yourself from calling it that, at least have the journalistic integrity of adding the word 'alleged' before saying it."

Xavier gave a silly giggle. "You have some real control issues, man."

"No, I don't. I simply like to advocate for information accuracy."

"Sure, let's call it that."

With an uncomfortable glance down at the mysterious tome, then at Xavier, Callum closed the book. "You're comfortable leaving this with me, then?"

"Of course!" Xavier stood up. "It's a loaner, but based on what you're telling me, you and your linguist girlfriend can do more with it than I can. And this"—he once more held up the folder—"this is gold."

Callum gave him a polite nod.

"Gotta get going. I ran here right after I wrapped up my morning livestream, and I have to make the most of my day doing some research before tonight's. It's gonna be a big one!" Xavier turned toward the door, took a step, then turned around and put his hand out to Callum. "Thank you."

Callum shook his hand. "Likewise."

9:40 A.M.

Already in the bedroom, lying in bed, shirtless, his legs hanging over the edge, Barry reached down to unbutton his pants, but Ray, who was standing over him, was quick to stop him, putting a hand on his wrist. This took him by surprise.

"Don't you dare," Ray said, giving him a wicked smile. "I've been waiting for thirty years. I've earned the right to uncover that myself. Now, take your hand away, or you might lose it."

He raised both palms and gave him an excited grin. "Yes, sir."

With swift, dexterous fingers, Ray unbuttoned Barry's pants as he covered his belly with kisses. He then hooked his hands into both his pants and briefs. Paused. Directed his gaze upward, in a "Ready?" expression.

"Both at once?" Barry asked, still grinning.

"So? This isn't strip poker. We're not going garment by garment." He gave a hard tug on his pants and underwear and it reached an inch below his hips. "Are you sure? Last chance to turn back."

Barry gave him a daring look. "If my pants aren't on the floor in ten seconds, I get up and leave."

"Is that a dare?" Then, in three hard tugs, Ray pulled his pants and briefs off, raised them up, triumphant, and let them fall to the floor, as he counted, "Seven, eight, nine, ten."

Barry laughed, blushing bright, seeing the naughty grin drawn on Ray's face as he removed his own clothes. Now, however, realizing he was fully naked and vulnerable in front of the man he loved, courage started trickling out from his face, slowly replaced by the old insecurities. *Fat, hairy, awkward, useless, cowardly. All I do is hurt people.*

"Wow." Ray's voice interrupted his thoughts.

"What?" Barry asked, his voice filled with worry. Was there something wrong?

Ray looked him over from head to toe, as if committing every curve, every tiny hair, every freckle to memory. "You are so beautiful."

He smiled sheepishly, called him over with his gaze.

Ray climbed onto the bed and approached him, positioning himself between his legs and, as he'd done what felt like an eternity ago, he kissed his thighs and ran his fingers through the tiny hairs on them. This time, he made a lengthy stop at those parts of his body he'd never seen in person, exploring, smelling, tasting, doing things that made Barry moan and grunt with incomparable pleasure. Things he'd never felt before—not like this, at least.

Ray continued his way up, kissing his belly, his chest, and his neck until he was kissing his lips. He paused to take a longing look in his eyes.

There was a wordless exchange between them—a question passing from Ray to him.

Barry nodded with eagerness. "Be careful, okay?" The bright, hypnotic grin his man gave him communicated so much love, so many things he never thought he deserved.

"Who do you think you're talking to?" Ray whispered and gave him a soft kiss on the lips.

"Well," Barry said in a playful tone, "if you do everything like you did the pants thing, then I'm in big trouble."

Ray chuckled, gave him another soft kiss, and shook his head. "Do you trust me?"

"With my life."

Everything flowed with such ease, was so natural, as if they had done this a million times before, but still with that thrill of the first time. Every touch was new, the intoxicating feeling of becoming one, that sensation inside him he had only ever dreamed of.

"*Faggot!*" The thought came out of nowhere in his mother's drunken, hate-filled voice. "*All you'll ever be good for is to get fucked in the ass!*"

"No," Barry mumbled under his breath. "Stop it!"

"I'm sorry." Ray stopped, puzzled, panting. "Should I stop?"

"No!" Barry shook his head and smiled, at once tender and filled with desire. "Please don't. Please, keep going."

Ray gave him a long, adoring kiss.

They got lost in each other's warmth until noon came.

11:30 A.M.

Callum had spent the last two hours using Sylvia's translation key to understand as much as he could from random parts of the mysterious book of the Circle—the Book of Uolmin. A full translation would take an extensive time, and given the previous night's events, he wanted to know more, sooner rather than later. He'd picked a few pages based on symbols and illustrations that caught his attention. This—though he wasn't sure—could help him stumble upon something useful. Based on other texts he'd seen, rituals would often be accompanied by imagery of some kind, not just text. If John Hitch thought he was following some kind of ritual, or a set of rules, it only made sense.

The book was now filled with post-it notes, sticking out between pages like slices of cheese in a sandwich.

The doorbell rang.

He debated ignoring it, but then, he realized, based on the hour, it was probably Peter at the door. He'd said he'd swing by before going to see his mother at noon. Part of Callum would've preferred he came *after* seeing her. He could only imagine what interesting tidbits of information his mother would've let out after the strange blackout of the previous night.

Peter greeted him, squinting in the bright sunlight, despite the chilly wind coming in from outside. He was holding an old, yellowed-out notebook in his hand. "You know? Waking up on time to come over was hard. I could've slept straight through the day."

"You and me both." Callum stepped aside, holding the door. "Come right in!"

After a bit of small talk—something Callum had never been fond of—Peter showed him the notebook. "I couldn't find a copy of the Uolminar in the attic, but I found this."

Callum took it, noted that the handwritten name on the cover was Peter Rojas, not Peter Lange—Rojas being his Costa Rican father's last name, before his mother changed it. He opened it to a random page and read, *"Manzana.* Apple. *Camisa.* Shirt. *Caballo.* Horse." He raised an eyebrow. "I think this Spanish course needs a bit of structure."

Peter chortled. "I should've probably explained first. My dad… uh, so, my mom put him in charge of teaching me how to read the Uolminar, but he actually used most of that time to teach me Spanish. He used to improvise which words he was gonna teach me, so that's how we ended up with apple, shirt, horse."

"Okay?"

"But he did teach me some stuff from the Uolminar. Some of the language. And in one of the pages"—he flipped through the book as Callum held it in his hand—"there's something about some kind of ritual. Something important I was supposed to know, but, uh…" He clicked his tongue and did a weird expression with one corner of his mouth. "I forgot about all this until now, to be honest. All that talk of rituals last night brought it back."

Callum studied it and found a doodle which matched an illustration from the book: a four-step diagram set in an incomplete circle, starting at the top with a crescent moon. A curved arrow then pointed from it to the second circle like a full moon. From there, another arrow led down to the third circle at the bottom, which was entirely black—a new moon, perhaps?—but what was most interesting was the last step: instead of another arrow leading to the last circle on the left, it was like the black circle at the bottom stretched, continuing the curve, until it reached the fourth step. This last one was a black circle with an infinity symbol inside. There was no curved arrow leading from this point back to the beginning, so it wasn't a cycle, it was a finite sequence. But then, why was there an infinity symbol there if it ended? Was it even an infinity symbol?

"I think this will be really useful. Thanks. Now, come with me. I know you have an appointment with your mom, but I promised I'd show you something today."

Peter followed him into his office, where he'd clearly been working before his arrival. The room smelled of the cold remains of coffee with cream at the bottom of a mug. "I'm guessing you didn't take the morning off after the late night?"

"Why would I?"

"Just saying."

Callum pulled a fold-out chair from behind the door, set it next to his chair in front of the desk, and sat down. "Sit."

Peter did.

"First of all. The families from the Circle. I mentioned Barry's family. I don't have the specifics, but during one of her benders, Yvette Giffen let out her late husband had been conspiring against your mom, and it got him killed. On its own, it doesn't sound like proof of anything, but the information on Logan Giffen's suicide letter pointed to him and his wife being part of the Circle. It kind of tells its own story. This is only conjecture, but it's likely Logan Giffen had been trying to get other members of the cult to remove your mother from power, and when she found out... Well, you know how she can make people do stuff."

"You don't know that for sure, Cal."

Callum eyed him with puzzlement. He couldn't understand if Peter was uncomfortable talking about the things he'd seen his mother do—some in front of the entire group— or if he truly had rationalized them to the point of complete denial. "He wronged your mother. He died. And it's not the first time it happens." His tone was assertive, which he felt was necessary if Peter was going to come onboard for the next part. "Which brings me to the Rockwells. They took advantage of your mother's condition and quietly left the Circle, and… Well, the entire family was wiped out."

Peter, still looking uncomfortable, gave a curt nod. "You mentioned another family."

"The Cunninghams, from what I can tell, are *still* part of the Circle, but I think Jess is oblivious to this. This one I have it from a credible source. Chuck Cunningham had a public argument with your mother a few years back, during which the words 'I'm leaving. Stay away from my family' were spoken. That year, Jess's brother died from alcohol poisoning at a frat party. No arguments since then, no conflicts, no deaths in the family, which tells me they fell back in line."

Peter kept his gaze down.

"I think…" Callum paused choosing his words, "I think you should try to remember what happened at the Vanek House. Every part of it." He let that sink in for a moment. "Including what your mom did when she came to take you away. I can't force you to see things the way the rest of us do. But you should embrace the fact there are things in this town beyond what we understand. I've gradually had to accept that, even though it's been difficult for me to shift my perspective. I want to show you what helped me shift it."

Peter eyed him with curiosity. "The video you mentioned."

Callum clicked around on his laptop, went on YouTube and opened a saved video, titled *DIMENSIONAL PORTALS EXIST!* "This was recorded by a tourist who stopped with her family at the Blue Overlook."

He clicked play on the video but moved the tiny ball on the progress bar forward about thirty seconds. The video showed a view from the Blue Overlook, moving around, recording the gorgeous surroundings. They could hear people talking. Joyful banter. The camera spun around toward the tourist's family—her husband and two teenage girls—who were making faces, smiling, and talking to her through her screen.

"It's important for you to notice the video doesn't cut at any moment," Callum said. "The recording never stops."

There was the sound of screeching tires. A white car came into view. It swerved, erratic, from one lane to the other, almost hitting another car coming in the opposite direction.

"What the hell?" the woman holding the phone said and focused the camera on the car.

Callum pointed at the screen. "That's Pam Rockwell's car."

Peter swallowed hard.

The white car made it past the sharp curve near the Overlook. It continued weaving in and out of its lane until it approached the tunnel. Right before the car entered the tunnel, it disappeared.

"What?" Peter stared at the screen.

"Wait for it."

The ticking of the video timer continued, second by second. Only an empty tunnel and the sound of people gasping and commenting in shock at the disappearing car.

Fifty-two seconds later, the car reappeared, in mid-air, beyond the edge of the tunnel and the cliff, already mid-fall toward the rocks. It crashed into them. One pointed, jagged rock pierced the windshield on the driver's side.

Peter gawked at the screen as peals of screaming from the people on the Overlook issued from the laptop's speaker. He stared at Callum. "Play it again."

Callum did. They watched it, beginning to end. Then they watched it again. Then, again. "One more time?" he asked.

Peter shook his head. "It's gotta be—"

"Edited? I thought the same at first. There are dozens of re-uploads of this video showing the disappearing, reappearing car. Most people consider it a hoax—but the *original* video was taken down—I suppose it was reported because it literally shows someone crashing their car and dying a grisly death. *That* video had a ton of comments, confirmed to be from *outside* White Harbor, in which people didn't see the car disappear. They only see a car drive up to the tunnel, stop at the entrance for about fifty seconds, engine idling. Then it moves, turns, and drives off the cliff. Everyone from White Harbor who saw the original video, saw the car disappear. So, of course, it might be some weird hoax, but there's this guy who has a livestream and a YouTube channel here in White Harbor—Xavier Poe Kane—he ran a test before the video got taken down. He confirmed it, live on his show. He streamed himself watching the video within town limits. The car disappeared. Then he got in his truck—all live—drove a few miles outside White Harbor. Played the video. The car was visible the entire time." He watched Peter's uncomfortable expression.

"Alright. So, even if I accept this isn't a hoax. What's supposed to be my takeaway from this?"

Callum shrugged. "The simplest one would be to accept there's something outside our understanding going on in this town and stop making excuses for it. We all know about the weird way this town works. I'd say, if you want to call it supernatural, or paranormal, feel free to do so. I think you should stop denying what's obvious."

"Alright. Fine. What's the other thing?"

"What I already told you. Remember what happened at the Vanek House. Every part of it. Sylvia and I never crossed the door on the second floor like you guys did, but somehow, we made it up a chimney to come out of a window in a hallway that didn't actually exist, and yet the fire within that hallway burned down the house." He pointed at the screen. "What you saw in the video is the same thing, but not contained within a building. The car approaches the tunnel, disappears for a minute, and appears in mid-air. Where did it go for that minute? Was it a minute where it went? This is just like the Vanek House. Space and time going crazy."

"I know *that* happened," Peter said, with reluctance.

"Good. Then, if you know it happened, and you know Freddie was able to tap into that power and control it to his will, what makes you think your mother can't? What if she used that to do things like paralyzing us and not allowing us to speak? What happened after the Vanek House burned down? Did we let that power out? Who knows? It might have even called you here for that ritual John Hitch was trying to prevent."

He surveyed Peter's face, trying to read his reaction or to understand what was going through his head.

Peter stood up in one abrupt move. "I gotta go." He turned to leave.

"Oh… Oh, yes, okay." He followed him to the front door. "Thank you for the notebook. It will come in handy."

"Sure." Peter was emotionless. "Later, Cal."

He let himself out, leaving Callum alone, thinking he'd pushed too far. He looked at his watch. It would soon be noon. He had to listen for the birds going quiet, like Sylvia said they had the previous day.

Chapter Twenty-Eight

The Closet

12:15 P.M.

B obby gave Royce and Jess the go-ahead, motioning toward the hallway. "Sorry I can't stay with you guys. I promised I'd meet Angie and Nadine at Seaside Park, and it's important I'm there. I know this goes against protocol, but if you need anything, there's Jodie"—he nodded toward a muscular security guard at the entrance to the cell corridor—"she's already filled in on why you're here, and she'll walk you back out once you're done."

"Don't worry, Bobby," Jess said. "You go give my girl the best day of her life."

He smiled at her, then eyed Royce and pointed at a cell's plexiglass wall, his smile quickly fading. "Cell 1408." He was ready to leave, but stopped and shot a hesitant glance at them. "Is it crazy that I'm going to an amusement park after what happened last night?"

The other two exchanged glances. "I think," Royce said, "in this town, since stuff like that might happen to you at any time, you gotta live each day the best you can with the people you love."

Bobby gave him a knowing nod, in which he communicated he understood, out of their entire group, Royce was a living example of how sudden loss could be. "See you later, guys." He shot a fleeting glance in the direction of Freddie's cell and walked away.

Royce marched down the corridor, followed close by Jess, who had agreed to come with him for support. The light shining through the plexiglass from the individual cells— some occupied, some vacant—cast soft squares of light on the plain tiled floor, which made the surroundings seem gloomy by comparison.

Freddie had his back to them, looking out his small, barred window at the blue sky. Royce knocked on the transparent surface of the plexiglass with the back of his fingers.

"I already heard you walking here," Freddie said with a smile in his voice. "The echo in that hallway is super loud. Might drive someone crazy, you know?" He turned to look over his shoulder and gave him a mischievous grin, giggling. "I was expecting Bobby to come visit after last night. Didn't expect to see you here, Leroy!"

Royce flinched. He hadn't anticipated it to sting this early on.

"Oops!" Freddie brought his hand up to his chest, as if mortified. "I'm sorry!" His tone and his malicious grin made it obvious he wasn't. "You're Royce, not Leroy! Did I do a racism?" He laughed. "I meant it because you were twins, and, in all honesty, I forgot which one of you I killed." His face twisted into a gross, demure smile.

Jess put a hand on Royce's back, and just then, Freddie noticed her.

"Hi there, Red Powerpuff Girl. Haven't seen you since you put a third eye in my forehead." He mimicked holding a gun and firing. "Bang."

She contained a shudder. Turned back to Royce. "Do your thing. Don't let him rile you up. I'll be here." As if to contradict that statement, she took a step back, out of the light cast by the large cell window.

Royce breathed out, slow, steady. "Hi Freddie." He gave a pained but sincere smile. "I came because I wanted to talk about a couple things. I...wanted to tell you, even though I don't think I can ever truly forgive you for what you did, I don't hold any ill will toward you. I know you weren't okay when you did those things." He paused, swallowed hard. "You're probably still not okay. I hope one day you will be."

Freddie stared at him. His jaw hanging open, eyebrows curved up, as if moved by Royce's statements. "Wow." He pointed a thumb toward the window behind him. "Did you catch the gulls going quiet a moment ago? I never get tired of it! It's freakin' awesome. It's like they're pausing in fear while God listens to the Mother's prayer." His face took on a fanatical, rapturous countenance. "*Tjenaf egoikaat gozun-Uolmin yggshe.*" He gave a wide-mouthed grin that gave Royce the creeps. "God will feed!" His eyes moved from one to the other, as if expecting them to understand the nonsense coming out of his mouth.

Royce exchanged a look with Jess, who didn't say a word. She motioned for him to ignore Freddie's ramblings and continue. "That's kinda what we wanted to talk to you about, Freddie. The birds?"

"Oh… What about the birds?"

"You know what's happening, right? The same way you had a hand in what happened at the Vanek House. You have a hand in this, too."

Freddie didn't answer. He only eyed him with an amused smile.

"A man named John Hitch said you went out to kill

four people last night, but you were here. So, that's nonsense, right?"

No answer. Just the smile. Just the stare.

"But, then again...you did things at the Vanek House that would make leaving this room a walk in the park. Maybe the power in the Vanek House wasn't only in there? Can you still tap into that?"

Silence. Royce pushed on.

"According to the news, three people went missing last night, and two others were found unconscious close to where they disappeared, Steve Felton and Maria Knox. You killed Maria Knox's kids inside the Vanek House. Did you have anything to do with this other thing?"

Freddie frowned, cleared his throat, went back to smiling.

"Is it already over? Will it happen again?"

"I'm sorry, Tweedle Dum. I can't answer any of your questions." Freddie regarded him with a look of polite calm, his fingers forming a tent, like a mortgage representative at a bank, telling a customer their loan has been denied. "The Mother forbids it. I'm her servant. I obey her. You won't get any answers from me."

Royce turned toward Jess.

"Alright, then," she said. "Let's go."

They nodded toward Freddie, and without even saying goodbye, turned and walked away.

He slapped his palm twice on the plexiglass. "Hey!"

They turned. Freddie had his full body pressed against the glass, speaking through one of the circular holes in it. "What, you're just gonna leave like that?"

Royce and Jess exchanged another look. Jess shrugged. "You have no answers for us. So, why waste our time?"

Freddie became upset. "You're just mad 'coz you don't know what's coming."

"Is something coming?" Jess said.

"Oh, I see what you're doing, Chuckie Finster. You and the clone are trying to pump me for information. I'm not that stupid."

Royce turned to Jess. "You heard the man. Let's walk."

They turned around again to leave.

"I killed three last night, but there's a fourth!" He let out a stupid-sounding mischievous chortle. "The fourth one I only helped, nearly shot me dead, that old bitch." He flashed his grin, false teeth replacing the ones Barry had knocked out. "Oh yeah. I guess it doesn't hurt to talk about what I *already* did. The Mother won't mind. What's done is done. Can't be taken back."

Both Royce and Jess pressed their jaws tight, not to let the disgust show on their faces.

"Will it happen again tonight?" Jess asked.

"I can't tell you that."

"So, it *is* going to happen again tonight," Royce said.

"I didn't say that. You did."

Jess turned to Royce. "So we can assume there's gonna be another blackout tonight. Four more people are gonna die."

"No, you fucking idiots, just one!"

They both flashed him a smirk.

"Fuck! Well, that's really all you get out of me, since I truly don't know who, and ultimately, that's the most important part of it, isn't it? Tonight, one person dies, and the fun part is, no one knows who. Not even I. I have nothing to do with it."

Royce gave Jess another nod toward the hallway, and they turned to leave.

"Hey! You haven't asked me who the fourth person was! That I can tell you. I *want* to tell you."

"Fuck off, Freddie," Royce said. "We're done."

"Hey, Red Powerpuff Girl! Talked to your mommy yet?" They stopped. He giggled, realizing he'd hit a bullseye. "Cole Felton, Sam Becker Jr., Stephanie Bilson. Those are the reported ones, but if you're asking me about last night, it means you still don't know your mom's gone."

He has to be lying, Royce thought.

"My mom's at my aunt's place," Jess said, flat out, her face a sudden mask of dread. "You're lying."

"Oh, I'm sure Chuck told you that. He left poor Maddie to die alone, while he went off to try to ambush me with your buddy John Hitch." He giggled. His "Hee-hee-hee!" laughter rang out louder than usual and echoed down the hallway. "'*Try*' being the important word here."

Royce took Jess's hand, trying to calm her down, trying to keep his poker face on, trying not to lash out at the notion the man who'd killed his twin brother might have also killed his best friend's mother. From what he could see, Jess was struggling to contain herself.

"C'mon, friendly neighborhood lesbian, give your aunt a call. Right here. C'mon. I want to see your face when she tells you your mom's not there." He shrugged. "Though, as you know, weirder things have happened." He pressed the tip of his index finger to the center of his forehead and giggled.

"Listen, you little shit!" Royce said, pointing a finger at him.

"Royce, cool it." Jess pulled his hand back to stop him from getting closer, as Freddie giggled maniacally. "He's lying. My dad would never lie to me about that."

"If I find out you hurt Maddie Cunningham," Royce said. "I'll do what Barry should've done thirty years ago and beat your ass until you're no longer breathing! You hear me?"

Freddie's response was more giggling. He turned a dark but ecstatic gaze to Jess. "Look in your mom's closet. I left something there for you."

Jess spun and walked away, expressionless, a shadow over her eyes. Royce flashed a killer glare at Freddie and hurried after her.

"Hey! Tweedle Dum! Wanna hear my impression of your brother?" He started letting out throaty gargling sounds which reverberated down the hall.

Once out of Freddie's line of vision, Royce caught Jess's hand again and pulled it.

She turned toward him. She was sobbing.

"He's only trying to get in your head. Don't let him rattle you."

"I have to see what's in my mom's closet."

The sound of Freddie's giggles followed them until the door to the criminal patient wing closed behind them.

12:25 P.M.

Ray was lying next to Barry, his head supported on his left hand, running his right-hand fingers over Barry's sweaty chest.

"How do you feel?"

Barry fixed his gaze on the ceiling's light fixture. There was a pleasant smile on his lips and a joyful glow in his eyes. He looked like the weight of the world had been lifted off his shoulders. His smiled widened a little, and in a brisk and peaceful voice, said, "Happy."

"Hmm." Ray squinted at him with curiosity. "Then why do you look like something's spinning around in that pretty head of yours?"

"It's nothing. Just thinking about what comes next."

"I get it." Ray adjusted his position on the bed to be closer to him and took his large hand in his. "In the movies, it's always so simple. As soon as the main character comes out of the closet, they're always so confident and empowered, their family and friends are so supportive. They usually throw in a full-town dance montage with rainbow flags all over the place—a couple drag queens for good measure. It's like they forget not all the good ol' U.S. of A is New York or San Francisco. They act like there aren't places where they actively want us dead."

Barry laughed, but there was some uneasiness in his tone. "Wow… 'Coming out of the closet'. Now *there's* a concept. Didn't have a clue that was a thing I needed to do. Guess that's gotta go on the list now."

"You don't have to," Ray said. "Not until you're comfortable."

Barry turned his light blue eyes from the ceiling toward him and smiled. "I do. I want to. You asked me how I felt, and yes, I feel happy, but mostly, I feel safe."

Ray smiled back, almost as if he could feel his joy himself. "Safe?"

He nodded. "I feel like me."

"Can I ask you something?"

"Anything."

Ray hesitated. "I could never imagine living my life as someone I'm not. But you... What has it been like for you all this time? You know what I mean?"

Barry nodded.

The glow in his eyes faded a little, the shadow of looking back at a darker time passing over his gaze. "When I was younger, I used to watch these movies, like *The Shawshank Redemption*, or shows like *Oz*, where characters are sentenced to life in prison, and I always wondered how they even survived. How did they cope with knowing they would never be free? Back then, the thought of myself in that situation used to send me into an anxiety fit. How do you live knowing you'll be locked up between four walls until you die? The world moves on without you, while you just watch the hours go by, trying to follow the rules and comply with what's expected of you, so as not to have a fight, or more punishment, or...worse?" He sighed and slowly shook his head. "I didn't have to wonder for long. I've lived in prison my whole life. Knowing I can't be me. I can't live, I can't express myself... Can't escape."

Ray ran a hand gently down his face. "You don't have to talk about this if you don't want to. I don't want to ruin the moment."

Barry took his hand in his and kissed it. "That's okay. It helps. Never had someone to talk to about this."

584

"You do now."

"I know." Once more, there was that glow in his eyes. His smile, framed by his brownish beard, recovered its beauty.

"How *did* you survive like that?"

He tilted his head to one side, thinking of an answer. "My children were the main thing. Without them, I would've lost my mind. The moments I was alone with them—no Maryann around—those moments, I was happy, at least in one aspect of my life."

"And the other aspects?"

He turned an inquisitive gaze toward him. "Do you believe in past lives?"

"No. Do you?"

"No. Me either. I believe in other universes, though. I kept telling myself, in another universe, maybe I was happy."

Ray's heart shrunk in his chest.

"I kept imagining, in that other universe, I was me, and I could live the life I always wanted to live. In that other universe, I didn't let the woman I used to call 'momma' make me feel less for being who I am, and I allowed myself to explore...*this,* earlier. In my mind, I never believed in the possibility it could happen in this universe." He gave Ray a warm look. "You grabbed that possibility from another universe and pulled it here."

Tears welled up slightly in Ray's eyes.

"Now, here, with you, I feel like me." Once more, he

took Ray's hand in his, squeezed it tight. He could feel his resolve come through in that gesture. "I'll never be that other person, ever again."

12:34 P.M.

Peter had spent the first twenty minutes since arriving in his mother's hospital room sitting on the edge of her bed, waiting for her to say something, while she sat quietly in her chair by the window. She'd ignored his greetings and any attempt at getting her attention. She clutched her strange black rosary as she gazed toward the garden. She wasn't in some unresponsive state. She'd noticed him, but turned her head away from him.

Noticing this, he'd thought, *The lights are on, there's someone home, but that someone's ignoring the doorbell, maybe hoping the visitors will go away.* Except the last part wasn't right.

Her silence unnerved him. Like at any moment, she'd lash out with some of her usual vitriolic remarks, but she first wanted him to feel anxious, for maximum impact once the inevitable strike came.

Is Callum right about her? Is she capable of such a thing? he wondered as he waited for her to either say something or visiting hours to run out.

He tried to process the thought his mother might be involved in the deaths of the Rockwells, of Barry's dad, of Jess's brother. Even if she was sick enough to wish those things upon them—not even his denial about her could deny *that*—how could she possibly have the power to do something like that? It defied all logic.

Logic has no place in this town, he thought.

She'd choked Jess outside the Vanek House without touching her. She'd paralyzed and muted all his friends as the Vanek House burned. She'd brought Royce to his knees and forced him to look into his brother's dead eyes. He'd witnessed all of these events up close. He'd seen her do it. But then, if she commanded such inexplicable power over others, why had she never used it on him? She'd always wanted to control him, so why hadn't she done to him what she'd done to the others?

She didn't need to, he thought, and even the voice of his own mind said it in a mocking tone.

Or maybe she couldn't? It was something to consider, perhaps. She must have been tempted a million times to force him to do as she asked, but she never did. Maybe she couldn't.

He turned a pondering gaze toward the enfeebled woman by the window. Her eyes were full of sadness, not her usual arrogant self. If he pushed all logic aside and accepted the things she did were powered by some supernatural entity, how was such a powerful woman trapped in a frail body with

587

a mind so clouded? Why couldn't she use that power to—

"You have a weak, pitiful son," she said in a tired croak.

Peter shook, as if woken up by a whip striking his bare skin.

She still gazed out the window, wistful. "I went to visit him last night."

She dreamed it. She must have.

"Rocket ships and stars."

Peter's blood froze.

"On his bedsheets and his room. Rocket ships and stars. Such childish concepts. There'll be no such things in the coming world."

William's bed covers at his grandma's home. Rocket ships, stars, and planets. How? She couldn't know this.

"There will only be God for humanity to prostrate themselves in reverence. The Moon—His ever-watching eye—and the bliss of eternal life under its glow. No more war, or hunger, or suffering, only rejoicing, living as part of God for eternity."

"Mother... What are you talking about?"

"I came to you last night, as well," she said. "Please, son..." Her voice sounded choked up as the onset of tears came over her, which alarmed him even more. "I don't want to suffer for you in my bliss."

"Mother?"

"When I cross over into God's glory, I don't want to

see you still here, suffering alone because you refused to listen. I don't want to see my bliss tarnished by your suffering. I came to you last night to plead. To beg for you to come back to me, to come back to God. After tonight, it will be too late. After tonight, I will have no choice."

He sat in stupefied silence, trying to understand what she was saying. Or, at least, what those words meant to her.

She turned a nasty gaze toward him. Her expression was no longer sorrowful or wistful, but angry. "What are you doing in my room, boy? How many more times do I have to tell you never to come into my room? Can't you see your mother is grieving? Can't I have privacy after your coward of a father left us?"

She was gone again. Any semblance of lucidity had vanished in a wrathful explosion.

"I have to carry the weight of everything since he left, and you can't even respect my space?" She stood up. She came at him, her hand raised, ready to slap him. "Get out! Leave! If I ever see you in my room again snooping around, I will cane you within an inch of your life! You hear me?"

"Mother! I'm sorry!"

She stopped. Scowled.

Her voice then turned into a vile hiss. "Go back to that bitch of yours and the spawn she birthed you. I don't need you." She went back to her chair, sat, and turned away from him. "God will bring you back to me. He promised."

From there, the conversation devolved into more rambling that skipped through the years at random. Memories of things long gone and recent events getting mixed up to create brand new memories, which happened today, but yesterday as well.

Then something she said caught his attention.

"Did you see it last night, Peter? God's eye?" She was smiling, her face molded into a rapturous expression, with glistening eyes full of unhinged devotion. "The Lord's awakening requires so much power, it can steal the light from the world. Every light dimmed by God stirring in His bed. He's not yet awake. He's merely turning over. The two nights to come and the eternal night to follow, God will rise to claim this world and reshape it. *Tjenaf egoikaat gozun-Uolmin yggshe!*"

A chill went up his spine at that moment, sitting on her bed, which appeared to continue now, as he sat in his blue Chevy in the hospital parking lot. It was nonsense, everything she'd said. It had to be.

(*Rocket ships and stars*)

But what if it wasn't?

(*Tjenaf egoikaat gozun-Uolmin yggshe*)

"God will feed," he muttered, a shiver climbing his spine.

He pulled his phone out of his pocket and called Jenny's mother. Three rings later, there was her warm, welcoming voice.

"Hi, Peter. How are you today?" Susan Morton said.

"Hi Susan, hanging in there, I guess." Even if he *were* alright, which he wasn't, he'd downplay it. He was uncomfortable telling Jenny's mother he was okay. How could he be okay when her daughter was dead? Not that Jenny's parents ever made him feel he couldn't be open about his feelings. This was his hang-up and his alone. "How are you doing today?"

(*My daughter's in the ground, buried, after a closed-casket funeral, how do you think I'm doing, you oblivious f—*)

"Fine, all things considered." She sounded deflated but soldiering on. "I cried three times before lunch. I suppose that's progress."

"I know what you mean."

(*How could you know what I mean? You cosmically stupid man! Did you carry a child for nine months, only to have her die in the most horrifying way possible? "Unrecognizable" isn't a word any parent should hear about their child, you piece of sh—*)

"William isn't home from school yet, darling. Did you need anything?" she said in her usual kind voice.

(*Why didn't you save my daughter? Why didn't you save my daughter? Why didn't you—*)

"I just wanted to check in and see how he's doing."

She let out a long sigh. "He didn't sleep so well last night, I'm afraid."

"Why? What happened?"

"From what I gather, he had a terrible nightmare."

Peter exhaled. He didn't want to ask, but he had to. "Did he tell you what he dreamed?"

"Oh, I don't mean to disturb you. But, he dreamed a woman—a *naked* old woman—with no eyes appeared inside his bedroom, saying horrible things. She said she'd 'gotten rid' of his mom, and she was going to get rid of him, too."

(*Rocket ships and stars*)

(*God will feed*)

"Don't worry too much about it. After what he's been through, nightmares are par for the course. However…" She made a pause that made his breath catch. "He has a bruise right below his calf. Fingernail markings. They broke the skin. He said she did that to him. I'm sure it was self-inflicted during the nightmare, though. No need to panic, but yes, he had a pretty bad scare last night."

Peter's memory went back to the weeks before the fire in which Jenny died. Her nightmares. Her night terrors. Sleepwalking. Setting the house on fire in her sleep as she held William by the wrist, nails digging into his skin. *The way Mother used to grab my wrist.* He pictured Mother paying nightly visits to his wife at night for weeks, filling her head with nightmares, leaving seeds of thoughts in her mind, leading her to set their house on fire.

No. That's crazy. That's beyond mental.

His mother's words repeated in his head: "*Rocket ships and stars.*"

2:10 P.M.

An eerie silence saturated Jess's parents' bedroom. The house was empty. It felt uninhabited, like she was walking through a prospective rental. Her dad was at the bar, covering for her. The room was quiet as a tomb and the dread of it actually *being* one weighed heavily on her mind. She stood in front of the closet doors, and all she could hear was a voice in her head repeating, "*If she's in there, I will die.*"

"Jess," Royce said, standing two steps behind her. "You don't need to do this. I can do it for you and tell you what I find. I'm sure Freddie was only trying to fuck with you. I don't believe—"

"I have to do it." Her voice was a soft whisper, as if she'd already resigned herself to finding her mother's corpse inside that closet.

"Then just—"

She threw the flimsy closet doors open, her arms wide to both sides.

Her mom wasn't there.

Shirts. Pants. Dresses. Shoes.

Why couldn't she let her breath out in relief?

Then she saw it.

In front of a pair of her mom's old blue shoes.

Her hand went up to her mouth and she let the breath out in a broken moan as her knees buckled and she let herself fall to the floor.

It was a bullet. A spent bullet, deformed from impact, with slight traces of old, dried-up blood. Next to it, in very tiny letters, written in red marker: "Just off the top of my head."

Royce crouched next to her and put his arm around her. "What is it?"

Weeping, but forcing herself to focus, she picked up the bullet and brought it close to her eyes as Royce watched in confusion. "Nine-millimeter bullet," she stammered. "It's not from my mom's handgun"—she breathed in and out, trying to get the words out—"I'm almost certain. This bullet is old. It's tarnished, and the blood doesn't look recent."

"What does that mean?"

She knew what she was about to say made no sense whatsoever, but the fact Freddie was still alive made no sense, either. "I can't know for sure, but I think this is the bullet I shot Freddie in the head with. He was here."

Royce stared at her. Eyes wide.

She gave him a teary, wet face, with a harrowing expression of pain in it.

"My mom is dead," she said, before collapsing in her friend's arms in heart-rending sobs.

??:???.?.

John Hitch walked along the dark, deserted streets of White Harbor—the version Freddie Parham had sent him to, at least.

Freddie had made a crucial mistake when creating this reality bubble. In his haste, he had left the time range too open, and the spatial limits too wide. He was, however, surprised Freddie had been able to do this with just what he'd taught him back when he was Ben Curling, and what he might have learned from Martha Lange inside his cell at Lighthouse Rock.

It was still amateurish work, he observed. Freddie had left the whole town at his disposal and literal decades for him to go over books at his home, books in the school library, and documents from many other sources people wouldn't even think to look for to find a way back.

John hadn't just found the way back. He'd found other crucial information, and he planned to put it to good use.

5:51 P.M.

After recording, taking notes, and writing his hypotheses on the bird phenomena—they had gone quiet at noon for almost fifteen minutes—Callum had spent the entire afternoon translating the page with the four-circle diagram. He'd also worked on translating the page before and the page after. He'd patiently interpreted the bizarre language, doing it word-by-word first, then phrase-by-phrase, then something that would approximate coherent sentences—or as coherent as he could get when he had a limited amount of words at his disposal—and most of those were educated guesses.

For now, he was focused on figuring out one of his greatest sticking points, which had to do with the fact what he was translating was called the "Ritual of the Four Nights", but the book only described three. It mentioned—or he believed it mentioned—a fourth, but the phrasing was different, and he only recognized the word "night" (*Uolvien*).

Il Uolvien: "The First Night."

Jin Uolvien: "The Second Night."

Kir Uolvien: "The Third Night."

Each of those headers was followed by a description of the requirements to complete the night in question. But then there was what he assumed was the fourth night. It was only a header with no description: *Goz Uolvien Viegozun.*

Viegozun wasn't a word in the translation key. He'd

need Sylvia to confirm his guess, but he thought he'd cracked it considering the infinity symbol in the last circle of the diagram—assuming it was an infinity symbol. If he considered *vien* was the word for time, and *gozun* was the word to denote immensity, enormity, or the unfathomable, putting those together (*viengozun,* minus an n, *viegozun*) it would be something like "unfathomable time". So maybe the symbol meant infinity, after all. "The Fourth Night is infinite", or "The Fourth Night is eternal."

His cell phone rang.

"I'm getting pizza!" Sylvia's cheerful voice said as soon as he picked up. "I don't mean to pump too much cholesterol into our forty-year-old arteries after the wings and onion rings last night, but I don't feel like cooking, and I'm sure neither do you."

"Where are you getting it?"

"Esposito's, where else?"

"We could've had it delivered."

"So, you're saying you don't want a hot Asian chick with a nice rack ringing your doorbell to deliver your pizza?"

"That's not what I'm—"

"I was planning on unbuttoning my shirt way down so you can see it through the peephole, and as soon as you open, say something like:"—she put on a badly-acted porn star voice—"Delivery for Mr. Baker. Careful opening this box. It's so, *so* hot! Unhh!"

Callum cleared his throat. "Well, um… That…doesn't sound so bad."

"I know what gets you going, baby."

He answered with an embarrassed chuckle. "Please, tell me you're taking an Uber."

"Why? It's not that far, and in a town this size there's like one Uber."

"After last night, I'm just worried about you. The day is unseasonably cold, and it's getting dark earlier."

"I'll be fine. See you in about thirty minutes, okay?"

"Okay… um, wait… If you could also get some whipped cream, that'd be cool."

"Whipped cream? For w—"

She stopped. He could almost hear the grin forming on her lips.

"Why, of course, Mr. Baker! Anything you want."

She giggled as she cut off the call.

He let out a long breath, trying to unscramble his brains after Sylvia turned them to gelatin with just a few phrases. He stared at the blank page of his notebook, trying to figure out what to focus on next. He looked from the page to the Uolminar, to Sylvia's translation key, then back to the blank page.

I'm drawing a blank, he thought. "Maybe—"

The doors to the closet behind him burst open, nearly startling him to death. He spun around in his chair to see

John Hitch standing there between two rows of old shirts and jackets.

"Wait, what the—"

Before he could say anything else, John Hitch took two strides forward, pulling his arm back, then pushing it into his lower abdomen. At first, Callum didn't feel the blade go in, but the impact was like a punch to the gut, and an explosive exclamation left his lips. Once the knife came out, there was burning heat spreading from the wound, as blood now poured from it, soaking his pants, and dripping off his chair.

Hitch pushed the knife in again. Higher this time, plunging it into his upper abdomen.

"Wait! Wait-wait-wait!"

Hitch shoved the knife two more times in his gut. Callum let out a panicked scream, like he was riding a rollercoaster for the first time, and having second thoughts right before the tallest drop.

"Wait-wait-wait!" His voice was coarse. Wet. Blood exploded from his mouth. "Wait!"

Hitch stabbed him two more times, going into his side. Something in Callum's body—his pleural cavity perhaps—was punctured and his lungs collapsed. Hitch raised the knife over his head, using both hands.

Callum could no longer scream, because he could no longer take in air. He pictured in a flash his lungs shriveling to the size of fists. He tried to raise his arm, eyes open wide, as his brain kept screaming, "*Wait! Wait! Wait-wait-wait-wait! Wait!*"

Hitch plunged the knife into his heart. He stared with piercing eyes directly into Callum's, then gave the knife a powerful twist, breaking through one or several of his ribs.

Callum took minuscule pathetic gasps, staring at Hitch with a mesmerized, terrified look in his eyes. The face of someone who knew they were about to die, of someone who was terrified of the unknown.

For as long as he'd lived, Callum Baker had sought answers to every question he could come up with. His obsession with understanding every minute detail of even the most mundane of things, often at the cost of his social skills, came from a deep fear of what he couldn't explain.

The events at the Vanek House had terrified him, but he took solace in knowing one day he'd have enough information to understand them. Blight Harbor was still a concept he didn't fully comprehend, but he took solace in knowing there had to be an explanation out there for him to find. But death, death was the great unknown, the huge guess, the huge assumption. Gods and religions had been created only to help humanity cope with the notion of death and what came after. *Guesswork*, he'd always thought with derision. *All guesswork.* Millions had died to defend what *their* version of that guesswork was, but in the end, now that he was here, faced with it, he found there was no explanation, no safety net, no time to process it.

Wait!

If there was an afterlife—and he'd always told himself there wasn't—he wouldn't know until the lights went out, and by then, could that be considered "knowing", when his brain was no longer functioning? That unknown, that unfathomable blank right after, was more terrifying to him than even the notion of there being nothing.

"This," Hitch said, "should not be personal. This should be just doing my duty. But you and that girlfriend of yours led that burning creature into the heart of the house. You burned my house down. Burned *me* down with it. I can't say this doesn't feel like justice being served. Now, I wait for her."

No, Callum thought, because he could no longer speak. He could no longer see. He could barely hear what the man had said. His mind was still in a frenzied panic over not knowing what death would be. That blank page from his notebook, now enormous, spreading quickly to every corner of his mind. *Don't hurt my...*

Blank.

Callum Baker was dead.

6:29 P.M.

Sylvia rang the doorbell.

There was no answer.

She rang again.

No answer.

Is he in the bathroom or something?

She rang a third time. When there wasn't an answer, she scrambled for her keys inside her handbag while balancing the pizza in one hand. *Dammit, Cal.* She pulled a cluster of about ten keys from the depths of her handbag, found the one with the yellow key cap cover, and slid it into the keyhole.

She opened the door into a gloomy apartment that smelled like burned coffee. The sun wasn't down yet, so there was some light still coming in through the windows, but for the most part, shadows owned Cal's place. Except for the office near the back of the house. The light was on there, but none of the paper-shuffling and typing and general "Cal-ness" of the place. The silence unnerved her.

Is he sleeping? she thought. Not likely. The bedroom door was open, and instead of snoring, Cal did this thing in which he blew air through his lips making a motorboating sound—it had annoyed her at first, but she'd grown to find it adorable—she should be able to hear him doing that in this silence.

She walked a few steps to the left of the front door

and placed the pizza on the small, round, glass table, along with her handbag and the tiny white grocery bag containing a can of whipped cream, then went for the light switch. The living area of the small house was bathed with light. Nothing moved. Nothing made a sound.

"Cal?" she called at last. Almost without thinking, she fastened the buttons she'd undone on her blouse to greet him when he opened the door.

The air inside the house was cold, unwelcoming, haunted.

Had he gone out? Maybe there had been an emergency, and he'd had to run out. If so, why not call her? Why leave the coffee maker on until the coffee started smelling like burning shit? She pressed the little red button on the coffeemaker to turn it off.

When she passed the table again, she reached into one of the small internal compartments within her bag and pulled out a tiny can of pepper spray, took off her shoes, then in slow, quiet steps, walked toward the office.

Please be okay. There were no signs of a break-in, but what if he left the door unlocked and some assailant walked in? *What about a heart attack?* After all, your forties are when you're the likeliest to have one. As she passed the bedroom door, she peered in, reached inside, and turned the light on. There didn't appear to be anyone there, though, perhaps in the bathroom? No. She didn't want to divert her attention from the office, with its foreboding light shining, when the rest of the house had been in gloom. She reached for the bedroom door and closed it. If there was anyone there, she'd hear them open it. *But then, I'd be trapped between the office and the bedroom.* She clutched the pepper spray with all her strength and proceeded, her bare feet noiseless on the carpet.

As she approached the office, she could hear the Pargin River outside, past the backyard, the sound of running water coming in like wet static through the office window, which she could see from the hallway. Once she'd reached the door, Cal's desk would be to her right, the closet and some bookshelves to her left. She stepped through the open door.

At first, as if to protect her heart, her mind flashed the notion perhaps he'd fallen asleep on his chair, facing away from the desk. However, that had been dispelled by the undeniable amounts of blood soaking his shirt, his pants, and the carpet at his feet.

She gasped. Held the air in. She walked without breathing to what she now knew, beyond any doubt, was her dead boyfriend. She could see the multiple stab wounds, the pallor on his skin, the glossy, red, sticky surface of the blood reminding her of a candy apple. She stepped forward and could feel the blood soak into her pantyhose as her foot pressed against the crimson—formerly beige—carpet. Sylvia went down on one knee, feeling tears welling up in her eyes, and put her hand on Cal's.

Cold.

She wept for a moment, holding his hand, thinking back to how, at first, she'd only felt an intellectual kinship with the saggy-cheeked kid everyone called "Droopy". That kid who had come from a humble home but had worked hard and found the way to continue pushing beyond what others believed was his place in the world. He'd become such an admirable man.

She remembered how she'd demanded to be included in their little group of weirdos, if only because she wanted to spend time with someone she considered an intellectual equal—someone she could truly respect. She'd expected him to be standoffish and reject her flat out, especially since she'd gone in with the threat of telling teachers and parents they had been breaking into private property, but he'd actually been excited to bring her onboard. He'd vouched for her when the others hadn't been so sure.

She'd found a place she could belong, at last, a place where she didn't feel so alone. All because that saggy-cheeked, bespectacled kid had seen through her posturing and seen the lonely girl hiding behind.

Still holding his hand in hers, she stretched up and gave him a soft kiss on the lips, even if this left a tiny stain of blood on hers. She didn't care. This was the man she loved.

She caressed his face, peered at his closed eyes, her heart completely shattered, and said, "Thank you."

Sylvia wiped her eyes and noticed his glasses on the floor. She picked them up, examined them. The way he constantly had to push them up his little nose was always endearing to her.

Something moved in the reflection of the glasses. Behind her.

She turned around, raising the can of pepper spray, as the stranger pushed his arm in a stabbing motion toward her. The knife slid into her abdomen, but a second later, the man was screaming, covering his face as the pepper spray did its job. He reeled back, leaving the knife inside her. As the pain truly hit, she recognized her attacker. *Hitch! That psycho, Hitch!* She knew taking out the knife from an abdominal stab wound was a terrible idea, but it was the only weapon she had available.

She reached for the knife, and just touching the handle sent violent jolts of pain through her body. Despite this, she grabbed it, and with a scream, pulled it out. She could feel the disgusting trickle of blood running down her stomach and thigh, but without letting herself be deterred by it, she stood up, brandishing the knife and ran it into Hitch's abdomen. She pulled it out and plunged it back in.

He screamed, and she was about to stab him again when he punched her in the face, sending her reeling back. She fell on her butt right on the carpet. He ran out, still rubbing his eyes.

She brought herself to her feet, aching and bleeding—she'd twisted her ankle, and it hurt like a bitch. She staggered out of the office to see Hitch grab her handbag, which had her phone in it, and run out the door.

As fast as her aching body allowed her, she reached the front door, but when she tried to pull it open, it wouldn't. It was as if some strange force was holding the door shut. She remembered the feeling. It wasn't a mechanical force holding it. It didn't even shake. It wasn't a lock, or some physical thing blocking it. It was as if it had been fixed in time and space and couldn't be moved. This had happened with the front door and the service room door at the Vanek House many years ago.

Sylvia ran toward the window, her hand pressing down on her bleeding stomach. Mr. Muschietti was outside in his driveway, bringing out groceries from the car. Sylvia shouted at him, screamed desperately, but it was clear the old man wasn't hearing her. He turned around and regarded her. He was seeing her behind the glass pane. He smiled and gave her a polite wave, like all he saw was his neighbor's girlfriend waving hello from the window.

She slammed her fist into the glass pane, expecting it to break, but her fist bounced back after a deaf thud, like beating on a drum skin pulled way too tight.

Realizing her predicament, she ran back to the office, searching for Cal's smart phone. She went to the bedroom and did the same. Hitch must have taken the phone with him. Callum had no landline. She was isolated from the world.

She took off her blouse, grabbed a towel and some duct tape from a closet, and went to the bathroom. She grabbed a bottle of rubbing alcohol off the medicine cabinet, poured generous amounts on the towel, and pressed it against the stab wound. The burn was immediate, and she grunted, trying to push through the pain. Using her teeth, she pulled a strip of duct tape from the roll, touched it to her skin, then rolled it over the towel. She wrapped herself with duct tape, as tight as she could, almost feeling like she was wearing a corset made of silvery adhesive tape.

Sylvia examined herself in the mirror. Unease washed over her as she realized this might not stop the internal bleeding. She was almost certain it wouldn't.

Back in the office, she rolled Cal along with his chair away from the desk, gently, carefully—as if to not wake him. "I'm sorry, baby. There's something I have to do." She grabbed the fold-out chair she'd sat on so many times while he worked—when she was on consultant duties—and sat, every move sending living tendrils of sharp pain through her abdomen.

No internet connection on the laptop. Fine. She expected that.

She wanted to understand what Cal had been doing before dying. He'd told her about the book and told her what he'd been attempting. She knew he'd be researching the Ritual of the Four Nights, which was the reason Hitch was coming for them.

Fucking stupid, she thought, berating herself for simply accepting the danger was gone. She'd lived in this damned town her whole life. The danger was never gone.

Cal had jotted down quite a lot in his notebook today. She flipped back from the blank notebook page he was on; she wanted to look at the last things he wrote. "Maledictions. Question mark," she mumbled, then went back a few pages. She needed to get a full picture of where her boyfriend's mind was before he died.

Someone might come and get her out in time. They might notice she and Cal hadn't messaged the group chat since she checked in that morning. But, even if they didn't, she resolved she'd work until she bled out, finding something that could be of use to her friends, to the town. Make sure if they found them both dead in this office, what they found here might give them a slim chance of averting whatever the hell was going on, or at the very least, catch the man who'd killed them.

Cal's death—and potentially hers—wouldn't be in vain.

Chapter Twenty-Nine

An Evil Dusk

Hitch had gotten lucky, and he knew it. First, for having left the sigil in the closet to return if he needed to browse through Baker's research. Second, for Freddie's amateurish understanding of how to create the boundaries of his reality bubble, which had given him invaluable knowledge. Third, for Baker being so invested in his research, he hadn't heard him step through the portal in the closet. Fourth, because Nguyen had twisted her ankle when she'd fallen, slowing her down and allowing him time to draw the sealing and isolation sigils on the front door.

Sunset was still about three hours away, but time was of the essence. Baker was dead, Nguyen would die of blood loss—as long as no one from outside saved her before she died. According to the research he'd done on that other side, he needed to kill three more before the Third Night—one more than if he'd killed them at the bar.

He peered down at his bloody hands, then back at the crimson trail he was leaving behind. Nguyen had gotten him good. Twice. He was gushing blood and wouldn't be able to keep himself going for long—even the protection sigils he'd drawn on his body wouldn't fully stop the bleeding.

The closest option, he thought—and the most satisfying for him—would be Jess Cunningham, the little bitch that had shot him in the heart when she was only thirteen. If anyone deserved his knife, it was her, he told himself, though he realized his rationalizations about who deserved it most kept changing. The reality was they all deserved it. It would've all ended in 1993, if they hadn't thwarted his plan at the Vanek House. So, he would forget about the word "deserve", and focus on the word "practical". Baker lived close to Cunningham's bar, so he figured she'd be the most appropriate target. She also had that cellar. She definitely had a first aid kit there. He could patch himself up, then he could kill her.

Two birds, one stone.

All afternoon, Martha had sat at her window, gazing out toward her house's backyard. The colors of her beautiful garden became desaturated, as the sun started its slow descent into the ocean and God's (currently closed) silver eye would soon rise over the horizon.

She couldn't remember why she was feeling this melancholy, like the strength had gone from her muscles, and her brain told her to sleep and forget about it all. But then, what kind of woman of God would she be? Not fulfill her duties? Never! Not in a million years.

And yet...

"Lord," she said in a diluted, weary voice. "Is there no other way? I will do what you ask, Lord, but he's my son. I know what I promised. I know what you will give me. But isn't there anything else worth your gift?" A single tear rolled down the craggy wall of her cheek. "Do I truly have to lose him to get him back? He's only a sixteen-year-old boy. Such a high price. Such a high price."

In her mind, while Peter had been taken away from her when he was thirteen, she'd been gifted a miracle—Peter's appearance in White Harbor today, in time for the Ritual of the Four Nights. For Martha, in two days it would be July 30th, 1996, which marked the blue moon. It wasn't just any blue moon, there was an unseen energy in it that wouldn't be present again for nearly thirty years, during a waning gibbous in July 2022—the actual present.

She couldn't wait almost three decades. It had to be done now.

"Such a high price."

A voice buzzed in her head, like gnats forming an annoying cloud. He was calling her. Freddie Parham, that cursed boy who wanted her to be his mother. That pathetic boy that clung to fantasies of a redemption that could never come.

She didn't need him this night. She would require his services on the Third Night, though. She had also made a commitment to him, and if she wanted to maintain his loyalty, she had to fulfill that commitment.

Freddie lay prone on the cold floor of his cell, his forehead touching the floor. His drawings and creations surrounded him, like nightmares that crawled out of his head to bear witness to their maker, prostrating himself before a painting at the center of the room. He'd replaced the other one—the one showing Steve Felton's street—with this new one showing a different house. He'd pulled this one from under his bed, where he'd kept it unmarked with his blood until tonight, when it became of use. However, whether he'd use it would be up to the Mother's discretion. She didn't need his direct help on the Second Night, which meant he'd have time to focus on more personal projects.

Now, on the floor, arms stretched forward, he called for the Mother. He called, he begged for her to appear. An almost inaudible sound reached his ears, a tiny crackle, like static electricity on a dry winter's day. He risked peering up.

It was always different, the way she materialized. It fascinated him to no end. This time, she started as a tiny thread floating in the air, almost a wisp of smoke that spun but didn't fade, then came another, and another, until there were thousands, millions of threads, joining, thickening, growing, weaving. Finally, he was at the feet of the glorious Mother.

"I have more pressing matters than to tend to you, Frederick. The Second Night is almost upon us, and you waste my time like this?"

"Please, Mother, forgive me." He groveled like a dog. After all, for someone as exalted as the Mother, he might be just that.

"You nearly failed me last night because you were arrogant, prideful. I should rescind my promise to you."

"NO!"

"What did you say?"

"No, please." His voice went down to a shameful whisper. "Mother, I beg you. The preparations for the Second

Night are ready. I worked so hard to make them perfect. To please you."

"Doing the most basic part of what's expected of you doesn't compensate for last night's missteps. Am I supposed to commend you?"

"No, Mother! Of course not! My work is yours. My work is God's. I am yours and God's. I only ask for this little kindness. This one request for myself."

He followed her with his gaze as she turned to the painting at the center of the room. While her eye sockets were empty, there were shifting shades of black and gray in them. She was studying the canvas.

"This is not relevant to God's plan," she said. "God will feed on them, anyway."

"I don't want to burden you with my petty revenge, Mother. You're above all that."

"Stop flattering me. Tell me why I should grant this, or I will deny your request right now."

"I know what I did in the Vanek House went against God's plan." He rose to his knees, tentative and awkward, and sat on his heels, as if meditating. "But, Mother, I didn't know that back then. I was only a child, and I was tricked by Ben Curling. I'd lost all my family. I had nothing. Doing what I did gave me a purpose, and above all things, it made me feel powerful, worthy. It wasn't about God. Not back then. I didn't know of Him until you showed me the truth, Mother." He looked up at her, and she responded with a nod. She was really listening, he realized with excitement. "For me, staying in the house, learning how to use its power, meant I had a reason to live. That was until he *threw* me out of the house and disconnected me from it."

Freddie glanced toward the painting, which showed a corrupted, deformed version of Barry Giffen's family home.

"So, what you want is to feel powerful? Is that all there is in your heart? Pride? Arrogance?"

"No, Mother, I beg your pardon!" He bowed his head. "I didn't want to feel powerful when that happened. I lost everything. I felt nothing. I *was* nothing. That power made me feel like I was something. Getting disconnected from that power was like losing my family all over again. A loneliness so complete, it wasn't worth living anymore. He took everything away from me. Think of how I could've better served you if I had learned to truly control the power. I wouldn't have failed you last night. I want him to feel the loss I felt when he threw me out of the house and broke every bone in my face."

The Mother regarded him with curiosity. "You can't kill him. You know that. He mustn't die until the Third Night."

"I don't want to kill him." He gave her a huge grin full of perfectly aligned fake teeth. "But I can kill his children. He can't experience loss unless he's alive, and I want him to experience that loss every second until the Third Night allows me to see the life disappear from his eyes." Freddie giggled. His sharp hyena laugh echoed in his cell.

The Mother stretched her hand toward the painting, touched her finger to it in a quiet, gentle caress. Gave him a nod, and he thought he could see something akin to a smile on her wriggling lips.

Her blessing given, the Mother disappeared.

The Second Night was upon White Harbor.

END OF BOOK 2

THE STORY CONCLUDES IN
A HOLE IN THE WORLD: WHITE HARBOR BOOK 3

Acknowledgments

It's easy to be cynical in this world sometimes, but throughout this process, I've learned there are people who will be supportive and nurturing and will propel you forward on your journey. I'd like to thank, in no particular order:

David-Jack Fletcher and Leeroy Cross James from Slashic Horror Press for saying, "We believe in your story and that you won't ruin our business (because we'll kill you if you do)." I promise I won't let you down.

Tanya Hagel and Rick Treon, from Book Talk on BookTok, who gave me a platform to reach others, and given me so much help in turning White Harbor into a TV pitch. You have both been angels on my journey. In this same regard,

Brian John Skillen, thank you!

Jacy Morris, for being the test subject for my writing and always making time in your schedule to be there with notes, support, and advice.

Jim Groves from the "Horror Movies and Shit Podcast" for being a constant fan and a long-distance friend.

Molly Rock, for lending me your voice talent. You are AWESOME.

Carlos Ruiz, Jose Villalobos, and Fabio Melendez, for being my cheerleading team. You have earned your place in my heart.

Chisto Healy, Mark Allan Gunnells-Metcalf. It's an honor to have you read my work and share your kind words.

And last, but absolutely not least, my wonderful husband, Jimmy Ballestero. My biggest fan, greatest supporter, and, in this book, even my idea contributor (one of the deaths in this book came from me saying "I want to do something different with this one", and him saying "how about this…?"). I love you. You are the best human being in this world, and I, the luckiest.

About the Author

Carlos E. Rivera is a gay author, born and raised in Costa Rica.

As an anxious, introverted kid growing up in a small town during the 80s and 90s, he always felt like an outsider. His refuge was escaping into and devouring sci-fi, fantasy, drama, crime thrillers, and, above all things, horror. For years, these books, movies, comics, and even video games became his life.

He dove into the horror-next-door of Stephen King, the ineffable cosmic abominations of H. P. Lovecraft, the disturbing atmosphere of *Silent Hill*, the dreamlike imagery of David Lynch, the sheer unnerving strangeness of Junji Ito, and many more; they got mixed in with his country's folk stories and his own experiences, resulting in what he describes as a peculiar blend readers might feel is familiar but askew.

And isn't that the foundation of horror?

Doesn't horror begin with something mundane that, seen from a certain angle, feels a bit off?

For updates on Carlos's work, follow him on Facebook, Instagram and TikTok at @carlosriveraauthor or his website criveraauthor.com